JOIN THE ARMY (
CALLA CRESS SE

What readers love

"**Takes you on a ride** and refuses to let you off until you reach the very end." *Marie*

"A brilliant read! I recommend this to anyone who enjoys mystery, suspense, thrillers, or action novels. The **detail is astounding**! The historic references, location descriptions, references to technology, cryptography....this author really knows her stuff." *Fran*

"An **action-packed adventure**, technothriller **across several continents** like a Jason Bourne or James Bond movie, but with an actual storyline!" *John*

"**Brilliantly written**. I loved the very descriptive side, which was a good way of visualizing and getting to terms with each new place, as the action takes place in several different countries." *Sean*

"The **description is so rich**, so immensely detailed that it just draws you in completely to its world." *Denise*

"There is **great tension and chemistry** between the two main characters, Calla and Nash, that has you begging for more." *Pam*

ALSO BY ROSE SANDY

The Calla Cress Technothriller Series

The Decrypter: Secret of the Lost Manuscript

The Decrypter: Digital Eyes Only

The Decrypter: The Storm's Eye

The Decrypter and the Pythagoras Clause

The Decrypter and the Beale Ciphers

The Shadow Files Thrillers

The Code Beneath Her Skin

Blood Diamond in My Mother's House

THE DECRYPTER AND THE MIND HACKER

www.rosesandy.com

THE DECRYPTER AND THE MIND HACKER

A CALLA CRESS TECHNOTHRILLER

ROSE SANDY

For those who are curious about the world, its history and the technology that runs it.

TEN DAYS FROM NOW
SEAPORT OF TIANJIN, CHINA
0517 hrs.

THE METALLIC STENCH in the forty-foot, transportation container churned Calla Cress's stomach, making her insides queasy. Its claustrophobic sensation filled her empty lungs as she focused on a glass-encased box.

She examined the case with the lifelike Tarim mummy, a defunct, male body with his intricate clothing and faint eyelashes covering his sunken eye holes. Her flashlight dazzled into the four-thousand-year-old face. With distinct, non-Asian features, there in the morbidity of the Chinese transportation container, he was perfectly preserved. Even after the passing of thousands of years, the red-haired mummy with Caucasian features rested in serenity. With recessed eyes, shut like a Buddha in meditation, he wore a black, felt, conical hat with a level brim. The mummy next to him glared back at her, his gape descending into the depths of her being.

"Give me a clue, my friend," she whispered.

"Is it here?" Jack said, her faithful friend and government colleague.

"That's what we need to figure out. I don't know why my mother chose these mummies. We've got to examine them carefully. They are our only lead," Calla said, her upper-English, London accent echoing off the iron walls.

"What if there's nothing here?" Jack said.

"Then, we go to where they were found in the Tarim Basin."

Honghui Zhou, the Urumqi Museum curator, observed Calla from a few meters away, with his back against the uneven façade. "Do you have what you need?" He checked his watch. "Your time's up."

Calla moved with caution and turned to Jack as he handled a high-speed satellite tracker.

"Is the emergency communications pod running now?"

"Give me a second," he said. "How can we fight a worm on global networks when our gadgets are the first targets?"

"We have to, Jack. If there's nothing here with these mummies, we must go to the heart of the Tarim Basin, and we can't do that without satellite linkup."

Jack shifted from his uncomfortable position between two stacks of freight, shipping boxes. "I can't guarantee that. The geospatial positioning in this fly zone is messed up."

"How many hours have we got on the current battery?" Calla said.

"Less than one."

"Not good. We'll need more than that to get to the exact spot in Xinjiang, where these mummies were found."

Aching with fatigue, he shot her a long glare. "I'm trying, Cal. She's not responding."

Honghui's eyes were on Calla's pinched face. A glacier of anxiety settled over her. She ignored him and set a hand on Jack's shoulder. "We're headed out to a deserted area, Northern Tibet, on the eastern side of the Himalayas. The desert is extremely dry as the bones on this mummy."

Jack smirked. "I wouldn't expect anything different on a trip with you. I gave up comfort when I met you."

Nash Shields, tall and strapping, stepped into the already crowded container and proceeded to the mummy case where Calla stood. "Not much to look at. I take it this one is not hiding clues."

Calla shrunk from the fervent gray of his scrutinizing eyes. Her search was linked to these mummies. She cast him a half smile. "They're incredibly well-preserved, but I doubt anything could fit between his decomposed skin and desiccated hunting gear."

Nash maneuvered to the next displayed corpse, dodging custom-designed cases of exhibition treasures. He slid his hand across the adjoining glass case. "The Beauty of Xiaohe."

Calla glanced at the intricate, wooden pins, fixed on the female mummy Nash was referring to and sidled over to the pristine case. "I don't understand why my mother picked these mummies. They're quite controversial and have mystified the curator world for years. The fact that some of them were blond with blue eyes says they could've been westerners that had settled in what is now Xinjiang."

Honghui raised an eyebrow. "Their origins are debatable."

Calla peered at him for all of two seconds, attempting to avoid a dispute in the massive metal-tank. "The Tarim mummies were, at least in part, Caucasians. We'll just leave it at that."

For the first time in ten minutes, Jack tore his eyes off his electronic device and sailed to where Nash stood. "Let me see that."

"Hey, not so close. The private tour is over. Time's up!" Honghui said. "Listen, Calla, I'm doing your boss at the British Museum a favor by letting you in here. Have you found what you need? I have to box up these mummies for departure. The boat leaves in an hour."

"Where are they going?" she said.

"If you must know, to California, for an exhibition in which I've invested many hours."

Calla couldn't tell if she liked the man. "Of course. We're done here."

"My obligation is now paid. No more favors."

"Favors?" Nash said.

"Calla authenticated some of our most valuable collections at the Urumqi Museum with Veda Westall, her superior. I'm just returning a favor. It was my job, not theirs. Now, if what you're looking for is not here, you must leave."

Jack set a hand on Nash's shoulder, and they gravitated toward the entrance. They lunged off the container onto the shipping park and took in the expansive space of the busy dock that assembled an array of shipping vessels. Their ears caught the hiss of prepped steamers queuing for departure from the largest seaport in China. A few popular cruise vessels docked as crews, and passengers made final departure preparations in the early hours of the October day.

"She okay in there?" Jack said.

Nash caught Calla's eye. "Yeah, she is."

Calla switched off the flashlight and handed it back to Honghui. "I take it, you've got my map?"

Honghui smirked. "This way."

They progressed to the door. Honghui pulled out his phone and paced to the edge of the container. He disappeared for several minutes before returning with a piece of paper in his grubby hands. "Our sources say that this is the exact spot. I've sent the digital file to Jack's phone, as you requested. Now I've never been there myself but..." He eyed Nash and Jack with a smirk. "You have two solid guys here, and I've asked our best archaeologists and two military men to go with you."

"We don't need company," Calla said.

Honghui stroked his chin and leaned forward as if to touch her shoulder. "You're in China. We have our regulations." His accented English was impeccable, British, mélanged with Eastern pronunciation, and to the point. "The area stays as it was found. Nothing should disappear. You get the drift."

Calla didn't care for the spiteful comments. For now, she would agree to his terms. "We're not treasure seekers."

"Are the Tarim mummies all you have to go on? Your mother must've left more information," Honghui said.

She gave him an alert gaze. "And their place of origin."

"Not much is it?"

Calla itched to escape Honghui's perturbing glare and proceeded to the exit. She leaped off the container onto the concrete, where her companions waited.

Honghui followed. "It's a long journey back to Urumqi and quite a strenuous hike through the desert."

She shot Nash and Jack a knowing look. "We'll manage."

Several minutes later, the trio jumped into a Toyota Tacoma truck and zipped to the airport, where they boarded a Gulfstream G150 jet that flew them to Urumqi, the capital of Xinjiang in northern China. Under Honghui's arrangements, two frontier-defense men, clad in infrared camouflage uniforms, and two resident archaeologists met them outside the Urumqi Museum. The men guided them to a military truck.

Hours later, on the back of the armored vehicle, Calla awoke, her head thumping the side of the off-road vehicle. They bore down the southern route of the Silk Road, the historic, international trade-route between China and the Mediterranean, whose arid nature had formed a vast wasteland in the autonomous region in northwest China.

She tugged at her thermal parka and adjusted her winter hat as they crossed into the Taklamakan Desert. Combative winds made their way through the back of the vehicle with fierce resolve. Calla glanced back along the road they had taken, observing the vast desert. No other vehicles lumbered the deserted climb. The transparent canopy above them flapped in the trail wind, their only shelter against Arctic gusts. Soon, the truck revved up a steep dune, on the southern route to Tarim that ran from Kashgar to Dunhuang.

Crossing the 'Sea of Death', as the locals called it, the place barely produced enough water for vegetation amid its harsh wastelands. She'd taken this risk with little thought. *This place is a death trap. What was my mother doing here?*

This wasn't how Calla had imagined the trip. Not venturing deeper into nothingness. And for what? A mother who had abandoned her at birth without a second thought.

When the Toyota ground its tires up the dunes to Hotan, nearing the citadel at Mazar Tagh, doubts crept into Calla's head. She leaned into Nash's shoulder, who sat on her left and studied the Hotan cross-desert highway, west across the Hotan River. Off a ruined hill fort, the site dated from the time of the Tibetan Empire. It meandered deeper into the nucleus of the Taklamakan Desert, the world's second-largest shifting-sand wilderness. The Toyota turned in to the interior of the desert basin where more mobile sand dunes dusted the plains, largely devoid of vegetation.

Nash whispered in her ear, unease lining his features. "Don't like this. We've been on the road longer than planned."

She moistened her dry lips. "We can't stop now. My mother's life depends on it."

Nash's head backed up against the truck's edge, his eyes firmly on the two military men. "Your call, Cal. Stay close."

Calla questioned the distrust in his eyes as they fell on the two *Tai Chi* swords the men carried. Was this typical of the frontier-defense army Honghui had organized to chaperon them? Nash was pondering the same thing. Had she dismissed the weapons altogether in their haste? Though reserved in demeanor, Calla wondered about their escort, especially the taller one with his angular build and slanted brown eyes that blazed at her like two amber gems.

The second man, short and stocky, gave her the impression he could physically slice any attacker in two, from the way he transported his weapon. He too gawked at her in silence, caressing the brass-handle in his hands, as he chewed a disdainful brand of tobacco. The two archaeologists had taken front passenger seats. One dozed with his head bouncing on the other's shoulder as the truck jolted, maneuvering the rutted roads.

Calla's face grimaced. Her eyes wandered over to Jack, whose satellite tracker had failed to pick up a secure British government satellite the whole trip. Their expedition depended on reliable communications systems. Calla owned up to the truth. They had no network signal. At the foot of their climb, Calla had detected the mixture of stone and sand along the highway, hardly a place for life human or otherwise. They could be out of communication with anyone who knew them. Their fates rested with the silent men in the truck.

Rigidness lined her brow. "Nash?"

"Yes?"

"There's no sign of civilization. I haven't seen a town, truck, cattle, or a camel for the last two hours. Not even a riffraff shop or temple."

His eyes lingered on the swords. "Thinking the same thing here."

She edged into him, the frigid metal of the side of the truck seeping through her skin as they hunched in the rear of the truck. A swarm of zone-tailed hawks squawked overhead in search of prey, crossing the sterile expanse.

How long? Had they been too quick to accept Honghui's terms? Nash's face set off a warning glare as he peered through the torn canopy. "Damn it!"

Calla lifted her head and squinted at the approaching menace of nature's force. Having never experienced one, the veiling dust that headed their way, dropped a weight in her gut. "A sandstorm!"

Nash's eyes narrowed, focusing on a cacophony thudding behind him. Close to a dozen, military men veered up the dune on horseback, the hooves of their beasts trudging the sand.

"Up!" the first military man bellowed at them. "We'll take all those tablets, phones, and any piece of wire on you that dares uses a byte or link to a satellite."

"No, you won't," Calla said.

His dagger edged to her throat. "Let's see how well you handle diplomatic relations in China."

CHAPTER 1

DAY 1
ROCKY MOUNTAINS
ALMONT, COLORADO,
0625 hrs.

CALLA WRUNG HER fingers and hovered them over the keyboard. She couldn't sleep and rubbed her eyes, scrutinizing the e-mail she'd composed hours ago. She'd send it through the little black box sitting in the corner of the room, a secure network, courtesy of the National Security Agency, or better known as the NSA. As a senior intelligence analyst at the agency, Nash had wired his Colorado home with every type of home and office security gadgetry in existence.

No one knew she was here with him.

No one should.

She reread the draft to her superior, Veda Westall, Head of the British Museum in London.

To: Veda Westall

Subject: Distorted!

I'm sorry, but I couldn't tell you the truth. I didn't go on an archaeological trip to Egypt. I didn't know I would be involved in clandestine, government procedures, too disturbing to retell. I have a secret.

A secret, my best friend calls a gift, the doctors call rare, the government would call a weapon and the one who wants me dead calls trouble!
Six months ago, I would have believed them all, but now I'm not sure.
Three years ago, the government asked me to take on a covert role as a cultural agent for one of their undercover agencies, the ISTF (International Security Taskforce). I was assigned with authenticating what we know as the Hadrius Manuscript, an artifact whose script didn't exist in any known human language. When I deciphered the manuscript, little did I know it would be a journey of discovery. That's why I had to leave the museum so suddenly six months ago.
I trust nothing the government has to say to me any longer. The search for my parents and the deciphering of the manuscript revealed a few things. I have a multimillion-pound trust fund with my name on it. I've no idea where it came from.
I discovered disturbing things about me. I accomplish physical feats most soldiers would kill for. My instincts and sudden awareness of danger are heightened above those of a dolphin. I was born with penetrating eyesight, scientists would call nature's only example of supervision.
Am I distorted? An outsider. You decide. My unclear past is the least of my worries, though. What I can't yet understand are these people who call themselves 'operatives'. I'm presumably one of them.
Operatives live above the state of nature and aren't subjected to

everyday, natural laws. Their technologies and science defy anything you can imagine. They are people with the secrets of the heavens, the knowledge and science, years ahead of anything humanity knows. I don't know who they answer to and why. They're trapped in our cities, our towns, offices, and in our ways. Their origin is as debatable as evolution theories and their legitimacy as that of the Shroud of Turin. Their secrets are known only to a few, perhaps the government. Though the secret intelligence services don't understand them, they need them. They've visited you often. You may not have been aware. You'd know. Because they leave their mark. Perhaps a stranger walked into a café. The girl who regularly checks her e-mails there. The politician for whom you voted. Your mother?
Mine was. And I am too...only, I wish I wasn't.
Veda, I don't know what I'd do if you don't believe me.

Calla glared out the window for a moment at the snowcapped Rockies. She could not send this nonsense to the head of the British Museum in London. Even though she trusted her with every instinct she had, Veda would not believe her.

Then again, who would?

CHAPTER 2

1242 hrs.

CALLA'S BREATH FORMED a steam film on the pane of the salon's grand windows. "He's out there, Nash."

Nash raised an eyebrow from his reading. "Who?"

"I'm not sure yet."

A few meters away, with his tousled, sandy-brown hair away from his face, Nash lounged on the upholstered couch, his feet on the glass table. He watched her curiously. Nash never failed to astound her. At six-foot-three, his lean build and posture spoke of years of military discipline, though that didn't rob him of the sparkle in his engaging, deep gray eyes.

Trendy and intelligent, he had just enough athletic physique to make her self-conscious by looking at him. Nash also had a quiet confidence that dazzled from the intent look of his stimulating eyes and a sharp sense of humor. Calla was awkward around men she found attractive, and as a rule, she avoided them. With Nash, that guard had dissolved without warning. Nash had made his feelings clear. He wanted a life with her. Yet Calla feared a steady relationship, although if any, it would be with Nash. There was no denying it; he was fiercely handsome. Athletic and chiseled in the right places, his sculpted arms revealed strength. Lean washboard abs tapered to a narrow waist—topped with broad shoulders.

He was good to her. Her instincts had made an unintentional decision regarding him. Though they'd been close friends for months, his being around gave her renewed strength, and she was drawn to him more than she cared to admit.

As a former US Embassy marine, now employed by the National Security Agency in human intelligence, Nash had been in London on and off in the last three years leading ISTF's classified intelligence analysis projects.

"There's no one out there," he rasped in his standard American tone. "This is private property. If anyone crosses the gate, the sensors will go off, and we'd know. See right there?" Nash's finger pointed to a wireless camera that sat idly on top of the entertainment center in front of him.

A raw sensation shot through Calla's veins. The ten mile-run that morning with Nash around Gore Lake Trail and the woods near the house had left intrusive thoughts. She leaned the side of her head against the warm cedar of the double-glazed windowpane, taking in the imposing, serrated ridges of the Gore Mountain range.

The protruding snowcapped mountainside, visible now in the early afternoon, provided much solace to her unsettled mind. Her emerald eyes glowed with the reflection from the slopes. She dug her hands deeper in the pockets of the cable-knit sweater she wore over a pair of dark-wash jeans. Removing a hand from her pockets, she ran it through her licorice-colored tresses.

At one end of the extensive salon, the stone fireplace

blazed in silence. Billie Holiday broke the otherwise quiet afternoon with a soft rendition of 'A Stormy Weather'. Calla welcomed the slow crackling of the pine, which reminded her of winters back in her native England and growing up outside London in Alderley Edge.

"Is there something you need to tell me, Cal? Is someone after you?" Nash asked. He observed the lines in her face from behind a worn volume on the origins of the Cold War, as she gazed out at the frozen yard.

Calla felt dryness in her mouth. "I don't know?"

"Do you want to talk about it?"

"No."

Her eyes followed the feathery snowflakes land on the lawn that bordered the edge of the covered swimming pool. The light floating was nothing compared with the squall they'd seen that morning, a typical occurrence in October.

She'd never imagined what Nash's getaway home might look like, a retreat he'd often spoken of over the three years they'd known each other. Set on the edge of a golf course, she'd spent that last six months in its opulent comfort, undisturbed and avoiding any mention of the events in London.

She glanced toward the Douglas-fir trees and wondered why Nash hardly spent any time in the alpine home that included a large main house, a guest bungalow, and a large lawn, the epitome of class and privacy. *A mirror of Nash himself.*

Nash paused his reading. "Believe me, beautiful, anyone who dares step on my property uninvited will be asking for it."

Calla's face tightened as she observed the high noon sun hit the mountain snow caps. Nash could keep her safe. He was a trained marine and had combat and intelligence analysis skills that the NSA prized in him when they recruited him three years ago. She bit her lip and mumbled. "I saw his footprints out there yesterday when you went into Colorado's NSA branch. Nash, he could be an operative."

Nash raised an eyebrow. "Why are you concerned with them? Operatives don't have anything against you. From my recollection, you were capable of handling anyone twice your weight. In fact, weren't they begging you to join them?" He stretched for a sip of chilled water. "Is that what this is about?"

When Calla did not respond, he flipped a page and continued reading. "Those footprints belong to the mailman."

The frigid glass cooled her flushed cheeks. She turned her attention to Nash's concerned face. He was not reading. He reclined his frame across the sofa, a body he kept fit by regular training, a residue from his military years. He wore a wool jumper above charcoal jeans that complimented him well. She studied the faint scar on his strong jaw, one she'd caused when they first met at Denver airport, three and a half years ago.

She was safe with him, her best friend who'd not hesitated to leave London on a whim at her sudden request. He'd taken several months leave, juggled his government assignments to work remotely for the NSA.

Not once had he asked her why they'd left in such a rapid hurry. *Not until now.*

Calla shifted with her back against the window and leaned on its wide edge. "I'm not imagining this, Nash. Someone knows I'm here. There's only one way up this part of the mountain, right?"

"This is private land and has been in my family for years. My grandfather built that road out there himself. The only people who come up are the mailman and delivery. I can't imagine you're expecting any of those."

He perked his upper body. "Who are you running from, and why? Don't you think it's time you told me?" Nash's eyebrows drew together. He shut his book and stood shoving his hands in his pockets. "Calla, I didn't ask why we left London in such a hurry." His voice trailed with resignation. "Can you come away from the window and tell me why I hired a private jet to fly us out of London without telling a soul? It's been six months. I think you owe me an explanation."

He was holding back his irritation at the riddles between them. She let out a quiet sigh. "I know, Nash."

"We didn't even tell Jack. He must be worried," he said.

A brooding gaze swarmed over Calla's face. *He's right.*

She recalled that last week in London. They hadn't spoken to Jack Kleve, their mutual friend, and colleague. She could not shake the words spoken of Nash by Allegra and Vortigern, two operatives she wasn't sure she understood.

Allegra's face formed in her mind. Wisdom exuded from the older woman, stemming from her experience as a highly efficient, British diplomat and the new head of ISTF. The agency was a clandestine, global, crime-fighting organization headquartered in London. Allegra's words continued to gnaw at Calla's conscience. *You can't be with Nash.*

Vortigern was a recent acquaintance and a lead operative, who'd been difficult to place as his conduct shifted like shadows. Yet, he'd revealed much about her past, including information about her parents. He, too, had given her unwarranted warnings about her liaison with Nash.

Calla disagreed with it all. That's why she'd left. She'd run from the responsibilities of a lead operative for people she didn't yet understand and ancestry she wasn't sure she wanted. The words spoken over Nash were treacherous. She had acted with intuition, on impulse and left that life behind. *But what do I do now? Can you blame me? I want to protect you from these people.*

When they arrived in Colorado, they were grateful to be alone, away from the events whose plausibility they could not explain. Her increased physical capacities were still a mystery. She hoped to make sense of a new relationship with a father she hardly knew and a new group of people calling themselves *operatives,* demanding she joins them. Calla had longed to find her parents—and why she'd been given up for adoption.

"You're right, Nash. It's been six months," she said.

"Do you want to go back to London?" Nash said.

Her eyebrows knit, penciling worry lines on her forehead. The truth about her past had been painful, and London reminded her of that truth. She shrugged. "I don't know. How can I? After twenty-eight years, I've finally met a father I barely know. A criminal behind bars wants me dead. I'm faced with the fact that I'm an undercover agent for an organization that's as enigmatic as far as the other side of the solar system. If I accept the operatives' terms, I'll have to—"

"What are their terms? You've never told me."

I can't. Because you are the bargaining chip! They don't want me with you. She reasoned. "Nash—"

"Must be hard to learn things you weren't expecting. I'm not so sure about the operatives either and their secret methods. Where do they get such knowledge to generate technological and scientific advancements that defy anything we've seen in the military and the NSA? But—"

Calla blinked at Nash's hesitation.

He continued. "Don't you want to get to know Stan, your father? Perhaps spend some time with him in England? You searched for him all your life."

Nash would not normally prod for answers. He usually let her emerge from her guarded self on her own terms, in her own time. He was patient that way. But his patience with her hesitation was wearing out.

Calla's voice cracked. "I'm not sure what I want."

"You didn't get to bond with him." Nash's face quizzed her. "You must have questions for him. Maybe more questions about your mother."

She rubbed her sweating hands on her jeans. "She's dead."

Nash sidled to the retractable doors where Calla stood. She observed his affectionate movement toward her. Her back turned toward him, as Nash stepped behind her and placed his robust arms around her frame. He glanced out the window, the sun hitting his strong jaw. "You're safe here. No one is going to find you, whatever you are running away from."

He brushed his lips over the top of her head and rested his chin on her smooth mane. "My father first sold this house when I joined the military. I bought it back from the owners a year ago."

She sensed hesitation in his voice when he mentioned his father. An irritation. He was changing the subject for her sake. She sank into his embrace. "It's beautiful out here, Nash. Why did your father sell the house?"

"It happened when I joined the marines. He didn't approve," Nash said, shrugging his shoulders. "Probably wanted to annoy me as he did my mother and drove her away. They split years ago."

Pain was evident in his voice as he spoke of his parents. She decided not to pursue the subject. "Thank you for bringing me here." She listened to Nash's soft breathing. Calla turned away from the window and looked into his gray eyes. "Okay. It's time I tell you why we *really* are here."

HER MAJESTY'S PRISON SERVICE
BELMARSH, LONDON

1700 hrs.

"That's the fourth visitor this month," said Hugh Kail, the prison guard in charge of high-security unit criminals at Belmarsh.

The tightly fortified prison stood in the eastern part of London. Kail surveyed Mason Laskfell's dark cell on the closed-circuit television monitors in the officers' quarters. Dark tobacco stains were visible on his finger as he ran it along the edges of the surveillance system. He considered the eminent felon, a silver-haired man whose physique defied his recorded age, an unusual criminal in his charge, and one with high, international status. He stroked his clean-shaven chin. Kail was used to notorious offenders, but not like Mason.

The man was daunting.

Kail pressed his lips in a moderate grimace. He took a seat at his desk and turned to Elias Koleszar, his subordinate, who'd just come in from a ten-minute break.

Elias's wide brown eyes shone in the bright lights. He'd been a prison guard for twelve years at Belmarsh, having been fired from the London Metropolitan Police for insubordination and violence on the job. Elias had spent seven months in prison himself. He'd left with one goal—uphold the law and community spirit, viewing it as part of his responsibility. So far, he'd failed. He extorted high-profile criminals for any money they could part with, in return for petty favors like extra blankets, cigarettes, or anything he could sneak into their cells.

Elias tunneled bony fingers through fine, gray hair. "Laskfell's behavior is odd."

"What else is new?"

"Has he settled in that isolation cell?"

"Seems fine to me." Elias knit his eyebrows. "He's one to

watch. Nothing like the others, you know. He has that strange, quiet knowing as if he sees what you're thinking."

"Don't get too close."

"I'm not. And off the record, he's the former head of ISTF. They wouldn't let me put that on his records. Something to do with keeping ISTF out of the media's radar."

"ISTF, huh? You mean the undercover group that intervenes in global, criminal investigations."

"I heard they only hire *wunderkinder*. You know, twenty-twenty vision, tip-top medical shape, IQs no less than 160. Sheeesh!"

Kail raised his head from his laptop. "ISTF has been under heavy investigation for years and yet is funded without the taxpayer's knowledge."

Elias pondered for several seconds. "Until we got this guy, we all thought it was poof! Long gone. That it had stopped existing months ago."

Kail didn't care for the exaggerations. ISTF had turned down his application years ago. And Mason was a sore reminder of that fact. "I don't think ISTF ever existed." His voice lowered as he set a finger on the mute button of his phone systems. "That's what the papers said. Yet one way or another, money keeps drifting through many hands to fund the blasted thing." He shot his colleague a deliberate gaze. "Some legit, some less legit. What do I care? I retire in two years. Doesn't seem as though Her Majesty's Royal Pension Service will be handing out gold coins."

Elias contemplated; his eyes fixed on the surveillance monitor. "That's what makes Laskfell's case fascinating. How do you incriminate a man for high crimes against an organization that doesn't exist on paper, again using taxpayers' money?"

Kail shrugged his shoulders. "They'll find something linked to other government agencies. You've seen these government types. So-called visitors have come and gone in the last six months, some coming from as far as Washington DC." Kail's eyes left the screen for the first time and wandered to where Elias stood. "That guy's got more millions than the welfare checks we hand out in this country, even after the government confiscated his personal funds."

"A billionaire behind bars. Milk it for what it's worth. You and I'll never see money like that in our lifetime, unless—"

"Every day, gifts from unidentified sources arrive for him. Have you been making a list? Make sure they stay in the confiscated pot. I'll find use for them someday. We need to cover our backs," Kail added.

"Certainly," said Elias. "But the governor authorized Laskfell's laptop in his cell."

"The magistrate denied him bail. She must've felt sorry for the geek and consented to a few belongings." He slammed his own laptop shut. "Heck! A laptop today is like having a book. Laskfell's laptop is generations newer than this piece of scrap. Did you disable the wireless and 4G networks? We can't have him engaging in any online activity. That was the magistrate's only stipulation."

"Yup."

Kail rubbed his chin. "We can't be careless, and none of the other prisoners should know about it."

Elias nodded. "I doubt anyone wants to be near him. The prisoners are talking. They fear him like the plague. I don't get it. It's not that he has the strongest build or even the worst criminal record. It's weird stuff, mate. They don't look him in the eyes. And when they do, they're gripped with fear of even coming within yards of him."

Kail rotated on his seat and glanced at the magistrate's list of approved visitors. He stamped a piece of paper authorizing Mason's next visitor, signed it, and handed it to Elias. "Solitary confinement will help with that little problem."

Elias glared at the slip of paper. "To imagine, that one man could be waiting for trial for murder. His report also lists offenses including the mishandling of classified information, kidnapping, criminal handling of government assets, and suspicion of terrorist activities against the state and international territories." He shook his head. "I had better check in his new visitor. This one's unusual."

CHAPTER 3

ALMONT, COLORADO
1512 hrs.

A FRONT-SNAP PUNCH slid past Calla's face. Nash studied her physique. "Always watch your blind spot."

She turned her head, having dodged a potential excruciating clout. She riddled back into fight stance, fists up, one foot forward, and guard in check. Catching the determination in his eyes, the floor beneath her bare feet was cold and dry. *Better for grip.*

Nash smirked at her insistence. "Coming back for more?"

The clock on the wall ticked audibly. She counted every second in her mind. *This one's for...*

Calla brought her left fist back, and struck at him with her right hand, twisting her hips to gain extra speed and power.

Nash broke her attack with his fists. "Now block me, quickly!" he said.

Nash launched a side fisted punch her way.

She blocked the strike with her left forearm, and stepped with her left foot on his, twisting him counterclockwise. With a firm hold on his biceps, she flung him over her outstretched leg.

Nash rolled on the floor and gripped her neck, bringing her down to him. "Good! But you need to finish your attacker."

Calla's frustrated look met his eyes. She glimpsed up from where she'd fallen. *I want this!*

It meant everything to learn to channel her strength, more for self-defense than anything else. She had to master skill. Skill in hand-to-hand combat, and defense while unarmed. Calla had vigor, thanks to her operative genes, but skill she could improve. "How do I finish him?"

"With an arm lock." Nash rose with Calla looking up toward him. "Here, let me show you. Like this." He reached for her hand. "Take your hand and place it around your attacker's right arm, behind the elbow. Then set your left knee down on their neck and the other on their chest. That holds them in a place of mercy. Keep them down. I feel sorry for whomever your attacker may be."

Nash pulled her to her feet and tugged at his black belt around his white, ju-jitsu suit.

Calla straightened her own ivory suit.

Without delay, Nash gripped her wrist.

She swung her head toward him in surprise.

"Use your strength, Calla, and use it against your attacker."

Calla rotated her wrist and thrust down his grip. "Gotcha!"

He grabbed her free hand. "Impressive. Listen, beautiful, build your strength from within. You're tougher than anyone I know, but you have to learn how to manipulate the opponent's force against them."

She threw a straight punch at him. Nash pivoted his right foot, moving his body out of the way of the straight fist's thrust.

Calla lost balance. His left hand reached for her, grappling the top of her wrist. Incapacitated, her hand didn't move, caught in Nash's grasp. When he sensed her vulnerable position, Nash loosened his hold.

Calla relaxed her muscles. "How do you do that? No matter what I do, you get me every time?"

"It's not about strength. The race is not won by the swiftest. A lieutenant learns that he can be forgiven for defeat. But he can't be forgiven for lack of alertness. You have to be one step ahead. Don't let your opponent surprise you."

Calla glimpsed up, mesmerized at Nash's skill. "How do you know all this?"

He gazed straight into her eyes and threw her a captivating smile. "It's a mixture of techniques learned along the way. That move is ju-jitsu. I trained US soldiers for six months in Japan."

"Was that when you were in the military?"

Nash nodded and gravitated to the end of the training room to grab a towel from the rail. He wiped his perspiring face and ran it through his hair. He smiled. "That's enough for today. You get it and a million times better than soldiers I trained. Calla, I've taught you everything I can about skill, accuracy, and tact. You're great, and training is strengthening you. Just keep an eye on your blind spot. The blind spot is more psychological than physical. Most soldiers ignore it."

"Thanks, Nash."

"You were already exceptional by my measure, my question is, why not train with the operatives?"

Calla glanced away and slid her feet on the bare wooden floor toward the door behind Nash. A slight chill had formed in her toes. "It's cold down here."

Nash regulated a switch by the door. "I keep it cool in here. This basement floor is for training."

Calla moved toward him and slid under his free arm as Nash turned off the lights.

"One more thing," he said. "I need to teach you how to use a firearm."

"I don't like firearms."

"Can you say that? After what happened at Murchison Falls and in London? You've been shot at more than once, Calla. You need to learn how to handle yourself with one."

She shook her head. "Nash, I really can't."

"It's still self-defense."

It troubled him that as a member of ISTF, she'd skipped much of the mandatory weapons training. The truth was she didn't like violence, though she could handle any fight that came her way. Everything she knew had come by instinct.

They plodded up the stairs leading from the sizable basement that incorporated a five-car garage, a training room, and an office Nash kept locked. She'd not set foot in there and had never asked him about it. One night about three months ago, when she couldn't sleep, she'd meandered to the kitchen for an apple. Startled by a noise, she caught Nash working in there with the door ajar. What did he do there?

Nash's work with the NSA was transparent to Calla most of the time. Her position within ISTF allowed her that privilege. She'd never imagined what his life was like outside of London, though they'd met when she'd come to Denver for an anthropological study many months ago. Here they were in his hometown if she could call it that. Nash had traveled most of his childhood, from continent to continent, owing to his father's work as a diplomat. Later his military career had taken him to the Middle East and Germany.

They reached the ground level, traversing the ultra-contemporary kitchen, fitted with natural wood cabinets and reclaimed wood floors. Calla followed Nash as they moved to the salon, where reset lights, fixed in the ceiling beams, provided an art-gallery-like feel.

"I want to take you into town for a celebration. I think we deserve one, no?" Nash said.

She knew what he meant. Her birthday had come and gone when they were in Africa. "Nash, you've done so much already, I—"

"Hey, let me do this."

An hour later, they settled in a restaurant that used to be a former hunting lodge. Nestled along East River, the exclusive restaurant cabin was only accessed by hired horseback.

Calla let the cool water slide down her throat as she took a sip, rearranging her words in her head. How should she begin?

They shared much of the gourmet offering. A jovial waiter served pan-seared pheasant breast, agnolotti, and wilted spinach. When the last course came, Calla had not raised the topic on her mind.

Nash was quiet for several minutes.

"What's eating you, soldier?" she asked.

He stretched for her hand and took it in his. "We don't have to think about this now...but what happens after?"

"After what?"

"After you find what you're looking for?"

"I'm not looking for anything."

"All right, then when can we talk about us... going forward...don't you ever want a family?"

Calla watched him bug-eyed. She fingered the thin gold chain she wore around her neck that Nash had given her six months ago. A simple piece set with her first initial.

She knew where he was going with this line of questioning. How could she tell him that after she discovered her parents abandoned her on the doorsteps of an orphanage, she'd sworn never to put any child through the same thing? If she could help it, she would avoid any commitment to a child. And help it she did, by considering major surgery. It was the only way Calla could guarantee never to repeat the faults of her parents.

Calla tunneled a hand through her long mane and glared into his waiting eyes that gleamed with admiration for her. She had to tell him. "Nash, I can't go there... It's not for me."

"Which part?"

"The family part. *Us* has to be me...alone."

LONDON, 1708 hrs.

Mason glanced up at the security camera. The cell reeked of disinfectant. Several meters from the officers' cramped quarters, curious gazes he'd often received, after being brought to Belmarsh, scrutinized him.

He leaned his six-foot frame against the cool cement. Fatigued with exasperated emotion rather than physical strain, his dark hair was littered with tiny streaks of gray. One usually guessed his age at forty-five. He didn't care. Age was not the authority on character and intelligence. A close look depicted a striking warrior, resembling a lieutenant in Napoleon's army, than the expert cryptographer and capable intelligence analyst he'd become. He'd risen to the ranks of chief of ISTF's research, signals intelligence, and linguistics divisions. Mason had served in the military as commander in the British Army several years ago. A fanatical workaholic, he'd thrived at deciphering puzzling codes, languages, accents, and handwriting. He'd once taken on the challenge of decrypting the coded Voynich manuscript, and like others before him, had failed. Upon joining ISTF several years ago, he designed and maintained government systems that kept sensitive data safe from outside threats, including impostors, identity thieves and those who caused cyber havoc. With

ISTF's focus on cyber criminals, eighteen months ago, he'd investigated the Stuxvet virus that targeted Iranian computer systems attempting to disrupt the country's uranium enrichment program. A case he'd intended to conclude. If only...

Rumor had it he could read minds, a reason many avoided him.

This had been his principal investigative procedure. Despite his accolades, he now was notorious for failed attempts at protecting global network systems. Some said he'd sabotaged them. What did they know? What did he care?

Mason rose from his stale bed. Though it was 5:00 pm., and his single opportunity a day to mingle with the other criminals, Mason had no time for petty socialization.

Besides, she's coming.

His monotonous cell, not the standard of the rest of the prison, boasted a flat screen television, its own toilet, a pristine shower, which came with large white towels.

Set on the outskirts of London, the rest of the prison blocks were minimalist, modern and efficient. ISTF offices had instigated the tightest security measures and technologies for particular isolation cells like Mason's. The rumor was this clandestine government agency stepped in where Interpol, the CIA, and MI6 stopped.

What did he care? He'd been a good ISTF leader. Illicit policing and global criminal investigation were now the least of his concerns. Yet, here he was, detained in his own handiwork. After he'd failed to make bail, Mason paid for the extras himself with a sizable donation to the prison charity. Though the state had confiscated most of his assets, his source of income was his own affair and not theirs. They'd barely taken a drop from his ocean of assets in seven offshore accounts in locations as far as the Cayman Islands, the British Virgin Islands and the Cook Islands.

He strolled to the private fridge, retrieved a firm apple, gnawed into its juicy core, and drummed his fingers along a steel cupboard containing his meager belongings.

Belmarsh housed the gravest offenders the country had seen and was a ruthless prison. Mason was yet to see a trial in court. How long would they keep him here? The case against him though plain, was not straightforward. So what if he'd attempted murder? Ordered it more than once? The Cress woman had walked, so had the NSA agent and now imprisonment itched his skin, like an irritating leach sucking on blood. Her Majesty's magistrates were up for a difficult fight, and the media had speculated whether ISTF would be dissected once the case began. He wouldn't make it easy for them.

Mason paced back to a pile of papers that created a neat stack on a pine desk against the wall. White magnetic pin boards and oversized, barred windows above the desk overlooked a brick wall. After furtive security, Belmarsh had authorized his laptop, but cut all online activity and connection. He finished his apple and flung the core at the surveillance camera.

How long had he endured? He calculated. *One hundred and seventy days. Twenty-four weeks and two days.*

He set a dry palm on his knee and continued a game of chess he'd started against himself. Most mornings, Mason's nostrils took in the strong aroma of coffee drifting through the latch from the halls. The scent was the first thing he'd noticed when he arrived. The coffee was always in plenty. It hit him when he walked the workshop areas, lingered in the games rooms and in the communal apartment-style areas where prisoners lived in groups of seven. Recently, the warden allowed him minimal freedom in the common areas.

The smell of after dinner coffee churned his stomach. He'd not had a proper meal in months. Though he reviled the nourishment the prison dared call food, he purposed to keep up his strength. As much as he detested the blasted routines, sometimes the warden came into his secluded cell with a tall stack of steaming, heart-shaped waffles and pots of jam, which he set on his metal table. He obliged most days, to manipulate the money-hungry mongrel.

It helped the time pass.

The lights out siren clanged in the upper quarters of the prison. Mason hurtled his unfinished game at the grilled peephole, sending two chess pieces to the other side of the cell. *Don't they know I was trying to help them!*

He checked the clock on the laptop. His next visitor would soon arrive, a late call owing to a ridiculous work schedule. His unusual status as an eminent government prisoner and the notable amounts of euros he'd arranged for the prison wardens in offshore accounts had legitimized the late caller. Mason was expecting eleven visits altogether and nine had crossed the gates of the contemptible establishment.

A wide grin grew on his face. The more fear he could spread in the prison staff and inmates, the easier his next effort would be. Discernment taught him they were watching him more than most inmates. Especially those two fools.

—

ALMONT, COLORADO
1637 hrs.

"I came here for your safety, Nash. They'll kill you because of me."

Nash's eyes glistened in the fire's glow. "Your protection, I'll take any day."

"I had to take you from London, especially after what

happened in Jordan and in Uganda. Mason did not hesitate to throw you over a cliff and—"

"Sh. .. I'm here now. That's over now. I want to move on. I can't work for the government forever. I want to settle down. I'm thirty-three and I think I've done my part."

She'd never seen his eyes so determined. "But—"

Nash lowered his voice as if reading her thoughts. "I don't want to know. .. whatever it is. All I care about is you."

She bit her lip as they settled in front of a fire. Flames beamed off Nash's face as he lifted a chilled water glass.

Calla tilted her head, with a penetrating gaze set on Nash. He was tired. Perhaps not physically, maybe something else. For six months, Nash had stopped all travel and battled with NSA and ISTF demands, mostly around signals intelligence. He'd rejected fieldwork where he could, and stayed close to her.

A recent cyber threat, involving a NASA spacecraft's, onboard communication system had kept him occupied most days. Calla had not followed the ISTF brief he'd showed her the other day. She still intended to stay away and neither would she entertain her obligations at the British Museum. She'd lied about a sabbatical involving a study expedition in Egypt and Greece for the museum's archives. A lie she could no longer deny. ISTF had not questioned her sabbatical seeing she'd been commended for apprehending Mason Laskfell, a conspiring criminal on constant watch in Belmarsh Prison.

As a superior linguist and historian, sometimes ISTF and the government called on Calla for her distinct flair in restoration science and her knowledge of the role languages and history played in social and cultural situations. The biggest topic on ISTF's agenda was global cyber crimes. Historic and language skills had also played a part in disarming recent hacking activity.

Calla raised her feet, slid them under her thighs and

settled on the couch. She gazed at the fire flickering in front of her. "Does anyone ever come here, Nash? It's such a big house for one person."

"I keep my life private, even from the government when I can." He reached for her hand. "So I can do things like bring you here without anyone's knowledge."

Calla smiled. "Does it get lonely?"

"I'm never here... just want to put down roots."

"Why the secrecy?"

"My father's public life meant living my childhood in newspaper columns and speculation. It was okay when the news was good, but once it turned sour, it placed so much stress on my mother. My father would have done anything for his career, even at the expense of my mother's sanity. I don't want to be like that, Calla." Nash edged closer. "People important to me come first."

Calla set a hand on his tightening jaw. "I know—"

He tilted his head. "I've always wanted to bring you here. The events in Africa and Jordan took their toll on you. We need a break sometimes. Perhaps a permanent one—"

Desperation rang in her tone. "I don't want to lose you."

Nash's hand stroked her skin and he gave her a strict look of affection. "You can't lose me."

It was probably best she kept quiet. According to Allegra and Vortigern, Nash had withheld information, which they thought put the operatives' interests at risk. She leaned into his arm. "Nash, when we were in Uganda six months ago, I learned much about me from this operative Vortigern. About my genetic and medical history, and my ancestry. When I met Stan, it was a dream come true and I couldn't be more satisfied until—"

He kissed her fingers. "That wasn't easy for you."

"But there's something I didn't tell you, Nash, before I do—"

Nash drew her hand toward him and placed it on his chest. "Calla, I don't care if you have the force of the Earth, or the strength of Hercules living in your veins. I also don't care what people like this Vortigern tell you about yourself. All I care about is the woman I first met at Denver airport, who charmed me for nine hours to London with her knowledge. And most importantly, her passion for the things and people she cares about."

Calla pursed her lips. She reached for Nash and for several seconds folded her arms around his neck, saying nothing. She released him and shot up before gravitating toward the fireplace and gazed into its soft blaze. "I need to know something."

He crossed his arms over his chest. "What's that?"

"Mason's an operative. The breakneck kind."

Nash leaned back against the sofa. "I don't believe most operative stuff."

"Why? But do you believe some?"

Nash rose and moved to her side. "When your father first asked me to protect you, I assumed that the British Secret Intelligence Service had denied his request to protect his family. Why come, and involve a favor from former CIA head, Ben Colton?" He watched her face with scrutiny. "Ever since you came in contact with the carbonado rocks the Hadrius Manuscript led us to, something happened to you and mostly physically."

"Nash, I never knew. I–"

"Maybe you've always been this way, strong, resistant... special. That's what I like to think. That you were already complete."

"You really believe that don't you?"

"Yes. Nothing missing. No additions necessary. Things people tell you about you do not define you. Calla, I trust you. I told you once that I was in for the long haul. You've special things about you that governments would covet for any of their marines." He paused and took a breath. "I fell in love with your spirit. That, Cal, no one can take away from you."

Calla's face flustered and she fell silent for several seconds. "Nash, have you ever investigated operatives in the CIA, NSA, or ISTF?"

Nash swallowed hard and turned his face from her. "Yes, and I didn't like what I found."

"What did you find?"

"I—"

A rapid shattering of glass exploded around them. It came through the window. Glass shards from the grand windows splintered in every direction. Cold, piercing wind shot into the room, bringing the sounds of the mountain valley into the large space.

Nash threw an arm over Calla's head and drove her to the floor. The lights went out, silence arresting the whole house, except for the cracking of the wood on the fire. They crouched on the floor for several seconds before Nash raised his head.

A can of discharging gas rolled inches from where they cowered.

Nash shot to his knees, pulling Calla up with him. "Let's move."

A deafening noise shuffled outside on the lawn. Their ears caught a rumble, sounding like the engine of a large vehicle or tank. With their backs against the wall, the armored vehicle, no bigger than a Jeep, scythed Nash's lawn, slashing shrubbery with its snow-crushing tires.

"Damn it! He broke my fence." Nash turned to the surveillance camera on the entertainment center and cursed under his breath. "He blew out my cameras, too."

Calla gaped out the window as the rapid, frigid breeze fluttered her loose mane.

"We're trapped. That's the only way down the mountain."

Nash swore. “Not on my watch.”

A silhouetted figure raced toward the house, crushing the frozen snow. Calla’s hands shook as she tugged at Nash’s arms. “I knew it, Nash. It’s him, the footprints. How did they find us?”

Calla crawled to the edge of the window for a closer glimpse behind Nash. The figure had stopped a few meters from the house. He raised a weapon he slung over his shoulder and pointed in their direction.

Nash pulled her away from the window and they shot to the far end of the room. “Got to get downstairs.”

His eyes narrowed with anger. “Your friend’s very daring.”

“What do you mean?”

“Let’s move.” He grasped her hand. “He’s got a damn bazooka!”

“What?”

“He’s going to torch the place!”

—

1715 hrs.

Elias scratched his itching bald head and departed to meet the feeble woman at the visitors’ gate. “Nice day for a visit.”

She did not respond but kept her head down, shielding her eyes from his questioning gaze. She lifted her head.

He scrutinized her oval face, dark and rather delicate. Her clothes were mismatched and form-fitting with her tweed skirt and a light-green blouse under an oversized sweater. She wore her limp hair in a bun.

“First time to Belmarsh?” Elias said.

She tightened her lips. “And the last.”

Elias registered her shaky, firm Northern England accent and took the calm woman through two air-lock doors. As the first closed, another mechanical door opened. Elias waited as an officer searched her belongings. The visitor, with a face frozen in calm, took off her hat, her coat, belt, and emptied all her pockets, then moved through an x-ray scanner. Her last subjection to a security check was a frisk with a metal-detector and a full pat down.

She frowned at the officers. "Surely by now, you would have found anything I might be concealing in this old tweed and perhaps, anything else I might be hiding on my person! Not to mention my thermal knickers! Are we finished?"

"Quite," said Elias.

The woman signed her name.

Elias peered down at the printed name.

First Name: Veda
Surname: Westall
Profession: Head Curator at the British Museum

Fortified doors dragged open and guided them to a second house block.

"This is our jail within a jail, only for our special prisoners," Elias said.

"I don't need your polite conversation. I need you to stay in there with me for three minutes for my purposes."

"Yes ma'am."

They arrived at a hefty, cell door secured with a grill-gated window. Mason glanced over his laptop. He lay on a freestanding single bunk, three inches thick, with a blue synthetic mattress and observed as Veda ambled into his cell behind Elias.

With her face pale, but proud, she scanned the pitiful environs, the relative darkness, the uninviting concrete floors, the steel toilet bowl, and the shelves firmly bolted to a wall.

"Unimpressed by the décor, Ms. Westall?" Mason said.

"Not quite in line with your keeping from what I understand, even if it's much more than most of your inmates I imagine. The power of cash flow knows no law."

"I'm glad you approve."

She smirked and turned her attention to Elias, who strode over to Mason and helped him to his feet. "Let's go. You'll be allowed a private consultation room for an hour. Private, that is, with us in there."

Elias bound Mason's feet with boot-cuffs and despite the restraints, Mason stood with the elegance of a gazelle as he reached for Westall's hand.

Mason set a gentleman's kiss on its upper side.

She jerked it back with the force of startled panther.

"Feisty, aren't we?"

Veda's eyebrows gathered. "I'm not your type."

"Didn't think so."

Mason observed Veda fiddle with her skirt as they paced the ten meters to an interrogation room with plain décor in dark glazed, bulletproof counter windows and minimal furniture. Veda's full dark hair, graying at the temples was as neat as a straight up whiskey. She was as short as he remembered, and barely came up to his shoulders. They'd met when he'd visited the British Museum to source a personal reference for Calla Cress's nomination into ISTF.

Mason and Veda took seats opposite each other. Kail, who'd now joined Elias, stood perched by the open door and observed the consultation, armed with incessant curiosity.

Elias shackled a computerized wire to Mason's left boot-cuff and connected it to a nearby computer in the security room.

"I don't think that's necessary," Mason said.

"Just procedure."

Must have been the NSA guy Shields. He alone could recommend this prison surveillance. *Damn it, I authorized it myself at the ISTF labs!*

The wire monitored his speech and conversation for aggression, much like a lie detector. He would deal with Shields when the time came. Mason eyed the two security cameras pointed at his face from two angles of the room, before turning to his guest.

"Ms. Westall," Mason began. "Excuse me, for the inappropriate hour. I imagine your work at the museum keeps you tied down."

"I didn't come to see you; I came for what you have for me," she said.

"All in good time."

"The magistrate ordered you to hand me the logarithms for the museum's security systems. Where are they? Who has them? At the moment, we are blind to any threat, should we wish to manipulate them."

"Straight to the point, I see."

Kail and Elias glanced from face to face, as Mason's persuasive manner with women seemed to wane with Veda.

Mason scrutinized their quiet snickers. He pored his eyes into Elias and then Kail. They took cue and took seats by the door, giving him the secluded consultation time he'd requested. He sensed terror spewing from them, also apparent in the shuddering fear in their eyes.

Fear gave Mason energy. In the months he'd been awaiting trial, guards around him were changed every four days, requesting reassignment each time. Fear was his finest associate. He had to work fast. "Ms. Westall, you sit on the London Board of Museums."

"What of it?"

"I've used my influence to acquire you that special piece,

Cézanne's Card Players. The only art piece you seek in the series, held in private hands."

"What're you getting at?"

"Experts say it could be worth as much as $100 million."

Westall raised an eyebrow. "What gives you the inkling that I would take any favors from a convicted criminal?"

"I've yet to be convicted."

"As far as I'm concerned, you are. Now, give me the logarithms I came for."

Mason ignored her insistence. "London museums need fresh collections to spur on their popularity and keep budgets where they need to be."

"Mr. Laskfell. What is it you really want?" She leaned closer. "My only purpose here is to obtain security coordinates memorized in that crisp brain of yours. You were the one who placed the British Museum under heavy security last year, a move I firmly resisted."

"Your museum is of much interest to ISTF."

"A threat ISTF called it. From what?"

"Intelligence." Mason studied her perplexed stare. "Do you believe in ISTF?"

Westall shifted in her seat. She struggled to focus under his gaze. "What do you mean?"

Mason's face broke into a wide smile. *Only a few more moments.* "ISTF has its uses and was on its way to greatness under my watch."

"I.... do...not care for—"

Westall's head shuddered, her bulging eyes focused on Mason's own. Her body launched into a quake of trembles.

Kail raised an eyebrow and tugged Elias's sleeve. They gaped at Mason, their eyes widening in unbelief.

Westall's uncontrollable movements intensified. After several seconds, she jolted back as if an intense, lightning bolt had thrown her back. She sat immobilized in her seat and stared blankly ahead.

Not once did Mason's eyes leave her.

Her tongue hung from her jaw, like a slack tail and for more than a few seconds, Mason maintained his gaze into her bugged eyes.

To the guards, he may as well have been studying her expression. With Westall's back to them, they could not grasp that her eyeballs had rolled back into their sockets.

Mason took a deep breath, unwavering in his glare. *Tell me what I need.*

She remained motionless, entranced by his unblinking eyes.

He edged closer across the table.

Kail shot to his feet. "Hey! No more physical contact!"

Mason recoiled analyzing Westall's unresponsive face, his fixed gaze blazoning.

Five seconds later, Westall collapsed to the floor unconscious.

CHAPTER 4

GRACE BAY, TURKS AND CAICOS ISLANDS
THE CARIBBEAN
1220 hrs.

"AFTER WHAT I did for you? You should be crawling to help. Come on, Tad," Jack said scratching his hair. At thirty-two, he was carefree than most, Converse shoes, Levi's jeans and sport jackets were his uniform, plus the shoulder-length dreadlocks he wore. A well-honed technology specialist, Jack could command any fee and any place of employment. With an impressive client list of government agencies, private corporations and security firms, Jack was an engineer and technology expert in demand.

Thaddeus Evick, a spacecraft designer for NASA, took a sip of his Mai-Tai, gulping the Polynesian cocktail of rum, orange curacao and orgeat syrup. He scanned the vast, white sand beach and aqua view in front of him. "We're lounging inches from the world's most blissful beach, by my count, and all you can talk about is work."

"Come on, man."

"Take a break I don't imagine you see anything like this in London."

"Technically, I'm not on a break," Jack said as he twitched his scorching nose. He glanced ahead at the sizzling beach that rivaled those in his native Seychelles, dipping into one of the first-rate coral reefs he'd ever seen, swarming with aquatic life. Yet all he could think about was the NASA meeting taking place next week in Washington.

Jack dug his feet into the virgin sand and took in Thaddeus' words as he reclined in the hammock overlooking the ocean. For a moment, he agreed with his old friend Thaddeus. He sat miles from the dismal October climate of London, on an island overlaid with white sand beaches, vanishing beneath the ebb and tides of turquoise waters. The Providenciales, part of the Turks and Caicos Islands, southeast of Mayaguana in the Bahamas, were beyond striking. Delighted to escape one of the wettest falls Jack had ever known in London, he observed the clear aqua ocean in the distance, sunk his feet deeper in the granular dust, cooling his toes. "Trust you to pick this spot for a reunion after seven years."

"It's the best part, the north shore of the island, in Grace Bay."

"I'm glad we can bask in this little paradise for a change." Jack raised an eyebrow and shook his head. "I need to ask you something."

Thaddeus squinted, the sun attacking his face. He pulled down his sunglasses, covering his dark gray eyes, a modish look, fashioned by neat, dark-blond locks. "Can't we talk about it later? By the way, how's your sister?"

Jack raised an eyebrow, aware of his sister's torturous liaison with Thaddeus. "She should have married you that day, man. I've not spoken to Fiora in five years."

"Is she still married to him?"

"The banker in New York?" Jack drew in a sharp breath. "Yeah, after she milked my US account, she's now in a loveless marriage with an idiot who thinks he can control tech stock on the New York Stock exchange. Tad, you loved her and she treated you wrong, but I've written her off."

"Forgive her, man. I did," Tad said.

Was he right? The woman had sold several designs to questionable tech companies making a fortune with his work. Jack gave him an impatient shrug. "I wish I could."

"If anything, know that she's not in a happy place."

"Is anyone? One day, I'll get my patents back."

"Is that all?" Tad said.

Jack squirmed on his hammock. "Something about her behavior has put me off women."

"You? Off women? I don't believe it!"

Jack grimaced, not wishing to pursue the matter any further. They'd met halfway, Jack from London and Thaddeus from Miami. Jack sat up in his hammock. The heat scorched his exposed belly, toned after dynamic, physical training, and a vigorous workout he'd requested of ISTF after his time in Africa. He drew in a sharp breath. "I leave tomorrow, Tad. I need your help now. Listen, I helped your father with his little problem with the British authorities. Paid for a legitimate lawyer—"

Thaddeus shifted in his beach chair and peered from behind his shades at his childhood friend. "Jack, what you've done for our family is invaluable. Come on, where we come from on the Seychelles Island and especially our corner isn't exactly the land of opportunity." He drummed his fingers on his thigh. "Jack, if I could bypass protocol, I would. But that NASA summit is an eight-member meeting and by invitation only."

It felt as though a slap had clouted Jack. He was not sure whether he should be content for his friend who'd left the

Seychelles at an early age, when the two were still boat boys. Thaddeus had pursued higher education in London thanks to a government grant. He later proceeded with a spacecraft design scholarship at Utah State University. NASA later scouted him from the university having read his thesis on 'The Future of the Ranger Spacecraft Design.'

A waiter stopped by with a glass of ice water and handed it to Jack.

He took the chilled glass from her hand and nodded his thanks before turning his attention to Thaddeus. "My intention is twofold. First, two nights ago, ISTF got word of a hack that has occurred on NASA's systems. The hackers I understand gained full access to the data network in one of the control centers, the Jet Propulsion Lab to be exact. I think I can help."

Thaddeus raised an eyebrow. "What's number two?"

"To improve space computer technologies, I've some micro robotic designs that NASA should look at. They're virtually worm proof. No hack can penetrate them. This meeting next week with the top designers and engineers is where I'd like to present the designs."

"Jack—"

"Let me finish. The importance and impact of artificial satellites and space systems on our lives cannot be underestimated. Think of it, everything we do depends on these processes. I don't need to be telling you this. Everything from telephones and Internet services, navigation and broadcasting, weather forecasting, medical assistance and humanitarian aid. Almost all facets of military operations are affected somehow by space and cyberspace capabilities. I've spent three years developing firewalls and intrusion detection systems and created patches for known and unknown vulnerabilities at the ISTF labs. System engineering is where I want to be. I need you to help me."

"So ISTF isn't keeping you busy enough. I thought they were a nonentity. What's *really* going on there?"

Jack ignored the question, "There's no time to kid about. I need to pick the brains of the brightest minds in technology and you can help me."

Thaddeus took another sip of his cocktail and held the chilled glass for several seconds in deep thought. "ISTF is keen on cyber crimes and I'm sure you've been helped set them up. I know the work you guys do. In fact, I'm not sure how the black hats, those blasted hackers did it. These intruders compromised the accounts of most NASA lab users giving them full access to the networks. They modified, copied, and deleted sensitive files. That's no joke."

Jack tilted his head. "So you see, you need my help over there."

Thaddeus pulled his sun cap down. "Can't your British counterparts help you get in on that meeting? They need British representation."

"ISTF is not exactly popular with some government agencies at the moment."

"I see. What about that keen observer of yours? What's his name...? Mason Laskfell?"

Jack's face twisted into a frown. "He's in prison, brother. Awaiting trial."

Thaddeus whistled. "And to think I had my hopes for future investment set on him."

"You're not doing too badly where you are. Spacecraft designs make a hefty killing."

Thaddeus threw his head back and belted out a deep-throated laugh. "Your designs and inventions fetch a hefty price too."

Jack folded his hands and leaned back on his hammock. "So you'll do this for me? It's my one chance to be part of future spacecraft design. I may also be able to help with the hack situation."

"Why is this so important to you?"

Jack raised an eyebrow wondering how much he could share. The NASA meeting would mean he could add space-technology architecture and innovation to his resume. He drew in a sharp breath. "There's a growing trend of adversarial use of widespread, space capabilities and technologies. Anyone today can buy images of targets on Earth and space. They can find accurate timing, navigational data and critical weather information generated by government-owned satellites and use it for their aims. We need to enhance these systems and give them heightened, protective capabilities."

"I know Jack that your robotics program has been instrumental to the government, but what can you add here? We're talking of mega-satellite programs, space robots, computer technology far superior to that of ISTF."

"You'd be surprised at what ISTF has to offer."

"Come on, ISTF doesn't cut it."

The words failed to bruise Jack's ego. He had something. Something worth sharing. What he didn't wish to tell Thaddeus was that he'd already invented the system that would stop such threats. He smiled. "ISTF may not, but I do. I just need to test it. I need to get in."

"I'm sorry Jack. I wish I could help, but I can't."

1609 hrs.

The lights were out making it impossible to see ahead of her.

Nash guided Calla in darkness with the skill of a man used to perilous situations. The only visible light came from the late afternoon's foggy sun rays that broke through the windowpane and beamed through the smoky mist that had filtered downstairs.

She reached with a free hand to grasp Nash's shoulder.

Once down the basement stairs, Nash punched in the code of the locked room. The steel door clanked open.

Calla could hardly see what was kept in the room. It felt colder than the rest of the house. Nash felt his way to the far wall shelves that Calla could barely make out. On the top level, he reached above the shelf and pressed a button that clicked open a small safe a few inches above a wooden desk.

Several cables ran above the safe and though the power was out, the wires flashed in neon blue lights indicating an independent source of electricity. Nash reached inside the safe and drew out a metal box. He clipped it open with both hands and pulled out its contents. Two semiautomatic pistols. Austrian-made by the look of it and standard issue at ISTF.

Nash turned to Calla. "Take this."

Calla hesitated at the gun he handed her.

A loud explosion rippled above them.

"Calla, please. Do it for me. I'll be with you the whole time. No time to argue."

Her hands tightened round her shoulders as Nash's strict tone sent an involuntary chill through her. This couldn't be happening again. Six months ago, they'd been ambushed on every mission. It was happening again. Fear had come back, lurking like a diseased animal. "Nash—"

"I won't let anything happen to you. Come on. We need to get down the mountain."

She slotted the gun in her denims.

They heard the intruder trudge with heavy footsteps on the floor above them.

"Who are they?" Calla said.

"Maybe you were right, someone is after you."

Nash pulled her in front of him and cupped Calla's face in his strong hands. "Or, perhaps as you thought, they're after...me."

"How are we going to get away? He has a tank and a bazooka. We don't know how many there are."

They scrambled to the far end of the room. "I've only got one set of skis," Nash said. He pulled two helmets from a small cabinet by the door and moved toward a large object covered in silver, pliable material. He grabbed two sets of snowsuit tops and tossed one at Calla. "Put this on, quickly."

Calla scrambled to fit it and slid the helmet above her head.

Footsteps stomped down the basement stairs, followed by loud bursts of sulfur from a firearm that rippled from behind the bulletproof door. Decked from floor to ceiling with a collection of armories, assault vests, patrol packs, and several field accessories, this was Nash's true hideout.

Once suited, Nash heaved the snowmobile off its rest. He found a remote control on a shelf and coded in a second password. A double door in front of them drew open and Nash started the ignition. Calla hopped on the back and tightened her arms around his waist.

The door behind them flew open.

Nash accelerated the snowmobile out on the sloping, snow-covered lawn, dodging Douglas firs until the vehicle found smooth ice.

The mobile raced down the slope.

Calla glimpsed back. The chasing figure stood at the entrance through which they'd escaped with a pistol in his hand. He aimed it at them.

"Quick, Nash. He's got a gun!"

"Here, take the handles."

Nash slowed the snowmobile, enough for her to get to the front and steer the bike. As she accelerated, he propped on the back, facing their hunter and drew his firearm.

A shot fired passed them.

The flash of fire, followed by a reverberating explosion, made Calla lose her grip for a second and the snowmobile waddled to the right, close to the edge of a ridge that lined the snow slope.

Nash leaned back, placed his hand over hers and angled the bike in a steady cruise down the slope. Calla regained her balance and continued zipping the snow vehicle off the mountain.

A second shot fired past them.

Filled with nausea, and realizing a shiver of panic, Calla tightened her grasp over the handles.

Nash tilted her way. "You'll be fine, from how I saw you handle yourself in Oxford and Rome. I know you'll be fine."

Calla could hear her heart pounding under her snowsuit as the biting cold slashed her cheeks. Why was she so afraid?

She'd been in worse perils.

Nash steadied himself on the bike, straddling his legs around the backseat for better grip. "There are three of them on foot and one in the tank," he said.

Calla glanced back and caught sight of Nash's house at the top of the incline. About four-hundred meters behind them, she caught sight of two men armed with pistols dashing out of the house wearing all white. The roaring tank they'd transported to the house had also started a steady decent their way.

Another bullet zipped passed Calla's ear and carved into a tree on her right.

Nash shifted his position and fired.

The bullet caught the slower pursuant in the leg. He collapsed and signaled to the pursuing tank to hoist him up.

The slope ended by an ice-covered stream. Calla swerved the bike around changing direction. Another bullet sizzled past her ear and tore through a twig that loosened from a branch in front of her and caught the front part of the snowmobile. The motion propelled them off their seats and catapulted them to the iced ground.

Nash pulled himself up, leveled his gun and pulled the unwavering trigger.

The bullet grazed the first man's arm; he jerked back and slid on the frozen path.

"Go, Calla. I'll take care of them."

She hesitated, eyeing Nash, then the last man on foot who'd gained considerable distance.

"Go." He handed her a piece of paper. "Call this number when you get to the center of Almont. Someone will come for you."

"What about you?"

"I'm right behind you, beautiful."

"Nash, I'm sorry.

"Why?"

"It's my fault. They're after me."

"We don't know that. Now, go!"

Calla shot to her feet. Her stride faltered as she set off at a race down the slope. She trudged the solid snow. As she drew near the bottom of the descent, her foot caught a tree root. She plunged forward, swallowing a mouthful of ice and caved face down on the frigid ground.

Pulling herself up, she gagged on the frozen ingestion and labored forward with a quick glance behind her. Nash was nowhere in sight.

A bullet ripped past her leg and hit a twig behind her, sending a shudder through her. She halted, riled by the coward who dared fire at her. She turned her head to face the pursuant that stood a few meters away.

He launched himself at her, slinging an arm round her neck and brought her choking to the ground.

She tore herself from his grasp. Before she could reposition her balance, he advanced with impulsive speed toward her and gripped her long mane.

Calla convulsed from the pain and booted her attacker in the shin. He slammed to the frozen ground.

Her eye captured motion from behind. Nash charged toward the assailant and knocked the firearm out of his hands, whose eyes followed the direction of the fallen gun. Before the assailant could retrieve it, Nash gripped his right arm and restrained it behind the goon's back, pivoting him farther to the ground.

Calla shot up, trembling with intensity. A suffocated cough left her chest. She targeted the gun Nash had given her, and held her breath as her eye caught movement in the attacker's hand.

Concealed in his grasp, a signaling device flashed a murderous red light.

Nash understood his intent. Before he could curb the man's grip over the appliance, his opponent activated the detonation with a savage gloved finger.

Nash's head spun toward his house.

Silence arrested the mountain.

Not a sound.

A fraction of a second later, a vehement explosion ripped through the atmosphere. Nash's house erupted in a violent explosion of flames. The force of the blast hurtled them back in one potent thrust.

When Calla opened her eyes, the side of her face was numbed by a bed of snow as it rested in the ice. A sharp pain ripped through her arms. Then she realized, her hands had been bound behind her back.

She glanced up. The hooded attacker, blurry in stance, stood above her and pulled her to her feet. A silver ski-mask concealed his face.

In one rapid motion, he jammed a white cloth over her nose.

Her eyes trundled with faintness. By the time she realized it was chloroform, the liquid compound had been ingested. Lightheaded, her eyes rolled backward, and she collapsed over his shoulder.

CHAPTER 5

TEN MINUTES BEFORE MIDNIGHT

MASON SHUT HIS EYES. The abstracts he'd seen in Westall's mind now rested interred in the secure compartments and files on his netbook, running on a questionable operating system. It would only be a matter of time before Belmarsh's, business systems expert discovered the hidden volume on his encrypted hard drive. He lifted the laptop's cover and ran his thumb over its tired keys before restarting the machine. It grounded through the drawn-out boot-up, stalling a few times, and churned at the start-up window.

Mason cursed under his breath. This wasn't the state-of-the-art technology to which he was accustomed. A quick inspection of the hardware configuration told him he was ready to try the clandestine program again. He'd worked all night after he'd returned to his cell, after his visit with Westall.

She'd been easy. *Too transparent.*

Though it was lights out, Mason labored, recalling each word Westall had spoken. *Her mind was open.*

Did he need more? *This should be enough.*

He opened an encrypted program, dormant and invisible in the bottom left corner of the monitor. A small icon, undetectable to the untrained eye. The murky screen requested a password.

He entered one.

A bad one he'd devised, something any business systems person would demote as too simple, his reason for selecting it.

MOTh5R

Any information technology, literate person could crack it. Its simplicity was its anonymity. They would not believe a once famed cryptanalyst would be imprudent enough to hide sensitive material in a folder lacking meticulous security. It was a trick he'd used often at ISTF and kept information hidden from prying eyes.

Mason's genuinely, sensitive finds were in a secret volume.

His intellect.

The hidden software was trite. The password cracked open an obscure screen of cyber gibberish. He scanned the data with caution, registering its meaning. Westall's information was as accurate as he could get. He had more data now.

Bloody idiots! An ingenious effort and bloody simple.

He scrolled through a series concurrent data flow, programming language.

He paused.

One section of scrambled information accessed from Westall's stubborn mind refused to decrypt.

Calla Cress.

Where are you, Cress? Westall doesn't know.

He keyed an icon at the bottom of the open window, shutting the program that shrank into oblivion on his notebook. His interaction with Cress would have to wait.

Mason leaned his silver-haired head against the cool concrete of the cell wall. How had he first discovered the clandestine program with resolve and proficiency? Was it the day he'd first met Westall? That was almost a year ago at the British Museum. He'd commissioned the ISTF team to install garrisoned, security systems in the museum vaults and important display cases. He called it a new way of preserving history as his men marched in the museum with cases of meticulous, laser security equipment, motion-censoring alarm systems and internal burglar-proof, display cases. They had all been engineered in ISTF's research and development center.

Mason's visit came with an ulterior motive. ISTF would one day require an intelligent, linguist and historian, possibly a curator from the museum to validate the Hadrius Manuscript. He had scouted the person who would surface from Westall's team. Calla Cress.

Damn it! The woman had been difficult then as she'd been hours ago. But Westall had the knowledge of a thousand curators and most important, she was Calla's superior. The agent ISTF had handpicked to join many cryptanalyst programs, all to prepare for the validation of the Hadrius Manuscript.

Westall was Calla's confidant by his measure. He shut his eyes and recalled what he'd studied in Westall's mind and the way she processed information. Afraid and disconcerted, hers was an intense anguish about her employee, Cress. Amplified concern about her whereabouts and an intensified burden about her well-being. *Yes, this is invaluable.*

When Westall talked with him, all he'd had to do was raise any casual topic, talk intelligently, and keep her engaged in topics that mattered to her, especially the security concerns at the British Museum. He pictured the words and emotions he'd perceived in her brain all geared toward one question, the whereabouts of Cress. He analyzed the three-dimensional, wave signal form of her brain activity. Why had Cress disappeared?

A sudden flashing from the laptop signaled that the program had registered new information. He launched it again and scanned the material.

He smiled to himself. The covert sequencer had not come at a stress-free price. He'd labored on it for ten years, having designed the interfaces and workings himself, but the fundamental parts were provided by a persistent overweight scientist. Mason took a deep sigh. "Now, Dr. Durant, let's see whether your research is accurate."

An image of the prodigy scientist came to him.

Dr. Durant, the French researcher from Marseilles, had been his first visitor. The shaky-fingered scientist, whose research was spearheading mind-reading programs, had by far, the most scholarly research on the topic. The study was elaborate in the way it harvested portions of people's thoughts, then decoded brain activity. This alone allowed Mason to enhance his extrasensory capabilities. Dr. Durant's research used a brain implant that could scan and observe a person's contemplations by monitoring haphazard words they said.

Mason's Belmarsh visitors, Dr. Durant, Westall and seven more had conversed with him as the implant claimed and registered their deepest emotions, thoughts and desires. He wore the implant on arrival at Belmarsh. Not one security scanner, guard, or medical examiner had picked up its existence. A surgeon would have implanted the device more competently, close to the cerebellum area of his brain, yet he'd accomplished the gruesome feat himself.

Mason was far from anatomically literate, but never winced at the sight of his own blood. He'd done the deed himself aided by a surgical knife. He gouged out a section of his scalp with the clinical instrument, cut a five-centimeter-long incision, in which he placed the transmitter, in front of the posterior bone.

"It needs to be close to the brain stem, near the cerebellum." He could hear Dr. Durant's instructive words.

Aside from a bothersome lump under his epidermis, the chip beneath his scalp delivered two things, the enhancement of his telepathic ability, and the proficiency to interpret brain activity of his visitors, by conversing with them.

Silence was the only reason Dr. Durant was alive. After paying him close to two million pounds in an offshore account, the beady-eyed scientist would concoct no trouble. If he failed to understand the mechanisms of Slate Mendes, the assassin sent to the high school of Durant's only child, matters for him would worsen.

Slate was another concern. The scoundrel had sold him out cold when arrested. The ungrateful orphan he'd raised and trained for years. *All for nothing!*

But Slate's knife had delivered the message and petrified every scrap of self-preservation the bald researcher could assemble.

Mason rubbed the bump—inches above his neck on the right side. Durant's proud face pictured in Mason's mind and his words stung Mason's conscience. Delivered with a Marseilles accent, they'd been accurate. "The research shows insight into how the brain processes language and thoughts. Though it's in its early stages, it connects electric signals using carefully selected chemicals to nerve cells. The stroked interfaces between nerve cells and devices permit direct involvement of electronically processed information into our nervous system."

Yeah? Now it's all here!

The imbecile had sold him the mind-reading sequencer, thinking it would fetch him a Bio-behavioral Research Award.

Mason massaged the chip, no bigger than a fingernail and snickered. *I own the very brilliance you used to script the program.*

He watched as the notebook continued to decipher Westall's brain activity and play back her thoughts in a series of notes it created. One thought drew his attention.

Cress.

Westall had been in touch with her. Perhaps soon after his arrest. He focused on the decryption.

I've not heard from you since the phone call from a London airport, six months ago...your research sabbatical...

Something is bothering you...me too...where are you? I talked with the curator at the Greco-Roman Museum in Alexandria...they haven't heard from you in six months...

1843 hrs.

Nash blinked the snow from his hurting eyes. He dragged the helmet from his throbbing head, raised his stiff neck an inch, and rubbed the agony of a burdening crank in his neck. Compact snow numbed parts of his hands, his right foot and one side of his left leg. A burning stench stole past his nostrils racing from the top of the slope from what used to be his home. It was the biggest investment he'd ever made, and a secluded hideaway.

He gazed through the smoke, and dense fog steaming from the burning debris of the safe house. Solitude and diversion from his unpredictable way of life were essential to him and the exquisite mountaintop retreat delivered that.

Until now.

He hopped to his feet, kneading his left leg for warmth and pain relief. He surveyed the area and the house that once stood on its own side of the mountain, away from intrusive eyes and wanderers.

Why had he picked this spot? Aside from he being born in Colorado, he enjoyed ski sports when he could find time. The decision to live here when he was off duty was an attempt at independence from his broken family. And by his standards, he'd succeeded.

A frosty waft of wind brought the stench of smoke and ashes to his nostrils once more. He coughed and rubbed his eyes in the slight haze.

Who were they?

Son of a gun!

What did they want? He couldn't recall much after the blast knocked him unconscious. The attackers had come for Calla.

His Calla.

The one person whose existence in his life had changed his perceptions about being in a relationship.

Damn it! He'd not listened when she'd try to tell him she was in danger. One thought reassured him. If they wanted her dead, they would have aimed better. They were capable of it.

It could have been an operative. He had to be sure and there was one way of finding out.

Nash wished he'd finished his conversation with Calla. Yes, he was familiar with the operatives and yes, he knew that they were not out for her best interest. He should know. He'd spent months scrutinizing their irregular activities in the US, such as the advanced weaponry the NSA confiscated in Great Barrington, Massachusetts at a hidden factory. He'd also investigated the unconventional, biomedical research labs discovered in Red Bank, New Jersey. That's when he'd been assigned to the operatives' case permanently. As the key US representatives for cyber crimes at ISTF, he was also assigned with investigating the hacking wave that surfaced in several government agencies and the Republican Party headquarters.

The classified nature of his work had torn his life apart often. He'd had to hide much of what he learned. This time, it was personal. It involved Calla.

The distressing operatives' report the NSA demanded of him, was past overdue. And he was not done. How could he protect Calla?

After today's attack on his house, he had to be sure it was an operative attack. The method in which the infiltration and been staged, triggered a thought he had the day he left London with Calla six months ago. Nash also sensed it in Calla, the day they'd deciphered the second code of the Hadrius Manuscript.

Calla had put to rest her worst fears and questions, like discovering what had taken her family away from her and left her helpless at an orphanage, and why the Cresses were connected to the manuscript. They'd only been too aware of why Mason Laskfell threatened Calla's life for it.

The resource, scientific and technological answers the coded manuscript examined and revealed to them, were astounding. Deciphering the manuscript led to a well of technological knowledge. The discovery answered many scientific questions the NSA wanted to get their cryptic hands on and keep hidden, plus five other governments.

The carbonados the Hadrius Manuscript led to were anything but mere black diamonds. Under a capable microscope, the carbonados veiled codes and logarithms into computing and scientific formulas no one organization should own. Not the NSA, not Britain's Government Communications Headquarters, ISTF, all who scrutinized every American or global byte in existence. Just as the

Pythagorean Theorem, an equation at the core of much of geometry that enhanced map-making and navigation and was a basis for GPS navigations, the codes discovered could change technology, spearing civilization years ahead, to a world that was not ready.

Nash understood his responsibilities at the NSA that liked to operate in the shadows and away from public view, an organization that monitored and decoded any signal transmission pertinent to the security of the United States. That the carbonados were in the hands of the operatives felt as if a bad dinner had wrenched his gut.

What about Mason? The ISTF boss he'd escorted to Belmarsh's high security prison. He'd also had a keen eye on every development around the manuscript and the black diamonds?

Could he have...?

Nash was not sure. The man could do anything.

He observed a set of footsteps in the subzero snow, trudged by the unwelcome assassin. Next to the solid prints, he studied a long, uneven trail. The man had drugged Calla and either dragged or carried her off.

Calla could handle herself. But she hadn't.

What had he used?

She'd trained well in the last weeks. Calla had learned to channel her strength and strike out with her closest weapon to the attacker's closest target. It was the best thing he'd taught her seeing she despised firearms.

They couldn't be ISTF assassins. The one he wrestled last had that accurate finesse, he'd seen in Calla. And if he were right, they'd vanished like vapor.

She could be anywhere now. He wouldn't be able to find her with ease.

Why would the operatives hunt Calla like a criminal? Shouldn't they be on her side? Using force meant theirs was a severe warning to him and to her. The last man he'd fought had eyed Calla with a look most bounty hunters use when in close contact with their target. He was no ordinary assassin and no ordinary operative. Nash had to find out why. The man analyzed Calla like a circus master trying to tame his overzealous tiger.

Agony from his injury shot through his side. What felt like defeat, washed away Nash's strength. A feeling he was unaccustomed to. His insides twisted uneasily. *I've failed you. You trusted me to protect you from whatever you were running from.*

Stinging rippled through his right arm. Must've been the fall. The blast had sent burning splinters of wood and glass flying and one had grazed his arm.

Thank God for his snowsuit.

He elevated his injured arm for a good look. *Nothing the emergency department can't handle.*

Darkness trimmed against the light from his burning lodge at the crest of the mountain slope. Except for the flaming debris stemming from what had been his home, he could barely see any structural remains of his house. Nash's mind raced through the recent events. *Who the heck dared...?*

He staggered up the slope toward the dwindling flames. A fierce explosion, detonated by the bazooka had demolished one end of his living room, and most of the top floor. The house's foundation remained solid as the fire died down. His lungs inhaled lethal gases that made his insides churn. Nash felt like gagging from the smell of burned wood, rubber and melting iron. He limped to what used to be the downstairs bathroom and grabbed a towel he wrapped around his mouth and nostrils. He waddled eastward around the burning property and stepped over what used to be his kitchen counter. His ears caught the faint sound of the sirens of rescue teams. *How am I going to explain this?*

Glad he had his insurance, he pressed forward. Before he

cleared the mess with the authorities, he needed to retrieve one item.

He tore his way through the ash, over scorched kitchen stools toward the basement door. The rubber on his sole melted as he vaulted from one safe step to another to his basement office. An unhinged door, hardly recognizable as it slung off the wall mangled in ash, steel and charred wood, covered his path to the room. He reached for the handle with a gloved hand and with one jostle snapped it open.

Once inside, he glimpsed round. The space was intact after the blast, except for a discharged force that moved several files and desk items. He brushed past the dismembered desk, tread for the metal shelves and fumbled for a steel case on one of the middle levels. Even with gloved hands, warmth from the singed metal seeped through to his hands as he tapped in his mother's birthday into the mostly intact, combination pad.

The steel bolt snapped open. He removed three envelopes and two hard drives he placed in his jacket. It was all he needed.

The emergency teams charged into the house through what was left of the scorched front door. He heard their hollers for survivors. Before he faced a succession of questions he didn't care to answer, he needed to make an important call. Someone out there could help him piece together the events of the last few hours.

He pulled out his cell phone.

Only one person had concrete answers he needed. And now!

CHAPTER 6

DAY 2
1133 hrs.

A HAND NUDGED her shoulder. "Get up!"

Calla's eyes rolled with heavy lids struggling to stay open. The dense liquid had repressed her. Her head pulsated as if her skull had been used for drumming practice. She wasn't sure how long she'd suffered loss of reflexes, sensation, and consciousness. After several attempts her eyes stayed open, barely making out the images in front of her. She gazed up, taking in the comfortable space, which after a few seconds she recognized as the empty first class cabin of a British Airways 747.

Calla rose from a semi-reclined position in one of fourteen seats, where she imagined she'd slept unconscious. Uncertain how long, she rubbed her eyes and mopped sweat from her perspiring brow.

Her eyes fell on a strong face. A man, probably in his mid-thirties with deep-set black eyes, short black hair in an uncomplicated crew-cut style above a square face and defined cheekbones. Lacking any empathy in his eyes, she didn't recognize the athletic individual whom instinct alerted was doubtless a proficient field agent. She should know. She'd been around enough field ops by now.

With broad shoulders and clearly less than twenty percent body fat in one lean physique, he gaped at her. He reclined in the compartment next to hers, looking something like a hawk with an agenda. A trained operative no doubt. *Mindless captor!*

Her first instinct was to fist his leering face. He wore worn dark-blue jeans, a smart shirt under a navy jumper and a stylish, black-leather jacket. His military boots looked new and Calla imagined he was methodical in his ways.

Convinced she could outmaneuver him by making a dart down the cabin stairs and off the plane, she decided against it. Yet questions infiltrated her mind. How had he forged a passport and transported her unconscious from the Colorado slopes? Who was he? How dangerous was he?

She recalled the blast... Nash... the gagging feeling.

Calla raised her head an inch. "Where are we?"

He rubbed his tight jaw. "You've endured quite a ride. How's your head?"

His English was faultless with a hint of an international, American twang, and tones not readily associated with any single state or city. Calla massaged her temple with her left hand and scanned the cabin. "Where are the passengers?"

"Disembarking."

"Where exactly are they disembarking?"

He remained silent, his expression revealing complete nonchalance. Her eyes wandered round the cabin before glancing outside the windows, where she caught sight of parallel east-west runways. "Heathrow."

She attempted to stand, then felt resistance from her arm. Her eyes wandered to her wrist, where her left hand was cuffed to his. She eyed the man in front of her, anger welling in her face. It was more proximity than she wished of anyone, although under other circumstances, she might have found him uncouth, almost intriguing. "Is this necessary?"

"Sorry, but my orders are to not let you out of my sight. I know you could make a quick getaway given half the chance."

Calla's eyes narrowed, darkening a shade. How had the thorough agent hauled her through airport security and on a plane, without interference in Colorado from border authorities? Was he working with the Metropolitan Police in London? Was she under arrest? For what?

She grabbed the edge of the seat. "What do you want?"

He smirked. "If it were up to me, I would make some rather thought-provoking requests right about now."

Calla straightened her neck to relieve the ache in her shoulders. "Watch it, errand boy."

He altered the position of his head slightly so he could observe her with depth. "Why you would choose to associate with someone unsuitable for you, I've no idea."

"No, I wouldn't imagine it to be in your capacity."

He raised his chin. "You could do better."

"You don't measure up to him. Nash is three times the man you are."

He moved in and touched her warming cheek.

Calla steered as far away as the restraints would allow. "Back off."

He drew back. "However, I've only been instructed to bring you in alive, and if need be, use whatever methods I consider necessary."

Calla despised his complacent tone and self-assured manner. She turned away from his musky smell, a man secure in his physique. He made sure every inch of him screamed of masculinity attempting to make members of the opposite sex idolize an encounter with him. Her stomach churned at the notion. "You need a sedative for that testosterone overdose."

She glimpsed at her disheveled clothes and noticed that

she still wore the same jeans and the knitted sweater she had on the afternoon Nash had taken her to explore Almont.

What had become of her snowsuit? Calla rose and studied the man opposite her who was a good few inches taller than her. "What did you do to Nash?"

"You need not concern yourself with amateurs."

"You mean like you."

She tugged at the cuffed wrist. The abrupt movement sliced a tiny tear in the leather of his jacket. "And you are?"

His face rearranged itself into a grin, taken aback by the strength in her tug. A gleam appeared in his eyes. "You can call me, Lascar."

"Get these off my wrist, before that cocky face suffers some minor scaring."

"Not likely."

"Tread lightly, Lascar."

"Calla Cress. That *is* your name. Here's how this will play," he said, glancing out the window at the last disembarking passengers who made their way into the terminal building. "You'll come with me, quietly."

He padded his coat pocket and exposed a concealed Sig226 handgun in the inside of his jacket. "I'll lead the way. We'll move through the diplomatic immigration line arranged for us, just as we did in Colorado. Keep your cool and I may have just enough fortitude to resist the urge to break your arm."

Calla crushed an impulse to resist. Was he serious? Did he think he could force her through Heathrow? Through London? Where would he take her? Where would the journey end?

Agent or not? How did you get a gun on a commercial plane? Perhaps, he was connected to the government or maybe ISTF.

Calla scrutinized the etched lines on his face, and shunned the permanent sneer that kept resurfacing. She could do little while still cuffed to him. She'd play along for now, and forced her rigid body to relax. "What are we doing in London?"

"This is your home is, isn't it?"

She shrugged.

Outside, the crew took leave of the aircraft. Lascar jerked her cuffed wrist. "Let's move."

She resisted for three seconds. "And if I don't."

He leaned forward, positioning his head inches from hers, his eyes fixed on her focused gaze. "I'll be more than willing to continue the journey the same way it began."

He heaved her toward the exit, a shove that bruised her upper arm. Lascar padded a small, medicinal bottle in his other jacket pocket, proving the lengths he'd go to obtain her cooperation.

Chloroform, no doubt. One of the original anesthetics used in early operating procedures.

How primitive.

Calla took two steady paces to the cabin staircase, then swiveled round as she set foot on the bottom of the stairs. "Where are we going?"

He pressurized her arm tighter nudging her forward. "Your questions are not mine to answer."

COTSWOLDS, ENGLAND
1145 hrs.

The taut, BMW S.X. Concept decelerated into the secluded driveway with its hardline nose moving toward the grand oak entrance. Set in the scenic, rolling countryside, the ancient manor lay in what Nash imagined were once attractive gardens, overlooking a sixty-four-acre estate.

The lights of the manor were on. Nash switched off the

engine, parked the car in the pebbled, parking space and pushed the door open. He stepped out on the dusty driveway. Stan Cress, Calla's ex-MI6 father was home.

Nash caught sight of several cement bags in the compound, a few meters behind a heap of light construction equipment. Was Stan refurbishing? He didn't strike Nash as one to stay home at any length, given his past in the Secret Intelligence Service or better known as MI6.

Nash's eyes moved to the west wall of the manor. Part of the Elizabethan Cotswold estate was singed with black soot, still visible from the chimney stacks and the gabled, turreted style of the front wall. He paused for a few seconds and stared at the door. So much for the break from this. He'd learned as much as he could from Stan about Calla's past, but much of it was still a mystery, especially her family history. Someone had taken Calla from him and she needed help. Stan hadn't given her all the answers. *It ends here, and today.*

He moved up to the front entrance and rang the doorbell. A few seconds later, a tall man of athletic build appeared at the wooden oak door. His aristocratic stance called for respect, which Nash assumed he'd often received.

Nash evaluated his emerald eyes, a shade darker than Calla's. Stan's hair was graying but evermore elegantly than most. He stood staring at Nash with a strong and rugged profile. "I was glad to get your call. Come on in."

Nash strolled into the entryway behind Calla's tall father. The interiors could have used help, even though the home had once been exquisite. Judging from the stone structure, Nash's historic interest in architecture told him the principal part of the house was probably finished in the sixteenth and seventeenth centuries. Partly timbered, the main construction was set in honey-colored, Cotswold stone.

They digressed through the Tudor-style wing corridor with its leaded windows, before settling into a light kitchen that had recently undergone modern renovation. The revamped stone floors, molded plaster paneling, colored marble finishing and refurbished stamp work, visible along the kitchen wall, all added to the recent repair works.

Stan strode to a glass cabinet and pulled out an espresso cup. “May I offer you something?”

“No, thanks.”

Stan studied Nash for a moment before reverting to his coffee making. “What brings you here?” he said, pausing as he brewed a shot of black espresso working carefully with the water, pressure and timing of his loud machine. “I’m glad you came. You and Calla disappeared with no trace.”

Stan bore a smooth expression as he swerved round to face Nash.

Not certain he wanted to discuss his little escape with Calla, Nash took a seat at the kitchen table. “That was her call. Perhaps you can tell me what she was running from. After all, from the minute she was born, you orchestrated events around her life.”

The machine frothed a strong scent of capao, a dark roasted Brazilian bean. Stan filled his cup with the caffeine and a dose of steaming water before taking a sip. “It wasn’t a decision we took lightly.”

“You wanted to keep her from the operatives. Why?”

“Nash, why now? What’s this all about?”

Nash ignored his drift and drew his brows together. “Isn’t that why you came looking for me with Colton from CIA?”

Stan grimaced twitching his left cheek. He guzzled the hot liquid and made himself another Americano before switching off the machine. “Hm—”

Nash felt a lump in his throat. Would Stan tell him more now than when they’d first met? “Stan, twenty-eight years ago you came to the CIA and asked them to help protect your family after you’d deciphered quite a large chunk of the

Hadrius Manuscript, and before you hid it. Colton was heading the government's Paranormal Espionage Program at the time and was a good friend. Wasn't he? He came to me and told me about your dilemma with British Intelligence Services."

Nash watched for a response before continuing.

None surfaced.

Nash's jaw tightened. "They wouldn't protect your family despite the years of service. You left Calla at the orphanage and two years ago, you and Colton, though retired sought me to find and protect her."

"And you did a splendid job."

Nash scrutinized Stan's face. "She's gone. And if I'm to help her, I need you to tell me the truth. I've come to get your help."

Stan placed the empty cup on the granite counter, his face thunderous. "Calla's gone? What do you mean gone?"

Nash pursed his lips. "Kidnapped."

Stan moved to the table and took a seat opposite him.

Nash leaned forward a sense of determination growing in him. "We started talking months ago when you asked me to protect her. You told me details about the operatives. Some were difficult to believe, some made complete sense. But I now need to know it all. The more I know, the more I can help."

"What do you need to know?"

"At that time, I didn't ask. All I cared about was making certain I understood whether the operatives posed any threat to US national security, especially around their guarded cyber activities. But that was before I met Calla."

Stan's face was carefully controlled as he watched Nash in silence.

Nash's mind swirled with doubts about the man, his motives and most important his feelings. He'd willingly abandoned his daughter, yet kept an eye on her from a distance, choosing not to contact her all her life, until six months ago.

Was he all right? He was struggling with something, especially when Nash had mentioned Calla's name in relation to the operatives.

Stan rimmed his coffee cup with a rigid finger, anger crossing his face. "Who took her?"

"I was hoping you could tell me?"

Stan dipped his head slightly. "Laskfell?"

Nash shifted in his seat, rotating his broad shoulders as he recalled the trouble Mason had caused them. He hadn't thought about him after he'd escorted the criminal with the Metropolitan Police to Belmarsh. "Mason's behind bars awaiting trial due to start in a few days and he'll probably be extradited to Langley. His are crimes under law in the UK and the US."

"Calla has never been safe the minute Mason learned of her existence."

Nash refused to register the significance of his words. "Mason can send an assassin after Calla, but this time, I don't think it's him."

"Then who is it?"

Nash shot up and ambled to the window overlooking a sizable conservatory. "I think it was an operative, you know, supposedly one of the good guys?"

Stan was silent for several seconds. His shoulders hunched in defeat. "So, they'll not leave her alone," he said quietly.

Nash swiveled to face him, an imperceptible tone of pleading attacking his voice. "Why, Stan? Why won't they leave her alone?" He tossed a hand in the air. "I closed my eyes to anything related to the operatives months ago. All I care about is her."

Stan gently drummed the cup on the counter. "You love her, don't you?"

Nash did not respond. He burrowed a hand through his hair. *More than she'll ever know*.

Stan stood and took the empty cup to the sink. "I'm not sure you're ready for what you're looking for. These operatives have ways that frustrated me for years. Calla has never been safe around them."

Nash squinted an eye as Stan's face hardened, blood rising to his cheeks. He spat in the sink. "This is exactly why we hid the Hadrius Manuscript. Calla and the Hadrius are like a cord linked at conception. She can't escape it. Her mother and I tried."

"I've listened to enough of that. Calla can decide who she wants to be. And from what I see, she has. She left London wanting to shove the whole operatives business behind her." He pushed his hands in the pocket of his dark denim's. "From what I've investigated of the operatives, I can't say I blame her."

Stan watched him with a squint in his eyes. "What bothers you about the operatives?"

Nash's expression shifted as a state of numb dread settled in his gut. "I used to think my job was to apprehend criminals, serve my country home and abroad. For a while, I did all right. But the moment I was asked to investigate the operatives and their cyber capabilities, somehow these operatives are—"

"Be careful what you say, Nash. I don't think it was always that way." Stan joined him by the window, laying a hand on his shoulder. "Maybe Calla can change that."

Nash searched Stan's thoughtful face. "How?"

"Have you caught the latest intelligence on Mason?"

Nash watched as the older man, though on in years, yet much lithe in build, tried to change the subject. "I've been on a plane for more than ten hours and drove straight here as soon as I found my car."

"I've been doing some investigating myself and follow British Intelligence coming from Belmarsh. Call it a curse, I can't leave the life of a spy, especially now when it concerns Calla. I owe her much."

"What about Laskfell?"

Stan meandered to a pile of papers on a table next to the wood-burner, perhaps the only decorative piece in his kitchen. "I came across this." He picked up the stash. "A day ago, a British Museum curator visited Mason, and she left Belmarsh incapacitated in an ambulance."

Nash reached for the papers and scanned them. "This is Veda Westall, Calla's boss. What's wrong with her?"

"From what you see there, it's not clear, only that she lost sense of reason and her body collapsed in shock. That top form is her medical analysis at the scene. She was the ninth person to fall victim to what is puzzling ISTF and MI5 at the moment. The baffling thing is, the whole time, guards are present. Mason has no physical contact with any of his victims when they are debilitated."

Nash felt his body tensing, recalling the look in Mason's eye when he'd hurled him over a boisterous African waterfall, in Uganda, leaving him to his death. "How's he doing it? I inspected his cell myself. Jack and I know every item of technology in that cell. Something must be on camera. Have all the visitors reacted this way?"

"They all leave in similar conditions."

"Why has the magistrate not withheld Mason's visitation rights?"

"Up until now, his victims have recovered. At least the doctors narrow it to shock. Except, Westall. She's in a coma."

"No. Not her."

"One other person has also been left unharmed. Allegra Driscoll. About the surveillance cameras, nothing is unusual."

Nash paced the length of the kitchen before settling his back against the sink. "I wonder whether the rumors are true—"

"What rumors?"

Nash studied Stan's face ignoring his query. "There is something authorities are not paying attention to."

"Like what? That's just it, Nash, no one so far can figure it out."

"Impossible. There's an explanation for everything."

"I hear you, Nash. But remember who we're dealing with. Laskfell is no ordinary prisoner. He has sinister ways that few know of, heightened capabilities and astuteness. And honestly, secrets best kept buried in that judicious brain of his."

"You mean like Calla?"

"Every operative is different and has different potencies. We need to figure out Mason's strongest ones and what he intends to do with them."

"But what has that got to do with Calla?"

"Mason is up to something, and something the operatives don't like." He eyed Nash, his face marked with loathing and pain. "The operatives need Calla. Hers are the only capabilities that match Laskfell's intellectually, physically, and psychologically. She's the only one whose genetic makeup is identical to his. And he knows it too."

Tightness formed in Nash's eyes. Any threat that came Calla's way depleted him in ways he was could not explain.

Stan was not done. "And Nash, she's in serious trouble if they plan to do what I think they will."

1202 hrs.

The walk through immigration had been swift with Lascar flashing a set of credentials in the diplomatic line, undisputed by the UK Border Agency. Once outside Terminal Five's international pickup point, a 360-Rolls-Royce Phantom waited with two discreet operatives lingering at the doors. Calla studied their nonchalant manner, as they acknowledged Lascar and waited for them to settle in the back seats.

The first man, a hefty Ghanaian, took the driver's seat, and the second, a slim, red-haired individual, settled in the passenger seat. *Is this how far Vortigern is prepared to go? Abduction?*

Calla set her head against the headrest of the limousine, her mind conspiring punitive thoughts. *What the heck is Vortigern thinking?* He'd sent a special operative in Lascar to find her. Why?

Calla glimpsed in the dark mirror ahead as Lascar sank into the seat next to her, nearer than she appreciated. She turned her gaze out the window at the drab, London, October mist.

They zipped on the M4 highway to London, and Calla avoided eye contact. She churned thoughts around her head. What would she say to Vortigern, the operative who'd revealed much about her ancestry and her special assignment as an operative?

Assignment? She wanted none of this. Just to move on. She'd just turned twenty-eight and had spent most of her life in doubt. She was making sense of it. *And now this!*

Her chance at a life with Nash, who'd been vindictively ripped from her side, was gone.

Was Nash all right? What had they done to him?

Mission? Calling? Calla didn't believe in such things. A rational individual, she'd always been an academic. Logic and reason had been her rearguard, until six months ago. Back then, her life had altered, discovering she could achieve feats most men and women could not imagine. Calla could combat with the forte of three men, defy gravity, and her acrobatic aptitude and heightened reflexes with danger were above normal. She needed Nash to help her hone this incomprehensible prowess. Nash, of all people, knew fieldwork firsthand, a former marine and lieutenant having trained soldiers and military ops for years. He knew the *real* her. No one else did.

Was she ready to face it all again?

Heck! They'd forced her to reconsider her decision, her anonymity and... She would need to use every restraint to face whatever Vortigern had in store. Calla bit her bottom lip prepared for their pending meeting. Whatever Vortigern wanted, Lascar was privy to and only too willing to assist in the endeavor. They exchanged no words for the hour's ride into the fatiguing, concrete, and glass intricacy of London City, a small part of the metropolis and a leading center of global finance. The historic core of greater London came into view, strewn with tapered skyscrapers, hoarded by a sea of focused traders.

What were they doing here?

The Phantom pulled up in front of the Gherkin skyscraper, with its spiraling pattern of diamond-shaped windows. The iconic landmark was recognized as one of the city's most important examples of contemporary architecture, given its spiraling diagrid geometry. She held back the urge to break the cuff restraint on her hand, outsmart Lascar and permanently wipe the smirk on his face.

If Lascar were an operative, how much did he know about her? Every operative was different, with varying strengths and proficiencies. Call it curiosity, she wanted to know what Vortigern wanted with her. This time she wouldn't be trusting. Anyone who interfered with her was to be kept at bay.

Did Vortigern mean harm? *I don't think so.*

Lascar tried to hide his intense inquisitiveness about her. Though hostile in every manner imaginable, she guessed he wasn't as hawkish as he seemed—just an overdose of masculine conviction. Though determined to sway her with his intimidation, it spelled out one thing. *Machismo*!

Lascar jerked Calla out of the Phantom. She glanced up the forty-one floors of the arch-shaped skyscraper with its alternating pattern of dark and light-colored glass. Minutes later, they proceeded through to the glass elevator. Lascar called the thirty-ninth floor, and in seconds, they meandered toward a spacious office, giving enough natural daylight and stunning views of the city, captured through floor-to-ceiling windows. And there he stood, tall and authoritarian. Like the first time she'd met Vortigern, the silver-haired, suave gentleman exuded grace and poise. This time, he was styled in a modish gray suit and not the blinding, silver-white, combat attire, operatives wore. He greeted them with malice.

The dour look with which Calla returned his greeting, bred diametrically opposed friction. Lascar pulled her forward.

"I wasn't aware you'd gone corporate. Have we abandoned coves, Vortigern?" she said.

"We too like to occupy presence in the more functional parts of society."

"I see."

Vortigern had not changed in the last few months, stunning and imposing with his tall frame and supple, silver hair. Vortigern studied Calla with an ageless, calm face despite the ruthlessness with which he'd authorized. "Forgive my methods, but when I heard you'd left London without a trace, I had to use ulterior modes to find you."

Tightness formed in her eyes as she observed him. Lascar

removed the cuffs.

Calla stroked her wrist and wheeled round to face him. Her next decision was brief but overdue. In one swift movement, she rammed her elbow across Lascar's jaw, a clout that caught him off guard.

He landed on the marble by Calla's feet, grappling his chin with a moan, before leveling his lower jaw with his hands. He tipped his head back and snickered. "I had that coming. Vortigern, operation completed, as requested."

With eyes still on Lascar, Calla placed a foot on the subdued operative's thigh and leaned forward. "What did you do to Nash?"

Lascar eyed her. "Aren't we done with that topic? Nash's no longer your concern. Don't you see that? I'd use your energy now to get to know... me. Your new best friend."

Vortigern interrupted the discourteous stares between them. "Lascar did as instructed."

Calla raised her chin to follow Vortigern's intent. Her tone, unreceptive and tenacious surprised her. "Oh, and was that to blow up Nash's house?"

Vortigern turned to Lascar. "You blew up his house?"

Lascar shot up in one brisk surge. "Just a little charred." He sidled toward Calla. "I don't see how they'll need it any longer. Without a place to hide, she stays here."

Calla calculated the agitated tone in his voice when he spoke of Nash with a look of resentment, and if she were correct, a trace of loathing, perhaps envy. *He despises Nash.*

Had Vortigern not been in the room, she knew what she would have done with that cocky smirk.

Vortigern's voice broke her thoughts. "Thanks, Lascar. Leave us. I need to speak to her alone."

Lascar shambled out of the office.

Calla hoped, in heaven's name, she wouldn't see him again. Her eyes bore into Vortigern. She needed straight answers from the head operative, one she thought she esteemed. "Why, Vortigern?"

"I warned you."

"Who is that six-foot slab of muscle, mostly in the brain, and very little respect?"

Vortigern strolled to his desk. "Good to see you, Calla. Lascar is more capable than you think."

"Really? Do you train operatives to abduct attack, shun and burn?"

"Sit. Lascar's my son and a capable operative who's been trained a long time to work with you. He was the only one I could trust to get you."

"Your son? I imagine like son, like father? I thought operatives were the good guys. What do you want, Vortigern? How did you find me?"

"Please, sit."

Calla remained standing. "How did you find us?"

"With the look, you gave Nash the last time I saw you, it wasn't difficult. We have a few operatives in the NSA. I must admit, your marine is quite thorough. It did take us six months."

"I'm not staying."

Vortigern raised an eyebrow. "I see."

A forlorn expression burdened his face as he took a seat at his desk. "I'm sorry, Calla. I ran out of options. *We* ran out of options."

"Options? For what?"

"Mason."

"What about him?"

"He's up to something fierce."

"And that's my problem because—"

"I know that I had no right to infringe on your decision."

"Finally, an apology."

"As I said, we ran out of options. A new hack has

penetrated global computers causing more headaches than we need."

"All because of a hack? Surely you operatives can handle a simple hack. You've had centuries worth of access to technologies the world knows nothing of. You can handle more than that?"

"Not like this one. Most hacks can be overridden. This one breaks the rules. Once we find a remedy, the algorithms shift, and we have to start again. It functions with its own mind."

Calla folded her arms over her chest. "A computer virus with its own mind? Sounds like singularity technology, you know the upcoming conception of technologies greater than human intelligence."

"Exactly."

"I don't buy it. Every hack is controlled by someone. Every piece of software has vulnerabilities."

"Not this one. It's so dissimilar to any worm we've ever seen. We've been following the activity on this distinct sequencer created by our operative base in Central London. The hack has manifested as an information altering, manipulating virus."

"Can't you override it as we did last time?"

His face surrendered no information.

"With impenetrable firewalls engineered by the carbonados' dynamisms and their matchless, sequencing formulas," Calla said.

"No. That's why we need you. Your mind can see patterns in technology, language, and logarithms. This virus attacks one day from one location and one day another and eats up pockets of valuable, global data. Financial, medical, and legal, you name it."

"You could isolate the activity on the systems mainframe that we conceived to spot any infrequent movement. Here let me see."

She marched to his desk and scrutinized the program. "This isn't just random data; these are global government records. It's using very sophisticated language to infiltrate computers across the globe... look here, that's NASA, and here, medical research centers in Kyoto, Seattle and Zurich, and even the UK government's own systems. There seems to be a pattern. It's stealing control of the Earth's best and most innovative networks and scrambling them using automated programming language."

"How does it work?"

"Not sure yet, but the language used is composed of a blend of social and alternating, linguistic forms and analogs used in dialects. That means its stealing known computer language and creating its own. It would take centuries to decode it. Who's doing this?"

"The activity escalated forty-eight hours ago. I'd say, Mason."

"It's very clever. It's like taking all language, human or computer, and creating a new processor language. I'm not sure how we would begin on a code to break this. What does he hope to accomplish? Controlling global computers is too easy for Mason. There's no challenge in it for him."

"We're not sure at this point."

Calla hit several keys and waited for a new window to open. She read the logarithms for a few seconds before settling into a chair opposite Vortigern. "I think I know."

Vortigern's eyes bore into her. "What?"

"Looks like Mason is using a sophisticated virus that automates by building databases of information to source from and thereby access malware that attacks the hardware layers of anything that uses technology. He has gained long-term access to every system and smart network on this globe that uses the slightest bit of technology."

"But, that's everything."

"Precisely, cell phones, power plants, government networks, and even your razor. He's figured the world uses technology for everything. Not even a child's toy runs without a battery or wireless remote control these days."

"This is huge, Calla."

"Sounds like big brother with not only a huge spying problem but an additive touchscreen habit. He'll be able to override any byte influenced structure that uses satellites, electricity, and generated power systems. If I'm right, and I sure hope I'm not, soon no organization will be out of his reach, even those of ISTF, the NSA, MI6, you name it. The question is, how did he bypass the firewalls of the most sophisticated systems?"

"Either someone helped him, or he stole the information."

"Exactly what I'm thinking and knowing him, it's the latter."

"How's he stealing it? He's been detained for more than six months with no access to any network. We've bugged the secret service, spy cameras in his cell," Vortigern said.

"Whereas your spying cameras have been operational for six months, Mason's plan has had its gears in motion for decades. That's how he does things. He's one of the most patient people on Earth. Never in a hurry, but at the right time, when the iron is hot, he strikes!" she said, her fist ramming the pristine desk.

"Hang on a second. We traced government intelligence from Belmarsh yesterday, Mason has been visited by innovative minds and people in society, like heads of state, Nobel Prize winners and—"

"Do you think they're working with him?"

"Who knows? It's happened before."

Quiet footsteps resonated from the hall and startled them as a figure approached. Calla never thought she'd see the face again that stood before her.

CHAPTER 7

MASON DABBLED WITH the program that had registered Evangelista Fiwa a few days ago, a Nobel Prize winner in Physics and the second person to enter his cell. Her groundbreaking experimental methods in computational physics were valuable, especially those she'd left out of her thesis. *My writing process starts with an idea. I can pick this anywhere...*

He skipped to the next person. The only victim, whose thoughts he was still trying to disentangle.

Allegra Driscoll.

She'd visited him two days ago, making a special trip to Belmarsh to retrieve the ISTF codes and passwords for the R&D facilities. Driscoll had to have them reconfigured, a privilege reserved for each new ISTF boss. Codes were personalized for their security and protection programs.

Mason cursed under his breath picturing Allegra in his ISTF office running affairs he'd engineered. Why could he not pick up any information from her? Operatives had proved difficult, but not impossible. All he could sense was disunity in Driscoll's mind. A struggle of wills. She didn't agree with a close friend, a confidant, or...

"Working into the late hours?"

The sound of the voice jostled Mason, and he sprung from the bed, scanning the dark room for the throaty male voice. "Who's that?"

Mason squinted his eyes, barely able to make out the form of the figure. A man sat at the end of the little worktable, and the dim work lamp concealed part of his face. "Damn operative!"

The late visitor's face moved into the light.

Mason shuddered back in disgust. He'd not seen the operative since Khirbat en-Nahas in Jordan. "Taiven! How the heck did you get in here?"

Mason looked to the door of his cell.

"You know me better than that," said Taiven. "When was the last time I used a door? What worries me is, why have you kept up this charade?"

"What do you want?"

Taiven rose and ambled around the spotless desk with casual movement, slithering a hand along its cool edge as he neared Mason by the bed. Taiven's wide-eyes were the color of coffee, and his charcoal-colored hair rode in waves on his large head. He tugged the collar of his tie-less suit, alerting Mason that his was a visit of a possibly hostile nature. "No bars can contain you, Mason, or what I believe is brewing on your laptop."

Mason snickered. Taiven was bluffing. The operative was of his generation, well-informed and difficult to read, like most. He despised the infuriating operative who made him doubt his plan for a second. But on second thought, Taiven had nothing on him. He arched his eyebrow, cautious. Taiven was a well-connected operative. Mason's nostrils twitched as he spoke. "What do you know?"

"Your plans always have one purpose and are driven by one name in particular."

"And who's that?"

"Your mother, who sits in a demented, psychiatric ward as we speak with, no contact from you."

How did the psychopath know that? "You're bluffing. She's dead."

Mason cursed and shot up. "I don't have time for this."

Taiven moved up to Mason's limit. "I believe time is all you have. She's much stronger than you think?"

"Who?"

"Calla Cress."

Mason despised the mention of the one person who'd surprised him, the one person who'd endangered everything he'd worked for. "Is that why she's in hiding? Or is she still trying to find Nicole Cress, who in her day went by the name of Bonnie Tyleman? I bet that deranged woman is exactly where I left her, rotting in obscurity."

The look on Taiven's face told Mason much. Taiven didn't know that Mason was the last person who'd seen Calla's mother. He stood solidly in front of Mason with a furrowing brow forming on his face. "I'm here to alert you. Your trial is in a few days. I'd start thinking about staying alive."

"I had no idea you were sentimental about my well-being. There's no capital punishment in this country, even if they decide to give me the highest sentence."

"Your crimes extend across borders? These court systems are not as lenient. Take the US, for example, the land of the free, but not for you. Halt your frenzied little plan because, in two days, the state will find you guilty and extradite you to the US to face trial there." Taiven edged closer, his nostrils flickering. "It'll certainly lead to capital punishment. Your eminent end."

Mason held onto the notebook that had sat on the bed since Taiven's uninvited entrance. "Get out of my way."

Taiven watched him push a finger over his mouse. "I'm

sorry to disappoint you, but I take orders from no one." He slammed down a key. "You know that. I never have, and as you can see, I have business to attend to."

Irritation crossed Taiven's eyes as he watched the notebook fire up with a screen displaying a transmitting box. He pulled out a P226, Sig Sauer handgun and fired at the churning notebook. It gusted into flames, burning a hole through the prison bed.

Mason snickered. "Your approach is tardy, my friend." Mason slammed the gun from Taiven's hands and slit him across the chin.

Taiven hurled to the floor and, with eyes burning with the fury of lava, glanced at the notebook. His eyes widened. The ticking words of the slow-functioning machine were clear.

TRANSFER COMPLETE

Taiven shot Mason a glazed look and observed as he maneuvered to the cell door. A whispery voice from behind the gated steel called out. "It's time."

Mason smirked as Elias jerked his head back at the sight of Taiven. "Who's that? How did he get in here?"

"The same way we are getting out!"

Mason seized Elias' shaky hand and shoved him into the quiet hall. "Lead the way."

Taiven waited until the hall fell silent of escaping footsteps. He lifted his hand and examined the item he'd come to retrieve.

A bloodied microchip.

—

1217 hrs.

"Mason intends to finish the hack he created. He's accessed the most influential minds in all society; scientists, musicians, politicians, authors, criminals, and the list goes on, so he can create software that can dismantle human innovation and every sphere of creative influence," Vortigern said.

Calla thought for several moments. "He'll bring the world to its knees subtly, destroying humanity. After all, without innovative ability, freedom to use technology, choice, and control of even one's cell phone, most people are incapacitated. Call it the technology curse. People can't live without it."

They heard a shuffle by the door. Taiven strode into the room and dropped a sealed plastic bag on Vortigern's desk.

"How's he coercing them?" Vortigern asked.

"With the chip in that envelope. It's only a matter of time before he gets another. I extracted it from an unusual place," Taiven said. "Mason asks the world's leaders to come to his cell and uses telepathy to milk their brain cells of intelligence, leaving the brain numb. He may have acquired powerful passwords, formulas, and the list is endless."

"Why do they come to see him?" Calla asked.

"Who's not intrigued by an invitation from a billionaire behind bars?" Taiven said.

Vortigern watched Calla. She knew they were waiting for a response from her. "I can't do anything about this."

Taiven set a hand on her shoulder. "You can. As sophisticated as Mason's methods are, he's never had an idea of his own. He mimics greatness. He's stolen ideas for years. He has vision and will see it through. Mason's processes are subtle, so subtle that people don't know they are coerced."

"I can't do anything. Look, the program has advanced. We may have ten days at best before it has engulfed every system known to us."

Vortigern rose and paced the room for a few minutes. "Calla, operatives are more knowledgeable than the average person. But somehow, you were wired with all the right skills to match Mason psychologically, mentally, and physically, like twins operating on opposing spectrums. For one, you have similar psychological backgrounds, and your thought processes are similar."

Calla reviled the idea. "I beg to differ. That's repulsive. How so?"

Vortigern zipped round. "You were both let down by people who should have been your biggest advocates."

"Who?"

"Your mothers. A child who's been let down by a mother can display certain patterns of behavior like—"

Calla shot up. "I don't believe this! Don't bring my mother into this. She died long ago."

Taiven interrupted. "There *is* another way." He addressed Calla. "You can find Merovec."

Vortigern shot him a warning glance.

Taiven ignored the response. "Merovec can help. He alone can interfere with the forces set in motion by Mason."

Vortigern pouted his lips and shot Taiven a defeated look. "There's only one operative who's ever communicated with Merovec, or even knows how to reach him."

Calla's eyes narrowed. "So, he's alive?"

Vortigern nodded.

"Who can reach him?" Calla asked.

The words shot off involuntarily out of Vortigern's lips. "Your mother."

1240 hrs.

Jack observed the programming processes and data

structures. He scrolled down his screen as he waited for a response from his recent command entry. He'd been in the ISTF information systems center since six that morning. He scrutinized the data transfer on the large monitor. This was the tenth time in a row he'd studied many files shift on global computer systems. The morning data traffic was busy. ISTF ensured that their operating systems were technically superior to most governments' data spy-centers. Jack enlarged the screen window. The systems had been replaced recently. They could intercept, decipher, analyze, and store vast bands of the world's communications as it voyaged down from satellites and shot through underground and undersea cables of domestic, foreign, and international networks.

The servers and network routers stored any attention-grabbing intelligence in near-bottomless databases. The recently installed software could break codes. Most days, the architecture performed flawlessly. This was in ISTF's favor as it kept an eye on criminalities in heavily encrypted financial information, stock transactions, corporate deals, international military, and diplomatic secrets, legal documents, and private communications.

Jack chewed on the end of a pen. He leaned back and typed a few algorithms in the mainframe. The commands brought down three new windows. He scrutinized the language structures, the compilers that translated complicated language, and dynamic information schemes on government and intelligence computers in Europe and Asia. He narrowed in on Athens, Abu Dhabi, and Tel Aviv.

A new window asked him for the exact data he required. Jack smiled to himself, realizing the privileged position he was in as he responded to the program's query. He needed the contents of private e-mails. Nothing was out of his grasp. Jack could monitor cellphone calls, Google searches, personal data trails, parking tickets, travel itineraries, software purchases, government payments, company security breaches, and digital transfers of the visitors allowed to see Laskfell at Belmarsh.

He chose all, specifically requesting the program to highlight major cities with unusual activity. A large bar appeared. *It could take all morning*.

Eight percent of the transfers were diverted through an Internet Protocol address, an IP on Santorini Island, where much data was shipped.

"This is bogus!" He stifled a curse. "A tourist island is not a top-hub for this sort of thing!"

He fired up the remote framebuffer, which overrode the system's architecture. His computer could remotely control the kernel, the system's input and output requests in Santorini.

Nothing.

ISTF systems bypassed any firewalls. *Not this time. Damn, it's sophisticated!*

He keyed in a series of commands. "Let's see if this'll work if you won't allow me browser access."

Jack connected to the Santorini IP address, hoping to spy for activity in listening mode. This allowed him admission, as the Santorini server hadn't configured its firewall to prevent him access. It meant one thing. The Santorini hacker was no computer expert, no match for him. Perhaps they were an *observer* as they called them at ISTF, people hired to keep a hacking computer alive in criminal activity.

With listening mode on, the island server sent him small rectangles of information through a video output device.

Incredible!

"Whoa... so that's what you are up to! NASA's security programs!"

But who the heck are you?

He scribbled notes and copied the received files on his

hard disk. Each time, data transfer started, he scribbled additional notes.

NASA, your door is wide open!

If only he knew where Nash and Calla were. They were good at investigating and cracking the genius behind cyber encryption—especially those who coded their activity in new languages. Together, Calla and Nash could piece links among cyber activity politics, history, and international communication systems.

He'd not thought about them in a while. *Where the heck did they go?*

It's been six months and no word from them!

He'd been discreet about their whereabouts. All he remembered was the phone call; the same day, he and Nash had escorted Mason to Belmarsh to supervise technological security breaches and procedures.

He fished out his phone, wondering whether he should call the emergency number Nash had given him during an awkward conversation that night at a private airfield outside of London.

"Jack, I have to take Calla away from here. She needs to get away from London," Nash had said.

"Where are you going?" Jack said.

"I haven't worked it out yet. I've just organized a private flight. We'll tell the pilot once we are airborne. I need to check we aren't being followed."

"What's she running from? She's just found her father. I'm sure she'll now get all the answers she was looking for when she deciphered the Hadrius Manuscript. I thought she wanted to find Stan and her mother."

"She's bitten off more than she can chew. Her parents were part of an underground, government operation, not only with the government, but I think with something deeper linked to the operatives. Calla has learned something painful. I noticed this yesterday at the St. Giles estate. She had a conversation with someone that turned sour. She's changed... more closed than usual."

"What can I do?"

"The little she's told me is the operatives her parents were involved with need her. By my measure, she's not willing."

"Why, Nash? You investigated these *operatives* at the NSA. If there were some sort of threat to her, you'd know."

"That's just it, Jack. I haven't finished my investigation, and the NSA wants my report, imminently. But there are a few things still baffling me. That's why NSA wanted me to get involved with ISTF as soon as possible, given the information ISTF had on Stan Cress and his dealings with the operatives in the past. The NSA is pretty doubtful about them."

Jack threw his hands in the air. "We've worked with them before. Vortigern and his counterparts have helped us to drag Mason to justice. From what I've learned in the last few hours, these operatives are no threat to international security. They have more sophisticated technology and science than ours. They're not affiliated with anyone. They see themselves as the police when it comes to global technology and scientific development. They work stealthy, efficiently, and take no credit for the successful operations they do."

Nash's hands and arms went limp. "I know, Jack."

"They're not on anyone's radar most of the time. Perhaps that's what the US fears, the fact they know little about them."

"I'm not sure, Jack." Nash handed him a sleek, thin phone, no thicker than a credit card. "Something still bothers me about them. Here, take this. It's a new government phone that runs only on secure networks and satellite space, leaving no traces. This one's pinned to me."

"My kind of clandestine work."

"I won't tell Calla. I want you to be able to reach me. Call me if you need me."

Jack set a hand on Nash's shoulder. "Be careful, Nash."

Six months ago, and still no contact. Jack had no idea where they'd gone and had not contacted Nash. In his type of work, Jack knew better than to leave evidence lying around. The shock, water, and temperature resistant phone had remained virtually plastered to his body. He stroked his chin and eyed the smartphone on the desk beside him. "What the heck?"

He dialed the number.

After three tones, he heard the voice of his good friend. "Jack?"

Jack leaned back in his chair. "How'd you know it was me?"

"You're the only one with this number, remember. You okay, man?"

"Yeah, but I need your help. Is Calla there?"

Nash was silent a few seconds. "I don't know where she is. But I think I'm on the right track to finding out."

"What happened?"

Tension exuded form Nash's voice. "She was taken by professional assassins. Possibly operatives. These guys knew what they were doing?"

"Taken? From where?"

"I took her to Colorado. Some moron came after her and torched my house. I didn't even live there much. The house was restored last spring. I'm not sure how they found us. No one knew of my or Calla's connection to that place."

"Do you think she's alive? What do we do? Where are you?"

"I'm driving to London now from the Cotswolds."

Jack checked his watch. "All right, let me know when you get here, and I'll meet you."

"I should be in London in an hour's time. Where are you?"

"ISTF offices. Watergate House."

"Okay."

Jack hung up and collected his things. It was approaching 10:00 A.M. He left the computer in his office running, purposing to shut it off remotely from his home office. He needed to locate the Santorini hacker in a secured room.

He rose and advanced to the door and paced into ISTF's bustling corridor filled with agents in clandestine discussions and cryptanalysts analyzing intelligence.

The Santorini signal vanished from the monitor. In its place, a new signal reemerged, gulping up more data. The coordinates of the location slithered in and out, stemming from a different place altogether—Spain. With no human interference, the signals reversed, and the hacker afflicted ISTF's network with an information-consuming virus on the main computer systems framework.

Seven seconds passed.

Jack's computer froze, and the worm tore through his system erasing all of his observation work, before snaking through the rest of ISTF's complete network.

"She's dead. My father told me she didn't survive her last mission." Calla peered from Vortigern to Taiven. "She died years ago."

Vortigern lowered his voice. "To him, she is. Stan Cress searched for your mother for years after she left you at the orphanage, but never found her. They left you there together, then she disappeared and has not been heard from since."

He's bluffing. A few minutes of pure thoughtless shock passed. Calla held her elbows tightly at the side, her stomach, stirring at the revelation. "How can you know that she is alive?"

"Your mother contacted me once when the Hadrius Manuscript was discovered in the sixties in Russia. She wanted to know whether the Hadrius mandate still held its obligations over you." Vortigern paced the floor. "She didn't reveal where she was. My hunch is she wanted to know whether we knew about you."

He took a deep breath. "So, you see your father lied to you."

"I don't believe you. How do I know you're not lying to me?"

Taiven approached Calla. "You should ask Stan."

"What's the Hadrius mandate, Taiven?"

"The Hadrius manuscript was a guide, and the Hadrius mandate is the decision. Will you accept what every Cress has feared?"

"And what is that?"

"Responsibility. Accountability to something greater than they are." His eyes gleamed with earnestness. Taiven's well-defined profile stood tall as his face showed a delicate dimension of sensitivity. "Calla, my sole purpose has always been to watch over you. To guide you where appropriate. To help you when necessary, so you can become the operative you are meant to be. But the decision to go ahead is yours. We point to the clues. I've watched you since you were little and believe you want what is right and have the determination. The choice is yours. You can step up to the plate, before technology disintegrates into something barely recognizable and before individual will and decision are coerced into puppetry."

"It's not up to me." Calla said. "That's a responsibility no one should have to shoulder alone. I'm just an average girl, born into an extraordinary family."

"You're anything but ordinary, Calla," Taiven said.

She shifted her feet. "So I've been told."

Taiven's unreadable features were more comforting than she'd witnessed in Vortigern. Taiven understood her, perhaps more than she did herself. He crossed the room in two strides. "I believe you can do this, even without your mother."

Calla sank in her seat. "I need to think about this."

Vortigern maneuvered toward her. "I understand, but keep in mind we don't have much time. Have you seen today's newswires? The growing easy availability of mobile technology and Internet-connected devices creates many threats. Recent attacks show that it's possible to hack devices other than conventional computers."

"That's exaggerating."

"Is it? Mason has shifted from Symbian and Java-based systems and is looking at more mature technologies, like government nerve systems."

"He won't get to them. We sealed them."

"Mason's trying to produce, and if we are unlucky, he already has fashioned a program that can intuitively control any machine on the planet. He's cloned the system drives of major government computers as a start. He's also tapped into a human weakness, dependence on technology," Vortigern said.

"His is a carefully orchestrated and designed attack, concentrating on localized and targeted incidents as we have seen with NASA, and pretty soon, we'll see the stability and security of the global routing infrastructures compromised. And this," Taiven added.

Taiven's words got her attention. He reached for the Guardian newspaper. "He's using many new and old avenues such as cloud computing attacks, aiming at monocultures where applications containing lots of valuable data are found."

Calla took the paper from his hand. Her eyes fell on an article, and concretely on a name she recognized. She studied it carefully.

Veda Westall.

She stood up and read the article, grappling the paper as if it was her last dinner. After a long pause, she turned to Vortigern. "I need a moment to process my thoughts."

Vortigern moved toward the door, followed by Taiven. "All right, use my office. I need to step out for a few minutes anyway."

When the men left, the room fell silent. Calla crossed her arms tightly over her chest. Something she'd read in the Guardian made her twitch. She slumped into Vortigern's chair, rotating round to face the full-length windows. *I can't accept this mandate. When will it stop? I promised Nash.*

She tried his cell phone and got an engaged tone. Calla slowly handled the paper before tossing it to one side and meandered to the window. She glanced out at London's traffic and drew strength from the city's atmosphere that she'd always called home. Taiven was right. She had to help, if only because it was the right thing to do. Was her mother alive? Why had Stan lied? What had happened between them? If her mother was alive, where was she? *Can I find her? But how? Will this Merovec reverse some of Mason's mess? Who is he anyway?*

Her eyes fell on the image of Veda's face on the discarded newspaper. She retrieved it and read the caption. Veda had been taken to the National Hospital for Neurology and Neurosurgery, a short drive away.

She studied Veda's face. *Why her, Mason?*

Calla swaggered to the door and hesitated when her ear

caught voices in hushed discussion on the other side. She held her ear to the wood frame, leaving an inch of viewing space.

Vortigern was in discussion with Lascar.

Calla dodged her head back into the room. The men's voices were still audible.

Vortigern spoke first. "Did you administer the memory repressant I gave you?"

Lascar's confidence had surpassed its level of tolerance with Calla. Even from behind inches of solid cedar, his sneer broke through with confidence and was becoming redundant. "Yes, Shields and Kleve won't know who she is by morning."

CHAPTER 8

1258 hrs.

CALLA CURSED UNDER her breath. Had any ounce of truth fallen off Vortigern's lips? Nash and Jack were in trouble. *Think, Calla, think!*

She was an ensnared individual between the operatives' purposes and her moment of decision. She edged back into the room and slithered toward Vortigern's desk.

Lascar and Vortigern appeared at the door.

"Had enough time to process your thoughts?" Vortigern said.

Calla winced, her mind resonating bells of caution as Vortigern approached, his silver eyes peering into her soul. "I apologize again for the way we brought you here. But I knew you wouldn't have come willingly."

Her eyes narrowed. Her mind worked frantically as she headed for the door. "Got to go."

Vortigern set a hand on her arm. "Where are you going?"

"To see Veda."

"Who's Veda?" Lascar asked.

Vortigern released her arm, a calculating look shrouding

his face. "Veda is Calla's boss at the British Museum and Mason's eleventh victim."

"Calla has a day job?"

Vortigern ignored Lascar's sarcastic remark and maneuvered his heavy body toward Calla. "Veda is under surveillance by ISTF. She's in an amnesia specialist unit at the National Hospital for Neurology and Neurosurgery, according to British Intelligence. We infiltrated their correspondence."

"Yes, and by the sounds of her condition, I'd better hurry," Calla said.

"You can't help her now, Calla."

"That's my call."

Vortigern shriveled slightly at Calla's bold expression. "Ms. Westall is being treated for transient global amnesia—a passing episode of short-term memory loss. She'll be fine. She should suffer no signs or symptoms of neurological impairment. I think you should focus on finding your mother."

What I do is my privilege. Calla strolled to the hefty door, dragged it open, and shifted away from Lascar's fervent stares. "All Mason's victims are showing one form of amnesia or another. I need to go before it's too late for Veda."

You've done the same thing to Jack and Nash!

Hypocrites!

Calla slowly left before Vortigern imposed another patronizing demand. She paced out into the hallway.

Damn it! She needed her things. Take a shower. Warm food. Change clothes. Find a non-traceable phone! Her feet hobbled in awkward steps on the carpeted floor as she shuffled to the exits.

"Calla!"

Vortigern's voice strained with authority she was frankly beginning to despise. "Lascar's coming with you. He is our martial arts commander, and quite versed as an operative."

So I gather.

Calla flipped her head around "No, thank you."

Vortigern narrowed his brows. "He can help you. Train you."

"I can manage."

"No, Calla, he goes with you."

She took one look at Lascar's fervent approach toward her and kept marching toward the elevators. "All right, tough guy. Let's go."

They careered out on the busy London boulevard. Calla considered the moderate traffic and shot Lascar a chilled look. "Should we take a cab? I've dealt with the hospital before. We're going to Russell Square."

Lascar handed her a set of keys. "Why bother with a cab. Taiven has your Maserati waiting in the underground parking."

Calla's eyes traveled back to the building entrance. *So, Taiven had it repaired after I smashed it on the A12 highway. Good old Taiven. One day I need to thank him, whoever he is.*

"Lead the way, Bruce Lee," she said.

They reentered the cucumber-shaped building and took the elevators down to an underground parking.

And there she stood, pristine, gray, and as tasteful as Calla remembered her at her best. Taiven had thought about every detail after her recklessness with Italian craftsmanship. The GranTurismo Maserati had all its prominent design fundamentals restored in the right places. Well-proportioned dynamism, an insistent grille grooming the prominent red-prolonged Trident. A set of new headlights with day-running, light technology stared at her as she prepared for a ride complete with a mélange of aggressive performance, personality, and comfort.

She drifted to the driver's side of the two-door sports car and hauled it open. Lascar lurked by the passenger side and placed his palm on the locked handle. "Hm, nice car... for a lady... did you pick it out?"

Calla inhaled the knuckles on her free hand tightening into a fist. She yanked the door and sank into the driver's seat crafted with a resplendent, ivory-leather finish.

Reaching over to unlock Lascar's side, she hesitated, swallowing hard. The permanent smirk on his face had to go. Her hand worked swiftly as she pushed down the lock and churned the engine into first gear. "I'm no lady!"

The ravenous engine roared, filling the underground parking with the hungry echoes of Italian artisanship. She swerved the car out of the parking space and growled the car toward the exit, leaving Lascar standing in the near-empty parking garage, his sneer molding into a muzzled scowl.

Calla checked her rear-view mirror. "I don't need tagalongs."

The last she saw of Lascar in the rear-view mirror, as she exited the garage, was his smirk shifting into anxious haste as he raced toward a parked vehicle. He would not give up. She took note as he leaped into a dark Spyker C12 Zagato, parked two spaces from where her Maserati had stood.

With her focus ahead, the garage door slid open, and Calla propelled the Maserati into London's afternoon traffic. She glanced in the rear-view mirror one last time, certain Lascar's rare automobile, begging to participate in a Formula One race, would shadow her every turn. She accelerated northeast on Bury Street before skulking toward Bevis Marks. *So it begins.*

Once on London Wall Boulevard, she lost him for six minutes until he advanced behind on Newgate Street. By the time she got on to Chancery Lane, in the heart of the legal district and the western boundary of the City, Lascar was determined not to be outwitted. She would have to take a less obvious route. Calla turned the thundering vehicle into Great Ormond Street where she sighted the National Hospital for Neurology and Neurosurgery on her right.

Lascar was not far behind. She nosed the car into a quiet road behind Queen Square, where the hospital stood. Even as she stole into the building, she felt her heart race. She needed to find Veda. Mason had gorged at a personal nerve. W*hy Veda?*

She waited by the entrance, scouting the reception area. Two lobby attendants sat discussing the day's celebrity gossip. Ahead she noticed the elevators a few meters from where the talkative women sat. She'd not seen Lascar when she'd entered. *He can't be too far.*

She hunched under the reception desk, stealing past unnoticed toward the opening elevators. A distracted researcher stepped out and failed to notice her disappear into the closing elevator. *Now, where would they put her?*

She scanned the interior of the sidewall for any information on the research patients' division. The wall bore three panels: one with the departments of research, one the emergency contact numbers, and one describing the escape route. Calla narrowed in on the department list. *This must be it —Neuropsychology, third floor.*

She pressed the button for the second floor. Seconds later, the elevator stationed on a bustling floor. Once out of the car, she leaned back in and pressed the top floor button. *That'll throw him off*!

Calla slinked past three doctors, followed by a horde of note-taking students as she stepped onto the floor. Lowering her head, she found the fire exit at the end of the hall and took the stairs to the third floor. If what she'd read in the newspaper was correct, Veda was in the Neuropsychology division specializing in amnesia. Her condition was unusual. The paper had highlighted the facility offered in-depth treatment for developmental amnesia.

Would Veda recognize her?

As she neared a busy corridor pointing to the Neuropsychology section, she apprehended him. Lascar stood questioning an intimidated student staffing the entry to the research patients' rooms. Calla slouched behind an information board that failed to cover her entire height.

She scooted down.

"You must have seen her," she heard Lascar say.

"Listen, Mr. whomever you are, unauthorized personnel are not permitted in this part of the hospital," said the student.

Calla peered from behind the board. From her angle, she observed the woman press a panic button under the nurse's desk.

"I'm not leaving until I see my colleague," Lascar said, his voice raising a decibel above cordial.

Calla calculated her next move. *You need a lesson in charming women!*

ST. GILES SQUARE, LONDON
1259 hrs.

Nash watched Pearl from his BMW. The pleasant, middle-aged Brazilian housekeeper to Allegra Driscoll entered the Victorian residence in St. Giles square in West London. From across the street, he drummed his thumbs on the leather steering wheel. Six months ago, he'd taken Calla out of this very residence the day they returned the Hadrius Manuscript to Allegra.

Allegra. He liked her.

She usually returned the same sentiment.

She was home. He'd called ISTF offices a half hour ago. He had not only been told that Allegra replaced Mason Laskfell as head of ISTF, but she also continued her duties as the Prime Minister's special representative on cybersecurity. To help Allegra, he had to make sure she was on his side. Not that he didn't trust her, but the day they'd left, she'd been uncomfortable around him and Calla, watching him from behind squared, reading glasses as if he professed a threat.

A minute later, Nash stepped up to the porch and rang the doorbell. Pearl's face appeared at the white door adorned with geometric and organic floral designs predominating the glass part of the wood. She smiled as she dragged the door open. "Mr. Shields, how nice to see you again. Is Miss Calla with you?"

Her cheery Brazilian accent had always entertained him. As she pronounced British English, a charm of aristocracy rang in her voice. Nash's eyes softened when he saw her. He stepped into the entryway and removed his navy pea coat he wore over a dark shirt and charcoal jeans. He shook her hand and smiled. "No, she's not with me."

Pearl furrowed her brow and tilted her head against the door frame. "Please come in."

Nash progressed through the familiar household, peeking around for any sign of Allegra's elegant face and illustrious, soft-spoken voice. Pearl shot him a glance, still inclined to converse further. "Miss Calla left most of her belongings. She left in such a hurry. Is she coming back?"

Nash's stride faltered. He shifted indignantly from foot to foot.

Sensing discomfort, Pearl dropped her line of questions. "I've kept all her things clean and attended to," she said.

He smiled. "I'm sure you have, Pearl, and quite impeccably, I imagine. Ms. Driscoll asked me to meet her here."

"Yes, she's in the den, Mr. Shields."

"Please, call me, Nash."

His invitation triggered a warm smile as he followed Pearl in the den.

Allegra glanced up from her work desk when she saw him. "Nash."

Even from where he stood, Allegra always astounded him. Though possibly pushing sixty or sixty-five, Allegra never displayed signs of slowing. She'd not lost any appeal or charm from her youth. Her range of accomplishments probably rivaled the Prime Minister's himself. Allegra was a former diplomat and traveled the globe like Nash's father had, negotiating diplomacy, from handling British relations with Palestinian authorities in Jerusalem to proposing plans for a Libyan no-fly zone, and sometimes representing the country at NATO Euro-Atlantic security meets. Today, she was ISTF boss, and his visit was about Calla and her safety.

Her eyes lit as he reached for a handshake. She embraced him with a hug that surprised him. "Nash, I'm so glad you are here. Thank you for calling."

He raised an eyebrow as she led him to the lounger. Nash ambled to the French Empire style, upholstered sofa, as a fatigued looking Allegra eased into the seat next to him. His eyes traveled to her face for a few minutes, determined not to be dissuaded. "You know where she is, don't you?"

Allegra avoided eye contact. Her head tipped back. Her voice, as always, was calm and encouraging. "I don't know where she is. But..." She hesitated for several seconds. "I knew they would come for her."

"How did they find us?"

"Vortigern was not exactly in favor of Calla's association with you, given her mission as lead operative."

"I see. And why?"

Allegra sighed. "He thinks in her role, she should be with someone else, perhaps an operative."

"Anyone in mind?"

"I don't know. Vortigern has always played hardball. He's not sure about you, given what you've learned about the operatives."

Nash felt a pang of betrayal. He didn't know Vortigern that well. Still, they'd fought Mason on the same side. He failed to sort his thoughts, but he had to know one thing. "Why doesn't he ask me what my intentions are?"

Allegra shifted uneasily in her seat. "You're right, Nash. When I'm wrong, I admit it. I'm sorry I entertained his notions. I don't agree with him."

Nash's gaze did not leave her face once. "How did they find us?"

"I don't know. They must have scrutinized Calla's e-mails, phone calls or even yours."

He slowly drew from her, his face pained. "Allegra, they blew up my house. If that's not an act of war...what are they trying to tell me?"

"They blew up your house?" She threw her head back in astonishment. "I didn't know that, Nash. That's too far."

Damn right, it's too far! Nash inclined his head slightly. "Allegra, please tell me the truth. What's going on? I know the operatives have played a daring card with me. But what do they want with Calla? Are you part of this?"

Allegra shook her head. "No. But I know their undertakings. Perhaps that's where my fault lies."

Nash loosened his jaw, feeling no emotion as a weakness seeped to his limbs. He edged back into the seat, his mind refusing to register the duplicity in her words. "I gathered as much. You have a few tricks up your sleeve. Calla told me you appeared out of nowhere in Masindi to help her when she was injured at Murchison Falls. Not to mention the swift removal of the Hadrius Manuscript from the Pergamon Museum. The bodily strength at your age impresses me."

Allegra offered a halfhearted shrug and rose to close the door, before settling at her walnut, kidney desk at the front of the impressive library—chockfull with ancient volumes. "I'm not your enemy, Nash. Calla's like a daughter to me, and I may have sat idly when she was ill advised, but I want you to know I'm sorry. Operatives are not the enemy, at least not all of us."

Nash pinched his lips together. Could he believe her? Had Calla tried to explain something the day she was abducted? *I want to believe you. Help me.*

Allegra fired up her laptop. "Nash, ISTF needs you more than ever. I'm confident Calla is unharmed." She waited for the program to fire up. "Have you seen this?" she asked.

She logged on to an ISTF intelligence portal well known to Nash. "How vital do you think the brain is?"

He leaned forward. "Excuse me?"

Allegra's face displayed a shade of amusement. "We're at the brink of what is becoming known as 'technological singularity'—important advances in technology, threatening to change civilization. I'd hate to wake to a day when scientists discover their machines are too powerful to control."

"If we're not there already."

"Mason can deliver it, unassisted. The brain is the center of the nervous system. Now, imagine how far the world has come by developing inconceivable technologies."

"*We* or the operatives?"

"Touché."

Wearied with thought, he sat silently.

Allegra continued. "Imagine what would happen if the human brain was no longer needed and technology took over. No power to think for oneself. No will or creativity innovation. Where does that leave humanity?"

———

1330 hrs.

"Is this man bothering you?"

The voice came from one of two bulky guards who moved toward Lascar and the woman at the desk. As they questioned him, his looming eyes caught Calla's own. The larger man gripped him by the jacket and hauled him off toward the ends of the hall. Lascar did not resist.

Bye!

A hand settled on her shoulder.

She snapped around with a jolt, and a heavy mass sank into her belly.

"May I help you, miss?"

Maybe?

At about six feet tall, a narrow, deeply seamed man considered her predicament. His thick, neck-length hair—worn in a neat style—was like black coffee. The strong-profiled doctor with two, caramel hooded eyes peered at her.

Calla dragged in a deep breath. "My name is Calla Cress, and I'm here on an investigation."

With narrowed eyes, he wore a troubled and stilled expression.

Calla bit her lip. "I'm with government intelligence."

The doctor's head flinched back slightly.

He doesn't believe me. Calla fished around her jeans, hoping what she sought had been left safe in the lining of her denim pockets. She breathed in relief when her fingers grazed her ISTF identity pass. "Look, here's my badge. I never leave anywhere without it."

With a mask of uncertainty, he joined his eyebrows. The doctor took the pass, then studied her face once more before returning it to her. The analytical stare eased, and his lips formed a temperate smile. "I thought ISTF was a journalist conspiracy theory. I wondered when one of you would show up."

Calla's eyes relaxed. "Do you know where I can find Veda Westall?"

"I'm Dr. Reuben Risebergl, Ms. Westall's physician, leading the research on her case. How do you know her?"

Calla lost all guard. "She's my boss at the British Museum and a dear friend."

"I thought you were with ISTF?"

The doctor's trusting smile warmed, allowing Calla to loosen the tightness in her gut. "I'm with ISTF. I'm what we call an authenticator, brought in for the more perplexing assignments concerning language, culture, and more recently cybercrimes that relate to language codes. You see there's much in anthropological language formation that can help code decryption."

"Really?"

She nodded. "More and more programmers draw inspiration from the brain. The result is cognitive computing."

"Impressive."

Calla let out a laugh, "Oh, there are new things every day. As a curator, I help ISTF to link history to the future and the other way round."

The doctor handed back her badge. "She's this way."

Calla kept pace with him as they neared an area of the floor sectioned off by a divider wall, manned by three security guards. The doctor fixed his eyes on her. "I'm sure as ISTF, you realize the classified sensitivity of this case."

"Yes, Dr. Risebergl."

The doctor pulled back the divider wall.

"Why trust me so readily, doctor?"

He paused for a few minutes and considered before replying. "Ms. Westall has mentioned your name repeatedly in her sleep. You must be close."

Calla ran a hand through her dark locks. "She's like a mentor to me."

"So, I gathered. She came out of the coma this morning. She's asleep, though."

Behind a mostly glass divider, Calla caught sight of Veda. Risebergl unlocked the glass door by fingering in a code in the latch that prevented access to her bed. "We've faced some debate as to the nature of memory loss in Ms. Westall. She's been in this condition for two days now. In some respects, her memories seem wholly lost and, in others, partially. We caught this from her brain wavelengths. I'm glad that you're here. You're someone she knows, and it may trigger something."

Calla followed the doctor into the exclusive area and glanced down at the still resting frame of her superior. A woman she admired and one who'd first mentored her at the British Museum, believing in Calla's ability to understand history at a whim. Calla sank into a stool next to the bed. "Tell me more about what she's going through?"

"She opened her eyes for the first time this morning. We think she's suffering from transient global amnesia or TGA. This means she may have significant problems accessing old memories. Sometimes it's recent memories. What's worrying is that her brain lapses. One minute she is normal and the next she suffers complete deterioration in thinking powers."

Not good. Veda is one of the biggest brains in international circles of anthropology.

"What sort of risk is she facing? I mean regarding her long-term health."

"She seems in perfect health. What concerns me is each time she relapses from one state to another, her heart undergoes duress, and therefore, we've had to set up this medical unit with heart specialists."

"Does she retain new memories?"

"In typical TGA, one almost has no ability to establish new memories, but hers seem mentally attentive and articulate. As explained before, she is moving through two or three conditions of amnesia. Hers is a worrying case."

Calla settled a cool hand on Veda's sleeping frame. "Can she hear us?"

"We've put her to sleep while we study the activity in her brain."

Calla stroked an itching eyebrow. "How does one get this way, doctor?"

His pained face showed struggle for an answer. "First guess, brain damage. Such as a blow to the head. But from the police reports, they say nothing of the sort happened while she was visiting the prisoner in Belmarsh."

Fiery tears and compassion wrestled in Calla's face.

Sensing Calla's struggle, the doctor shuffled his feet and moved to the head of the reclined bed. "Her brain is deteriorating to a state we typically see in later patients of amnesia or dementia. It doesn't make sense."

"I hear she was fine one minute, then this happened," Calla said.

"If she were older and maybe had suffered this sort of thing for a while, I'd have assumed it was natural memory loss, seen in older patients. Her condition has only developed in the last forty-eight hours. She's only forty-nine according to her employment records. Look here at this data."

Calla followed his finger to where it pointed to a screen with a beeping line. "Heat is developing in her head. We're monitoring that heat with this apparatus. See this?"

She observed the steadily mounting line. It ascended like a healthy sales line on a chart. "What is that line doing? What does it reveal?"

The doctor fingered a few buttons on the machine. "The

apparatus stabilizes the temperature in her brain. However, it's moving faster than I'm comfortable with."

A grave look engulfed his face. "The heat might cause a burst in her brain."

An involuntary gasp left Calla's lips.

He turned his face toward her. "We're trying to steady the swelling as best we can, but at this rate, I don't think she will last a week, ten days at the most."

—

1359 hrs.

"I'm sure you're going to tell me," Nash said, feeling his muscles relax for the first time since entering Allegra's home. Tension left his face. "Twenty months ago, I was part of an ISTF research team that studied the human brain, all attempting to better understand signals intelligence... how the two are related. None of our research was conclusive."

"What did you find?" Allegra asked.

"It's an ongoing side project. Some of it is controversial. We've shared the program with MI5. We like to keep an eye on proprietary electronic equipment that analyzes electrical activity in human beings." Nash leaned over to study the screen. "These are computer-generated brain mapping programs that continually monitor all electrical activity in the brain. But what's this all about?"

Allegra set her palms on the table. "I'm sure you realize that Calla is a remarkable person." She caught his concentrating eye. "I'm the last person who needs to convince you of that. As an operative, Calla, with her aptitude for linguistic form, history, and technology plus her genetics, put her in an exceptionally, strategic position for Merovec."

Nash crossed his arms over his chest. "Merovec? Who's

Merovec?"

"Who he is, isn't important. What we need are his designs for technical and linguistic programming of the human brain. Mason has launched a war on the human brain using sophisticated, neuron altering schemes."

Could the rumors of telepathy Nash had heard be true? Nash breathed in heavily, fatigue seeping into his muscles. "If this Merovec is so versed in comprehending Mason's war, why doesn't he step up? He's an operative, I take it?"

"The head operative. His argument will be that Calla was the one wired to do so. Whether she likes it or not, she was the one he nominated to do this. Her talents match Mason's hostility. Unfortunately, Calla and Mason are genetically matched."

"Have you shared this with ISTF?"

"So far, the intelligence comes from the operatives. The operatives want to work with ISTF, only, it's yet premature." She gripped his arm. "I want this to work for everyone. Calla can be an instrument in bridging the two sides."

Nash thought for a moment. "By my measure, this only works if the two sides walk together."

Allegra pulled up another file. "Taiven retrieved a microchip Mason designed with a scientist named Durant. ISTF confiscated his computers. Let's say Taiven unceremoniously retrieved it from Mason's skull."

Nash flinched back. "Serious?"

"Mason self-implanted that chip. We don't know yet what it does, but what we saw when it was analyzed at one of our London coves, is that Mason's victims all suffered from neurological problems. We assume he wants to attack innovation at its core. This'll threaten technological advancement. Any creator today uses computing technology. That goes for researchers, software engineers, and developers."

Nash squinted in the early afternoon light that poured into the den. "I'm not so sure. Mason must have another ulterior motive. It just doesn't add up. The NSA looked at similar programs. What will he do? Retrieve human thought with a telepathic chip that archives memories?"

"Yes."

"If that chip does what I think, he'll be able to send and receive electromagnetic copies of thoughts and direct them anywhere, another being, a computer network—"

"So that's why the operatives need Calla. Disarm him and his train of thoughts," he said.

"Taiven informed me she was taken to one of their London offices this morning."

"Do you agree with that sort of behavior? Abduction? She could be hurt."

Allegra's face lowered with a downcast pout. "No."

"Is she all right?"

"I'm sure she is." Allegra changed the subject. "The human brain has progressed over the last two-hundred thousand years responding to the interaction between environmental challenges and activities—"

"Yes, and it continues to do so at a natural pace."

Allegra tilted her head. "Not any longer. That natural pace is what is at risk if Mason finishes his worm. First, he targets technology then the brain. The future may be more directly in Mason's hands."

"No one will be safe," Nash said more to himself.

"Forget the NSA spying on PCs. Mason will have our thoughts. The information we're deciphering here shows that in less than fourteen days Mason could have computers writing books, performing medical procedures, commanding the armed forces, business politics, culture, and recreation... in essence, humanity."

"Have you analyzed how he's running the program? For

instance, is he tuning in remote frequency emissions from his personal computer circuit boards? I assume he left the computer behind when he escaped Belmarsh? If we could retrieve the machine he used, it might help."

Allegra scrolled through her online notes. "Not sure. What we do know is that the system he's creating automates by building databases of information to source from. So far, this has been the brains of some of the world's greatest minds. The system then custom-tailors a query about a topic and creates templates of packaged information. The program mimics the thought process an expert would go through to create, to rule, command, and do their job. Mason is the only one who controls the software."

"We can hack it."

"Nash. Mason's technology is at least fifteen years ahead of any government. It's not as easy as it seems."

Nash returned to the desk and eyed the information on the screen. "So to recap, Mason steals human intelligence, scrambles it like eggs to re-create a network grabbing hack that in turn thwarts global computers off track without our knowledge, all trying to create a mechanism powerful enough to read human thought. Damn! We're sitting ducks! He will use human intelligence to create an even greater threat."

"We need Calla to find Merovec. If I know Vortigern, she's under his supervision at the moment."

Nash took a slight step back. Only a few months ago, Calla had found the thing she'd longed for most—information on her family, her parents. Instead, she'd walked into a ploy that had waited to ensnare her all her life, and personally, he didn't blame Stan for what he'd done. It now made sense. Who was this Merovec? What the heck was wrong with these operatives? An unusual superior portion of the human race, amassing skills and technologies for years, and here they were stunned at a threat created by their kind. Yet their very same weaknesses make the human race vulnerable. *Fear*.

Allegra wanted swift answers to eliminate Mason. She feared something. Like this Merovec perhaps, who refused to make an appearance. Or even Mason himself? A name he'd hoped to forget. He owed someone a visit—the woman who'd charmed Mason and brought him to his knees.

"Allegra?"

She raised her head.

"One question. Why weren't you affected when you went to see Mason in his cell? The notes here say you were one of the visitors."

"I—"

Nash set a hand on his temple. Waves of crushing agony beat against the back of his eyelids. A sudden pain throbbed on the right side of his head. He recalled the wound that had grazed him in Colorado. The throbbing intensified, slowly dropping to his neck. He ignored it.

"Are you all right?" Allegra said.

"Yeah." He slumped back into his seat, rubbing his temple.

The desk phone rang. Allegra pressed down the speakerphone. "Yes."

"Ms. Driscoll," said a woman's voice, "I've the PM for you."

Allegra shot Nash an inclusive look. "Put him through."

A matter-of-fact, upbeat male voice commanded the cracking speaker. "Ms. Driscoll."

"Mr. Prime Minister."

The PM cleared his husky throat. "I need to discuss something urgently with you."

Allegra set a finger over her lips, warning Nash to remain silent. "Please go right ahead."

"I'm ordering you to shut down UK's ISTF operations,

resign your position as head and contact the other four governments with Britain's disposition on the matter. ISTF is no longer of use to national and global security."

Her lips tightened. "Why, PM? We've progressed in our investigation in this new cyber threat. We can't stop now."

The PM's voice interrupted. "As far as I'm aware, the cyber threat originates from the last person who led ISTF. I've ordered a full investigation of ISTF, and I need you to redeploy resources and funds to the Secret Intelligence Service."

"But PM—"

"I'll expect ISTF to stop all operation in a month's time when I'll make a public announcement and frankly, an apology to the cabinet."

"PM—"

The line went dead. Allegra glanced out the window, a frail hand settling on her trembling lips.

With his upper body in agony, Nash was quiet for several seconds. He knew what this meant. The member countries would not cooperate on this new cyber threat. ISTF, the only organization capable of uniting them against Mason, had been incapacitated.

Nash altered his position on the sofa to relieve the pain. "He doesn't mean that. It's a political ploy, someone in his cabinet is not happy and its seats shuffling time." He stroked his temple and curled forward. "I need to go."

"Where are you going?" She hesitated. "Nash, what's wrong?"

To find Calla, then her mother. She's the only operative with any sense to disappear from all this madness. He hobbled from the seat. "I need to get to the US Embassy. I'm sure I can discover more about what's going on with ISTF."

Allegra rose. The news had hit her hard. ISTF was the only organization ever to cooperate with the operatives. "Nash, be careful."

"Thanks. I'll contact you soon."

Nash scrambled out of the house and staggered the few meters to his car. The throbbing deepened. He took a deep breath. He'd come here in a hurry. *Why?*

Come to think of it, he wasn't sure he knew anyone who lived in West London. Had his memory suffered a slight setback?

RUSSELL SQUARE, LONDON
1520 hrs.

"Thank you, Dr. Risebergl, for all your help."

The doctor's voice weakened. "I wish there was more we could do."

Calla plodded beside him as they made their way back to the elevator before returning to the main lobby. She reached for his firm hand and gave it a gentle shake. "I'll be back soon to see her."

Out of the corner of her eye, she caught the outline of the Skylar, parked in the hospital entryway. Calla edged back toward the elevator, taking the doctor with her. Lascar remained outside like a hungry cub waiting for a lionesses' feed. She pursed her lips and caught the doctor's eye. "Dr. Risebergl?"

"Yes?"

"Could you do me a favor?" She scribbled Allegra's residential number on a piece of paper. "If Veda's condition changes, could you please let me know by calling this number."

"Of course, Ms. Cress. You really care about her, don't you?"

The compassion in Risebergl's eyes eased Calla's nerves.

Her lips stretched into a smile. "She's phenomenal with a prodigious mind. The world needs more people like her."

The doctor stuffed the paper in his pocket. "I'm certain it does." He tilted his head. "Who's your friend?"

Calla's eyes traveled to the entrance. Lascar had been out there, probably since security had curbed him outside. She set a hand on the doctor's arm. "Is there another way out?"

The doctor followed her gaze out the front, spotting Lascar drumming his fingers on the dashboard. "Friend of yours?"

"More like a stalker."

"I don't blame him. You're a beautiful woman."

A slight flush crept across her cheeks, and she ran a nervous hand through her dark hair.

"Come this way. You can leave by the staff entrance," he said.

"Thanks, Dr. Risebergl. I don't need to deal with him now."

Calla stole out of the back entrance and gave the doctor she'd come to appreciate a wave. She almost jolted into a bevy of nurses on a coffee break as she scurried to the Maserati that waited in a small alleyway behind the hospital. She fired up the engine and, within minutes, raced down Marylebone Road on her way to West London. Calla waited at a stoplight and took in the pungent scent of her clothes, a mixture of sweaty struggle, cabin discomfort, and lack of fresh air. The thought that she'd been wearing the same items for close to two days repulsed her.

Famished and needing a shower, she reached for the car's in phone system and switched on the untraceable application. Was Nash okay? What about Jack? *Damn it, I need my things!*

What sort of drug could have put Veda in such a state? She wasn't even pushing fifty. Veda was more than a prodigious curator. A linguistic genius and unparalleled historian, who'd studied Hebrew, Arabic, Mandarin, Greek, and if Calla was right, all before the age of twenty-one. One of Veda's important accomplishments was her published work in linguistic anthropology, all stemming from her controversial theory about the origins of language, which continued to be a matter of debate in scholarly circles. Her theory explored language as the unconscious, vocal imitation of movements in one's natural environment. Veda also argued that language was ingrained in one's DNA.

Is that what Mason was after? Her theories? Her undiscovered ones? How far would he go?

Veda had supported her theory by comparing fossil records and archaeological evidence from numerous ancient languages. Though her theories were not shared by most, they had raised eyebrows. Aside from her riveting mind, Veda was a guru to Calla. One who encouraged Calla's potential and curiosity, given her access to all she'd learned as they worked together at the British Museum.

What did Mason want with her mind? Determination gripped Calla's will. She faced a choice and pressed her head against the secure headrest, realizing fatigue would set in if she didn't have a decent meal soon.

She had no choice. She'd been pulled into a hunt for her mother and a neurotic loose criminal. And without doubt, the former frightened her more than the latter. *Why did you lie to me, Stan? What father does that?*

The Maserati nosed into St. Giles Square, a few meters from Allegra Driscoll's residence.

This was it. She could no longer run. So many people's lives depended on cornering Mason and dismantling his worms.

CHAPTER 9

1616 hrs.

The Maserati parked in a quiet square in West London Calla now called home. The Victorian residence stood among its peers in a garden square located north of the Thames River. Calla had moved here after her flat in West Kensington was vandalized when the government came in search of the Hadrius Manuscript, memories she wanted to shelve. Though Allegra had told her the home was now her own, a luxurious estate enough to house an army, Calla wondered how long she would stay. It didn't matter. She had all she needed. All she owned was here and in an offshore account sitting in a trust fund her father had put aside for years, a fortune amassed by the Cress family over more decades than she knew to count. Without her key, she rang the doorbell.

"Ms. Calla?"

Pearl took her frigid hands. "You're back. You don't have a coat or anything with you. Come in, come in."

"Thanks, Pearl."

Warm air from the interior caressed her face. Pearl was

right, she'd literally run around town without a coat, or anything warm. The only important items she had on her were the keys to the Maserati and minor identification she always carried, usually in some undisclosed pocket in her denims.

The smell of fresh *tarte tatin*, a French delicacy Allegra enjoyed, drifted from the kitchen, reminding her of her ignored hunger. "Mm... Pearl, I'm famished."

She heard light footsteps on the stairs and glimpsed up at the spiral, cedar stairs that dominated the side of the entryway. Allegra descended the grand staircase, her elegant hand sliding along the magnificent detail on the railing.

Allegra lingered at a midway step veering to the end of the staircase. "Calla?"

The tone in her greeting was warm and cordial as she stepped to where Calla stood and took her hands in hers. They exchanged a genial glance before Calla pulled away from Allegra's gentle grasp.

"Are you all right?" Allegra said.

"Shouldn't I be?"

Pearl broke the aloof stares by shifting toward the kitchen. "Ms. Calla, all your things are exactly as you left them. Would you like me to get you something to eat?"

Calla glanced her way. "The tarte you just made smells wonderful."

Allegra moved her head slightly as if trying to avoid some dazzling light. "I had nothing to do with it. Vortigern—"

Calla moved quickly past her and started a slow mount up the stairs. "I'll just collect a few things."

Allegra's face contorted into a complex set of wrinkles. She tailed the younger woman. "Wait, Calla. What do you plan to do?"

Calla wasn't sure how much Allegra knew about her ordeal. Usually, nothing went past Allegra. Calla held her hand to her forehead, sighing deeply. She owed her cherished friend a little trust. She stopped on the second step, her hand resting on the banister. "How did they find us? You were the only one who knew where we were."

The narrowing of Allegra's eyes told Calla she was pained. Allegra's eyes softened, filling with an inner glow. "I didn't tell them where you were. I'd never do that. Vortigern must have his connections. In fact, I envy you."

"Why?"

Allegra's gaze lowered as did her voice. "Because you stood up to them and.. . I didn't."

Calla faced her. "I'm scared, Allegra. Scared for the lives of my friends and what else the operatives are capable of."

"Nash was here earlier."

"He's here? Is he okay? How—"

"He went to see your father earlier. He's worried about your safety." Allegra heaved a sigh. "Nash guessed right. He knew the operatives had a hand in your abduction."

"I should have told him from the start," Calla said the words to herself, hurt and concern creeping in her heart. "Where is he?"

"He was going to ISTF and to the US Embassy."

"Did he say why?"

Allegra shook her head slowly.

With an apologetic glance at Allegra, Calla drew in a yawning breath. "Listen, Vortigern has attempted to harm him and Jack with some sort of memory sedative because of me."

Allegra's face reddened. "Vortigern will stop at nothing. If he dared use the same repressant they used on my former husband Aston, as I imagine he may have, there's something you can do to stop it taking effect."

"Aston. You took a huge chance, didn't you by marrying him."

"As much as I believe in the good we operatives do, I

decided our human emotions sometimes outweigh reason and logic."

Calla resumed her march up the stairs, with Allegra keeping step. The first floor housed an array of state-of-the-art bedrooms, one of which Calla occupied when she moved in. She pushed open the ivory carved door and marched into the room. She headed for the closet and peeled off her travel clothes. Fingering a pair of burgundy leather pants, a black turtleneck, and a pair of new riding boots, she dumped the items on the bed, before heading into the ensuite bathroom.

"What do you plan to do?" Allegra said, taking a seat on the French design comforter.

Calla sailed into the adjoining bathroom and started the shower. "I have to find Jack and Nash. Then... my mother," she said, peering back into the bedroom to see whether her statement had forged any response from her usually blunt friend.

None.

Allegra would not give much away. Calla left the door ajar so she could converse. She stripped off her underclothes before stepping under the flow of the warm stream. Her preferred moisturizing shampoo and conditioner were within arm's reach, and foamed in her dark locks, bursting the smells of lavender and vanilla into the spacious glass cubicle.

"So you'll do as Vortigern requests?" Allegra asked.

Calla poked her head toward the bedroom. "If I do, it'll be for my reasons."

"May I ask what those are?" Allegra hollered, sliding a hand over Calla's trendy all-weather leather slacks.

Calla finished her shower, grabbed a large soft towel, and wrung a smaller one over her dripping hair. "Do you agree with Vortigern?" she asked as she searched for the low-set hairdryer.

"Not exactly."

The rumble of the hairdryer filled the two rooms. Allegra watched as Calla ran a comb through her tresses before slinging the drying mane into a high ponytail. "Let me help you with what you're about to do."

"Vortigern has wiped Jack and Nash's memories. An operative by the name of Lascar and his team were sent to Almont and must've accomplished it somehow. Nash is probably suffering memory loss... and God knows what poor Jack must be going through. From where I stand. .. not too different from Mason's tactics."

In minutes, Calla was dressed. She grabbed a medium-sized backpack and quickly congested it with some toiletries and a change of clothes.

Allegra rose from the bed. "At least take this to wherever you're going." She left the room and returned with a 9mm, Colt Defender handgun. "Take this—standard issue for ISTF agents in the field. I don't know where you're going, but I can't let you go without some help. I assume Lascar used the special ops diplomatic service at the airport. We reserve it for special purposes. ISTF has used it often." Allegra raised her chin. "I'll have a new passport for you tonight. We'll declare the last one lost."

"Thanks, I don't do guns. Never could."

—

1635 hrs.

Calla moved closer to Allegra and fingered the gun. It felt like *déjà vu*. But this time, she would take it. Her face softened. "Thanks, Allegra. How can I reverse what Vortigern has done?"

"If he used the standard operative chip for temporary or selective memory loss, then there is something you can do."

"What? Does it have side effects?"

"That repressant is reversible, but it'll take some skill." Allegra grasped her hand. "It might be too late, Calla. I saw Nash, and he kept rubbing his temples as if he had a headache. Those are some first symptoms."

Calla frowned. "All the more for me to help him. Nash plays by the rules. It's spineless for anyone to slink on him like that."

Clamor from downstairs caught their ears. They listened in dread as unexpected voices argued. They heard the front door slam shut.

Calla was first to the bedroom door. They caught the sound of Pearl in dispute with a deep-throated voice. Calla whirled around and shot Allegra a deliberate look. "Lascar."

She tilted her chin up, scuttled out of the bedroom, and along to the top of the staircase, pausing when she saw a face that was becoming all too recognizable. "What do you want, Lascar?"

He glanced upward. "I'm tied to your hip bone, Cress."

Calla summoned every shred of calm and coasted down the staircase to where he stood. Lascar's stare was punitive. He placed a hand on the wall, blocking her forward passage. "I'm gonna stick around longer than you wish."

His tone was more than she could bear, his musky scent, intolerable. Shifting her eyes to the wall against the stairs on her left, she caught sight of two nineteenth-century South East Asian spears. Her hand moved swiftly as she drew one from its hold, and with its speared end away from her, she slung it under Lascar's robust legs. "Bugger off."

He plummeted to his knees.

"Not the ones from the Vietnamese ambassador!" Allegra's

voice came from above them, amused by the display of boldness.

"I'm just borrowing it," Calla said. "Don't worry; they're not the ones at risk of damage."

She stepped over Lascar's agonizing frame as he writhed on the marble of the landing. Lascar groped her heel and launched her to the solid floor. He arched suddenly to pull himself upright, stretched for the second spear above her, and pointed its blade at her throat. "Ready for lesson one?"

"Maybe it should be yours. And one in manners would not hurt either."

Still cleaving on to her newfound weapon, Calla rose in one fluid motion, regaining her feet and alighting inches from him. Their hardwood poles clashed in a violent struggle. With strengths matched and faces fuming, Calla carved her foot under him, breaking his hold on the priceless pole. She leaped onto the second stair.

Lascar clambered after her and thrust the nineteenth-century weapon toward her midriff. She blocked his thrust. A tremor shook through her spear, rising to her upper arm as she plunged backward.

Lascar charged his way up, leveling the spear for attack. Calla crawled back with one hand along the stairs, combating the barbaric pole, as she held her balance. Lascar's spear insisted on taming her as he threw his weight into his strikes.

Once up the grand staircase, Calla slammed her back against the tiles of the upper floor. She was trapped between his weapon, and the lack of ascending space. She swerved her foot across his jaw, lunged over the banister, landing at the bottom of the stairs in a steady touchdown.

A frightened Pearl, who'd carried in a full tray of tarts, smashed its contents on the polished marble, before scrambling back into the kitchen.

"He's not staying for afternoon tea, Pearl."

Wiping the blood from his jaw, Lascar lurched down over the banister after her and burst in front of her face. The moment his feet touched the floor, Calla rounded her body backward in double flips that carted her to the front door.

Lascar barged for her, anger crossing his pained face as fumed breath seethed from his nostrils. His pole charged in her direction.

She halted his approach with a momentous clash that sent him spiraling backward, before landing with a thud, his shoulders crashing against the tiles. Calla barreled forward until her spear spoke louder forms than any words she could use. Its tipped edge hesitated against his Adam's apple. He drew a sharp breath, a split lip spattering drops of blood as his face displayed thunderous spite.

Setting a foot on his heaving chest, she leaned forward. "Looks like you're the one who needed training." She stepped away from his trained physique and held out a hand to help him up. "Now, have I made myself clear? I don't need tagalongs."

Lascar took her hand and rose slowly.

She turned on her heels to return the unharmed spear to a gaping Allegra. Calla sensed movement from Lascar. Without delay, his hand claimed her back. He swung her around and pushed her to him before forcing ambitious lips over hers.

Revolted, she kneed him in the groin. He released her abruptly and fell back, coiled into defeat before slowly raising both his hands in surrender.

A short laugh left Allegra's lips. She'd witnessed the heated match, joined them at the foot of the stairs, and pierced disapproving eyes at Lascar. "I take it this means you leave her alone now."

Allegra chuckled before catching Calla's interrogative eye.

"What's this all about, Allegra?"

Allegra's look approved her victory. "Where did you learn to focus your skills like that?"

She smiled down at Lascar. "Nash."

"You're definitely ready. Lascar is the head commander and trainer of the operatives' special weapons and tactics team. If you can thrash him, then you can take on *anyone* and *anything.*"

Chagrined, Lascar rose, took a seat in an adjoining hallway chair, and attended to his wounded lip. Pearl reentered the hallway and picked up her discarded tray.

"Pearl," Allegra said. "Please show our visitor to the door."

After Lascar left, Allegra set a small gadget, no bigger than a car key, in Calla's hand. "You'll need this to set back the memory loss. This radio device controls the chip grazed under Nash and Jack skins. Vortigern doesn't know that I made this after what they did to Aston."

Calla fingered the small, black gadget.

"You can maneuver the chip on the front of the interface," Allegra said. "Try to get a good aim, without interference, so the wireless signal has the best chance. Once you do so, destroy it. Even Merovec believes in free will, and that's why you have to find him. Vortigern is right about one thing; you must find your mother for everyone's sake."

Calla gazed at her with questioning eyes before taking the wireless control. Her mother had outwitted them all, Mason, ISTF, MI6, the operatives, and Merovec. She had to find her if she would live the life she wanted and protect her friends. "Am I ready for this, Allegra? You know, unearthing the past again. Will I like what I find?"

"Only you can judge that. It has to be your choice."

"Where do I begin?"

"Find Mila Rembrandt. She's the only one ever to contact

your mother. And unfortunately, your mother is the only one who knows how to contact Merovec."

Mila had been puzzling from the minute Calla learned who she was. Mila was the operative charged by her parents to watch over Calla from a distance and was a cousin of her mother's. Calla knew little about the woman who shifted like shadows from continent to region.

"Mila's in Greece," Allegra said. "That's where she was last seen."

Allegra seized Calla's hand. "Know that Mason will stop at nothing. Even if it means eliminating your mother. Right now, it's his only way of getting to you."

Calla's eyes narrowed.

Several minutes later, Calla wolfed salty cod with tomato and chorizo sauce that Pearl had prepared and grabbed her backpack. She placed the gun, an untraceable smartphone that Allegra arranged for her and the device in secure compartments of the carry-on.

Allegra escorted her to the door. "It's time Mila told you about your mother."

CENTRAL LONDON, 1658 hrs.

Calla sped the Maserati east on the M4 highway. She turned on the car radio. Perhaps Chopin would calm her nerves or Beethoven. But even as Classic FM churned out several arpeggios, her mind focused on her next feat. *What will it be like to see Nash, as if for the first time?*

If Allegra was right, Vortigern had followed through on his threat. As an operative, Calla was not supposed to get close to non-operatives. Not in personal or dependent ways. She had to get to Nash and Jack before the microchip's behavior took effect. Allegra had explained that initially, the memory repressant contained in a pill, had been scuffed under their skins by a tranquilizer gun. It was a drug that erased painful memories, such as witnessing a ferocious crime or suffering major trauma. The repressant was developed by scientists in the operatives' labs several years ago.

Allegra had developed it into various forms of memory manipulation, using beta blocker, or as she'd been told by medical operatives, a medication used to treat several conditions, often by reducing heart activity. The blockers could interfere with how the brain made and reformed memories. There'd been side effects with the first tests the operatives had conducted, mostly around personal identity, because people were linked to their memories, but only had it set for over forty-eight hours. *When did you do it, Lascar?*

"The drug sits in a chip administered by a tranquilizer dart. Once it's had enough time to stabilize, it transmits neuro-activity through the bloodstream, then to the brain, beginning with memory deterioration," Allegra had explained.

Cowards!

She could reverse Nash and Jack's repressant activity, given the chip was discovered in time and that its transmission was halted, or the chip was removed.

Classic FM tuned into a piano arrangement of Bach's Orchestral Suite No. 3 in D major, a piece she'd often played as an ambitious teenager. The music numbed her anxiety as the Maserati slid onto the Mall, running from Buckingham Palace toward Trafalgar Square.

The pacifying arpeggios took her mind to when she first met Nash all those months ago at Denver airport and Jack in Edinburgh, at a TED Technology conference. With both, she'd felt at ease instantly. Jack... first, he was always running from some inner ambition he had to conquer, all surfacing into some prodigious innovation in technology, like the rotor robots that ISTF had used for military purposes.

Calla guessed Jack's eager, yet healthy ambitions probably stemmed from his upbringing in the Seychelles. Raised in near poverty, but now one of the richest technology entrepreneurs in the United Kingdom, Calla admired Jack. He could be insecure yet unaware of the insecurity. Even though in her eyes, he was brilliant, he always wanted more from himself. Extroverted, he could start a short conversation with anyone, anywhere. He made her feel sane. She was often intrigued by how his creative mind worked, resulting in new and wild inventions in computing.

She turned down the music and reached for the cell phone in the front pocket of her backpack, and dialed Jack's number.

No answer.

She tried Nash's number.

No response.

Had he switched to his UK cell?

Nash, a choice athlete, was like air she needed to inhale daily. His was a rare mix of perceptual and physical strength, right principles, and humor. Perfect for her, though she'd never told him. She'd known no one incredibly attractive, with his smiling gray eyes. Nash possessed an arresting presence, supporting that quality with mesomorph power. It was only when she met Nash that she'd felt the ability to embrace affection. Feelings she'd run from all her adult life. Recently, she'd understood. It was Nash, or no one else. Six months with him in Colorado had solidified that stance. She sometimes shuddered around him. He was an idealist, always desiring to make the little extra difference in everything he did. Like the time he'd put his life in danger to save his colonel lieutenant friend, Masher, her life repeatedly and even Jack's. Frankly, anyone in danger.

Calla breathed deeply, inspired by Nash's sense of sacrificial commitment. *He never thinks of himself first.*

One thing bothered her though—something he'd asked her to do for him in Almont. The one thing he wanted was the only thing she wouldn't give him.

Inside the Watergate building compound, Calla angled the gray sports car in the staff parking. She was early. Allegra's assistant was to meet her and reprocess her with a new badge and all she needed to get her ISTF credentials and access codes. Her ear caught the newscaster reporting on the BBC station. She placed her phone in her pocket and turned up the volume.

> *"NASA has reported that they've lost control of Lincoln International Space Station. The station is the largest artificial body in orbit, launched several months ago for a crew made up of mostly US and British astronauts conducting research experiments in biology, physics, astronomy, and meteorology.*
>
> *"It's unclear how the computing problems began, but what NASA determines is that an onboard virus took control of the station's main onboard computers.*
>
> *"What concerns NASA now, beyond the financial implications, is that the shuttle with nine crew members is at the mercy of an unknown hacker. The safety of the crew is of utmost importance, and British and US intelligence have launched counter precautions."*

Calla switched off the radio and jumped out of her car.

So it had begun. Mason was starting where it hurts. *International relations!*

ISTF OFFICES
WATERGATE HOUSE, CENTRAL LONDON
1721 hrs.

An incoming call interrupted Calla. "Ms. Cress. Hi, I'm Scarlet Lorens, Ms. Driscoll's assistant. I understand you'll be joining the Karachi Brief program."

Calla didn't recall the details. She assumed Allegra had prepped the staff. "Yes, that's right," Calla said.

Your clearance and credentials have been updated and will be ready for you when you arrive."

"Thanks, Scarlet. I've just arrived."

"Great. The operation team on the Karachi Brief is in place, and you'll join them. I understand it's being led by Nash Shields, I'm not sure whether you've met. I'm quite new here."

"Karachi Brief?"

"Yes. The code for the investigation of NASA's hacked computers."

"I see."

"I'll meet you downstairs in a couple of minutes, Ms. Cress."

Calla hung up. After arriving at the grand lobby, Calla gave her name at the reception and was met by a delightful Middle Eastern woman with olive skin, dark-brown eyes, and shoulder-length, elaborately styled brown hair. Her clothes were formal, and she wore a vintage Bedouin Hirz pendant, a vintage form of jewelry.

"Miss Cress. I've heard so much about you." Scarlet handed her a set of cards, keys, and documents. "Your cryptic skills are legendary here. Seems the organization has missed you."

Calla's face abandoned all pretenses as they marched toward the glass elevators. "Jack Kleve is not here at the moment. He left saying he'd go meet Nash Shields. An update on the Karachi Brief will begin in about an hour. I assume they'll all be back then," Scarlet said.

Calla placed the credentials in her backpack. "Thank you."

The elevator stopped on the fifth floor. Calla knew the place like the tattoo on her ankle. Much of her professional work around authenticating and cryptology, manuscripts, and coded language outside the British Museum took place in the confines of this clandestine establishment. ISTF remained an organization that played by its own rules, known officially on public records as the Government Research Agency. Such a name had raised little eyebrows, and no one came in or out without considerable security scrutiny.

ISTF retained its position as a secret, five-government member agency that fought to dismantle various types of crime, recruiting its own teams from various fields and training its agents for fieldwork. Although crime erupted in all forms and manners, ISTF had mostly focused on cybercrimes in the last several months. The escalation of cybercriminals' heightened computer and network intrusions included identity theft, spam, stock manipulation, financial fraud, and telecommunication scams that led to various forms of criminal activity—from international art thefts, terrorist activity, and most recently cyber hacking. These attacks showed ISTF that artistes could compromise and control millions of computers that belonged to governments, private enterprises, and ordinary citizens.

Once on the fifth floor, Calla and Scarlet sauntered past the file room. Calla had heard of the fire that had taken place seven months earlier. She turned to Scarlet. "Just tell me where the meeting will be. I need to attend to something first."

"By all means, Ms. Cress. The meeting will be on this floor in sector three, room five.

"Thank you."

Calla waited until the assistant was out of earshot before sliding her pass through the card slot of the file room. The room was empty.

It was after five, and most staff had left for the day. From the inside of her bag, she withdrew a thin file of no more than six to seven pages. She pulled out the stapled papers and inched to the shelves labeled under the letter D.

She filed through the memo and located an ISTF stamp in a nearby desk. This was her version of the Hadrius Manuscript case that had begun over seven months ago. No one knew the document belonged to the operatives. She'd erased that information from the servers before going to Almont, and now she held a hard copy of the report. She read the file again, fingering the stamp, and rammed it over the document.

FILE CLOSED

"That should do it," she said to herself.

For an office as hi-tech as ISTF, it was perplexing that everything needed to be documented on paper. Calla placed the file on the shelf, glanced around the dark room, before exiting and shutting the door behind her. With twenty minutes to kill before the meeting began, Calla tried her father's phone. "Stan... I mean, father?"

"Calla? Where are you? Are you all right?"

"I'm fine."

Her thoughts meandered to the disturbing question that had inundated her mind since that morning. "Father?"

"Yes?"

"Why did you tell me that mother was dead?"

A long silence drew out on the other side of the line. She

heard shambling before Stan cleared his emotionally congested throat. "I've wanted to talk to you about this. I regret lying to you, after all, you went through."

"Why did you do it?"

"Let me come and see you." An imperceptible note of pleading surfaced in his voice. "Let's have a proper talk, sweetheart. Where are you?"

She closed her eyes and leaned back against the wall, letting the dappled lights play across her face. Footsteps behind her told her that Scarlet had returned. "I need to go. I'll speak to you later. I'm at ISTF, in London."

She set the phone in the back pocket of her slacks and managed a smile as Scarlet approached.

"This way, Ms. Cress. I believe Jack and Nash are waiting for you."

Forty-eight hours ago, she'd been taken from Nash with the possibility he wouldn't remember who she was. A concentrated swallow trailed down her throat as she followed Scarlet to the spacious room.

"Mr. Kleve, Mr. Shields, this is Calla Cress," announced Scarlet. She'll be working with you on the Karachi Brief. I'm sure you read her bio that I handed you earlier. She's versed in several languages, classical and modern history, and understands cryptograph and signal intelligence systems. Did I mention she is a curator at the British Museum in charge of the Byzantium and Roman collections?"

Jack moved over to Calla, his face alight with charm. If she knew no better, six months had morphed Jack's physique in distinguishable ways. He'd gained lean muscle in a way most military men do after lifting heavy weights for several months. He tossed her a wink. "Quite a resume. We need more of you around here." He grinned. "You know, brains and. .."

Calla's heart lifted for a moment, delighted that Jack would be

Jack. But almost as it had come, her receptive sentiment altered. She fought back the choking sensation forming in her and groomed a fragile smile. For someone who didn't remember her, Jack was everything she recollected and cherished. "Mr. Kleve—"

His face brightened as he took her hand. "Call me, Jack."

She smiled. "Jack, I'm going to like working with you."

Jack turned to Nash. "Nash is from the NSA, part of our two governments working together in the ISTF maze."

Nash ambled over toward her, strong-eye contact fixed on her, poring into her depth, and if she hadn't known better, her soul. She'd not seen him since their ordeal on the slopes of the Rockies and their escape from Lascar's gun missiles. Even now, he made her flush as his eyes smiled at her. Would there be a connection? He reached for her hand and gently took it into his for a sociable shake, not once blinking. "I hope you'll like it here."

Calla shook his warm hand and held it longer than she should have, all the while searching for clues of acquaintance, familiarity, recognition. Attraction? "Nash... I'm glad we'll be working together," she said as she sank slowly into a seat by the table, certain her face bared a hint of disappointment. *They don't know me.*

—

CENTRAL LONDON, 1730 hrs.

Calla pressed the back of her head against the leather of the chair in the room, arranged around a white coffee table. Her hand rested firmly in her backpack. She slithered the bag to the floor and unzipped the front compartment, fumbling around to find the correct buttons on the wireless devices. Sweaty fingers slipped off the gadget several times. If Allegra was right, she could just set off the button. This would offset a signal to the transmitter and disengage it.

She raised her head and watched as the men exchanged a few words by the door. Her hand found the small plastic button and pressed it down. She watched for a response. The men continued talking before Jack picked up a hard copy of the Karachi Brief that lay on the table by an Mac.

"I'll be right back. I need to check a few data statistics in the systems' room before we begin," Jack said as he stepped out of the room.

Nash tilted his head to one side, watching her. "You all right? First days are always tough."

Calla drummed the tip of her fingers on her knees as Nash ambled to where she sat. He halted about a foot from her chair, uncertainty creeping into his eyes. She raised her chin, sensing his height and alluring presence, as she rose to speak. "Nash—"

He placed a tame hand around her waist and drew her a few inches toward him. The gentle move startled her. Calla watched as his other hand wrapped around her other side, accelerating her pulse quicker than she could think. About a head shorter than his six-foot-three frame, she questioned the tenderness in his gray eyes.

His face, calm, and adoring contradicted the firm hold he had on her back. With unwavering eye contact and their faces in alarming proximity, Calla braced herself for the inevitable.

Nash bent over until his face was only inches from hers. Her chin inclined forward. No words exchanged, and no questions raised, his lips flickered over hers and settled for several seconds.

Calla found her eyes closing and her body relaxing. She felt the weight of her hair slide over her shoulders as he loosened her firm ponytail. The fruits scent from her mane enveloped them. Nash's embrace was as affectionate and fervent as it had ever been. He released her and smiled. "I never left you, you know."

"Charmer... smooth, Nash." She bit her lip. "Very smooth."

He unrolled his fingers, and her eyes caught an object lying in the well of his palm. A small silicon, chip, checkered, and half the size of a fingernail.

"How did you know?" she asked.

"I've learned a few things about you operatives along the way," he said.

Relief swelled in her. "They came after you and Jack because of me."

Nash let out a short chuckle. "It'll take a lot more than that to separate you from me, beautiful."

Calla's eyebrows knit. "How did you disengage it?"

The puzzled look on her face caused another grin on his face, stressing the single dimple in his left cheek.

"Surprised?" Nash said.

"Impressed, actually. You dumbfounded Vortigern's intent."

Still holding her, his hand laced through her hair as it glowed under the reset lighting. "When we were in Colorado, you asked me whether I'd investigated the operatives at the NSA. I never got the chance to respond."

"How much do you *really* know about the operatives?"

"When I met Stan at the CIA a few years ago, he agreed to tell us about them. That was the deal to getting CIA to help protect you... and why I came back to London after leaving the marines."

"You knew all along? I mean about the operatives' types of technologies."

"Some things I ignored, some things were hard to believe. Some things fascinated me." His eyes lit. "Like you."

"How did you know about the drug in the chip?"

"Stan told me about Allegra and Aston. How she defied the

taboos, and the kind of tricks operatives use. When that gun on the slopes hit me, it didn't feel like a gun wound should. I should know. I had to make sure the bullet, or should I say the drug, was removed at ER before it took effect."

The door burst open.

Calla and Nash turned as Jack rambled in, clasping a printout he read.

She paced to him. "Jack?"

He glimpsed up. "Yeah—"

His face betrayed a hint of mockery. "What's with you two?"

Calla and Nash exchanged a humorous flash.

"So," Jack said. "Are we going to find out what this whole NASA mess is all about, or are you just going to stand there and watch me."

"Jack, you okay?" Calla said.

"Damn right, I am."

Calla held her hand to his forehead and played with his mid-length dreadlocks. "Where did they plant this thing? Any damage that's not already there?"

Nash let out a laugh, sensing the jesting in her voice. "I called Jack when I left ER. I was actually late. He'd already been hit. But he made it to the emergency room on time."

Calla folded her hands. "You two are the biggest bloody jokers in government circles," she said, her voice erupting in upper-class, English tones.

The men smirked at each other. They were ridiculously absurd together and smartest together, a contagious camaraderie with which she felt at ease. "It was fun while it lasted," Jack said. "You know, we sort of wanted to see if we had you back."

She patted Jack on the shoulder. "Glad you're okay and sorry for leaving you out of the loop. I mean, with the last six months."

"You two had much to work out anyway."

Nash pulled the printed sheet from Jack and studied it with a critical eye. "What are the latest stats on the NASA worm?"

Jack dropped into a seat. "The computers on the space station are still not responding to any of our efforts."

"I know why, and you won't like it," Calla said.

She traipsed to the full-length window and leaned her back against it.

"I saw Stan this morning," Nash said.

Calla's eyes lit. "You did?"

She turned her head to look out the window. "Stan's not who we need. We need to find my mother."

"Your mother is alive?" Jack asked.

"And my father chose to not let me in on it."

Nash studied her carefully.

"Why?" Jack asked.

Nash moved forward. "Because he doesn't know where she is. He hasn't found her in close to thirty years."

"Since they left you at the orphanage..." Jack added. "Why would she disappear?"

"I don't know Jack, but we need to find her because she has the keys to unlocking Mason's behaviors and telepathic idiosyncrasies."

CHAPTER 10

DAY 3
OIA, SANTORINI ISLAND
AN HOUR BEFORE SUNSET, 1747 hrs.

CALLA STEPPED ONTO the narrow street in Oia, a town that covered the whole Greek island of Therasia, the northwestern part of Santorini. The local attractions were closing being October. The late afternoon sun brushed her face as she hustled through the narrow street, her mind scouring house numbers of the low-lying, lime-washed condominiums concentrating on why they'd come. *Find Mila.*

She strained her eyes toward the Mediterranean, observing as tourists shifted in front of her from shop to café, soaking in the island's glamour, relishing Greek cuisine, all the while mesmerized by the stunning sunset about to form around the next bend.

Cooling heat bore on her bare shoulders, signaling that the nights at this time of year were crisp. She glimpsed to her left and caught the hillside where Oia stretched. The bustling town was marked with traditional white houses, boasting blue window frames delved into the porous rock, with views to the belly of the volcanic caldera of Santorini, and the deep blue of the Aegean Sea. White, red, and black sand beaches adorned the island, marking Santorini with its own appeal after a large volcanic explosion centered on it, possibly before the fall of Troy, sinking the center of the small island.

Jack seized her hand. "Mind if I wait for you guys here?" To her right stood a souvenir shop with its trinkets priced two-times their worth, and a run down Internet café. "Call me when you find Mila."

"All right, Jack. Keep your cell phone handy," she said.

She continued moving with Nash down the single street coursing along the entire length of Oia that had only two sets of cliff-side stairways, descending to the bays of Ammouda and Armeni. They ambled their way through a sea of throngs arriving simply to watch the legendary sunset. Calla observed as every space comfortable enough to sit on, or not, wall, step, or patch of ground was seized by masses who anticipated an unforgettable display of the Cyclades.

"You'd think I'd come here on vacation, instead of hunting an operative who doesn't want to be found," Nash said.

"I'll make it up to you, Nash. I hope Mila is where Allegra said she would be." She set a hand on his shoulder. "Nash, I'm really sorry about your house."

He shrugged. "Hey, we made it out alive."

Several minutes later, Nash and Calla stood facing a blue iron gate on the main pedestrian path with white steps leading to a luminous yard. Calla pushed the entrance open, and they tread down the steps toward an entryway of a house built in the traditional Santorini style—vaulted roofs, arched entryway, and a whitewashed façade.

She pounded on the door.

No answer.

They glimpsed through the kitchen window, whose shades had not been drawn. The house was set deep in the rock, with little natural light in its inner recesses, tunneled into the soft volcanic cliff, a feature that kept the residence cool in summer and warm in spring or fall.

She stepped back and checked her smartphone. "This should be the place. Mila moved here two months ago."

Nash peered inside the window. "You positive?"

Calla nodded. Her eyes traveled to a knob they'd missed, the doorbell. She rang it. The chime reverberated for several seconds with no answer. They glided back up the stairs to the pedestrian path, and gazed back into the quieting alleyway, abandoned as the hordes congregated at the tip of the island. The descending sunset settled on the horizon, an orange orb bathed in lavender and amber luminosity. Last stragglers roamed toward the viewing spot as dread crept through Calla's spine. If they didn't find Mila, they had nothing.

Something made her turn her head toward the roof of the house, several meters above them.

Movement drew her chin up. There was just enough time for her to arch back as ruthless projectiles zipped toward her before she noticed they'd been fired.

Nash rammed an elbow in the nearby wooden hedge, ripping out a plank of wood. He drove her out of the line of fire, and they landed on the stone path in a hammering thud. The bolt had been swift, quiet, silenced by the late afternoon sounds of the tourist town.

Their attacker was not done.

The assailant's missiles landed one by one in Nash's shielding wooden slab he raised above their heads to screen them from the onslaught.

Mounted on the uppermost point of the white house, the

camouflaged man cocked the bow of his compound crossbow and fired a hail of shots.

Nash barely regained his balance before he could fire his gun toward the assault.

A furtive hand reached between Calla and a propelling arrow. It snapped the aluminum bolt in half. "Let's go!"

The voice belonged to a veiled woman, dark eyes visible through the otherwise full-body, white cloak-over attire, tan combat trousers, and a white T-shirt. Her strong build flexed able shoulders, her deflection marking accuracy. Under her cloak, she concealed a similar crossbow.

The woman bucked against the wall between them, glimpsing toward where the onslaught had come. She released three bolts one after the other.

The attacker on the roof plummeted face down and rolled off the tiles, colliding on to the stone by the steps.

"This way," said the woman. "We can't talk here."

Calla glanced in her direction. "Mila?"

"You're late."

1759 hrs.

Calla and Nash plowed behind Mila, past the side of the house and down the 235 cliff-side stairs, ripping down to Ammoudi port. Once their feet hit the pebble beach, Calla glanced back, catching sight of two archers perched on adjoining rooftops of two flat-roofed houses. "We're being followed!"

She scanned the small harbor with its fishing boats, waterfront taverns, and restaurants. A path led from the beach around the base of the mountain.

"We're exposed," Nash said.

A bolt sliced into the soil, missing Calla's foot by a finger breadth.

"This way," Mila said. "To that boat."

Nash and Calla spurted in the direction she was pointing in. Docked on shore, they spotted the state-of-the art, two front-seater speedboat.

"In here," Mila commanded. She rocked around and fired off another malicious arrow that slashed one attacker on the wrist.

Calla's gaze narrowed in on the two men. They were swifter than most attackers they'd encountered. Speed and accuracy was discharged with every fired shot. She flashed forward to the boat behind Nash, scuttling to climb on the speed vessel as it buoyed in the water.

Nash ignited the surface drive propulsion, capable of touching speeds of eighty knots.

Behind them, a miniature arrow sliced into Mila's arm, generating an agonized outcry from her lips. Calla scaled off the boat, darted toward Mila, and reached her in time to break her fall. She rolled her behind a protruding rock.

Nash launched off the boat and raced to where the women cowered. His gun leveled at the first archer. He fired.

The bullet caught the man's chest. Nash watched bewildered as the man shot up unharmed. The archer shot down the stairs after them taking two steps at a time, his companion in tow.

"Let's go," Nash said. He hauled the women to their feet.

Calla retrieved Mila's discarded bow and arrow from where it had fallen. She aimed it at the first archer who'd hurtled to the bottom of the stairs and started a dash in their direction. She fired a projectile that caught one man in the leg. He recoiled, grasping his hamstring.

She sizzled a second missile at his companion. Calla's

attention turned to Mila. The arrow had entered her arm. Nash broke the tail off. "We need to get her to the hospital."

"No!" Mila yelled. "They'll find me there."

"Who are they?" Calla said.

"Mason's science project."

Nash reached under Mila's body and hoisted her off the ground before scurrying to the boat. They reached the speed vessel just as the other archer regained his balance. Joined by his hobbling companion, they loped after the trio.

Nash scanned the mini cabin for any sign of keys. With eyes barely open, Mila pointed to the joystick that steered the boat. Cramped for space in the two-person boat, Nash maneuvered the power system behind a split–display screen that set the vessel's cylinders in motion. The boat waded out a few meters into the open sea before he fired the engine at full throttle. Soon the vessel, created for the serious-minded racer, roared as it gained speed, carving the current and nosed toward Athinios port.

Calla raised her head. The two archers hesitated at the edge of the water and aimed for a few seconds before lowering their weapons. Out of their firing range, Calla breathed a sigh of relief as Nash barreled the boat with marine skills, Calla didn't know he had.

He pulled out his phone. "Jack? Listen, change of plans. Meet us at Athinios port. I'll send over the details. Make it a half hour. Be careful."

A blast of headwind hit them as the boat bounced off on heavy water, tilting Calla off balance. She hunched on the deck floor by Mila. Instantly, a yelp left Mila's lips.

"Nash, she's badly hurt."

"Here, take the stick." He said. "Can you ride one of these?"

"Try me."

They exchanged positions on the high-performance,

unique hull, and Calla gripped the joystick, zipping the boat forward. Nash dipped to Mila's side and raised her head before lifting her to the hydraulic seat under the nose of the boat.

Calla glanced back briefly and observed Nash as he searched above Mila's head for a First-Aid kit. He found one in a compartment above the seat. Mila drifted in and out of unconsciousness, her head swooning from side to side as Nash stabilized the arrow wound. He applied adhesive tape to the base of the shaft, keeping the arrow still and minimizing Mila's discomfort. He observed her for a response to pain, then wrapped clean gauze around the base of the shaft, before applying direct pressure on the bleeding wound. Blood seeped through as Nash held the gauze on top of the first. The blood loss eased. He rose and searched more compartments before hauling out a blanket and wrapping it around her shivering frame.

Mila's eyes settled on his face. "Looks like you know what you are doing. Thanks."

He smiled. "You're welcome." Nash turned to Calla. "I can take over."

Calla returned to Mila's side as Nash navigated the boat on a calming sea. She studied Mila's face and helped her remove the veil, revealing a soft, pale face. "Why does Mason want you?"

Mila rose to a seated position, barely able to breathe. Calla suddenly realized she had shut her eyes.

"Are you sure you don't want to go to a hospital?" Calla said.

"There's no time. Let's get to the shore and find our way off the island. Those archers, Mason's recent recruits won't be far."

"Who are they?"

"Mason has trained a new breed of assassins, three

operatives to be exact, who can eliminate any operative hands down. I'm afraid our defenses are a little inferior to his. They have immense resilience to most hand weapons, except theirs."

"When did he do this?" Calla asked.

Nash slowed the boat, steering into the mooring and turned briefly.

"My guess is he's been at for years," Mila said. "I had the cove build this crow-bow when we discovered the kind Mason was developing."

Thirty minutes later, they docked into Athinios. The stunning shore, belted by elevated volcanic cliffs, accommodated the ruins of an old lighthouse. Mila was silent but breathed steadily. As Nash leaned to carry her off the boat, she held a hand in front of him. "Wait. From here, we can get a car to your plane."

Calla took a seat on the leather beside her as Mila reached in her pocket and drew out a worn package. "I've kept this long enough. This is yours, Calla. Your mother told me never to give it to you unless it was necessary."

"Why?"

"Find her, Calla, the last time Mason came on with such force at the operatives, she was the only one who could thwart him. She stole a blueprint of something he was working on, just before—"

Mila fell deathly still.

"Before what?" Calla understood that Mila didn't intend to take the topic any further. She fingered the enveloped note. "What is in this?"

"That's how you find her," Mila said, her eyes rolling.

The package dropped to the deck floor. Calla retrieved it before it sailed into oblivion. She fingered it with cold hands and glanced at Nash, recognizing the size of the moment. Would its contents reveal the whereabouts of a mother she'd searched for all her life? She slowly ripped the brown envelope. Her fingers drew out a microfilm. She ran her eyes over it and pulled it to the diminishing light, catching little, yet some symbols stood out. "It's coded with incomprehensible characters, like the Hadrius Manuscript."

Mila smiled. "Trust her to take extra precaution."

Calla scanned the symbols and remembered the mystery it had been decoding the Hadrius Manuscript. She found Nash's gaze. "I need the journal with my parents' codes."

Nash nodded.

Calla blanked at him. "I've no idea what it says."

1813 hrs.

The cramped room was not ideal but gave Jack the anonymity he sought and the ability to scan Santorini's network on location. Jack slid his index finger over his tablet. He would switch to British government networks if he couldn't find a strong enough signal.

The network signal in the café wavered. One by one, frustrated users left the tiny Internet café until only two, fervent social media addicts remained. With his tablet connected to the café's low-level Wi-Fi system, Jack took a risk. It was not a secure network, but he had to verify something—the location of that hacker.

He logged in to his account at ISTF. It was the only way he could look closely at data, having detected a processing signal from Santorini Island. *Who was controlling it?*

It was not a strategic location from a military or diplomatic perspective, yet a network on this island was operating an

Internet address allowing a hacker to upload worms to steal identities, control NASA systems and copy sensitive stock-market files.

Damn it!

The signal from the Wi-Fi router went out. Jack slammed a fist on the desk, drawing a questioning look from the bearded café owner. He needed to remain on the hackers' network.

"Everything okay there?" the heavyset man asked.

"Yeah. Can I connect to the landline?"

The man shrugged. "The wire stations are downstairs," he said, pointing to a narrow staircase in front of Jack.

Was there time? He had to meet Nash and Calla. Jack rose to take his tablet and headed downstairs. The dim room confined three filthy desks. Jack settled in one and hooked a connection to the main router with a smaller tablet he drew from his bag. Its power was a lot stronger than the tablet. He failed to link up to ISTF satellites but could reconnect to the clandestine network. He charted onto the UK Space Agency framework, before dialing Scarlet in London on his cell.

"Scarlet. I need you to document something for me." An incoming call interrupted his conversation. *Nash.* "Hang on, Scarlet." He tuned into Nash's call. "Okay, I'll head there right away."

He hung up on Nash. "Scarlet, are you still there?"

"Yes."

"Okay, please jot this down."

"Yes?"

"The web portal I'm loading to ISTF systems now manages five spacecrafts conducting active space missions including those to Mars and Saturn. Hackers have compromised the accounts of most users. This means their networks are wide open. It's a security lapse. Did you get that? I'll advise on when, or whether they need to be shut down, but we'll need the cooperation of the UK Space Agency. Got that?"

"Yes, sir."

"Thanks, Scarlet. I'll call if there's anything else."

He hung up the phone and tried the ISTF satellite again, finally connecting remotely to his computer-tracking program. He swore. A computer within radius was disrupting NASA signals, and those of the UK Space Agency, which was affecting satellites belonging to those two nations.

Jack attempted to program a worm that could isolate the hacking signal. "No use! I can't infiltrate the system."

He tried another tactic. If he could mimic the program, and transfer a copy to his netbook, perhaps he could get to see how it functioned.

His battery was draining out. Scrambling under the dust infested desk, his fingers found a socket. He slotted the tablet into the power and connected the other end to his machine. Jack fingered several buttons in a coded language he'd developed. The laptop constructed a program, mimicking each function of the hacker's activities. *How is this hacker bypassing firewalls and protocols?*

Once the program was done, he encrypted the logarithms. Jack unplugged his laptop and sat for several seconds, thinking. The hacker was gaining unauthorized access to computer systems in the United States and the UK. It could log in to NASA networks. What would be next? The military? Defense systems? All the while negotiating unidentified scripts.

Some language he understood. Parts of its scripts were programmed using ANX, a high-level, dynamic programming language. He'd worked on the program with US and UK signal intelligence agencies recently. He'd helped develop ANX as a general-purpose scripting language to make report processing easier. ANX code was powerful, smart, and unbreakable. Until now.

His eyes were drawn back to the screen. The Santorini

signal had stopped. Had someone pulled a plug? He had the information he needed to investigate further. Was it enough? He checked the time. Nash and Calla would be at Athinios port by now.

The ISTF program flashed, registering the IP address he'd tried to identify since entering the café. The computer was registered to an ISTF account holder. He scanned the new IP address and tried to align it to a name in ISTF's database.

A name flashed across his screen.

Mila Rembrandt.

1912 hrs.

CALLA HELD MILA'S frigid hand. She was alert, perhaps delirious. The operative had only spoken in half whispers since they'd fled Oia. With eyes glassy like beads, skin ashen white, her skin lax with fatigue, Mila's words had been incomprehensible most of the ride.

The tangerine-colored sunset slipped behind the horizon, and darkness enveloped the popular island. Calla rubbed her bare arms. The evening evoked a seasonal chill that sent a shiver crawling down her exposed arms and face. Nash placed his jacket over her shoulders.

"Thanks, Nash."

She patted his hand before examining Mila's wound. More blood had caked through the tightly wrapped gauze making Calla more determined to get her the pressing attention of a physician. Mila's fists tightened each time a pang of pain shot up her arm, with the arrowhead still nestled in her arm. Calla's eyes confronted Mila's. With every passing noise, whether the horn of a leaving ferry or the laughter of night travelers, Mila's eyes blinked open.

Uneasy eyes mirrored her mounting concern as Calla leaned into Nash. "We should get her to a hospital."

Nash killed the boat's engine, vaulted off the hull, and tied it to the pier. He approached a mule owner whose eager interest in the trio signaled the desire to earn some euros by renting his animal.

"Where's the nearest hospital?" Nash asked him in Greek.

He shot them a mystified glare, but when he observed Nash return to the boat to heave a perspiring Mila in his arms, the man understood the urgency. He nodded and pointed up toward the winding road that led off the busy port. "Up a few hundred yards, there's an emergency clinic there by the post office."

"Thank you."

The man stared after them as they trudged up the small stairs that left the dock. They crossed the active parking lot and took another set of stairs onto the busy road, strewn with arriving and departing tourists. The miniature building the man had indicated was burrowed deep in the side of the hill, and from its outdoor terrace, Calla supposed it had once served as a tavern, now converted into a small emergency unit. A bus depot neighbored to one side and a café to the other. Odd as it stood amid the hubbub, Calla's concern was for Mila. The clinic entrance stood ajar as they advanced past a desk in the reception room.

"Can I help you?"

Calla's eyes moved to the Greek doctor, who stood tall, clutching a clipboard. He surveyed them, a quizzical look crossing his bearded face. Soon, lines of worry creased his face once he heard moaning from Mila. His eyes fell on her anguished body as Nash carried her in like a limp doll.

The doctor dropped his clipboard and turned his attention to the groaning patient. "This way, please. That looks bad. What happened?"

Nash and Calla exchanged a consented look before they accepted the doctor's offer to support Mila's weight. Two aids scurried into the congested space, with one pushing a wheelchair. Within seconds, Mila was wheeled into an adjacent room. Calla stayed back and took a seat in the deserted waiting room, wondering if the arrow had been lethal. It had caused more swelling than a local wound. She twiddled her thumbs and listened to the rotating fan on the little desk.

Several minutes later, Nash appeared through the doors. Calla lifted her head and searched his tense face. "Nash—"

He took in the strain of her voice and took a seat next to her as he placed a hand over hers. "She'll be fine."

"She's out of harm's way. May I ask what sort of weapon caused the wound?" The doctor returned into the darkening room.

"It was a hunting accident," Calla lied.

The scouring look in his eye told Calla, he was not to be fooled.

"I'll arrange for a car to take her to the hospital in Oia."

"No," Calla said. "We're leaving tonight. She'll be taken to a hospital in London."

"But—"

"Thank you, but no." The words poured off her lips more quickly than she'd intended.

Nash set a hand on the doctor's shoulder. "Thanks, doctor. I'm sure you can give us whatever medication we may need for her. It's only a couple of hours' flight to London on a private plane," Nash said. He reached deep in his pockets and pulled out several hundred-euro bills. "I think this should cover your fee."

The doctor's glance fell on the generous amount of money.

"Make sure you take her straight to the hospital when you land. I'll get her ready and give you some medication for the journey."

Nash deviated to the door and pulled out his phone. "Jack...where are you?"

Calla sauntered to his side as he set the phone to speaker mode. Jack's voice sounded hurried. "I'm in a cab to the airport. I thought you'd be heading there."

"We'll be there in about twenty minutes," Nash responded.

"By the way," warned Jack. "I found something you guys might want to check out before we go any further. You may not like it."

CHAPTER 11

DAY 4
ST. GILES SQUARE, WEST LONDON
0811 hrs.

"YOU'VE GOT to believe me, Allegra," Jack said.

Her eyes didn't give away much.

Jack removed his hand from her mahogany table, nearly knocking over a prized lion statuette carved out of pure gold she'd once mentioned was from a royal official in Bhutan. His arm muscle throbbed, having spent the last twenty minutes perched over her well-organized desk like a ravenous pelican.

Ever the diplomat, by profession and in manner, Allegra's stance remained calm.

"I'm sorry, Allegra, but I didn't get much sleep last night after jetting out of Santorini, and by the time we left the hospital, it was late."

Allegra leaned back against her chair. "I understand."

I wish I'd brought Calla with me. She has an edge with Allegra. Firm, but an edge.

“That computer was registered to ISTF under Mila Rembrandt’s name,” Jack said.

“How did that happen if it wasn’t you?”

Allegra was polite. “Mila is no more a hacker than I am. Let the poor girl rest in hospital. I’m sending my physicians there in a couple of hours to check on her condition and have ordered ISTF protection for now. What we need to consider is why Mason sent his operatives after her.”

Hadn’t she heard him? Her words stung Jack like cobra fangs. Didn’t she understand the gravity of his dilemma? Jack wiped his beading brow. The anguish of his Santorini discovery was more than he could take.

His tone relaxed. “I’m sorry, Allegra, maybe I’m not making myself clear. ANX is a top-secret program used by government, military, and defense agencies. We developed it at ISTF, then licensed it to NASA and the UK Space Agency, among other select government agencies a couple of months ago. You signed it off.”

She took a sip of her aromatic, peppermint tea that had sat brewing on her desk for the last several minutes. Her eyes stole a glance at his face. “Yes, I realize that.”

“But what you may not know is that the code was created to be impenetrable, so a hack could only have come from an inside informant or aid.”

“There’s no such thing. I’ve spent the last seven months weeding ISTF of Mason’s ill influences.”

Jack took a breath. “With all due respect, I understand that. But see my point. ANX is a difficult program to hack. You’d need the right code, encrypted and accessible only to three people. NASA and the UK Space Agency don’t even know how to control its dynamics. That’s how they wanted it. We alone control its dispensation. We’ve been trying to gain entry into the very systems that have collapsed.”

"We must have some skill here." Trained technicians? Plan B."

Jack shook his head. "No, Mason deauthorized further development." He dipped into the cream chair in front of Allegra's desk. "This proves my theory further. The hack was an inside job."

"Exactly. Mason."

His eyes narrowed. "How?"

Allegra placed her china cup on the saucer and shot up from behind her desk. "Mila accessed Mason's mainframe computer. Mimicking everything ANX does in an attempt to stop him."

The blood nearly left his face. Ashen like chalk, Jack could not believe the operative had hacked his program. It had taken him months to create the world's first anti-hack system.

Jack didn't like holes in any of his creations. ANX programming was at least fifteen years ahead of any known computing technology. *What has this operative done that I, its brainchild, am struggling to piece together?*

He edged back in his seat and laced his hands behind his head. "Mason must have apprehended her plan. Those where his operatives in Santorini weren't they? Mason knows she was onto him. If I know him, he'll change tactics. The Santorini signal was my first break in the case, and now it's gone."

"Where to?"

"I don't know. This is the first known breach in ANX. But I can find out if I get your authorization to override the systems within the UK Space Agency."

"I'm afraid I can't do that, Jack."

"But our whole defense and government systems are wide open. We've no idea where Mason is or from where he's controlling the virus. The quicker I can access those systems, the better."

"No, Jack. Even if I wanted to?"

Provided the information remained confidential, that's how they wanted it.

"This means we are back to the drawing board," Jack said.

"Not necessarily." Allegra circled the length of her desk, moving to the edge, before taking a seat on it in front of Jack. "Jack, I believe in you. You can fight this. Just find a way to override the hack."

"But—"

"I can't, Jack. ISTF is shutting down. If I authorize your entry, it'll raise suspicious eyebrows from powers above me."

Jack shifted in his seat. Even though the tone in Allegra's voice resisted, her eyes said something else. *She's in a tight bind.*

Jack leaned forward. "Allegra, I don't know how long we have until Mason's starts manipulating every computer, gadget, cell phone, and network system. This hack is spreading."

Allegra thought for a few minutes and clasped her hands together. *What's holding her back? She's taken risks before. She kept the Hadrius Manuscript from ISTF, why can't she do this. She has only to sign the bloody paperwork!*

Had she lost her confidence in her job as head of ISTF? Her authority?

She rose and paced to the back of the room, leaving Jack mincing behind like a hunter whose prey had fled. Allegra swiveled around Jack, her eyebrows pinching together. Her voice had a hesitant tone to it as she spoke. "Mila spent years investigating Mason and his tactics."

Jack hesitated. "When we broke into his house seven months ago, we could get onto his motherboard and disengage all his programs. That's how we overrode the original hack. Perhaps, I should've looked around for other gimmicks. He must have planned this a long time. He failed to secure firewalls around his systems, thinking no one would suspect him."

"Longer than you know, Jack. Much, much longer than we all do."

Jack scratched his head. "We checked Mason's home, accounts, and systems thoroughly, even the laptop he was allowed in prison."

"Mason is not an amateur. He is an operative who's been anticipating payback for something much deeper than we understand. We need to find what that is. A simple reprogram will not suffice here. He knows how to conceal anything and keep it buried even while it stares right at us," she said.

"So, where does that leave us?"

Allegra slanted a glance Jack's way. "We'd better decrypt Calla's mother's note. Mila told me Calla's mother once obtained information on Mason's weakest vulnerabilities. How she accomplished that all those years ago, we don't know. But she must have pissed him off, and he's still sour."

0945 hrs.

CALLA'S FINGERS FILED through a charcoal journal. Its velvety cover, smooth under her touch, despite its age. The aging journal had remained well-preserved under the conditions she'd put it through while in Sub-Saharan Africa during a plunge in the crocodile-infested Nile. She'd kept it in her office safe as she'd done repeatedly with antiquities she needed to authenticate. Responsible for the Roman and Byzantine collections from the Eastern Mediterranean, from the late third to the mid-fifteenth century, her collections boasted metalwork of gold, silver, and bronze, treasures coming from places as diverse as Esquiline, Carthage,

Lampsacus and Cyprus. Calla also handled glass, textiles, ivories, and pottery, including Byzantine, Greek, and Russian icons.

A head peered through the half-open door. "Sorry, Calla, but we used your office for storage. We weren't told when you'd be back."

"That's all right, Hera. Not sure I'll be using it extensively at the moment."

"Was Egypt all you expected?"

Calla smiled at her colleague, a curator of horological collections with her passion fondly around French provincial and American clocks. "Quite."

"Next time, take me with you."

Hera shut the door behind her as she left. With a contented smile, Calla clammed the journal shut. She edged back in the light wood chair, her arms folded in contemplation. Before she'd been assigned on the team to authenticate the Hadrius Manuscript, she'd been thinking of moving to her first love, linguistic anthropology, and perhaps finding a post in the Anthropology Library. Nothing amused her more than handling books, pamphlets, journal titles, microfilms, maps, and sound recordings, especially as it concerned lost languages and codes.

It had been easy to accept ISTF's request to join their signals intelligence arm. Understanding riddles and programming was second nature to Calla.

The quiet room, with scattered shelving space, needed a good tidy up. It hadn't been touched in months, and Calla's eye caught sight of a film of dust along the sturdy desk. Her blue Bathysphere and the scores of antiquities in boxes lay on the floor, waiting to be indexed and possibly shelved for lack of room space. She sometimes wondered how staff at the British Museum were expected to work with priceless artifacts in such cramped spaces. Confined in the basement of a

Georgian building, in quarters historically servants' quarters, Calla longed for the opening of the new conservation center. Here she would continue her research into rare languages and their effect on civilization.

Calla threw open the journal, having spent the best part of the early morning reading its carefully indexed symbols, symbols that should have been second nature by now. The journal was worn, but had opened her eyes to historical possibilities of language structures' she'd never imagined.

She smiled to herself, wondering how the little book had survived a forty-foot drop at Murchison Falls and the rapid currents of the Nile River. Calla fished for the microfilm Mila had given her, and scanned it through the microfilm reader on her desk, producing a legible printout. She jotted down codes from the journal, translating symbol after symbol in her mother's work. The letterings were foreign, indecipherable, but at least now she knew they were meant to be, and the journal would get her there in the end. The microfilm had come with a note from her mother, handwritten and hurriedly by the looks of the graphology, especially the strokes along the more rounded hieroglyphics, mimicking the symbols of the Hadrius Manuscript.

Her parents had interacted with the manuscript for years, and as they deciphered it, and successfully, it seems, they'd marked all their findings in this journal, then hid it for years. Without the journal, she couldn't have unraveled the mystery of the Hadrius Manuscript. Her heritage. Her legacy.

She heard a knock at the door.

"Your colleague thought I may find you here." Stan's distinguished face peered into the room.

"Fa...father?"

Stan brushed into the room. "So, this is where you work?"

Calla set her reading on the desk and nodded as she observed Stan's curious gaze around the office. Tall, commanding, and green eyes like hers, framing a handsome square face, she'd only found her father seven months ago. There was much he didn't know about her, and the impression was mutual.

Feeling apologetic about her disappearance without telling him, in hindsight, she guessed he knew why after his own absence from her entire life.

Stan seemed at ease as he swaggered from artifact to book, commenting on her accomplishments. Her eyes suddenly narrowed, watching him as if he were a hawk. She bit her lower lip. *Why did you not tell me the truth?*

Calla glanced down at the microfilm and printout on the table. She quietly hid the items in the pages of the journal. Stan concluded his exploration and sagged into the padded sofa by the door. "I see you like working in solitude."

"Maybe I get it from you."

"Touché. I deserve that. I'm proud of you, Calla. This place is astounding, and what you do here."

"Most times, it's quite inspiring."

"It's easy to know why you like working here," Stan said. "You've got a mind that makes history relevant to the present, take the best from it and reinvent it for a better world. I can see why the operatives desperately needed you, and why ISTF came knocking, asking you to drop your curator brush."

"I really haven't." Her eyes narrowed into his. "You'd probably have had me work in some clandestine, mendacious, agent organization. Let's see, possibly, at the Secret Intelligence Service like you. I imagine secrecy and lies become a habit there."

Stan shifted in his seat and leaned forward, his eyebrows burrowing. "I deserve that, and I'm sorry, I didn't tell you everything about your mother."

A tear welled in the corner of his eye. He wiped it away with a white handkerchief he pulled from his tweed jacket, despising himself for revealing his gentler side. Calla's heart suddenly felt heavy, sympathizing with the burden of responsibility, guilt, and mistakes he'd carried.

"Stan...father?" She hitched herself on to the desk and smiled. "I'm still not used to calling you, father. I know there's so much that we need to—"

"I don't blame you one bit. Your mother and I fled operative life. And rightly or wrongly, we tried to hide you from it too."

She slid to the sofa next to him and folded her warm hands over his chilled knuckles. "I know."

Uncertain how much he knew about Mila's microfilm, she took the handkerchief from his hand and dried a second growing tear. "I forgive you. But right now, I need you." She knew the words meant more to him than life.

His eyes lit. "What can I do?"

"I came across something recently that I think you can help me with." She watched him attentively, choosing her words carefully. "Was my mother's name Nicole?"

CHAPTER 12

US EMBASSY LONDON
0927 hrs.

THE CORRIDOR WAS deserted. The building had changed little, from the vivid entry rotunda, modern lobby, and a four-story interior atrium with a sweeping, spherical stairway. The US Embassy always had a sense of mystic and duty, all intertwined in one. Nash had to get to Masher's office before he fell into a lap of prying questions. Why had Masher not returned his call? Lieutenant Colonel Masher was a senior officer he'd fought along in Syria and later came to serve under at the London Embassy.

He strode past the bureaucratic consulate section, accessed via the staircase, whose entrance faced the seemingly endless set of stairs. Nash quickly glanced at the consulate's interior, displaying the art of forty artists from the United States, mostly modern. He never cared much for modern art, or for most art displayed in the Embassy hallways. His taste included classic and purposeful strokes, rather than spur-of-the-moment creations, or at least that's what it seemed to represent. He crossed two lengths of expansive office space on the quiet floor. Masher's office was at the end of the hallway.

"Commander Shields?"

That voice. It felt too familiar. Nash halted as a marine ambled out of the adjacent room.

What was he doing in this part of the building? His impeccable uniform and stance reminded Nash of the days he'd been in charge of the protection of classified information and equipment, vital to the national security of US diplomatic relations at the London Embassy. He wouldn't take an assignment here again were it offered.

He purposed to pace right past the marine, mind, and eyes fixed ahead, perhaps a courtesy nod.

The uniformed marine saluted him. "Shields?"

Nash acknowledged him with a single nod. "Major Chidson."

"Thought you'd been relocated. What're you doing here?"

Nash didn't have time to explain his priorities to the junior officer he'd once commanded. That Nash left the marines, joined the NSA two years ago, worked alongside the CIA as a *'watcher'*, and was then planted in ISTF as a US agent, would not settle well with Chidson, a marine who envied him. Only because ISTF recruited the best marines, spies, analysts, and recruits from all fields they considered necessary. That fact alone was not popular around Embassy circles any longer. Chidson didn't understand the classified nature of ISTF, and that the appointment had given Nash what he'd desired most, the chance to be back in London, to protect Calla.

Nash stopped and saluted him back. "Nice to see you again, Chidson."

"Good to see you too. Will you be here long?"

"In London? Who knows? I'm here to see Masher."

Chidson turned around and pointed him to the door at the end of the hall.

“Thanks,” Nash said.

Chidson threw him a half smile and resumed about his business navigating toward the staircase. “Be seeing you.”

Nash minced toward Masher’s door. So far, his NSA credentials had raised no eyebrows on entry into this part of the building, but he needed to be cautious. At Masher’s, door he knocked twice, the sturdy door sliding open behind his fingers. Nash glanced both ways before peering into the darkened room.

“Masher?”

Silence.

It was against the norm for unoccupied offices to stand ajar. His investigative senses alerted, Nash drove the door open, casting a backward glance.

Masher was a tidy man, but he’d never kept his office as impeccable as this. Nash’s eyes scanned the space, from the US flag by the shaded windows, the set of level files under the front section of the desk, the three desk phones each with a different strategic purpose, the gold-edged, picture frame of the US President and, the miniature desk next to the window behind the mahogany work desk, where Masher usually kept his computer. Nash hunched over the desk and examined the environs closely for a minute.

Masher’s laptop was gone.

He eased around the desk and dipped into the padded chair. What had happened to his friend? Where was he? His office was clean. Tidy. *Too tidy! What am I missing?*

His eyes traveled to the top of the glass-covered desk and scrutinized the far corner nearest the door. He caught sight of a crack, a centimeter deep—no bigger than a thread of hair in the glass. That told Nash all he needed to know.

Masher had been taken by force. The chip in the table had been caused accidentally. *Like something crashing into it.*

What?

Nash ran his fingers over the cut glass, his eyes diverted up, then behind him to the steel flagpole. From the angle the flag stood, it had come down on the desk glass like a landing pole vault.

Not too long ago.

Nash's eyes swept the room again.

Transferred?

Possibly.

Killed? Don't want to think about that.

Early retirement? His stuff would be gone with him.

Nash shot out of the chair, scouting for any extra clues.

Nothing.

He back trailed behind the desk and reached for the top left drawer. He tugged at the handle.

Locked.

He then searched for a laptop. A cell phone? A diary? A notebook. *Gone.*

The desk stood devoid of personal belongings. Nash sidled to the cabinets on the far right of the room and grazing his fingers along the shelves, he stopped at a photograph taken in Syria of Masher and him. Eyes smiling, shirts turbaned around their heads like senseless schoolboys, an effort to cool their blistering skin, Nash smiled as he recalled how much Masher was like the father he always wanted. He was nothing like George Shields, his father.

Masher had lost his son in the Gulf War, a younger version of the colonel lieutenant. He'd told Nash his son was like Nash in every manner except Masher junior had been stubborn and impractical.

Nash had never met the soldier, yet acknowledged the fondness Masher used when he spoke of him. His smile disappeared quickly, overturned with apprehension. Masher would never have left the Embassy without telling him. The last time he'd seen him, Nash had handed the older man a memory chip in a sealed envelope that contained all Nash's analysis and codes on the operatives. One detail had made him want to keep that file safe—*Calla's one weakness as an operative.*

Nash feared she didn't know what it was, and the consequences should it be appropriated by desirous hands, like Mason and the government.

He didn't want to consider that option. He couldn't take that risk. Perhaps that's why he'd been so ready to make a crummy deal with Mason. If Mason were ever extradited to the US for trial, which would happen once caught, the current administration would eventually have him executed in some capacity. If they seized the information on the memory stick, they would know how to annihilate the operative, if it ever came to that.

He hastened his fruitless hunt, wondering whether he'd endangered Masher's life by trying to save Calla's. His ears caught insistent footsteps thudding the hallway. He narrowed his eyes into the door, alert.

Once the smothered voices disappeared, he glided to the shelves and ran his palms over books, trophies, and memorabilia in the middle sections. Grazing a small opening between a volume on US diplomacy and a hand-to-hand combat manual, he pulled out the two-inch volume. His hands steady, eyes fixed on the volume, he recalled an incident and something he'd seen behind the book. He hated himself for prying into Masher's private affairs and wished he'd never accidentally seen Masher place controversial photographs behind the volume.

Curiosity settled in him. When he opened the volume, his eyes glanced past the title credentials until his attention fixed on a small bronze key taped to the front flap. He eased the key from the adhesive, his hand trembling slightly, not wanting to tear the pages. Nash rotated the key for several minutes in his palm, marched to the door, closed it, and scrutinized the room.

His boots slid unintentionally across the carpet, and a rip in the woven Persian almost caused him to trip. Nash nearly abandoned his search when he loped back to the shelves and stopped. He retreated, then moved forward two steps. His feet grazed over a slight rise, barely noticeable, a lump in the floor surface as he neared the seat of the main desk. Nash fell to his knees and grazed his palm across the carpet under the desk. *This must be it. Masher wouldn't have taken the envelope out of the Embassy. It's safer here.*

He tugged at a partly loose carpet, careful not to rip it. It lifted effortlessly in his grasp as if held in place with Velcro.

And there it was, a rectangular, steel covering amid the wood panels that fashioned the floor. In its core was a keyhole. He hastened to unlock the latch. Once turned, the key activated a small digital window he'd missed altogether in the corner of the small safe. The reader sprang to life and asked him for a six-digit code.

He searched his mind for a code Masher could have used.

A birthday? An anniversary? Too easy.

His first day in the army? Too simple.

Think, Nash! You've known this man for close to fifteen years!

What if?

He fingered the numbers.

A date.

The day he'd saved Masher's life while rescuing refugees in Syria. Masher had always maintained he'd never forget the day he got a second chance at life.

The counter failed to respond.

Nash's heart sank into his gut. Not sure what to do next, his eyes darted around the room in frustration.

The safe snapped open. He lifted the small steel flap, and

his fingers discovered his envelope, just as he'd given it to Masher. *Sorry, Masher. I need this!*

He locked the panel, patched the carpet, and rose. With the letter safe in his coat, he turned toward the window, his back away from the door.

Was it the slight whisk of air that grazed past his ear, or the rapid senses of one so accustomed to covert missions? He rotated his body to one side and stole a slanted look behind him. His muscles stiffened, arrested by the cold steel that grazed his ear. He cast his eyes toward the frigid sensation.

"Not so fast, marine."

Chidson's Beretta M9 jabbed against his ear.

—

Stan's face froze. His lips twitched. "How do you know that?" His eyelids fell to his shirt, and he surrendered a sigh. "Yes. She was born Nicole Jefferson and used Bonnie Tyleman as her alias."

Calla returned to the desk and retrieved her mother's items.

Stan's shaky hands took the worn document as his body went rigid. "Where did you get this?"

"Mila. Do you recognize it?"

"No. When did Mila give it to you?"

"Yesterday, in Santorini. Father, she'd hid this note from mother for years, at least twenty, the last time she saw her."

Stan sank deeper in his seat and examined the note's edges, the script, and the symbols. He drew the microchip to his nostrils and inhaled its scent. Calla observed his face and the way his lips moved as if in silent prayer. She placed a hand on his knee and dropped slowly to the floor beside him. "Do you know what it says? What it means?"

He shook his head. "No, but she's clearly imitating the Hadrius Manuscript's style. If only I had the journal."

"Mila said she left it for me. Mother wanted me to find her someday."

Stan brought a hand to his eyes and wiped them dry. "She must've known she wanted to hide, to get away."

"From what? Surely, she wanted to be with you."

"Oh, my brave, beautiful child. I'll never forget the look in her eyes when we left you at the orphanage. She hated me for it. Yet, at the same time, she was determined not to get your life mixed up with the operatives. She didn't trust them. She trusted no one."

Calla thought twice before venturing on what could have been sensitive ground. "What about you? Did she trust you?"

Stan's finger traced the lines of writing on the paper that grew smaller and cramped toward the bottom.

"Were you in love with her? Did she love you?" Calla asked.

Stan eyed Calla, his lime-green eyes adoring his daughter. "We were so irrationally in love. The day she learned she was expecting you was the happiest day of our lives. We knew the Hadrius Manuscript and what it required. It was a responsibility we weren't ready to place on you."

"But why did she leave you?" Calla insisted hoping his answer would explain her difficulties with commitment.

"I don't know, Calla. I've spent the last twenty-eight years, asking myself the same question."

So that's why you told me she was dead?

Stan turned his attention to the microfilm in his hands. "Can we view this?"

"Yes, here," she said and pointed his attention to a microfilm scanner on her desk. "I had that brought from the archives this morning and have printed a copy of what's on the film. Here."

He took the printout from her hand and fingered it as if the act would bring Nicole back to him. "Have you been able to decipher it?"

"Almost."

He watched as Calla rose to get the journal from the desk. "I've translated the symbols, thanks to the journal you wrote."

"I knew you'd find it. It's not easy to keep anything hidden from you. We thought we were crafty by hiding it. Who'd have known fate had another plan and that you'd inherit skills that led you to your destiny."

"It's not my destiny. Living is a choice, not destiny. I have my reasons for wanting to find her. Not theirs."

"What about Mason?"

"If I can help, I will...then.. ." Calla stopped mid-sentence. "Here, father. This is what I've been able to translate. Can you tell me what it means?"

She read the scribbled notes aloud.

AMENDABLE TILLER

A linguistic victory for one so fair.

AWAIT EMBANK OAT

A model of modernization, a cry from my dwelling charred to the ground.

RAM SKIN NU

A mystery out of ten,
a mausoleum of inexplicable men.

Calla's eyes bore into him. "It makes no logical sense."

"Neither did the Hadrius Manuscript. But you worked it out." He sighed. "Nicole liked reading about mysteries in history. In fact, as COPPER J21, her MI6 code, she was remarkable at deciphering mysteries, cryptography, you name it, and anything encrypted was easy. It was her special gene as an operative, and she passed it on to you."

"What did I get from you?"

"I think you know. Have you ever lost a sword fight or hand-to-hand combat?"

Calla trailed her mind. He was right. She'd fought a few fights with those her size and those much bigger and belted her opponents.

Stan's voice interrupted her musings. "Anyway...during the Cold War, with Soviet codes still unbreakable, Nicole gained considerable access to their encrypted communications during the late 1970s. We all admired her, and that's why they gave her the tough cases." He smiled at Calla. "You two are so similar."

"At the bottom, she says: *'Find where I lay and there my heart will be'. There I leave a trail for thee,"* Calla said.

"She wants you to unravel this. Maybe she's referring to events in history or location coordinates. I could check some of my files from—"

"Hang on a minute." Calla retrieved the notes she'd spent all morning scribbling, her hair cascading over her face as she spoke. "Part of this is an anagram."

"Clever girl. Nicole didn't want her location to be compromised. She probably figured if you ever found the answers to the Hadrius mystery, you could also find the answers in this note, and if you didn't, then you wouldn't know any better."

Calla scrutinized the note again. "We may not be as far off as we think." She read the first two lines again.

AMENDABLE TILLER

A linguistic victory for one so fair.

"We may not have far to go. That's only a few doors

down," Calla said, her mind churning through the history of language. Ancient and modern.

"Come again—"

"The answer may be in this building. The 'linguistic victory'. It's the Rosetta Stone. That's right here on the ground floor."

She reached for her badge. Stan grasped her hand. "Calla, wait!"

Looking down at his arm, her face crimped with puzzlement. "Wait? Why wait? Surely you of all people would want to find her?"

Stan paused, reluctant to move. "Calla, you may not like what you find."

"Why?"

Was Stan afraid to find the woman he'd lost years ago? Was he suffering from fear of meeting her again? Calla settled a gentle hand on his shoulder. "We can do this together. Don't you want to know where she is?"

"Yes and no."

"Why?"

"Because she's always known where I was. We bought the manor in the Cotswolds together and planned to retire there together." He swore insults that filled the small office. "Now it sits half livable, a faint memory of what it used to be, and I've been unable to release it all these years because I foolishly thought she'd return one day."

"It still can."

His face raged. "She's never attempted to come home."

Calla's eyes softened. "Maybe she's afraid?"

Stan glanced at her and straightened his shoulders, his eyes hopeful. "Nicole was never afraid. Not once in her life. And if so, of what?"

Calla pecked his cheek. "That's what we need to figure out, father."

CHAPTER 13

0725 hrs.

MASON BUFFED HIS hands for warmth as he waited outside a shabby warehouse, several hundred meters from the passenger building at the Port of Dover. The blare from a departing ferry caught his ears. He breathed in the morning air, inhaling in his freedom, his face displaying a witty-smirk, a degree above gratitude. With a free hand, Mason reached under his shabby full head and scratched his scalp. A few degrees higher in temperature than he wished. A false mustache rested above his upper lip. It would draw little attention from onlookers, having been carefully selected to match the repulsive wig on his head.

He paced the little cobblestone compound. "Damn it! Where is she?"

Quiet footsteps behind him startled him. He zipped his head around and cocked a MARK 23 handgun with its suppressor toward the approaching sound. Three figures emerged from behind the building.

"You haven't lost your touch, Mason," said a woman's voice.

Her tone smooth as hot caramel, she was more seductive than he remembered. Her Mid-Western accent was fortified with a melodious twang. He lowered the firearm. "You came in person. Not the kind of errand I would expect from someone of your ranking."

She'd always made him think of a lost and wandering spirit, her narrow eyes the color of smoke, luxurious, soot-black hair worn to cause whiplash. She was tall with a curvy build he remembered well. She smiled at him with rouged lips. She stepped forward. "I had to see you."

It was an attempt at weak affection. She winked an eye. "Make sure you were all right."

With the speed of a terrified fly, she gripped his arm and forced a hungry kiss on his indifferent lips.

Mason succumbed to the forceful domination before he tore her away. "This is business, not pleasure."

"Perhaps.. . I see prison has kept you as unbreakable as an obelisk."

She grinned shamelessly and zipped her head around to two armed men behind her. Embarrassed, she straightened her shearling-lined jacket. The first man handed her a small packet, which she ripped open and turned to Mason. "Okay, here's your passport. You're now an American citizen according to this, under the name of Aron Zeel. These documents have been authenticated, based on the photographs and specifications your aid dropped by last night. I have also organized all your tickets. Have I missed anything?"

Mason took the packet from her and rummaged his hands through the contents. He drew out a set of keys and peered behind her at a parked A3. "An Audi? Really?"

"You wanted to blend in."

"Yes. Like a banker, not a masseuse."

"That's a matter of perspective."

“Then, it doesn’t look like you forgot anything.”

She held on to his arm as he pulled it away. “When will I see you again?”

Probably never, though. . .

He removed her had off his arm. “Our business is concluded. I’ve given you the access codes to the personal computers and systems of the Democratic Party. Actually, I’m surprised you didn’t want more from me.”

Her distinguished face became brooding as she grabbed his collar. “I do want more.”

The two Marine Corps security guards turned their backs to them, trying to allow privacy, however obstinate.

Mason frowned and turned his attention to the ferry dock. “I can’t give you anything. I never could.”

He kept to his rules. No accessories, no loose ends. He worked alone, and he liked it that way. He took *baggage* when it suited him and only when he needed their services, like this woman. So what if they’d indulged in a trivial affair. It was never serious. She knew that.

He hid the packet in the lining of his winter coat and marched toward the Audi.

“Where are you going?” the woman asked.

“If you must know, I’m driving to Paris. From there on, I’ll take the private plane you’ve arranged for me from Orly Airport. Our agreement was you’d provide the plane. I’m my own pilot. So I think the rest is my business. Yours ends here.”

She kept pace beside him, her three-inch stilettos pinning the concrete pavement. “Mason, you need me!”

He jeered.

“Let me help you,” she said.

“I don’t need anyone.”

He dipped into the driver’s seat and rolled down the window, studying her angry face. The car angled toward the loading dock, leaving the woman scowling, her hands fisting at her sides.

She turned back at the two men, lit a cigarette in her shaky hands, and inhaled. "You."

The security guards scurried in her direction. "Did you plant him?"

The tallest one spoke first. "Yes, ma'am. You'll have linkup when he scans the passport at any port and when any business is conducted in the car or the plane."

She blew the smoke in his face.

His nose twitched, and his eyes shut in revulsion.

Margot Arlington, the former US Republican candidate and the US ambassador to London, finished her cigarette and stamped it out. "Good. I'll expect a report every hour."

UK SPACE AGENCY (UKSA)
SWINDON, SOUTH WEST ENGLAND
1011 hrs.

"So, that would set off an alarm?" Jack gave the astronaut a long shrewd glance over a pair of uncomfortable spectacles he'd disguised over his face.

"Yes, it would," said Orson Rand, head engineer at UKSA.

Jack lay a hand over the system. "May I?" he asked.

"I'm sorry, Mr. Baruch, but this tour is an eyes only tour." Incidentally, what is your interest in the UK Space Agency? You seem a little mature for the graduate groups we usually invite here. But who am I to judge?" Orson checked his tablet. Says here you're from McGill interested in a career in the Information Technology Center."

“Yes, my background is in mathematics.” It was a lie, but so had his entire charade been since wandering into the UK Space Agency, after an hour and a half drive west out of London to Swindon.

Orson Rand, a tall astronaut of graceful build, came from Australia, Perth, to be exact, Thaddeus had explained. His slanted brown eyes were like two splotches of mud that studied Jack with heightened interest. Jack scanned the system in front of him. “Can you tell me more about the systems aboard the ARGUS-B satellite? I understand you’ve been having trouble with them.”

Orson’s burrowed eyebrows told Jack he was astounded at his knowledge of the satellite’s demise. The media had mentioned no details about satellites. The deceitful, graduate student that Jack had effortlessly tried to pass as all afternoon was working.

Orson shifted his feet. “You should not believe everything you read in the media. The satellite was launched as part of Europe’s Galileo satellite navigation system. ARGUS-B carried onboard the most accurate atomic clock ever flown into space. Together with ARGUS-A, it will test new technologies for future Galileo systems.”

“Hasn’t that mission now been compromised?”

“Listen.” He read Jack’s visitor’s badge. “Mr. Baruch. I know that you’re also considering a career with NASA, let me assure you your student credentials are quite impeccable, and even if you seem more experienced than most graduates, I don’t want to discourage your application here. Our systems are the finest in the globe. Satellites are the foundation of the UK space industry. You’ll find that our engineers are among the world’s leading designers and builders of satellites.”

“I see. I could find lots to put my hands to here,” Jack said.

“You should know that our scientists carry a reputation for

expertise in space instrumentation. You would lose nothing in being part of the team."

"Are you trying to give me a job?"

"Mr. Baruch, I'm trying to steer your curiosity in the right direction. We receive funding for a range of technological developments."

Jack smirked. His plan had worked, and Thaddeus' recommendation and direct access to Orson had facilitated an audience and entry into the facility. Orson was one of the Space Agency's most experienced astronauts.

A natural talker, Jack, attempted a smile. "Yes, but your systems have been down. I'm interested, if I were to choose a career here, how would one go about avoiding hacking problems in this establishment? Could I have a peek?"

Orson brought his wrist up in front of his face and stared at his watch, eager to get to his next appointment. "All right, this way."

Orson continued his lecture as he strolled, fascinated with Jack's knowledge and comments about computing technology. Jack's sharp invasion in matters Orson considered beyond his concern didn't bother the astronaut for the moment. He stifled a grin as they walked. "Every satellite launched into space has a 'payload' and a 'bus'. The payload, or carrying capacity of an aircraft, is all the equipment a satellite needs to carry out its duties," Orson said.

"You mean the tools for the task? This can include antennas, cameras, radar, and electronics."

Orson raised an eyebrow. "Exactly. The 'bus' is the section of the satellite that carries the payload and all its equipment into space, such as the subsystems that drive the spacecraft, coordinate the instruments, provide electrical power and permit the satellite to communicate with Earth."

So the bus is where the problem is. "Could I see a demonstration of the system?" Jack said.

Orson winced before leading Jack to a second room, which housed *a* small, microsatellite spacecraft bus. "This will normally carry six experiment payloads to low-Earth orbit," Orson said. "Such a system would be manipulated by this panel here." He pointed to a row of computer systems, electronic circuit boards, and several monitors along one wall.

An engineer sat with headphones communicating with astronauts on the space station. Jack scrutinized every piece of technology in the room. *Where's the mainframe?* "Tell me, Dr. Rand, if by chance systems started failing, or such as the news reported that the last Space mission, involving three British astronauts, went quirky, how would one go about identifying the system failure?"

"That would all depend on the nature of the failure. In that particular case, the onboard systems lost power."

He was speaking in half-truths. Orson would not reveal company secrets. *Fair enough.*

Jack tapped the end of a pencil on his chin. "Is there a possibility that there could've been outside interference? For example, could the systems have been hacked with a firewall bypass?"

"Impossible. Sure, any computer program is liable to hacking but not in this case."

Liar!

"But is it possible? And if so, where would the vulnerabilities be?"

Orson stammered. "Mr. Baruch, let me assure you our systems, as I mentioned earlier, are the finest in the world. ISTF's recommendation was—"

He moped his forehead, having said more than he intended. "I'm not sure what your interest in hacking is, our government is in full control of the recent crisis, so no need to concern yourself about that. Should you join our graduate program, I'm sure you'll learn that we train and produce the finest here. A hack is improbable."

"Please elaborate?"

"First, if there were a real problem, we would know. In this case, we would have known prior to takeoff."

"How can you be certain?"

"Well, for one, we have an agreement with the US that includes cooperation on Earth science and the use of ground networks. Heck, any airborne mission and space-based technology possible, we collaborate on. If a problem had existed before takeoff, we'd have been alerted."

"What about on the UK side?"

"Our side was all clear."

Jack's noted Orson's irritation at his probing. But what the heck? He knew his ANX system inside out and could isolate the problem. *If only I can get a better look.* "Thank you, Mr. Rand, for your time."

"A pleasure. And rest assured. We know how to handle such rare cases. Incidentally, you didn't tell me how you know Thaddeus, he and I trained together."

Think! Jack, think! "Tad and I are old fishing buddies. We fished in the Indian Ocean as boys."

Orson led Jack toward the elevators to the exit on the ground floor of the establishment. Jack had noted two rooms where IT engineers worked feverishly. One room drew his interest, the Space Telescope Operations Control Center. A space bursting with monitors, and kept under watchful eye by a dedicated team of highly skilled engineers. He saw three men argue over a malfunction as if deliberating the hacks.

He was certain that was the room he needed.

1030 hrs.

"Move!"

Nash's hands rose to his shoulders. He turned slightly and glared at Chidson's shaky grip of the weapon.

That gun could go off! Chidson's not a good shot.

Nash considered deflecting the firearm and slamming it from Chidson's grip. Calculating the fear in his opponent, he could swipe the gun without qualms. He bit his lip. "What's this all about?"

"You're under arrest, Shields. You're on US soil now."

Nash knew the protocol. He might as well have been in Red Bank, New Jersey. Still, he'd done nothing wrong. His chin turned slightly toward his left shoulder. "What's the charge?"

Chidson didn't respond. Instead, he edged the gun deeper into Nash's temple and radioed in his mouthpiece. "He's here."

Who was on the other line? Must be whoever had taken his position when he left the Embassy marines close to two years ago. They'd possibly take him for questioning as he was under the jurisdiction of US courts. Still, he couldn't help concluding Chidson was out of line. He couldn't arrest him without a formal charge. As dire as his predicament, Nash knew this was the least of his worries. His concern was the envelope in his jacket. How much had Chidson seen?

Nash slanted his head slowly away from the cold steel. "Chidson, I'm your former superior, and I'm unarmed."

"I know. We confiscated your gun at the entrance."

"Exactly. And if you go through the standard procedure, you'll see that it's registered to the NSA. We're on the same side."

"Let's go, Shields. You're trying my patience."

Chidson guided him out of Masher's office and pointed toward the main corridor. With the gun now in his back, Nash glanced over his shoulder, estimating the marine's courage. *He doesn't have the nerve.*

Chidson could do nothing. He could not shoot him. This was pure power play. "Chidson—"

"Just keep moving!"

The marine led him through to the elevators by the spiral staircase. Once inside, he pressed the button for the ambassador's floor, a tightly defended area that needed the highest security clearance, palm scan, fingerprint check, and coded doors. He should know. He'd authorized most of it himself after a few briefings with Internal Security a few years ago. The only people on that floor were the headman himself, his deputy chief of mission, and the defense attaché—the executive wing.

Nash caught Chidson's reflection in the aluminum doors. He took a deep breath and pivoted to face him. "I know you won't shoot me. You don't want to do this."

The armed marine gulped, holding on steadily to his gun.

A sudden hand swipe from Nash, allowed him to distract Chidson for a second and rout his grip over the weapon.

Chidson froze his face ashen. Nash gently removed the gun from his clammy hand. He secured it and handed it back to Chidson. "I'll face whatever I have to. There's no need for this."

The elevator halted, and the door slid open. Nash stepped out before him. He knew these corridors like the interiors of his favorite jacket, having been responsible for the security of two ambassadors. "I assume we're to go through Ambassador Westbrook's security procedures?"

Chidson said nothing. When they reached the door, Marine Corps security guards stood alert on the executive wing. Chidson nodded to them, and the two bulky men stepped aside. Nash's eyebrows drew together as he tugged his collar, not recognizing the two marines.

The first security guard dragged the door open as Nash and Chidson marched into the executive room. Nash noticed a newer décor of light-colored curtains, French-style chairs, desks, and Persian influences on the floor and the cabinets. A diplomat who'd spent time in the Middle East, similar décor to those Nash had grown accustomed to while in Syria and Qatar. A person whose back was to him, spoke with an impressive affirmative voice as they faced the window. They spoke into the secure phone he'd had installed on his last assignment with the Embassy. This was a different ambassador altogether.

"You may leave us, Chidson." It was a determined woman's voice.

Chidson started for the door tossing Nash a scoured look.

Nash turned his attention to the person behind the desk. *Well, I'll be damned!*

"I told the gate to alert me should you ever walk through these doors again," Margot Arlington said.

Nash drew a huge breath. *What's she doing here?*

He'd not realized the ambassador had been replaced in the last seven months. Nash frowned. The last time he'd seen this woman, he'd read her rights, so to speak. She'd collaborated with the enemy, trying to buy her way to the White House. He stepped forward, as Arlington set the phone in the receiver.

"London suits you better than campaigning for a seat in the White House," Nash said.

She swung her chair around and beamed at him. Dignified in a cashmere tweed dress, she'd not changed much, elegant clothing and incurably persuasive speech. She twiddled her fingers around an elongated metal necklace, embellished with paint-stained pearls.

Nash ambled toward the desk. "What do you want with me?"

"You're on my territory."

"And I'm under arrest, *because?*" he said, loathing her playful voice.

"That was just a little gimmick to get your attention, Shields. You're the one who personally escorted Mason Laskfell to his cell."

Nash scratched his jaw. "Laskfell escaped prison twenty-four hours ago."

Margot eyed him curiously. "That's why I wanted to see you."

1050 hrs.

Once outside the glass elevators, Orson fingered in a code.

The code to this floor. Jack's disguise glasses, armed with a microcamera in the left corner of the frame, captured the delicate details. A mini gadget he'd created himself, registered the movement. They straggled into the lift and descended to the ground floor. At the lobby turnstiles, Jack turned to Orson. "Thank you for the private tour, I'm certain this place ranks higher in my books than NASA."

Orson nodded. "Good day, I'll see you out, Mr. Baruch."

Jack turned toward the turnstiles as a male receptionist reached out for his visitor's badge. "Could I visit the men's room before I go."

The receptionist smiled. "Go back through. It's to the right of the elevators."

Jack turned to Orson. "You don't have to see me out. This gentleman can point me in the right direction. I still have my visitor's card here."

"E-mail me if you have further queries," Orson said before plodding to a side staff entrance adjacent to the elevators.

Jack hastened to the men's room. Hurrying into a cubicle, he removed his eyeglasses. He carefully locked the door and leaned against it. Using his smartphone to manipulate the micro camera in the eyeglasses, he downloaded the photographs on to the mini screen. He quickly memorized the eight-digit code he'd need to get into the observation room. That had to be the room he'd seen. All he needed was to connect his tablet to the mainframe systems in just sixty seconds. *Tops!*

He straightened his jacket, set the *faux* glasses above his nose, and hustled out of the restrooms. Once in the main lobby, the unmanned desk gave him the few seconds he'd calculated were necessary to return to the elevators unnoticed. Unable to control his heavy breathing, he pranced quietly through the lobby. A chatty receptionist returned to her station. He persevered, not daring to glimpse back at him. This was not his territory. Covert spying was the sort of thing Nash could do—eyes closed.

The elevator failed to respond.

Damn it!

"If anyone stops you, just act like you belong," Nash had said. "Most people don't know everyone who comes in and out of any building. Don't draw any attention to yourself."

Yeah, easy for you to say, Nash!

Jack hung on to Nash's words. He heard the receptionist's jabber on the phone behind him, hoping their attention would not shift to him. His eyes caught the slow glass elevator descend. *Empty!*

Once outside the Space Telescope Operations Control Center, on the same floor where Orson had let him scrutinize their equipment, he fingered in the code. Orson must have used one code to get to the main rooms, something they'd advised at ISTF. A good, sound code it was too.

The door snapped open.

Jack poked his head through the ajar door frame. Three engineers carried on about their tasks, oblivious of his entry. The engineers worked seven days a week, 365 days a year, monitoring the telescope's operations.

Large, and lodging several terminals along seven rows of sophisticated computers, he searched for the furthest terminal on the last row. Interred into the desk, the digital design of its mainframe and quantum computing connected to a server projecting an image on the desk before him. *Clever, just as I would do it.*

The device relied on ultrafast manipulation of billions of bits of information as it received data on spacecraft flight operations. Jack scrutinized the processor as it performed tasks such as in-depth subsystem analysis, simulated tests, database integration, and updates to flight software. *The hack must have entered via the software on this machine.* He raised his head forward.

His stealth appearance remained unquestioned. A man, three rows ahead, evaluated a prototype, an innovative, oxygen warning system. He had on headphones as he worked. At the far end of the room, a woman spoke on the phone.

Jack withdrew his electronic tablet and dialed into a wireless connection to the computer's terminal. The tablet booted a black screen written in ANX that coded the space center's aircraft management information systems. He scrolled through the lines of programming language detailing precise, real-time aircraft operations and logistics support. He reached the security control line with its list of ANX commands. *I just need to bypass the firewall, imitate the program, and transfer a copy to my system.*

He fingered in commands.

The firewall restricted his efforts.

He tried again.

Silence settled in the room. He needed to focus.

On the third try, it acknowledged his command, replicating files to his tablet. He drummed his fingers and peered up again. *Thirty more seconds!*

Twenty-nine seconds later, his counterfeiting progressed, nearing ninety percent.

Damn it!

He drummed his shaky fingers. *Done!*

Phew!

"Hey!"

Jack swiveled his head around, only to confront Orson's irate eyes.

CHAPTER 14

1057 hrs.

"THAT'S IN THE HANDS of the British Metropolitan Police. My duties in London are with ISTF and the recent cyber threats to NASA and the UK Space Agency," Nash said.

"I had you checked out with the NSA, myself. They view you so highly, and that's why I need you."

"To do what exactly, *your excellency*?" Nash smirked, his stress on 'excellency' sounding more sarcastic than intended.

"If you sit, I'll tell you."

"I'm afraid I don't have much time. I need to get back to my duties."

"Then, why are you here?"

How would he disguise that one? No one had ever questioned his movement about the Embassy, not even an ambassador. There were new players now, and if Margot was sore about his investigation of her personal files, she showed it. Arlington was doubtless sour at his last encounter with her. He'd caught her dealing with Mason in matters that could incriminate her for life. Ready to pay a high price to enter the

White House. By his standards, the FBI had let her off easy. If she'd resurfaced as an ambassador to a high post like London, she had friends in higher places than he'd climbed. That she was the ex-Republican candidate meant she was someone Americans cared about.

Not many, but some. And influential ones. People who threw around dollars hoping it could buy them the influence they needed, revolted him. He was not sure how, but Margot's influence had paid off and won her a station in the US Embassy in London.

The Republicans needed her.

"What do you want from me, Ms. Arlington?" he said.

Arlington rose from her seat and coasted toward him. Not his style of woman; nevertheless, many would consider her attractive. In her late forties, she was young for her political achievements. She placed a finely manicured hand on his shoulder. "We Americans need to stick together. I need a favor."

The scent of her floral-fragranced perfume crossed his nostrils. He turned his head slightly and removed her hand from his coat. "What sort of favor?"

She studied his build from head to boots. He sensed Arlington had anything but diplomatic affairs on her mind. She caught his disapproving eye before gravitating to the window. She glanced down for several seconds at the Roosevelt Memorial fountain that stood outside the Embassy grounds. "You may not know this, but Mason and I had an affair."

And there it is.

"Does that surprise you?"

Nothing about Mason surprises me.

"It's none of my business," he said.

"I have no misgivings about it." She turned to face him again. "I need you to find Mason for me."

"As I said, the British are handling this."

She tossed a lock of ebony hair from her face. "I need you to find him. .. because, if you don't, he'll come after me."

"Why?"

"I stole something from him, and he needs it back. Desperately." She waited for a response from him.

He gave none.

"I need you to come back and protect me."

"You have enough protection here from the Bureau of Diplomatic Security. And besides, why me?"

"Because Mason will not touch you, or Cress. At least for now." She held her head back arrogantly as though sniffing something. "So long as you still hold his secret.. . you know, the one you used against him in Belmarsh."

How could she know that? She's not kidding! They were lovers!

He inclined his head. "I'm not sure I follow?"

"I can help you ISTF people stop Mason's attack on information technology. He told me himself where the holes were."

"Why would he tell you?"

"Let's just say it slipped out of him when he could barely remember his name."

Nash didn't care for the details. Their love affair was her business. She was bluffing. He knew it. Not a single soul knew of the transaction he'd had with Mason. And Mason wasn't one to repeat his affairs to a lax woman like Margot. *Mason trusts no one, not even his own mother.*

Nash inched a few steps in her direction, his eyes studying her behavior. As a trained marine and a confident analyst, he knew what signs to watch for. She was unduly concerned about what others thought of her. Her values and opinions floated and morphed, depending on whom she was with. It was all in her files. *Liar!*

"Why do you want to get Mason so bad? I doubt he's about to launch an attack on the US Embassy."

"Because he used me. He used my influence, made me look like a fool!"

And broke your heart.

Nash had investigated Mason's criminal file and knew it like his mother's birthday, but he'd never contemplated the magnetism Mason had, or lack of it, with members of the opposite sex. Something she'd said made him stop and consider. The woman didn't want to launch a premeditated war on an international criminal. She was nursing something more dear to her than her country—*a bruised heart.*

Arlington sighed. "If you protect me from him, I, in turn, will protect Calla Cress's affairs."

"Come again."

"Mason told me about her and you."

It was blackmail but only were she telling the truth. Perhaps Mason had surrendered something to her while he was vulnerable. Or had he? She could not only ruin him with what she knew, but she could also hurt Calla.

Is she lying?

1112 hrs.

Jack raised his head. "Mr. Rand."

Orson's face rearranged itself into a frown. "I'm calling security."

"No, wait! A hacker has full-functional control of your systems. I was trying to isolate the problem."

"I don't believe you!"

Orson seized Jack's tablet. The three engineers in the room glanced up from their work. Jack wasn't sure whether they knew what had transpired. The woman shook her head at the rude interruption and set back about her programming. The other two engineers jerked their heads forward, anticipating a considerable dispute. Orson's tone was even. "You don't leave my sight."

He flung Jack toward the door. Blood drained from Jack's face as he shifted his weight from one foot to another. His one thought was about retrieving the tablet. Damn it, he'd almost had the logs.

Jack debated. He could run. *No, too risky, too guilty!*

Fight? No! The beefy astronaut was probably at the gym more times than he was.

He longed to seize the tablet from Orson's giant hands. Orson held onto it tightly, sensing his intent. They reached the door. Jack turned with a quick snap of his shoulders.

Damn!

"Hey, Orson, come in here. The system is acting up again." The voice came from the engineer seated in the front row.

Jack shot Orson a knowing glance. *What's he going to do?*

Torn between turning him in and examining the imminent, system problem, Orson eased his frown and held tightly on to Jack's arm. He pulled him back into the room. "This better not be your mess."

The engineer spoke in hurried tones. "The hacker is at work. Look here. There's more activity, Orson. We can't contain the destruction and its gaining speed."

Orson released Jack's arm and leaned over the terminal. His eyebrows knit in a frown. "We can't identify the Internet Protocol addresses. They move from one location to another. I've never seen this before."

Jack drew in a deep breath and strode to where the two men stood. He hunched over the monitor. "Here, let me see."

"Hey!" yelled Orson.

"Do you want to isolate the hack before it eats up the entire backbone of UKSA's systems, or not?" Jack said.

Orson moved back, muttering punitive curses under his breath. The engineer eyed Orson, waiting for instructions.

"Trust me, Orson. I built part of the program you guys use," Jack said.

The engineer shot Jack a quick look without comment, his face carefully neutral. He slid out of his seat, allowing Jack to proceed with his analysis. Jack straightened his shoulders to relive an ache that had surfaced on apprehension. "She's a nasty one. These hackers are not just testing their skills at breaking into UKSA's systems; they're attempting to shut it down completely."

He asked Orson to key in passwords before he could penetrate the program's computing system. "I need to implement security improvement," Jack said as his fingers flashed against the keys, scripting language the two engineers tried to follow.

He hit the enter key.

The keyboard failed to respond to his commands.

He bypassed the system lock with a few more directions. This time, the system responded, allowing him to isolate several commands being written remotely by an invisible hand from heaven knows where. He overrode the commands and placed a shield that reversed the hack, implementing a lock over UKSA's two main systems and IT infrastructure. "Okay, looks like it's contained for now."

The engineer sneered at his work. "How did you do that?"

"As I said, I built your programs. I'm with ISTF. It's only a temporary fix. I would need to analyze the data more concretely to completely isolate the problem."

Orson dropped into a chair next to him, not sure which way to look.

Jack shot him a sideways glance for several seconds before rising from the engineer's seat. "I wouldn't feel too bad, Orson. This is the first breakthrough we've had in forty-eight hours, and we've been working at it for several days."

"I knew you weren't an ordinary graduate."

Jack clasped his hands together. "Now, do you want my full help or not?"

BRITISH MUSEUM, GROUND FLOOR
ROSETTA STONE DISPLAY
EGYPTIAN SCULPTURE, ROOM 4, 0001 hrs.

"It has to be the Rosetta Stone," Calla said.

She eyed Stan, her face lighting up. His glare focused on her, then back at the stone, with its dark gray-pinkish tone and a coral streak running through it.

Calla fingered the lettering and traced it over the reddish-brown undertones that adorned the front side of the stone. The Rosetta Stone, a basalt slab with three languages carved on it, Greek, demotic, and hieroglyphs, covered its surface with ancient decrees. It stood among various Egyptian sculptures on level zero of the British Museum. Encased behind protective glass, it was one of the aspired stops by Museum visitors, and on any single day, they would channel their way close enough to glimpse its gradient surface.

Calla's determined stance set her circling the famous stone that had been in the Museum since 1802. She'd chosen this hour specifically when cleaning was done, and Lester, the security guard and an admirer she'd once given a private tour of Roman collections not on display, allowed her access to the cases in this part of the museum. Later, they'd worked on

ISTF security at the museum, and now, Lester had looked the other way.

"We need to move it," Calla said.

"You're joking, right?" Stan said.

"No."

"Darling girl, why are we moving the stone?"

"I want to examine every inch of it."

"This is an important historical artifact."

She slid on her latex gloves and tossed him a pair. "Exactly, and I'm quite qualified to handle it."

"Has it ever been moved? It must weigh a ton."

She sneered at him with a skeptical eye. "Seven hundred and sixty kilograms to be exact. It was moved three times, once toward the end of the First World War in 1917, and when the Museum was concerned about heavy bombing in the Second World War. They moved it to safety with other important artifacts. The third time was in 1999, to be cleaned for an exhibition called 'Cracking Codes'. And that's what I'm here to do."

"Yes, and I'm sure it took more than you and me."

"Father, when has lifting weights been a problem for your operative genes. Remember, I get it from you. Listen, this is important. Mother must've hidden a clue here?"

"What clue?"

"That's what we need to find. A clue to her whereabouts."

Stan watched mesmerized. "It's remarkable how much you remind me of her—determined, stubborn, and intelligent."

Calla smiled and surveyed the gallery floor. She took a deep breath. "Are you ready?"

He nodded slowly.

"Okay, let's move it. I've disengaged the alarms. This time, on my own accord. I still need to discharge the lighting diffuser and the magnetic contacts fitted to its opening panels.

Otherwise, we'll wake the magistrates and possibly...her Majesty," she said with a sneer.

"Can you do all that from the central security room?"

"As an employee, no. As an ISTF agent, I can do anything. As an operative...who knows?"

He could not argue with that.

Calla decoded the magnetic contacts, disengaging the display light altogether and shed darkness on the Stone. She slid the nonstandard panel glass open, and with socked feet covered with plastic bags, she slid into the case like a slithering cat. Stan followed, and together they crammed into the small space. She curved her arms over the tablet. He edged to the other side, butting his head on the top section of the glass and stretched his arms over the celebrated rock.

It felt sharp under her touch, nestled on a slab of concrete that held it in place. Calla glanced at Stan. "Ready."

She closed her eyes, and in her mind, she pictured the stone moving. *If I can will it, I can move it.*

That's what she'd learned about her physical strength. Vortigern had described it like that of *Shimshon,* the Nazarite, or Samson. *'Man of the sun'*. She'd been compelled to research that detail, being slightly less familiar with theological history. Shimshon, she'd learned, was a Nazarite granted supernatural strength by God to combat his enemies and perform heroic feats. Her research revealed he'd wrestled a lion, massacred an entire army with only the jawbone of an ass, and destroyed a pagan temple with his bare hands.

Eight months ago, it would have all been a passionate myth to weave into some museum tour. Now she was not so sure. Was there truth in it? Shimson's strength and weakness were in his hair. Where was hers? Did she have one? An *Achilles' heel*? Did anyone know of it?

Stan's own strength mirrored Calla's, sharing a gene that operatives had engineered in his family line decades ago.

"Perhaps, her message is in the lettering of her note and not physically here," Stan said.

"No, that's too simple, don't you think? I think she left something physical."

Calla inhaled a breath, and together they heaved the stone an inch. It slithered readily in their capable arms with tenacity beyond ordinary strength, beyond science.

Nothing. Not a clue.

They replaced the stone with the might of two wild buffaloes towing a boulder.

"Why would she choose this stone, father?"

They carefully withdrew from the cramped case, and Calla reinstated the alarms. Stan stood stunned, watching her. "So it's true? You do have the Cress strength like that of Shimshon, the ancient Nazarite."

"Nash was one of the first to notice, actually."

"I tried to suppress those genes for years. You're a strong operative, stronger than I thought you'd be. You've managed to balance that and still stay undetected for years," he said.

"Must've got that from you. I'm sure it was because I didn't know. So as they say, what you don't know can't harm you. Knowledge of my ancestry or the lack of protected me for years. But I can't ignore it any longer, father. Nash's right, I need to channel it. It must have been given to me for a reason."

Stan glimpsed at his hands, unable to look her in the eye. "It's always been a Cress gene and maybe a curse as your mother and I thought."

"Is that what you think of the operatives' responsibility, the Hadrius mandate?"

"It's what we thought." He managed a weak smile, skirted round the other side, and watched her eye the stone. "Satisfied?"

"I just want to see what's beneath."

"There's nothing there."

A frown fell on her face. "Father, how did you ever keep your operative life undercover?"

"Thanks to MI6 secrecy customs, it was easy. And then, you learn to get on with it, until the day the mandate came looking for you. MI6 had kept our operatives identities secret, but they couldn't' keep our personal lives protected. That your mother and I could not handle. Anything else, we could even face danger and death."

They heard a small can drop behind them, followed by male voices. Two museum night workers walked by in the next room, unaware of their presence. Calla held her breath. The noise ceased as instantly as it had begun. Her eyes suddenly fell on the plaque to the stone, engraved in the glass. "Wait, father," she whispered.

"What is it?"

She reread the Rosetta plaque engraved in the glass. Calla slumped on the floor in deep thought. "You're right. There's nothing here because we're looking in the wrong place."

He smiled. "Now, you tell me. Now that I've nearly broken my back."

Calla smiled to herself. "Doubt that."

All her life, she'd wondered what it would be like to have a father, and despite his mistakes and absence, she adored him more though he'd been absent most of her existence. She admired the way his silver hair showed age, but his face showed the grace of a handsome lad, who'd lost something long ago. It pained her she couldn't undo the things in his past. And here she was, conversing with the father she'd found barely seven months ago. "Father, come with me to find your Nicole."

His face rouged with pain, and he angled his back to her. She reached for him, setting a hand on his shoulder. "Father, once I made a mistake. One thing I learned when I was looking for you was that sometimes we give up on people close to us. Don't do that. Let's find her. I think it'll give you the closure you need. Believe me, I tried 'alone' for so many years. I pushed away people that wanted to change that in me, thinking I had to be alone because my parents left me. But I took a chance."

"You mean with Nash?"

She nodded slowly, carefully avoiding difficult emotions. "I couldn't accept what Allegra and Vortigern told me. Nash's different from me. He believes in life and living it to the full. It's in his makeup."

"Have you told him how you feel about him? That man would do anything for you."

With six months in Colorado, the allure was always there, but why they'd shied from it, Calla didn't know. Yet, they were inseparable as a unit.

Stan's eyes were proud as he watched his daughter. "Nash has my approval. I knew that the moment I met him."

"All the more for you not to give up on Nicole, on my mother. Whatever her mistakes in leaving you or staying hidden were, if we find her, she can help us. We can find Mason, and father, finally, settle what began decades ago. We may not have started it, but we can finish it."

She hesitated. "And maybe, just maybe, we can carve out a normal life for ourselves. Let's challenge the mandate. Let's find these answers together."

Stan's shoulders relaxed. "Where do we start?"

"In France."

"France?"

"Why France?"

"Because the French first found the Rosetta Stone."

Stan's eyebrows knit. "Enlighten me, curator Cress."

Calla fished her printout from her denim pockets. "Here, read this again."

Stan scanned it. "Then, Paris is where you need to begin. Remember, this first part is an anagram. There are three, and I know what she means by A-M-E-N-D-A-B-L-E T-I-L-L-E-R."

Calla's eyes glanced up at his photographic vision working intensely as it scoured the anagram for answers. "But that could be anything."

"Not anything, someone. It's Danielle Lambert's name, unscrambled."

"Who?"

"Danielle was your mother's partner at MI6 before we were paired. They were sent there to Paris to observe the investigation of De Gaulle's assassination attempt in 1962. It was one of her first missions. She was barely nineteen."

"Why would MI6 get involved?"

"MI6 always got involved. After the war, they needed eyes and ears everywhere."

DOVER FERRY TO FRANCE
0120 hrs.

Mason drummed his fingers on the deck railing as he watched the ferry leave Dover. A waft of smoked steam brushed his skin, filling the air with a petroleum stench. His gut welcomed a sigh of relief at leaving English soil as he expected no problems before docking in Calais.

He padded his pocket having changed several pounds that Arlington delivered from his offshore account, obtaining euros at the busy *bureau de change* below deck. His journey would be devoid of technology–no chips, no phones, cards, or byte interference until he arrived where he needed to go.

The rocking of the large vessel aboard choppy waters triggered his motion sickness, and nausea crept to his throat. The English Channel, largely gray and the smallest of the swallowed seas around continental Europe, was unusually storm ridden. He leaned forward on the railing. "Shields, what am I going to do with you?"

Mrs. Hawke, a trump, middle-aged bodyguard he'd hired and trained twenty years ago, loped toward him on the deck overlooking the English coastline. "All arrangements have been made as requested."

"How soon can we get started on the cyber files? I need everything to work without hiccups."

"Yes, sir. In forty-eight hours."

"Did you open the files I wired as I asked?"

"Yes, we have all of Cress's files."

"Good. That's where we will start."

"I also have the other problem taken care of. You know the one at the NSA and the US Embassy."

Mason glanced at her. The woman had aged vehemently in seven months, possibly gained weight. However well she'd served him, he couldn't let this one slip. New blood was needed, the kind to stand up to the operatives.

He sighed deeply. Everything was right on schedule.

So much was at stake, and he knew exactly who he could use to pierce Cress and Shields where it hurt the most.

CHAPTER 15

PÈRE LA CHAISE CEMETERY
PARIS FRANCE
1412 hrs.

"DANIELLE LAMBERT. Not a single Secret Intelligence Service, ISTF, or government record on her. Who's this woman? I've tried the French authorities." Jack leaned against a decomposing bench opposite an impressive headstone. "Yet, here we are in a graveyard, Miss Cress, may I ask why?"

"Danielle Lambert was my mother's secret-agent partner. She was born British to French parents. I doubt you'll find anything in any records. She went undercover after they were pulled off the Charles de Gaulle case."

"Why?"

"Don't know. They never finished the case, according to my father. My guess is, Danielle wiped herself off the face of the Earth."

"Listen, the only Danielle Lambert that remotely resembles the description your father gave us is listed as a textile dealer whom we've been told passed away ten years ago. All we have is a will by a shady guardian of her estate."

Calla looked back at her friend. "Come on, Jack, we need to look deeper, she left a will. Can you boot it?"

"I don't speak French."

Calla rose from her scraping off a mossy tomb and took a seat beside him. "Let me see."

Jack angled his tablet toward her.

She studied the screen. "Here, look at this. It's the same riddle in French as in my mother's note."

"Seriously, I wouldn't know that."

Jack glimpsed up above at forming clouds. Though the day remained warm for early fall, a chill ran through the largest cemetery in Paris. Burrowed in the twentieth *arrondissement* of Paris, on Boulevard de Ménilmontant, it housed the remains of prominent figures from authors, to composers. Gravestones littered the hill ranging from somber, unadorned headstones to towering monuments and ornamented mini chapels, accessed via several leveled paths.

"It still does not answer why we are here," Jack said.

"These spies, Danielle and my mother were partnered together, probably because they thought alike. My mother trusted three people in her note. I still don't know who the other two are, but Danielle's family, like many prominent French families, has been buried here for centuries."

"Getting creepier, Calla, *and?*"

She slid on latex gloves from her backpack. "Let's just say she took the secret to her grave or someone else she was close to did."

"Is that her tomb you're looking at?"

"Not exactly? I need Champollion's tomb. Danielle left whatever my mother wants me to find with this French scholar most associated with the Rosetta Stone. Because he died in

1832, I figured his grave was the next best thing. That's what's implied by my mother. Danielle left it for me. She knew the riddle referred to the Rosetta Stone, and who better to hold onto the secrets than Jean-François Champollion?"

Calla shot up from the bench and crossed the pebbled cobblestone to the other side of the path. She leaned over the grill-gated grave, with an obelisk in for a headstone. "This is his tomb."

Jack followed her and stood gazing at the obelisk. "This is Champollion's grave? I can barely pronounce the name."

Calla giggled.

Encircled by a metal rail, the renowned graveyard remained quiet. A decaying rose reposed at the foot of the tomb, next to a plastic bouquet of pink carnations. Armed with an archeological tool roll, Calla opened an excavating case and pulled out a narrow leaf-trowel. She reached over the grill railing and scrapped at the base of the grave marker.

"Should you really be doing that?" Jack said.

"Not exactly, but I need to see something, I'm trying to find anything unusual."

"The only thing out of the ordinary is us, in broad daylight, scavenging a tomb. So why is it called the Rosetta Stone?"

Calla smirked. Jack's humor was always well-timed and welcome. Frankly. .. because it kept her sane. "Champollion's interest in Oriental languages, especially Coptic, led to him being assigned the task of deciphering the discovered Rosetta Stone."

Jack snickered. "Could he be a distant relative of yours?"

"Only if I were French in a former life," she said. "French scholars worked at Napoleon's request in the town of Rosetta, or Rashid, in Egypt during a French expedition. They found the Stone. As a cryptographer for the secret service, my mother took inspiration from him. This cemetery is its own who's who list. You see?"

"Yeah, yeah. .. we're literally on a walk of fame," Jack said.

"You could say that. It's the largest cemetery in Paris."

"I've never understood why people flock to a graveyard when they've no friends or relatives there. Are we done here?"

"This place is no ordinary cemetery. It's a *hall of fame* museum, only its occupants have been renowned for centuries. It's the most visited cemetery in the world by reputation. The graves of thousands of lives that have enhanced French life over the past two hundred years. Chopin, Bizet, Collete, Molière—"

"Jim Morrison," Jack said.

Calla giggled.

"Why didn't your father come?" Jack asked.

"He still finds this all so difficult. He feels guilty about many things and is not sure how to cope with me wanting to find my mother."

Calla retraced her steps and wiped her brow. She took a seat on the bench across from Champollion's tomb and studied the obelisk that stood close to two meters high. Nestled between two moderately sized graves, the wind whispered as it beat against the concrete slaps carrying a fierce fall chill. She tunneled a hand through her loose hair. "I don't think I've missed anything," she sighed. "It would be easier if I knew what we were looking for."

Jack smiled. "Remember the carbonados. They found their way to you. This, too, will come."

He was teasing. This was different. Her mother left clues baffling her more than history had ever done. It was easier to decipher cryptic clues in time than trying to understand the mind of a woman she'd never met. *Even still, I do have her genes*.

Calla moved back to the tomb and squatted in front of it. She scrutinized the mausoleum for several minutes and leaped on the grave. Her feet touched the inscription of the Egyptologist's name.

"Hey, I'm not sure you can do that," Jack said.

"Only for a second," she said, dusting moss off the top left corner of the tombstone.

"Hurry before someone sees you."

Calla stole a look behind her before lifting the plastic bouquet resting in a dented circle in the bottom corner. "Flowers to those who have passed on are our way of gracing their memories with a fragrance of goodwill. Sorry, Jean-François. Please accept my amity."

She scraped at a dent cast in a circle of iron. "Jack, do you have a Swiss Army knife?"

Jack fished around his backpack and produced a small, Wenger Swiss Army knife. "Here."

Calla took the knife and drew out the large blade. In the corner of her eye, she caught sight of a few tourists who'd stopped to observe her actions.

Jack followed her stare. "Ah! No need to be alarmed, people. She's a historian and is doing some conservation work."

The elderly couple shook their heads, not having understood him. They observed Calla for a few seconds before moving on.

Jack flipped his head round. "Hurry; otherwise, they won't be the only audience we'll get."

Calla shaved the covering, then placed the edge of the blade on the dent. She shoved it down a circular iron slab, the size of a credit card.

It popped off. She glared down the narrow crater beneath, about ten centimeters deep.

"Pass me the gloves in your backpack, please."

He tossed a pair of latex gloves her way.

Ridden with moss, plant roots, and mud, she grated at the interior of the shallow cavity. Calla supposed it hadn't been part of the original grave, sadly, an ingenious piece of vandalism undetectable to the naked eye. She dipped her fingers in the moss and stretched them in the cool earth until they hit the edges—a *dead end.*

She sighed.

Wait.

Her eyes caught a red cord the size of a shoelace visible under the moss.

"I have something."

"What?"

She tugged at the string and noticed that it was attached to a rolled-up, leather bundle. She retrieved the roll and replaced the iron cast over the lid, heaping moss and earth over it before stamping it down with her foot.

She drew off her gloves, jumped off the grave, and back on to the main pedestrian path. "Look."

"What is it?" Jack asked.

"Not sure."

They took a seat on the bench across the tomb. Calla unrolled the hardened leather, and disinterred a tiny metal grid, resembling a memory chip, and a section of browning cloth kept dry by a plastic bag. She unrolled the cloth no bigger than her palm. Calligraphic German words, half-finished sentences, and large straight strokes in a pattern of writing stared at her. Calla unrolled the entire roll of cloth. It had been perfectly preserved.

"What do you think it is?" Jack said.

"I'm not certain of the date, maybe medieval, the cloth is older, though. But these half-finished words seem to be old German. I recognize some letters, but the words don't make sense. Can you look at this, Jack? It's a vintage computer chip."

. . .

She leaned back against Jack's shoulder and trembled against his warmth. She watched the clouds scroll in.

Not sure how long she sat contemplating the bizarre nature of her mother's mind, nor how long Jack studied the chip and researched it on his tablet, Calla sensed defeat. *What's this cloth? An artifact, with old German and sprinkled strokes.*

Her eyes fixed on the clouds. Then, motion drew her eye.

SEVILLE, SPAIN
0600 hrs.

Mason's eyes opened with an abrupt jerk of his upper body. He checked the time. He'd fallen asleep in his clothes the minute he had set foot in the house. He pulled himself off the bed and staggered to the window like a drunkard. He'd consumed sleeping pills to help him unwind after reaching Calais, proceeding to Orly Airport in Paris, then to Arlington's private jet. A pilot on his own payroll had driven him from there to the Andalusian capital, Seville.

He glimpsed outside the window. The traditional house, usually known as a *hacienda,* grew olives and oranges on a commercial scale, a guise he'd insisted on. Surrounded by fifty hectares of land outside Seville, Mason had bought the property for his mother but now kept the house as part of his estate under a different name. Originally from the eighteenth-century, the property had undergone a careful refurbishment program over the last five years.

Mason had not felt this weak in years. Seven months in prison and poor nourishment had weakened his physique, from his feeble arms to his shaky legs. Perhaps age was catching up. He tossed the idea away. Yes, he'd lost weight. Too much weight. He could see it around his sunken eyes.

And now, the nightmare. Mason was now an international fugitive. He shook his head, trying to relive the memory.

He trusted dreams and knew the psyche always had something to say. Some of his best ideas had come from dreams and some from nightmares.

He'd been lost for clues to destroy the oncoming evil. The evil of the Hadrius Manuscript. Its secret was out, but not the secret of what it had done to him and his mother. No one would find out, and now with Cress on the loose, his senses were alerted. He'd known as much when the woman had looked for Merovec–his other bad dream. It was time to act. *Nicole Cress must never resurface.*

Not after what she'd done—played with his mind and his mother's. He'd seen his mother again in his nightmare. That's what had woken him. Her snarling voice, her poised elegance menacing him. The woman in his dreams held her hands around her neck, shrieking for help. She sat imprisoned in a ward surrounded by people who didn't understand her, people who didn't care.

Mason rubbed his bleak eyes, relieving the pain of his hallucination. It took him back forty or was it fifty years when he was still a young man by the world's standards. He'd walked into his home, only to lock eyes with a woman he didn't recognize. Long, ravenous hair cascaded down her back as large, chestnut-colored eyes, unfathomable in their murky depths, glared at his mother. He'd stood by the door as the woman patronized Dena Laskfell.

"The arrangement is off, Mrs. Laskfell. I'm taking the Hadrius back! I've learned the true purpose of its intent, and I'll not let those plans surface."

Mason's mother stretched for the Hadrius, a fiery look in

her observant eyes. "No, Nicole! We'll finish this! It's important."

Nicole fingered the seven-page Hadrius Manuscript. "You've translated part of the document and unleashed God knows what in Southern Europe. Your hunger and thirst for the manuscript's secrets have nearly killed a hundred people in Great Barrington, Massachusetts. How many more? It stops here. No, I'm taking this manuscript to the tormented place it came from."

"You don't even know where that is," Mason's mother said.

"I'll die trying."

"Give me that, or you die now!"

The following struggle of the battle of feminine wills left Mason paralyzed as he witnessed a knife appear from under his mother's garments. A twenty-minute, physical brawl ravished the house as the women wrestled from room to grounds, injuring Mason's prized, tracking hounds. Mason watched as Nicole displayed physical fitness and energy that no one had seen or known possible in a woman. She was a belligerent fighting tiger, her vigor taking a toll on his mother, who'd been no match for Nicole Cress. He remembered the muddy boot on his mother's chest and those words. "We won't discuss this again!"

Mason bolted to his mother's side as she lay unconscious but alive on the floor.

Nicole shot him a look that made his breath leave his body. She'd stomped out with the manuscript, and he'd never seen it again until her barefaced child had found it in Berlin.

Mason rubbed his eyes again. He understood why the Cress girl could put up a good fight. He didn't recall exactly when he knew she was Nicole's daughter. But when he'd seen her at

ISTF on her first day, he'd recognized that fire in her eyes, that hair, those wild jade-green eyes. Then in the African wilderness, how she'd handled herself.

He sent a fist into the window.

It sliced a little cut in his thumb. Mason straggled to the bathroom for some tissue paper before settling at the work desk in the somber room, wired according to his specifications.

"It will do," he muttered to himself.

He fired up the hidden camera linked to a remote location in a Washington Prison for the mentally ill, where Dena Laskfell had been imprisoned, thanks to Nicole's undercover work at the Secret Intelligence Service.

Moisture from his brow dropped to his chest as the woman gripped her knees on her little bed. As the former head of ISTF, he'd authorized a hidden camera in her ward, so he could keep an eye on Dena. Her downcast face masked heavy-lidded eyes.

Dena never communicated with the workers around her, confined in an institution for the psychologically challenged, within a prison establishment. A white-uniformed man strolled in with her medication. He started a conversation with her. "Mrs. Laskfell. Here's something that'll make you feel better. Your son used to send you the best medication out there, although that's not happening anymore."

"I have no son!" the woman screeched, her eyes poring into the nurse's. "If I did, I wouldn't have been here for forty-three years!"

The words stung Mason like poison in his gut. It didn't matter that his mother had been imprisoned for singlehandedly destroying the technology infrastructure of half the NSA.

What have they done to you? What did Cress do to you?

"It's time to get you out! If the Cress woman's alive, she'll serve the rest of your sentence."

PARIS, FRANCE
1412 hrs.

Whisking with the force of a Peregrine Falcon, a steel circle catapulted their way. Small and swift Calla hurled Jack off the bench as the violent ring landed by her boot, sliding off the cobblestone ground at turbulent speed. Calla's eyes widened, recognizing the instrument on the ground.

She was not mistaken. It was a Rajput warrior *chakram*. Circular in shape, with a sharpened outer edge, the 'circle of fire', as it was known in India, was about twelve inches in diameter. A weapon of India's first line of defense against foreign invaders in the eighteenth-century. It was a throwing weapon mastered by Rajput warriors among a multitude of lethal weapons.

Calla and Jack hunched against the bench. A figure in dark attire stood on a hill in the adjacent alley of the cemetery. He twirled a second circle of fire on his index finger and tossed it with a timed flick of the wrist.

"Jack! Run!"

Jack hauled Calla off her feet with a tug. "No, wait!" He drew out a Colt pistol, and they dropped behind the moldy bench. "If we run, he'll toss another."

He set an index finger on the trigger and spied through the wood of the bench.

Calla peered above them. "He's heading this way. We can make a run for it."

They scrambled to their feet, and the pair bolted up the pedestrian path. Behind them, the man pursued and lanced a *chakrum,* slicing over their heads. Jack swiveled around and fired.

The man dodged the bullet.

They hurtled the length of the path along the edge of the cemetery that led to the exit. Their pursuant leaped on the two-meter circular wall that bordered Père la Chaise cemetery and tore after them, his steady strides scudding on the brick from on high.

Calla glared back, her frown deepening. He was no ordinary assassin. He employed the skills of an ancient warrior, with an over-muscled build. His arm reached for another *chakrum,* a smaller one.

"Jack! Down!"

Calla pulled Jack to the ground.

He turned, leveled the gun before firing a shot that caught the missile midair. He fired a second bullet. The shot erupted and caught their opponent in the leg. He slid off the wall frame.

Calla eyed Jack. "That's impressive."

He helped her to her feet. "It rubs off when you hang around Nash long enough. Let's go."

They bustled as far as Alexandre Dumas Metro station and gasped for breath. Two travelers, a man, and a woman wound down the stairs as Calla leaned down to tie her boot.

She glared up.

Perhaps it was the contrast in traffic clatter or the scent of danger. She turned and faced the looming presence behind her. His eyes were still hidden by dark glasses, slate-silver in color. He seized her arm, and a sharp edge dug toward her middle, its jab forced by the vigor of the Rajput warrior. Short of tearing through her clothes, it had to be a *Katar* that pressed into her middle, an Indian dagger. The man swung Calla round until she faced Jack, who stopped in his tracks.

Stay close to the attacker. Her mind repeated Nash's words.

Strength was on her side. Was skill? From the glare in Jack's face, she read the intent in her attacker's nudge.

Jack held the gun at his side and exchanged a look with Calla.

No, Jack. I'll be dead before you can raise it.

Jack's hand tightened around the gun. With no option to pacify her attacker, she could not focus on the Indian knife. It would be deadly.

She drew in a rooted breath, angled her elbow with a violent snap into her opponent's forearm, and gained control of the dagger. She wielded his hand for a moment, diverting his attention. He plunged to the ground and, as quickly as he'd fallen, fetched his ankle into a kick. Calla leaped over his leg and slammed his neck, rendering the assailant unconscious. She moved to the floor and retrieved the *Katar* from where it had fallen. She folded it around a discarded plastic bag and placed it in her backpack. "Thanks. For my museum collection." She turned to Jack, whose gun was still marked at the opponent. "It's all right, Jack. I think he's down."

"I wouldn't be so sure."

Motion behind her drew Jack's head as a second warrior appeared behind Calla. The watchful goon, with a clear resemblance to the first man in build and stance, pierced a savage look into her. He rounded into her and jabbed a pistol in her rib.

Sensing Jack's thought, she glared at the unconscious man on the floor, who'd come to, and rubbed his agonizing neck. The blow had not been severe enough.

Jack and Calla exchanged an underline look, and with a wink from Jack, Calla tore herself from the gunman. They fled down the Metro staircase, slamming into distressed passengers leaving the station, who shrieked at the armed man.

At the foot of the stairs, Calla lost Jack amid frantic travelers. She saw police officers trying to suppress the disorder of screeching tourists, a cacophony of voices over droned travel announcements. As she charged toward them, a hand seized her leg, and she thumped to the ground.

Jack pushed his way through the crowd and reached a hand to pull her. A blow to Jack's shoulder sent him to the floor.

As feet rushed in a bustle around them, the two friends glared straight up. The attackers stared down at them. Transportation police, unaware of the trigger of the commotion, subdued frenzied crowds, before disappearing behind the ticket office.

Calla's cheek numbed against the cold concrete as she exchanged a defeated look with Jack's fainting eyes.

—

ALEXANDRE DUMAS METRO STATION
PARIS, FRANCE
1512 hrs.

The assassins peered down at them. Menacing eyes, relieved of dark glasses, they studied Calla and Jack's cautioned faces. In one instant, they hauled them up and shoved them toward the trains. Trapped in the Paris subway and heralded to the platform by malevolent warriors, whose fighting capabilities were deadlier than any effort she'd yet encountered, they waited cautiously.

Were they Mason's men? Calla held on tightly to her recently discovered bundle, retrieved at Champollion's tomb. Had Mason sent them, that's what they were after. And her neck.

"We're going for a little walk," bellowed the amber-eyed twin.

That's it. *They are twins.*

The first man gripped Calla's arm and thrust her deeper into the depth of the subway. The second secured Jack's gun and heaved him hastily down the stairs. Within seconds, they stood on the platform. Calla glimpsed at the information board. An incoming train nosed on the platform heading toward Châtelet. The fierce nudge from the grip around her arm told her the assailant intended to either joust them onto the tracks or take them toward central Paris. They wouldn't dare think the unimaginable in daylight. Calla had to be sure, though.

She wished she'd listen to Nash and Allegra's advice and trained with firearms. It was no use. She hadn't carried the one Allegra had given her, a last-minute decision she now regretted.

A waft of wind smacked them as the train slowed on the tracks. She gave Jack a knowing look. He returned her stare and winked. *What's he saying?*

Jack kept eyeing the oncoming train emerging from the tunnel. *Does he mean...?*

In an instant, she understood.

More travelers crowded the subway platform as the train slowed on the tracks. When it sailed past Calla, she twisted around and lunged at the giant with a straight punch.

His gun rolled to the track. The twin behind Jack swiveled her way in anguish. She hunched low and with both knees, pushed off into a somersault, her feet bearing off the halting train. The slowing speed delivered the right momentum, and her right foot landed in the jaw of the man restraining Jack.

Jack turned around and slammed a punch in his captor's ribs.

With both men on the ground, several gasps were heard. Calla seized Jack's arm, and they tore back up the stairs. She turned around, only to spot the fully responsive attacker level his pistol and fire in the air. Panic-stricken travelers dropped like blocks on the concrete. Some attempted to flee the ominous menace.

Calla and Jack scuttled up the stairs, only to clash eyes with a third assassin. She blinked twice. Was there another?

Jack pulled her to him as the man mined a pistol into her belly.

Calla shut her eyes, calculating her next move.

Without warning, a loud eruption of sulfur, its stench stealing past her nose, arrested her hearing for a few seconds. When she threw her eyes open, she took in the sight of crimson, only too aware that the blood she smelled, could have been her own.

Then she saw him.

Nash.

He'd grazed two of the attackers with one bullet, an accurate marksman. As the French transportation police cuffed the sedated giants, Nash bucked them down, his knee on the back of one assassin. With his pistol against the goon's neck, he held him down cautiously until he was certain the man would not stir. When the police took control of the incident, their faces showed gratitude as Nash handed them the offenders' weapons.

Nash put away his pistol. "Is this the sort of sightseeing you two do in Paris without me?" He thrust his hands in his pockets with a smirk. "I thought we were meeting in a graveyard?"

CHAPTER 16

PARIS, FRANCE
1502. hrs.

CALLA SLUMPED TO THE stairs. The Paris police inspector, a caramel-skinned, gray-eyed robust man in his forties, named Salvert, finished his interview with witnesses. He wore civilian clothes, possibly jostled into action after being informed of unusual criminals in his commune. He thanked Nash as they spoke in a quarantined area at Alexandre Dumas station. "*Merci, monsieur* Shields."

"*Pas de problème, Inspecteur Salvert*. Contact French ISTF if you need help with this, I suspect you might," Nash said. He joined Calla and Jack. "They're working for Mason."

"You mean the twins?" Calla said.

Nash nodded. "Actually, they're triplets."

"Come again," Jack said.

"They're triplets according to ISTF files that I've come across, but I would need to look into this further," Nash said.

Calla examined the Rajput warrior, having been heavily sedated by Nash's gun. "Do they know where Mason is?"

Nash shook his head. "Too easy. If I know Mason, he sent them, and they don't know it."

Calla drew the folded bundle from her bag and eyed the strip of cloth covered with ancient script. Nash watched as her fingers handled the paper and the microchip. "What's that there?"

"This is what we found at Champollion's tomb," she said.

Nash grinned. "So the trip there was not to pay homage to anyone we know." He took the items from her hands. "What's this microchip? It's old, like some of those first used at the NSA years ago."

"I'm not sure. We'd have to scan it. The cloth, however, is scripted with ancient writing. It's old. I need to date it," Calla said.

"Should we stop by the Louvre? You could ask one of their curators to help with dating materials?" Nash added.

"True. I could ask Madame Josseline Foss. We've worked on several projects together, but I have a better idea."

Jack shot from the stairs as police carried the assassins off on stretchers. "Man, you two speak a language of your own. How can you know such a simple cloth has that much historic significance?"

Nash and Calla shook their heads at him, amused. "The same way you can make sense of bytes."

The trio stepped out of the Metro station into the October afternoon. Calla hailed a taxi. A cream-colored Peugeot nosed to a halt as a chatty Parisian driver swung the door open for them.

"Marché aux Puces de St. Ouen, s'il vous plait," said Calla as she and Jack took the backseat and Nash sidled to the front.

"Where are we going?" Jack said.

"I asked him to take us to Paris's largest flea market."

"Don't tell me selling it is your best idea?" Jack said.

Calla managed a smiled as the taxi accelerated into Paris traffic. "No, I know a man there who looks at artifacts. I don't want the Louvre to question the origin of this cloth."

The taxi cruised through the nineteenth *arrondissement* and sidled into a busy street at the top of St. Puces market at Porte de Clignancourt. Assumed to be the biggest flea market in the world, the seven hectares grouped more than a dozen flea markets, a complex of thousands of open stalls and shops on the northern fringe of the city. What had begun as a scavenged, rag-and-bone shantytown on the fringes of the city limits, was systematized into bounded villages, some covered and others open-air, bordering streets and several boutiques of antique trade.

The market sold everything from relics to classic cameras, furniture to ceramics, new to vintage clothing, books, prints, and kitchenware. A gigantic garage sale in the eighteenth district of Paris with something for everyone. Designers, tourists and bargain hunters, motivated by the activity, flocked to the alleys of the Paris flea market to take in the latest trends.

The inquirers from London stepped out of the cab and proceeded toward the stalls until they reached the main street of the market, the rue des Rosiers. Turning left, vendors barraged them, bellowing their offerings. Calla watched as smaller merchants proved a greater desire to sell to them. They marched further inland to the antique sections of the 120-year-old market and stopped at an art shop–past the high-end Marché Paul Bert section and into a motorcar garage, the Marché Serpette, offering its top of the range interior design merchandise. Several eighteenth-century, imitation portraits were mounted at the entrance, with dated cellos and violins. A few Persian rugs hung suspended on the ornamental walls.

"This is it," Calla said.

They meandered into the interior of a classic furniture shop, and Calla greeted an attentive teenager who perched over an eighteenth-century desk toying with a smartphone.

"Est ce que monsieur Fabien Chastin est la?" Calla asked, wanting to know whether a man called Fabien Chastin was around.

"C'est mon grand-père," said the teenager who switched into English when she caught the puzzled frown on Jack's face. "That's my grandfather. He's in the back."

"May we see him?" Calla asked the spirited girl.

"Calla Cress!"

The deep-throated voice bellowed from behind the teenager coming from an older man of plump build with dark skin, dark eyes, and short, lank black hair. His full lips curled into a hospitable smile as he moved over toward Calla and kissed her on both cheeks. "What brings you here?"

"Fabien, it's been a long time." She glanced back at her companions. "Meet Jack, and this is Nash."

Fabien dipped his head. *"Enchanté.* Delighted."

Calla stepped toward them. "Guys, Fabien used to work at the British Museum in London specializing in 'Portable Antiquities and Treasure', an initiative to record archeological objects discovered by members of the public in England and Wales."

"Oh, and a job it was too. Here, I work for myself," Fabien said.

Calla glanced around the tiny space. "You have a remarkable shop. It allows you to finish your research. Listen, Fabien, I wonder whether you could help me with something." She hauled out the artifact she'd discovered earlier in the day and set it in Fabien's thick hands.

"What's this?" Fabien asked.

"I'm hoping you can date the cloth. And help me with some of the symbols. They are out of my preferred centuries."

Fabien ran his fingertips over the fading cloth. For the first time, Calla beheld the intricacies of the figured fabric as Fabien examined it. "This is incredible. I don't recognize the symbols. They're quite large, but it could be an old letter. Maybe a manuscript, or a legal document crafted on fabric."

Calla shot Jack and Nash a hopeful look, as Fabien took the artifact with him through the door behind the counter. "Come with me."

He took them around the back to his congested office–a tools and easel room filled to the brim with restoration equipment, arranged around a suction table for larger artwork. A work lamp and a myriad of heated spatulas, magnifying glasses, and radiocarbon dating equipment lay on the cramped table. The men watched as Fabien and Calla threw on latex gloves and laid the organic sample across the well-lit table.

The curators clipped a small section of the cloth and submerged it into nitrogen and waited for a reaction as they mixed the contents.

"This usually takes longer than you have time for, but I'll do my best," Fabien said.

"We'll take what we can get, Fabien."

An hour later, Fabien drew off his gloves. "Still early to determine, but here's my take. I think it's from the seventeenth century. It's an old type of figured fabric. Possibly first made of silk in Damascus. The fabric contains satin, and the surface's design flows in the opposite direction from that in the background."

"What does that tell us?" Nash asked.

"It was used mostly for furnishings, table linen, towels that sort of thing. It was rarely used as dress fabric and even less as a calligraphic fabric."

"Merci, Fabien," Calla said. "Then it is from Champollion's time. The Rosetta Stone was found in 1799. I initially thought the cloth could be from the time of the Rosetta Stone, around 196 BC, given its charred and delicate state."

"No, it is definitely seventeenth century. But I also think it's in pieces. A bigger part is missing. You only have about a square inch. Here, I'll keep a sample of it, just a few threads," he said, carefully clipping off a microscopic section. "And if I think of anything else I'll let you know."

"Thanks, Fabien."

"Not a problem. It's definitely European, similar to manuscript scrolls used then for more elaborate artwork around here."

"That's what I imagined, Fabien. Thanks for your confirmation," Calla said.

The three friends stepped out into the market's congested alleyway.

Jack rested a hand on her shoulder. "It confirms one thing. We're looking for two other pieces like this. Your mother must've really taken inspiration from the Hadrius Manuscript."

"Do you blame her?" Nash said. "It was a well-kept secret for thousands of years."

They traipsed to the pavement terrace of a nearby café and slid under a shaded canopy. The waiter took their orders.

"Just tea for me," Calla said.

Nash and Jack both ordered *café au lait*.

"I wonder if ISTF files..." began Calla.

She fired up her tablet and logged on to ISTF's network. Her eyes fell on her flashing inbox to an incoming e-mail from a sender she didn't recognize. "Wait, there's a message here."

Nash leaned over. "From?"

She opened the e-mail. "Mason. Mason Laskfell."

UNDISCLOSED LOCATION

Mason observed Calla's face, tight and grim. The message had been delivered with precision. Nothing could make her apprehend the technology with which he'd used to pry on her activities. His fingers flashed across his keyboard, firing off a second message.

I understand you seek information on your
mother, Nicole Cress.
Meet me at the Eiffel Tower in an hour to know what happened
to her.
This offer is only good for an hour.
Come alone.

Would she meet him? Calla fired off a reply:

Where are you?

He responded.

That's unimportant.
Don't bring your tailing companions.
You have one hour.

1511 hrs.

He was watching her. How? She wasn't sure. She drew in a sharp breath and turned to Nash, showing him her correspondence with the criminal. "Mason's watching us now. He must be here."

Nash took the tablet from her hands. "I can't let you go alone."

"But, I have to."

Jack motioned forward, his hands settling on the table. "Do you think it's really him? Let me see if I can trace it."

He took the machine in his hands and flashed a new message.

This is a setup. Mason.

Mason responded.

You've never seen a picture of her, have you?
There's a man who worked with her in Paris
and he has her picture on his wall.

Hop over to Galleries Chevalier in the fifth arrondissement. Give the owner your name. He'll give you a photograph.

Decide then whether you want to know.
If so, come to Trocadero, on the viewing
platform of the Eiffel Tower.

The clock is ticking!

"It's a trap," Nash said.

"What does he stand to gain from giving you this information, Cal?" Jack asked.

"I wouldn't do it, Cal. Find your mother on your terms. How does he know you're after your mother?" asked Nash.

Jack glanced her way. "Calla, don't go."

She peered outside. "I can handle Mason."

Nash hunched his shoulders and bent his mind to the futility of the argument.

The Galleries Chevalier stood in the heart of the fifth arrondissement, on the left bank of the River Seine, dominated by esteemed universities and institutes of higher education. Owned by a dealer of museum-quality, twentieth-century decorative arts, it specialized in French Art Nouveau, furniture and objects, lamps, and French cameo glass.

Calla moved past the well-displayed objects toward a man of hefty build, dressed smartly in a vividly colored suit. He arched behind a walnut-stained, French-style desk, with dovetailed drawers and a tooled leather top.

With eyes firmly on the stocky man, Calla approached the desk. *"Bonjour monsieur. Vous avez un message pour Cress."* She wanted to know whether he had a message for her.

His eyes pored over her for close to three seconds. Stroking his chin, he regarded her carefully. *"Vous êtes Calla Cress?"*

"Yes, I'm Calla Cress?"

"This way."

He directed her through the main gallery hall and toward the end of a row of original photographs mounted on pristine, ivory-colored walls. "That's her. I think she's what you're looking for."

Her eyes meandered to a wall-mounted, black-and-white photograph of a woman whom, had Calla not known better, would have thought was an image of her own face. The woman, like her, had a mane of dark locks cascading down her back. She sat at a café table, skimming out into the streets of

Paris. The tightness around the woman's lips suggested she was in deep contemplation.

"She looks like you," said the man, his French accent deep and melodic.

"I don't understand. How do you have this?" Calla said.

"The previous owner of the gallery acquired this picture, and his one stipulation was to leave it here. The picture was never to be sold out of the gallery."

"Who was the owner?"

"I believe it was... let me see. I may have more information in my files."

They plodded back toward the front desk, and the man reached behind the counter. He tossed an envelope on the desk. "That's a framed copy of the same image ordered just a few days ago. I'm not sure who sent the order."

She ripped it open, and her eyes caught sight of the woman. Nash, who'd stayed in the cab, skimmed into the gallery behind her. "Is that her?"

Jack stepped forward. "Except for the lines around her mouth, you're the spitting image of your mother, Cal."

Calla raised her eyes at them, sensing a sudden shiver of uncertainty. "It's the first time I've seen her."

Nash interrogated the man behind the bar in French. "Who gave this to you?"

"The replica was mailed here three hours ago by messenger."

Jack pursed his lips, his frame leaning against the wooden desk. "Mason knows where we are and what we are up to. We need to be careful."

Nash's fingers took Calla's arm with gentle authority. "Still sure you want to meet him?"

She shrugged her shoulders. "Mason's on the run. He has few places to hide. I can handle his manipulation."

Nash straightened his shoulders. "I know you can. But he's telepathic too. I'm still coming with you."

Jack jerked upright. "Me, too."

"No," she said. "Just me."

Nash peered into her eyes, his jaw tightening. "I'm sorry. I can't let you. I don't care what you say. I'm coming."

"Okay. Just keep your distance when we get to the Eiffel Tower."

She gave them a brief nod. "Let's go." Before moving to the door, she paused and zipped her head around to the gallery owner. "*Excusez moi monsieur,* who was the previous owner of this gallery?"

"Someone who let my uncle run it for him. A monsieur Stan Cress."

They hailed a cab and Calla instructed the driver. "*Champ de Mars Brassiere, avenue de la Bourdonnais, s'il vous plait.*"

"Why are we going to a café away from the Eiffel Tower's viewing point?" Nash asked.

"Mason will know if I'm with you. That way, you guys can stay out of sight. I'll stay in communication using this smartphone app. You'll know where I'm at all times."

"Fine," Jack said. "Make sure you activate it and switch it to global positioning locating and have the microphone on. That way, we'll be able to hear anything that goes on."

They headed out in a cab toward the *Champs de Mars,* a sizable, public green space and formerly the site of a French Revolution massacre, *the fusillade du Champ de Mars.* Huddled between the Eiffel Tower to the northwest, and the military academy, the École Militaire to the southeast, the cab gravitated past the grassy park, dropping the men off at the café before edging up toward Trocadero hill.

Calla marched onto the Palais de Chaillot Plaza, across from the Seine River and Eiffel Tower. With the time approaching four o'clock, the fourteen degrees Celsius felt like eight as a steady wind from the south caressed her face. Trocadero hill included more than just the plaza. It had two theaters, a restaurant, and several museums, yet its most visited area was the watching plaza across the Tower.

Calla glimpsed forward the length of the grounds leading to the Eiffel Tower as she rested her hands along the edge of the platform. The wallowing cacophony stemming from the array of fountains drowned the drones of the tourists, as they streamed up and down the renowned hill.

Jack and Nash observed from the Champs de Mars Brassiere, a crowded café on one corner of Avenue de la Bourdonnais, near enough to the Eiffel Tower to observe its environs, yet far enough to remain discreet.

Calla understood why Mason would pick such a place—public and perhaps the most tourist-infested place in the world. She glanced behind her at the busy street, looking to the Eiffel Tower. Where would Mason hide in this crowd? Would he be bold enough to show his face in public, even as he remained the most hunted fugitive in Europe?

She ambled past tourists from Japan and a group of students from the Sorbonne as they trailed behind an eager Art History professor.

Nash peered through a pair of mini binoculars. He'd not wired Calla. Mason would expect that, yet a panic button remained on her cell phone, and she could alert them if necessary. She just had to press nine, and the cell phone would alert not only Jack and Nash but ISTF.

Nash sent her a text message.

Any sign of him?

She replied.

None.

Calla slumped against the edge of the concrete border of the viewing platform, overhearing an argument between a Swedish couple on their honeymoon. Distracted by the squabble, a man zipped in front of her and dropped a smartphone in her hands.

"What the—" She called after him. "Hey!"

He charged past the crowds, disappearing past the fountain as Calla plowed behind him, bumping into startled tourists. Calla studied the phone in her hands. She noticed a text message. Thin, sleek, state-of-the-art, a flexible LCD screen flashed menacing words.

I TOLD YOU TO COME ALONE!

The communication disappeared, and the screen opened a live video feed on the smartphone's interface. Calla gasped, nearly dropping the phone in the fountain as her gaze shot toward the café. The image recorded Jack and Nash at a table.

Waiting for her.

She fumbled with her own cell, phone her fingers, searching for the panic button. The phone slipped out of her hand and splattered into the fountain. Armed only with the stranger's phone, a chill shivered through her senses as she caught his next message.

A countdown timer.

She set off at a run toward the café and glanced down at the remaining seconds.

9...8...7...6...

"No!"

5...4...3...

Does Mason have the...?

"Coward!" The October wind scoffed up her voice as it cut across her face. She took one more peek at the counter.

2...1...

Silence.

EIFFEL TOWER VIEWING POINT
PARIS, FRANCE
1615 hrs.

Stillness.

The plaza and the drones were muted by the heaviness in her chest. A flock of doves shot from her feet as she thrust in a dash toward the café. Her limbs trudged with heaviness as if they no longer belonged to her.

With her heart thrashing against her ribcage—boisterous and overpowering, the sounds around her diminished. Her thoughts were on one thing.

She waited.

No detonation came.

Foot-travelers hustled along the sidewalk, undeterred by the proceedings churning in her mind. Calla assailed down the stairs, jolting into confused pedestrians. The café seemed further than the ten meters between her and the front entrance. The faster she ran, the quicker her breath zapped out of her lungs.

Three ambulances zipped past her and screeched to a halt at the brasserie.

How?

Seven seconds passed before she crossed the street to the café's outdoor terrace. Smoke oozed out of every window of the café as men and women tore out of the space, coughing and shielding their nostrils with napkins and items of clothing.

There'd been no blast. *What is this thing?*

Curious passer-bys gasped at the panorama of tormented café-goers. Calla scrutinized the dust cloud. It wasn't fire smoke.

She shook with anger, her hands unclenched in the pockets of her slacks. It had been a chemical or biological explosion.

Subtle.

Deadly.

A silent bomb. They'd disarmed many at ISTF for the five global governments. Whoever it was, had access to ISTF or was igniting a careless, missile of terror.

Calla scurried through the front entrance, slithering past medical staff who attended to several coughing victims. Other authorities attempted to evacuate the brassiere through every exit.

"Non! Mademoiselle!"

She swiveled her head around. The commanding gendarme of the national police jostled her out and back onto the sidewalk. *"C'est très dangereux, mademoiselle!"*

I know it's dangerous! I need to find my friends. Her thoughts countered the rough policeman's words who'd warned her of danger. Calla stood outside, paralyzed by that sense of futility, unable to know whether Jack and Nash were hurt. Yet again, she'd jeopardized the lives of her friends.

Calla closed her eyes. Could I? Maybe?

She concentrated. What was it the doctor had said? The boy with x-ray vision? The same x-ray vision she possessed that penetrated solid surfaces. This came from inherited DNA that profited from genetic enhancement of her operative ancestry. Operatives, in their research and development labs, she'd been told by Vortigern, had engineered a special silicon chip. The chip had obtained energy, much like that contained in the carbonados they'd found while in search of the Hadrius Manuscript—a map encrypting the location of three hidden carbonados. The operatives had guarded the document for centuries until it disappeared during the Cold War.

The chip engineered by the carbonados, when implanted under her skin, realigned the molecules in the epidermis and her central nervous system. When her body sensed contact against gravity, the chip acted like an engine, reversing the natural physics of gravity. A side effect that gave her eyes x-ray vision.

She would try.

Though she'd not used the ability in the last six months, Calla shut her eyes and her mind before drawing in a deep breath. Her mind unlocked, releasing penetrating vision beyond human capacity. It made no difference whether her eyes were opened or closed.

Open, she could see through objects better, and those she could see, she could also hear. Her attention steered to the door, then past the few emergency staff, using the bar's countertop as a place to hold medication for the troubled victims. Is this how far Mason would go this time?

"There's no one else here," she heard a female paramedic say to the two paramedics who stood by one wall. "Everyone's been treated and accounted for, I think?"

The man in front of her replied in French. "Thank God, no one else was hurt. It was a good thing we were on standby and could react to the toxic gas."

"What was it?"

"Not sure, but possibly a very sophisticated bio-warfare program."

"Contact la Sûreté. The Department of Territorial Security will love this."

Calla squinted. Where are you guys?

She observed as one paramedic treated a blonde woman with oxygen. Smoke subsided in the café.

"Are there no more customers?" a policewoman asked the bartender in French.

"No, we weren't full. It's the post-lunch hour, and we only had a few tables going." The man paused. "Come to think of it, there were a couple of guys here at this table by the window. English speaking, but I'm not sure if they left."

"Has the bill been settled?" she asked the tall waiter.

He swung around the counter and checked his machine. "No. .. they may have evacuated when the smoke hit. It happened so fast."

He turned her focus to the table Jack and Nash had occupied only minutes earlier.

It had to be.

Nash's coat still hung over the back of the handcrafted chair. "No, maybe they left before the blast, then again, I'm not sure."

Calla shivered despite the warm coat she wore. She blinked twice. Had she not known the way he liked to trend dark colors over natural tones and his broad shoulders, allowing a strong, masculine form, it easily could've been anyone else's coat.

No! Not Nash!

A brief shiver rippled through her. Trembling with fury at what Mason was capable of, her vision broke through a wall divider where two telephone cabins stood behind an Internet terminal. Her eyes settled on the masses on the floor. There next to Nash, Jack's head faced the concrete wall, with his back to her.

No oxygen had gotten to them.

No treatment.

No paramedics.

CHAPTER 17

MIRABELLA, SPAIN
1620 hrs.

"AND?" MASON STUDIED the confident woman.

"Yes—"

"What proof do you have?"

She slid a tablet broadcasting news from Paris on the antique table.

"That doesn't tell me anything. Get out!"

Mason fumbled with the video software on his screen. The signal disappeared. Shields had to be eliminated. With him out of the way, the easier it would be to get to Cress and eventually her mother. The video stalled, unable to bring up a decent image. He longed for the days where he could access his own equipment and not rely on amateurs. Shields was holding on to a detail no one was supposed to know. That arrangement he'd made. That blasted NSA file. Had he not been on the run, getting to Shields' NSA, employment file would have been simple. That file would die with him. That deal would die too.

He longed to get within ten feet of the marine. It would

make reading his mind easier. Shields' mind would give him access to the secrets of the Cresses. Somehow, that girl had him in her alluring grasp. He would expunge them. Shields and that tagalong Kleve.

He reached for his scotch only to find the chilled glass empty. Mason called to Mrs. Hawke as she set about cleaning his pistol. "Get me a real drink around here!"

BRASSERIE CHAMPS DE MARS,
PARIS, FRANCE
1712 hrs.

Nash raised his head. His stomach heaved as he staggered up and tried to grasp the radiator above him for support. His eyes fell to his feet, where Jack moved in slow movements, barely able to sit.

A shaft of pain swept through his temples. Had he fallen? Been shot? Hit his head? He could not recall what had happened until he saw the half-burned photograph on the floor. Cracked glass from Calla's picture frame had sliced through his hand. Numb to the pain, he pulled out thin splinters and rapidly recalled his ordeal.

Calla had left the framed photograph of her mother with him. He'd laid it on the table until he'd noted a sluggish, gas cloud shooting from one corner of the sliver frame. His nostrils were used to a variety of lethal and incapacitating biological agents. He'd learned about several during his military training and once led several soldiers out of a building in the Ghouta area of Damascus infected with chemical agents. This was a nerve agent that would attack the nervous system and affect muscle control, vision, heart, and lung functions. He'd prepared for the worst, yet he'd only thought of the people enjoying their café afternoon.

A stern fog cloud gushed into the room, stemming from a burning corner of the picture. With little reaction time, Nash had seized the photograph, covered his nostrils with a cloth napkin, and bustled for the nearest exit. The semipermeable fabric allowed minimal inhalation, yet he had to remove the toxins from the café where there was little air movement to dissipate the gas. He had one thought.

Deadly.

Following his intent, Jack pursued. Nash located an exit by the phone booths in the back. He tore through the door, darted to three garbage containers, and stashed the exuding biological agent in the large cans. A sensation of intense sickness and desolation swept over him as he returned to the door. He'd barely had time to react to Jack's heaving frame when nausea crawled to his throat and knocked him out unconscious.

Nash checked for residue glass-splinters in his hand. Certain that no toxins remained, he slumped to Jack's side.

Jack gasped. Next to him, a female paramedic held an oxygen mask to his nostrils. "Monsieur," she said in French, turning her attention to Nash. "Do you need this?"

Nash's hand slid to his temple and rubbed the side where he'd hit his head. "*Non, Merci*. I'll live."

The woman rose with an insistent glare in her face and reached for an icepack from her medical bag. Nash placed the frigid compress over the small bruise on his forehead and turned when he heard her voice.

"*Ce sont mes amis. On est venu ensemble,*" he heard the voice say.

Calla.

She was telling them they were together, and her upper English, unyielding, French-accented tone told him; she would get her way.

Thank God, she's okay.

Calla burst to his side, her eyes moving to Jack's recovering frame. Nash took her hand and sensed her pulse beat in her wrist. "Cal? Did Mason come?"

Calla shook her head slowly and turned to Jack. The woman had removed the gas mask. "Jack? I'm so sorry," she said, the words barely escaping her throat. "Could this day get any worse?"

Nash drew closer, and Calla set a soft hand over his bruise. "Ouch."

Her eyes registered horror. "Nash, I'm so sorry."

"I'm fine. It's just a graze, like the one you gave me at Denver airport when we first met."

Calla managed a weak smile. "I can't keep doing this to you guys. I lost you once. It broke my heart, my spirit, my mind. Nash, I can't. We have to stop pursuing this nonsense. .."

Nash took her in his arms. "It's not nonsense, Calla. It's your life and that of many others. We've come this far and must see it to the end."

The emergency woman asked if Calla needed medical attention, sensing her borderline hyperventilation. Jack turned on his side and willed himself to stand. "Cal, Nash is right. If we stop now, then everything we fought for was in vain."

Calla stared at him through agonized eyes. "Jack, I couldn't live with myself if I lost either you or Nash. You two are the best friends I've ever known. I can't go through another episode of not knowing if Mason's gonna come for me or you first."

. . .

They moved outside the café. The commotion had subsided, except for one ambulance and a handful of eager spectators, oblivious to the near brink, act of war Mason had begun.

Nash took Calla's hand. "Let's go for a walk." He patted Jack on the shoulder. "Hey, here's an address." He found the location on his cell phone. "Do you mind going up to this place? It's government-run. NSA used to call it the home away from home. It's known as the Dalbret. There's a man there who runs the private hotel and club. You won't find it in any guidebook. From the outside, it looks like a private house, so don't be fooled. If we need to stay off the radar, Dalbret will get it done."

"Smooth, Nash. One of your NSA friends, I imagine?"

Nash threw him a cocky grin. "I never reveal my sources. Give them my name. Let's stay there tonight and decide where we go from here."

Jack nodded. "Where are you guys off to?"

Nash shot Calla a quick glance. "There's some training I omitted—one more lesson. We'll meet you for dinner at the hotel. Dalbret will know the procedure. Thanks, Jack."

Calla and Nash headed to the avenue lining the river and soon found themselves on the Ponts des Arts, a pedestrian bridge in Paris that crossed the Seine. The evening was setting in slowly. They walked arm in arm in silence. Nash couldn't think of anyone he would bring to Paris but the woman beside him. He held her hand as they strolled along the southern bank, the *Rive Gauche*. They crossed graceful gardens, palaces, intimate parks, a flower market, and a congested bookshop. Only when they passed a street painter did they speak.

"Cal, let's breathe for a moment. I don't want to discuss what we do with Mason tonight. He thinks I'm dead and that you're alone somewhere, possibly dead too. We can do that tomorrow. I want you to breathe."

Calla found the phone the man had given her and threw it in the river.

"What was that?" Nash said.

"A bad memory."

Nash saw the fatigue in her eyes. The edginess he'd known when he met her had returned. He hated to see her like this. The months they'd spent alone in Almont had been his best. For the first time in his life, he saw a future. *Damn it!* Perhaps, someone he could settle down with. Here she was, battled, and her brow creased with worry.

He held her trembling fingers and kissed them. "Beautiful, I know you want to give up. I know you feel afraid. But you don't have to be. You're much stronger emotionally and mentally than any of the people who are after you."

Calla watched him through pained eyes.

"You can do it. You can rid society of people like Mason. Don't always be hung up on how you'll do it. You have a gift that many would kill for," Nash said. "In fact, that's all he's doing. Believe in yourself. For whatever reason, someone had the confidence to give you a well-loaded gift, because they knew you could do it. I want to help you."

He placed his jacket over her shoulders. "Is that better?"

They hopped into a Parisian cab and cruised down a straight line from l'Assemblée Nationale, navigating through Neuilly before nosing into La Defense—Europe's largest, custom-built, business district, bordering the outskirts of Paris.

Calla stepped out of the cab and paid the driver before hurling her gaze up the Grand Arche de La Defense. As the cab sped away, she glanced over at Nash. "What are we doing in front of this twentieth-century version of the Arc de Triomphe—Paris's own symbol of victory?"

"After your little escapade at the Shard in London, I figured you'd like an architectural tour of Paris." He reached for her hand. "Come on. It's award-winning, architectural design."

She tossed him a skeptical look. "Are we here to admire architecture? I thought you said something about training?"

"I did. Let's go."

LA DÉFENSE, PARIS
1921 hrs.

Calla studied the monument, constructed to honor humanity and humanitarian ideals rather than military victories. Shaped like a cube, the Grande Arche de la Défense projected its elegance on to a three-dimensional world, with its emphasized, concrete frame formed with glass and Italian Carrara marble. The desolate concrete landscape at the western end of Paris had needed an iconic centerpiece. Former French President, François Mitterrand's answer had been the Grand Arche, positioned at the end of the *parvis,* a central, pedestrianized plateau shaping La Défense's main boulevard. Twice the height of the Arc de Triomphe, it stood in a straight line, six kilometers to the center of Paris, at the height of 361 feet.

The Arche was at the end of a line of architectural testaments that ran through Paris, known as the *Axe historique.* Nash smirked at her admiration of the building. "Like it? Did you know the Grand Arche forms a secondary line with the Eiffel Tower and the Tour Montparnasse, the two tallest buildings in the French capital?"

Calla armed herself with a twinge of curiosity and followed Nash. "If I didn't, I now do. All right, lead the way."

They traipsed through the entrance. Nash was met by a tall, black-suited man with cream skin, light-brown eyes, and frizzy, black hair. The man handed Nash a pass with no words exchanged. Several minutes later, Calla stood frozen in a stunned tableau, on the roof of Paris, skimming the 'triumphal way'. As if intentionally, the sunset permitted startling crimson and velvet views all the way to the Louvre. Her eyes veered toward the Eiffel Tower in the distance, before settling on the sparkling river Seine as a calm breeze grazed her face. She stood before Nash completely submissive. "You certainly have friends in high places, Nash."

He balanced on the edge of the concrete structure, where they hovered on the ridge, the equivalent of the second floor of the Eiffel Tower. They'd taken the sky elevator to the three-story rooftop, arranged around four courtyards. A roof closed to the public and only accessed via elevators in the north and south walls. Admissible only to authorized personnel, Nash had called in a favor, and Calla smiled in gratitude. The view had the serenity and calm her mind needed at the moment.

Without forewarning, Nash gently removed a calla lily from his pocket, having kept the flower's delicate form intact, despite the ordeal it had suffered in his black jacket. "I promised you a real date months ago. A small reminder that I haven't forgotten."

"Hm. .. one flower?"

"A special one that stands for magnificence and beauty. Both of which you have."

Calla stood motionless, her cheeks rouged as she smiled and took the trumpet-shaped lily, native to Lesotho and Swaziland in Southern Africa, and after which she'd been named. "That's thoughtful, Nash. Thanks."

"All right, are you ready for your last piece of training?"

"Don't you think I'm ready?"

"Oh, you're ready physically. We need to work on mentally."

"What do you mean?"

Without answering, Nash leaped onto the roof border, balanced his lean frame on it, and reached for her hand. "Up here."

"Nash, are you mental?"

He threw her a confident smirk. "Come on. You want that kiss, I promised. No date is complete without one," he said. "But you're gonna have to come up here and get it."

Her bearing rigid and questioning, Calla placed the flower behind her ear, her pulse racing. Nash was incredibly handsome, and a shiver of attraction shot through her. She reached for his hand and mounted next to him onto the apex of the building. With feet firmly planted, Calla balanced her body smoothly as the diamond-lit city sparkled beneath her. Nash stood so close she could feel the heat from his body. His expression held a note of playfulness as he pulled her to him, not once losing her gaze until his nose caressed hers. "That wasn't so hard, was it?"

She leaned in, questioning his intent as the hum of the city nightlife faded in her ears. Nash glanced down and slithered his feet away from the edge until all that held him were her loose hand and his firm feet, only balanced by the front part of his boots. He eased his hand slowly out of hers, his face carefully neutral. "The calla flower symbolizes rebirth, according to some historians. It's time we renew your mind."

A quizzical look crossed her face. "Rebirth. .. renew what?"

"Your fear of taking chances—"

With that, he glimpsed down at the hundred-and-ten-meter drop and caught her eye again. "I'm taking a chance on you, beautiful. Will you take one on me?"

Without warning, he loosened his hold of her and leaped backward, plummeting headfirst to the ground.

Calla's heart froze, and with instinct kicking in, she plunged her body at ninety-degrees in a skydive after him, her eyes fixed on Nash's dropping frame. Within a fraction of a second, her feet veered to the glass wall of the building and slammed against the glass. She bent her knees and forced her legs to slide down the smooth wall at the speed of a discharged missile.

Not once did her eyes leave Nash's free-falling body. As gravity lost its power over her operative genes, she sliced through air at twice the speed of gravitational pull, until her flashing frame matched Nash's falling speed. Blasting past him by a few feet, with no time to reflect, she swiveled at a breadth of a second, faced heavenward, and willed her feet to fasten to the façade in Nash's falling path—a meter above the plaza floor.

Nash's weight crashed onto her, yet her body remained fixed against the side of the wall as she caught him with a circle grip. Neither his weight nor hers, made her lose her footing at the flat angle. Her heart pounded faster than she could control. For several seconds, she held him tightly, as if unsure they'd made it to safety.

Perched horizontally on the south side of the building away from prying eyes, Calla understood. She took in a deep breath as she realized the safe height at which they were suspended.

Stretched over her, Nash raised his head. "I'm sure glad I calculated your speed accurately. You were one zipping bullet!"

Calla's eyebrows drew together. "Hm. .. is this your idea of a joke, soldier?"

"I knew you had it in you."

In one instant, she released her feet off the structural wall, and they landed in a mass on the concrete. Nash rolled to one side, in uncontrollable laughter.

"Oh, you think it's funny?" she said.

"You're better than I thought. What I would do with your skills!"

The contagious laugh caught Calla's lips, and for several moments they convulsed in hysterics on the frigid ground."

"I wanna do that again," Nash said.

"Don't you dare."

"Thanks, beautiful. You saved my life."

"Nash, you're crazy. You could have been killed!" Her heart pounded avidly in her ears." What if I—"

"You wouldn't. Besides, I had an escape plan." He removed his jacket and tugged at the back. "A small, ISTF parachute. I was right, you have a significant depth of accuracy and speed. I wanted to prove it to you. Doesn't it feel better?"

"Better? You mean me having a heart attack, sliding down a bloody French monument just to save your back end!"

"Don't be sore, gorgeous. Training is over."

"You call that training?"

Nash grinned as he rolled to his side, facing her. "One, you took a chance on me, not knowing if you'd survive. Two, you conquered your fear of your abilities." He pushed a loose lock from her face. "Calla, embrace your strengths, don't fear them, and don't you dare give up as you did earlier today."

His face lit with malicious amusement. "Belief is half the fight. That's how you win. Every soldier knows that, and if they don't, they should. Any fight or struggle is first won in the mind before it's won on the battlefield. That's what I meant by rebirth."

He set a tame index finger on her forehead. "If I can believe in your abilities like now, so can you. You have to do everything with intent, not by default. Even when it comes to. .. to *us*."

She nodded slowly, her long, dark hair hung loosely over her shoulders as her eyes glistened under the Arche's evening lights.

They rose and strolled to the La Defense fountain, nestled within the ultramodern kingdom of concrete, steel, and glass. Its jet springs shot up, radiated with bright mottled lights. Nash and Calla let their feet hang over the fountain's edge. The shooting waters glistened before them as darkness set over Paris, and a mild breeze teased through her hair. Calla's hand crawled to grip Nash's warm fingers as he leaned back. "What would I do without you?"

He watched her carefully as an unwelcome blush stole to her face. "No Cal, what would I do without you? I think I'd stop breathing."

2003 hrs.

Nash found satisfaction in studying Calla's profile. His hand lightly traced a path over her skin. Her eyes confronted him quietly as he clasped his arms around her waist, and his mouth smiled against her lips. With a soft sigh, he settled a kiss on her lips." She edged into him.

Nash's pulse quickened. Calla was extremely unaware of her enigmatic beauty and had stolen everything in him long ago. He couldn't explain what it was. The emerald mystery in her eyes, the appetite for justice in her heart or was it that ebony hair that cascaded over her back like the dark nights of Arabia. He gently stroked her mane and drew back. "I don't know whether I've ever told you—"

"I know, Nash. You are the one thing in my life I'm sure about, and the only one I'd return love to."

He smiled. She'd read his mind.

Calla grazed a hand on his clean-shaven jaw and stroked the little wound above his eye. "How could I not?"

He clasped her hand as it stroked his face and set a warm kiss in her palm. "Then you know the only way you and I will make it through. .. depends on two things."

She let out a quick laugh. "Does everything come in twos with you? What two things?"

"Finding your mother and. .. kicking some serious donkey hide.. . together."

She chuckled. "Yes, commander."

He shot up. "Let's go find Jack and bolt out of sight. Dalbret will make sure we stay in and leave Paris undetected."

They walked to Dalbret's—hidden in Paris's Latin Quarter. They took close to an hour as they navigated through Paris's tight and entangled streets, strewn with historically accurate details. When they meandered into the secret lobby, Dalbret met them, checked his three guests into the state-of-the-art suites and alerted them to a complimentary dinner in the private basement club.

Calla left Nash and Jack as she took leave to her suite to change. Later, the three friends dined in one of Paris's most secret clubs, complimented with upscale cuisine and a romping dance club, graced by global undercover agents and prominent individuals on government protection programs. By invitation only, clients were rich enough to demand it and stay off the globe's radar. Hours later, nearing midnight, Nash walked Calla to her door. "Jack's already settled in for the night. I didn't see him leave the club. He'll meet us at breakfast. He's still battling your anagram. He hates any puzzle to defeat him," Nash said. "The man never sleeps."

"That's why he's good," she said.

Outside her suite, Nash squeezed her hand. "Get some rest. Dalbret put me in a room opposite yours."

"Hey?"

His eyes glistened under the hallway lights, and her mouth curled at the corners. "What other nocturnal tricks do you know?" she said.

He tossed her an amused smirk.

She reached for his shirt collar and pulled him toward her. "I have training for you too."

Nash stared at her, his eyes loving her. A shudder ran through her as he backed her against her suite door. Her strapless back felt cool against the door, contradicting the heat rising in her. Nash's nearness had always puzzled her, but tonight she would fight it no more. His closeness was a drug, lulling her to euphoria. She wanted him more than anything she could think of and settled back, enjoying the warmth of his arms around her. Their lips touched, and a satisfying flutter flowed through her skin. Nash tasted of a perfect combination of longing and possession, firm yet tender.

He lifted his head slightly and glared into her eyes, stroking her hair. "Calla, I love you."

She traced her fingers over his eyes and couldn't miss the musky scent of him as he pressed her close. "I know. I've known for a long time."

His breath fanned her face. "I've always loved you."

In one forward motion, he unlocked the door to her suite with her security key and led her by the hand. He shut it behind him.

"My place it is," she said, smiling.

In the darkness, he drew her to him. Calla welcomed his kisses, his gentle touch in her hair, her back, his strong arms around her, and his persuasive body against hers. Nash pulled away and removed his jacket, then his shirt. She'd seen his upper body countless times, from his sharply shaped shoulders to his well-proportioned torso and defined biceps. She let her fingers glide along the crests of the toned muscles. Her breath was shallow, her senses drugged. She reached for his arm, this time pulling him her way until she felt the edge of the bed against her calves. His kisses had always been deep and with intent, but tonight his hands and mouth took command and explored places she'd never let him. The magic of his sensitive hands overrode her inhibitions as she sensed the thundering of his heart pounding against her chest.

She smiled, staring into his deep gray eyes, barely able to breathe.

Nash eased her backward into the silk cushions of the luxurious satin, his hands moving with slow inevitability.

Calla relaxed and sighed deeply. She sank into his cushioning embrace and covered his face and neck with soft kisses. Why had she pushed him away for years? He loved her. Always had.

He took her hands, encouraging them to explore. She was his tonight—the only place she'd needed to be. Calla heard a soft murmur of gratification as sincere hands explored the hollows of her back. She felt his fingers on her elbow, then an arm was around her shoulders, easing her out of the silk tank top she'd worn to the club. The delicate straps crisscrossing over the open back loosened. Soon nothing stood between them. Months of restrained attraction morphed into sensual, slow lovemaking. She welcomed the wildly masculine sensation of his passion until their bodies came together with deep, sensual commitment. Soon a quiver pulsed through her veins. She took in every moment, every heartbeat until she heard him breathe with gratification.

Calla raised her head. "I bet you couldn't do that again."

His eyes smiled at her. "Wanna bet?"

Her body vibrated with new life a second time, and when it

came to a third, she collapsed in his arms and drifted into a deep, exhausted sleep.

Two hours later, Nash was awakened by his phone beeping. He turned it off and settled on his elbow. His eyes fell on Calla's resting frame as she slept beside him. She reclined on her front. Her glossy mane cloaked part of her back, revealing a soft shoulder. With her breathing soft and rhythmic, he stroked her head. Perhaps it was in sleep, she knew no conflict.

He had to protect her. To rid her of struggle. He feared for her life. Mason had raked in some resilient operative attempts. *I will let nothing happen to you.*

He thought of his cache, on the memory stick he'd rescued from the Embassy, the contents firmly ingrained in his head. Mason had infuriated him too often and had a deadly disadvantage despite his overall muscle and intellect.

And Mason knew, Nash knew his little secret. The same handicap that could destroy Calla—her will.

His eyes reverted to the beeping. That was the third time that untraceable number had found his phone. It always hung up when he reached for it and had called him one other time in the last few hours. He had no idea who it was and where it came from, a signal he failed to locate even with NSA and ISTF resources within reach. Nash dismissed it for several seconds, but could no longer ignore the intrusion.

He reached for the cell phone. This time, an encrypted text message stared back at him. Nash decoded it using a sophisticated NSA encryption code and read the message.

Nash,
I need to talk to you!
Nicole Cress

—

DALBERT PRIVATE GOVERNMENT HOTEL
0821 hrs.

Nash sipped his black coffee and stared into his cup. The hotel breakfast room, ideally hidden in a vaulted cellar, stood away from prying pedestrians and secure from circuit television cameras. He'd chosen this hotel specifically because it belonged to a French family related to Masher and had found a prestigious clientele in secret service circles. Masher's sister could be trusted, who ran the business with her French husband, Dalbert.

Nestled between the Latin Quarter and St. Germain des Près, the hotel once was a residence dating from the end of the seventeenth century. In the sixth arrondissement of Paris, near numerous monuments and museums, its stone walls reminded Nash of a monastery. Rumor had spread that Franciscan monks once made their home in the historic thoroughfare of the Latin Quarter.

He had slipped downstairs, alerting Calla and Jack to join him when they were ready. His phone rang—a US number.

"Hello?"

"Nash?"

"Mom."

"Why haven't you called? I just heard from your lawyer about your house. What happened?"

Nash tugged at his collar. His tone softened at the woman he'd always wanted to protect from his overbearing father, governor of the Federal Reserve System. A woman, who for years, was married to an inaccessible man, emotionally and physically. Somehow, despite his travels, Nash tried to make time for her. Divorced, his mother lived off a significant alimony check in Cherry Creek, Denver's most admired neighborhood.

He tuned into his mother's quiet, insistent voice. "I'm okay. No one was hurt."

"Where are you?"

"Paris."

"When do you get home? Will you be home for Thanksgiving?"

"Perhaps. I'm on assignment."

"All right. Could you try? Your brother will be here, and he needs you."

Nash's jaw tightened, betraying a deep frustration stemming from a brother, a cousin actually, and one of the closest relatives Nash had. He was six years his junior and lived in Rome. The man couldn't keep a job, although he was a trained lawyer, yet ironically couldn't stay out of trouble with international law enforcement. How often had Nash bailed him out?

"I'll try to make it."

"What's holding you?" A silence arrested the line, and she cleared her throat. "It's her. The exquisite British girl. Isn't it? Did she agree to what you asked?"

"I need to go. I'll call you when the assignment's done."

"Be careful, Nash."

"I will."

"I know you are good in the field. I meant, with your heart."

Nash hung up the phone, his eyes depressing as he recollected a conversation he'd exchanged with Calla in Colorado. *Will she ever change her mind?*

What was she so afraid of? How he hoped Calla would meet him halfway and not be so terrified to repeat the disastrous history of her parents.

As he set the phone on the breakfast table, his eyes caught

Calla coming down the narrow stairs to join him. How striking she looked that morning?

Calla meandered into the café, hair loose, swinging an inch or two above her petite waist. Tight jeans hung below a low V-neck sweater, and she strutted in elegant hunting boots. She wore nothing that purposefully accentuated her femininity, but somehow, she always came off more attractive to him and extremely sensual, no matter what she wore.

Calla slipped into the seat opposite him and flashed him a flirtatious smile. He took her hand in his, recalling the unforgettable day they had had yesterday.

"Sleep well?" Nash said.

She nodded. "Mm...like a box turtle in hibernation."

Nash's shoulders dropped as he watched her. He waited until she ordered a cup of Ceylon tea and a fruit salad before saying what had been on his mind all morning. "I'm sorry about last night."

Calla frowned. "Sorry? About what?"

"I was not thinking right and was not myself—"

"I don't understand, Nash. We had a fabulous time—"

"That's not what I mean. Listen, I know what we talked about in Colorado may not be important to you, but it is to me, Calla."

She sighed. "Nash, why is it so important. Can't we just have what we have, each other? Can't you make an exception?"

His hand tightened around hers. "Cal, there'll never be anyone for me, just you. I've always known that and I accept it, but—"

"Nash, I don't think I can be that person. I'm not cut out for that sort of thing. I can't do what you ask. I've always known that. It's who I am. We talked about this in Almont, please Nash. Why bring it up now?"

"Cal, don't let the bad examples you had around you

influence your decisions. We all have things our parents did that we want to change in us. We can rise above their mess."

"You're asking me to change who I am, Nash." Her voice was gentle. "My parents left me as a baby at a questionable orphanage and never looked back. I'd hate to repeat that? What about my job at the Museum? ISTF? The operatives?"

The words hit him harder than she'd probably meant. The last thing he wanted was for her to change who she was for him. He didn't need the answer now, just a hint at the likelihood. "I'm sorry, Calla. It's okay." He kissed her hand and set it down gently on the table. "I accept all of who you are. I'd rather have that than nothing. Let's not talk about it anymore."

She leaned forward, gazing at him for several seconds. "You sure *you* don't want to change your mind?"

Before he could answer, he saw Jack approach the table.

"Morning," Nash said.

Jack glanced from one face to another. "What'd I miss?"

Calla shook her head, an embarrassed look glistening in her gaze as Jack shrugged his shoulders and dipped into a seat. "I've something here. I did some research last night—"

Nash quickly stole a glimpse at Calla, whose attention had shifted to Jack's conversation. It was then he knew she would never see things his way. Her mind was set on leaving everything as it was.

Jack turned to Nash and fired up his tablet. "Nash, have you ever seen anything like this? I've run the anagram through a computer program at ISTF. We may have some luck."

"Let's see."

"Okay, Calla. Remember when your father said that he thinks the anagrams are names of people who worked with your mother or had close links with her, like Danielle?"

Calla's eyes lit. "Yeah?"

"Look here. The anagram for A-W-A-I-T E-M-B-A-N-K- O-

A-T has unscrambled a few possibilities, and this name T-A-M-I-K-O W-A-T-A-N-A-B-E is a very convincing option."

Nash's eyebrows knit. "There must be at least a thousand people with that name."

"Exactly. I've screened the names through ISTF and British Secret Services files and have narrowed it to four people."

Calla leaned forward. "Who do you have?"

"One is a stage name for a Japanese movie star, whom MI6 surveyed for years thinking he was aiding terrorism. The second is a real estate businessman from California who acted on behalf of the CIA for covert Asian missions during the Cold War, namely, in Tokyo and Hong Kong. The third is on FBI's and Interpol's watch list for smuggling drugs from Indonesia into the European Union and the US." Jack scrolled down his list. "And the last owns a shop in Tokyo."

"Who do we pick?" Calla said.

"Well, that's just the thing," Jack said. "The first three all would be around your mother's age. The shop attendant is the odd one and has a huge appetite for gadgets and electronics. My money is on him. He's barely a day older than seventeen, though."

"Why would he be on any government's watch list?" Nash asked.

"Because he knows someone, *and* possibly something that someone doesn't want him to know. ISTF monitor all kinds of suspects," Calla said as she drew out her mother's printout and the translation she'd inscribed. "We want the teenager."

"Because?" asked Nash.

"It's a hunch. ISTF would not have him on file if he were not a lead," she said. "Jack, we must be rubbing off on you. Great work."

"That boy better have an interesting alias," Nash said. "He wasn't even born when your mother disappeared."

CHAPTER 18

AKIHABARA ELECTRIC TOWN
TOKYO, JAPAN
1630 hrs.

CALLA'S FINGERS RAN along the display of electronic gadgets exhibited outside of a disorderly stall in Akihabara. Tokyo's largest congregation of obsessively interested masses flocked to the shopping area that accumulated hi-tech, electronic appliances, and devices from across the globe.

The bargain-hunting area in the Chiyoda district of Tokyo had acquired its nickname—*autumn leaf field*—shortly after the Second World War. Back then, even as a center for household electronic goods and the postwar black market hot spot, to Calla, there was no difference to what she witnessed in the contemporary setting. Anime and manga enthusiasts crawled the congested alleys sampling the range of merchandise looking for 'newer' or '*newest*'. Crowds, ravenous to buy, scoured the unclassifiable collection of stock. Eccentric and rare electronic items had found a niche, somewhere in the intriguing cultural center.

Her mind could not fathom how such cutting-edge electronic gadgets, superior to any found in ordinary stores in London, were on the market for sale like 'bric-a-brac' in a flea market. An aroma of spicy, *gyudon* beef-and-onion bowls crept past her nose as she proceeded past a chain restaurant. The temperature, mild on the skin hovered at 45°F, and earlier rain had reduced visibility by twenty percent. Several young people ambled past them, kitted out in die-hard, manga fan culture.

"This is Tamiko's shop. It's the address listed at ISTF," said Nash picking up a high-class electronic action camera, half the size of his palm.

Grateful for the men's dedication, Calla scrutinized the congested shopfront. "Nash? You think that'll replace the one you lost in Almont."

"Let's see if he's here," Nash said, grinning.

"Tamiko Watanabe is, no surprises here," said Jack, "Tamiko Watanabe junior. ISTF records him because they don't know where his father is."

"Let me guess," said Nash. "His father was the one who worked with Calla's mother."

Calla pursed her lips. "But does junior *know* that?"

Jack shrugged his shoulders. "He may know where his father is. That'd be a start. But with regards to knowing about his father's undercover past, well, let's find out."

Nash glanced behind him.

"What is it?" Calla asked.

"We're being followed."

"By whom?" Jack said.

"Not sure yet. My guess is Kane, Ridge, or Sage."

"What are you talking about, Nash?" Calla said.

Nash pulled the two deep into Tamiko's tiny, electronic shop. "Our friends from Paris and their *sister*."

Calla found her back edged against a row of finely exhibited microcomputers. No more than two meters wide, the three could hardly move along the shop without ramming into some display. Tamiko, a young man looking to be in his twenties rather than a teenager, glanced from his computer game, cramped behind a wall of micro-cameras. His solemn comportment, true to anime culture and hidden among his goods, revealed hooded, tinted grass-green eyes and thick bleached hair of medium-length. His attire, simple and street-like, revealed plenty of orange and black.

"Listen," Nash said, lowering his voice. "I didn't have a chance to tell you this on the flight over, while I was researching. Kane, Ridge, and Sage are triplets who volunteered for ISTF training programs when they were close to seventeen. They were orphans that had been in Britain's social welfare system, handed from one foster home to the next when Mason came calling. Two of them we've already met."

"You mean the assassins in Paris?" Jack said.

"And Santorini, Calla. They're not ordinary assassins. They are human-hybrid soldiers," Nash said.

"No way," Calla said as she tilted her head and paused. "What does that mean?"

"From the reports, the triplets were found mysteriously as babies in a Roma Gypsy camp. The acting parents claimed they found them on their doorstep. Social services took them under their wing and later sent them to foster homes. Soon they started displaying really odd behavior," Nash said.

Jack's brow wrinkled with puzzlement. "Like what?"

"Like immunity to pain and emotion. They were enhanced and, by age four, were able to lift weights weighing nearly ten pounds, out to their sides. That's when they got on the radars of researchers who began a series of tests on them."

Calla rubbed the back of her neck, thinking of her own abnormal capabilities. "Did the researchers find anything?"

Nash's eyes communicated he understood her concern.

"Initially, and this is where the research ended, they recorded that it could have been the result of a mutated gene intended to restrict the production of myostatin that limits the growth of muscles. Since they couldn't find the parents, they could not compare the DNA structures and whether relatives had mutated copies of DNA as well. The government later protected them by changing their names and raising them under the social care system in the UK until they were sixteen."

"So how did they come on Mason's radar?" Jack said.

Nash drew in a sharp breath. "I think he further bioengineered them into soldier assassins. The ultimate killing machines. That's why I doubt they're still with French police."

"Who knew about this?" Jack asked.

"It was classified. ISTF proposed to use a similar technique to Spartan soldiers. These triplets have endured a vigorous regime involving incessant physical violence, severe cold, and lack of sleep."

A chill ran down Calla's skin. "You are serious, Nash?"

"Yes. When I joined ISTF, I was given an induction into all R&D projects, even the classified ones. Mason trusted me then to be one of his recruits. There was this one classified project that had been shut down by all five governments, and I was surprised to see it surface on Mason's accounts when we arrested him."

"The triplets," Calla said.

Nash nodded. "It started out as a training exercise to transform them as spies and agents with new skills, but Mason wanted more. He thought more could be achieved physically with them, so he reopened the project under another name."

"Where did he hide this information?"

"In India. He hid the project in Rupert Kumar's global

empire of corporations and specifically in his R&D labs. The era of a flawless robotic killing machine may be decades away, but scientifically, ISTF has experienced a breakthrough with the next best thing, the creation of human eliminators. The triplets sense minor pain, less terror, and less exhaustion than 'non-improved' soldiers."

"So, no one ever discovered where they came from?" Calla said.

Nash leaned away slightly. "I don't know how to tell this to you guys, but it is one of the fastest-growing areas of science. The Pentagon alone spends close to $400 million a year investigating ways to enhance human fighters. My take is when Mason found these triplets, his sick mind thought they would be the ideal candidates."

Calla felt like she'd been slapped a thousand times. These triplets challenged any operative ability she'd seen, and worse, they probably had no consciences. "How do these triplets operate?" she asked.

"It's tricky. The triplets volunteered, wanting to serve their country, but when Mason got hold of them, he took them under his assassin wing. He used chemistry to attack fatigue, using a drug like Modafinil. One way Mason eliminated post-traumatic stress disorder after intense training exercises in them, was to erase unwanted memories. And with his telepathic capabilities, we know he can. After many tests and experiments, they were fit to start, but they really didn't know what they'd signed up for. He'd used a beta blocker–a drug that can erase the effects of terrifying memories."

"We live in a sick world. It's highly unethical and, in essence, mental kidnapping," Jack added. "He's wiped their entire humanity."

Nash took a deep breath. "It was initially called Project POG before it was shut down—Perfect Operating Guerrillas—new types of spy assassins. Kane's body was loaded with several drugs, and part of his skeleton was replaced with titanium after a biking accident. He was then sent to be trained by the Indian army with the skills of the Rajput warriors."

"What about the other two?" Calla asked, sensing her body stiffen with shock at every revelation.

"Ridge's brain activity accesses a wire nerve of artificial intelligence implanted in his nervous system. Research intended to aid the medical field. Mason stole it and used it for his own purposes."

"What can we expect from Ridge?" Jack asked.

"He was wired and drugged to act faster than most, and be quicker in thought and action. He was trained with ninja, or Ninjutsu, fighting tactics. Lastly, Sage, the only woman to undergo the program, and my guess is she *was* in Santorini, uses the fighting knowledge and skill of Apache Indians, and her body is passionately advanced with steroids. Her files say she can hack any computer."

"So unless we all have a heightened level of muscle and intelligence, we're screwed," Jack surrendered.

"That's right," Nash said carefully, eying Calla. "Cal, you have to be careful. Mason knows about you, and these cutthroats are ruthless and act without thinking. Mason controls all their activity with a thought. They use modern and ancient weaponry, the best of both worlds, and do whatever it takes to execute their missions."

"And we're that mission," she said, more as confirmation, rather than seeking information.

Nash shot a quick glance at an eyeballing Tamiko. "The government shut POG down. It was not ethical. ISFT was never meant to infringe on agents' human rights. Mason went overboard, and now, he sits back, God knows where, and uses the arms and legs of these triplets to terrorize technology and our freedom to use it."

Tamiko glanced their way. "Hey! May I help you?" he said, attempting his best English.

"Thank you, we're just browsing," responded Nash in Japanese.

Jack studied his electronic tablet. "Look at this. Mason's now infiltrated the UK's new nuclear station. They can't control the virus there, the plant is barely functional. I need to alert them and even give them a temporary fix until we find Calla's mother and hopefully the permanent fix."

Calla eyed the computer. "Should we contact Allegra? We may be able to get a conference call with her at the British Embassy."

"I'll go. What about you guys?" Jack said.

Nash rolled his eyes over to Tamiko. "We have a few questions we need to ask that boy. Jack, be sure to load the address for the Embassy in your global positioning app. It's tricky getting around Tokyo without Japanese."

Jack picked his way out of the tiny shop and disappeared into the market's alleys. Nash and Calla turned toward Tamiko. "You have a fascinating gadget display. Has the shop always been in your family?" Nash said.

Tamiko shrugged his shoulders. "I bought it a year ago."

Calla got to the point, "Where can we find your father, Tamiko Watanabe."

The boy did not respond but shriveled at Calla's stare.

"Could you tell us where he is?" she insisted.

Tamiko thought for a moment, scratching his head. "Listen, you either buy something or get out of my shop."

Had they touched an untreated wound? Calla inched closer to his counter. "Your father knew my mother. Please, I'm trying to find her."

Tamiko rubbed his forearm across his face. "I don't know my father!" He thrust a hand across several small boxes of gadgets on the table, sending some tumbling to Nash and

Calla's feet. He burst out, rambling punitive words in Japanese, many of which Calla found difficult to follow. "What's he saying, Nash?"

"Something about a rich coward. .. and a father who discarded responsibilities. .. oh, and a Ginza Tower."

"Isn't Ginza an area in Tokyo?"

"Yup," Nash said, scrutinizing Tamiko's eyes.

Something in the boy's expressionless face alerted Nash's reflexes. Without warning, Nash spun on his heels, to avoid a ninja *shiruken*, a sharp throwing star, and a deadly weapon as it carved past him with the fury of a barbaric army attack.

Calla dove to the ground, pulling Tamiko down with her. With her limbs stiff and awkward, she hauled him away from the cash counter, shielding him from further attack. Her eyes fell on his limp body.

The *shiruken* had scuffed his right shoulder, and the steel spike had lodged in Tamiko's neck.

—

1712 hrs.

Nash scudded to the entrance and slammed his back against the shop's inner wall, with one eye spying out into the alley. Calla removed her silk scarf and padded the seeping blood from Tamiko's wound.

Nash felt round his leather jacket and located a knuckle stun gun. He peered once more into the street. His eye caught the *shinobi* sharpshooter many would call a ninja. *Ridge!*

The assassin clipped to the shop across the alley, and half concealed himself behind a stall of electronic equipment. If the *shinobi* had undergone the brutal training Mason had authorized, he was 'a fight-till-the death' type. Not only was he genetically fierce, but the man had also probably been boosted with potent hormones and drugs, and trained in the systematized, Japanese martial art.

Nash shot a second glance in the alley. The marketplace thrived with hordes of shoppers. If he could get close enough to Ridge, who stood three meters away, he would stun him as a first move. He took another glance. The stall was empty. *Damn it!*

Ridge had used pure *shinobi* genius. The most effective ninjas were the inconspicuous ones like those who sat next to one on a bus, incognito, blending into their surroundings. Nash hadn't gotten a good look at the man's attire. He could be any of the men pretending to browse. Ridge was probably alone. Under any circumstance, Ridge would be a clear target, but Nash had to be alert. What other weapons did Ridge conceal?

Think, Nash! The average human reaction was four seconds. Would this work for Ridge? Nash took his chances. Crouching on the ground, he galvanized into action, moving in a military crawl to the outside of the shop and cowered against an outdoor display table.

Ridge shot to his feet and barged into the alley.

Alerted, Nash rose and moved forward, rupturing into the ninja's space. Ridge swung a *kubaton* overhead, a throwing spike with concealed missiles that threw off Nash's approach, knocking him to the ground.

With his face to the gravel, Nash struggled up, a severe pain shooting through his back, as the *shinobi's* feet remained planted, inches from Nash. He tasted his own blood, vinegary from a split bruised lip, as Ridge grappled his neck, choking him to his feet. He edged an elbow into Ridge's midriff and the triplet curved. As Nash had guessed, the ninja sensed no pain.

Nash assumed a ready position, as his opponent shot up for another strike. Quick as a flame, Nash twisted his body. His leg stretched, and he slit it across Ridge's feet. He tipped him over, then hobbled a few steps as a violent pain shot up his leg. *Damn, he's all titanium!*

A crowd had gathered around the commotion, many muddled by the confrontation. Ridge reached for a second weapon, a *kunai*. Attached to his leg, it resembled a masonry trowel and hung in his holster.

Nash calculated the damage the weapon would impose. He gave Ridge no time to draw it, as he wrenched himself away and crashed a fist in the ninja's face.

Ridge failed to react, unable to sense pain. Nash had hit a titanium plate that released violent waves of agony through his arm.

Crowds of stunned shoppers stopped in horror as the two men wrestled. Ridge drew his weapon and thrust it toward Nash's chest.

Inches from his chest, Nash edged back until he was caught up against the shop's wall front. Trapped, fury minced through his veins, seconds before motion drew his eye.

What was that?

Ridge's hand dropped the *kunai* in a rapid movement. A projectile from Nash's left side smacked Ridge's blade and sent it flying from his hand.

Calla burst out of the shop toward the cursing ninja. As Ridge sensed her charge, he plowed in her direction and seized her backpack.

Writhing on the cold ground, Nash shuddered in soreness as Calla wrestled Ridge for the strap until it tore, hurling her into a stack of manga video games.

The *shinobi* ripped open the bag and overturned it.

Is that what he'd come for?

Nicole's items. Her mother's only words to her.

Ridge held it high as he maintained poise, towering over Calla for several seconds. "This woman is dead! You'd better end your search here. This was just a warning."

Nash glanced to his left as a flash from the crowds, a second *shinobi,* this one more tactical, surged from behind him. The unidentified man tossed a *shiruken* that caught Ridge in the back.

Ridge swiveled with rage. He eyed the martial art attacker. In one heave, Ridge pulled the *shiruken* out of his back, tossed it to the road, and spat a mélange of saliva and vindictive curses before barreling through the market.

"Quick, this way!" said the Japanese man as he dragged off his face cover and frowned. He aided Nash to his feet and proceeded into Tamiko's store, where he caught sight of the teenager's flailing body on the floor. He dipped to the boy's side and felt for a pulse.

"He's breathing. Let's get him out of here," said the Japanese man with a confident command of the English language.

The fearless ninja slung the youth's arm around his neck and hauled him to the door studying Nash and Calla's faces as they waited. "Come on. I heard you're looking for me."

GINZA TOWERS
SHAMIKO ELECTRONICS, HEADQUARTERS
1937 hrs

Calla reclined in the lounge chair by the office window and gently massaged her arm. "Why would he want my mother's note, Tamiko-san? It means nothing to him." She'd used *'san',* imparting respect to Tamiko senior with the reverential Japanese title before a person's first or last name, regardless of gender or marital status.

Tamiko stroked his graying goatee that graced a round jaw as he faced the elegant, sky-rise window. He glanced down toward a boulevard facing the backside of a central street in Ginza district, an upscale area of Tokyo. He was a slim, yet muscular man with raven, sleek hair, voluminous and progressed down to his waist. Tall as a gazelle, nothing in his face gave away his age. For a sharp businessman accustomed to commanding his affairs with tact, by the way, he'd led them to his tower office, Calla found him poised and suave.

Tamiko sipped jasmine tea from a porcelain cup and strode toward her with astounding swiftness. "Probably not, but it stops you from getting to her."

Nash stood several feet away, admiring a hand-forged, Samurai sword that hung in Tamiko's lavish office. Tamiko had brought them here after attending to his son in hospital.

"How did you know where to find me?" Tamiko asked.

"My mother," Calla said. "She left a riddle and an anagram, and we unscrambled it. Your name, quite a common one at that, came up. We cross-checked it with ISTF and MI6 files seeing you were one of their own. But one thing that edged me further in the direction of Tokyo besides that fact that whenever we searched for your name, it only yielded your son."

Tamiko slowly straightened his shoulders. "What was the riddle?"

"A model of modernization, a cry from a city, burned to the ground," Calla said. "After the Tsukiji area of Tokyo burned to the ground in 1872, the Meiji government decided to build Ginza–*a model of modernization*."

"Right where we stand," Tamiko said.

"Exactly, I checked that little detail on the British Museum's online archives and figured you couldn't be far."

Tamiko shrank toward the window. "Your mother, Calla, was a very brave woman."

Calla didn't like that he'd used the word *was*. "Tamiko-san, where is she? Is she alive?"

"I'm afraid I've not seen her since she gave me this." He swerved to a closet concealed in the wall and coded in a password before dragging a secret safe open.

Nash stopped his admiration of the blades of the Kaeru and slipped into the chair opposite Calla. Tamiko pulled a wooden box from the safe and paced to where Nash and Calla sat.

"This is yours, I believe. I've never known what it was, but your mother was like a sister to me. We worked on some serious undercover work, especially in this part of the world," Tamiko said, his voice raspy with a faint British accent.

Calla took the box into her hands. "You were also with the British Secret Service, right?"

"No, Japanese. As you see, I've run this electronics empire since 1969. I was not really an active agent, so to speak. I was an *observer,* as we called them, an informant for the British government."

Nash set his right elbow in his left hand. The hospital had bandaged two bruises on his arm when they'd taken Tamiko's estranged teenage son. "They passed on information to you and vice versa?"

"Not quite, Nash-san. They used my factories and my offices as guises for some of their infiltration work. Your mother was assigned to me. I was her protector, and she used this building as her hub when on duty in the Far East."

"Was my father ever around on those missions?"

"No. I think she'd left him by then."

"This must have been after I was left at the orphanage," Calla said.

Tamiko hitched himself on the edge of his executive desk. "We became good friends and worked on many cases together. Until she suddenly disappeared, but only after giving me that there."

Calla eyed the box in her hands. What had Nicole left her this time? What secrets? What lies? What pain? She lifted the lid, her pulse increasing, and a visible bead of sweat appearing on her forehead. She moped it with her hair and unraveled her mother's secrets.

She stopped short of removing its contents. "What happened to my mother? Did she ever tell you where she was going?"

Nash sat still, his eyes narrow as Tamiko shifted his hip slightly. "Nothing. She trusted me with that box, and that's all. I wish I could be more helpful."

Calla dove her fingers into the wooden jewelry box. Ornately stamped with a garden scene on the sides, the box was vintage, finished with relief lacquer. "Just as the last one," she said as her fingers found a similar, medieval cloth rolled in a bundle.

"I don't understand it," she said. "I'd hoped the answers would come crashing into my brain as easily as they had with the decryption of the Hadrius Manuscript."

"Keep trying, Cal," Nash said. "You'll get there."

Aside from the congested symbols scribbled on the exterior of the cloth, it resembled the first in weight, thickness, color, and encryption. This time the symbols were slightly larger and felt more like drawings than actual script. *What is this thing?*

"What's wrong?" Nash asked.

"It doesn't make sense. I thought this clue would help clarify matters, but nothing is coming to me."

Nash examined the cloth, spreading it over his knee before handing it back to her. "We have to keep going. She still has one more clue for you. Maybe it'll make sense when they're all together."

"That's just it, Nash. I can't figure it out, and from the looks of it, in a little less than three days, the world's technological systems will be exposed to a criminal of disproportioned insanity, unless I find her."

"I know, Cal," Nash said. "Jack just sent this message. Eighty percent of the US, German and British government systems have been compromised. Mason is out for the final lap."

Nash's cell phone rang, startling them with its loudness.

Nash glanced at it, a stern frown settling on his face.

"Who is it?" Calla said, studying him.

He let the voice mail pick up the call and retrieved the message. When he spoke, a hoarse rasp arrested his voice as his eyes met hers. "Eva Riche. She says she's in trouble and needs my help."

Calla's face grimaced. "She won't leave you alone, will she?"

"Wait, there's more," he said, leaning into the cell phone. "Says she ran into your father and has done some investigative work through Riche Media, her news media company. She has information that will help locate your mother."

CHAPTER 19

DAY 7
GINZA, TOKYO, 2012, hrs

A SWIFT BREEZE blustered their way. Calla observed the glint against the skyscrapers' dazzling billboards, publicizing everything from branded goods to chocolate as they plodded past the clock tower of the Ginza Wako building, the symbol of Ginza district in central Tokyo.

With Tsukiji fish market on one side and downscale Shinbashi district on the other, Ginza presented a thriving and prosperous commercial center with an animated flair of its own. One of the most lavish pieces of real estate in Japan, and possibly the world, Calla, Jack, and Nash meandered through the characteristic destination, strewn with pedestrian sidewalks, built alongside skyscrapers and well-heeled, side-street boutiques. Small shops merchandising traditional crafts found their home among galleries, landmark department stores, enticing locals and travelers.

Calla's neck and arm throbbed from her struggle with the *shinobi* the day before. Her mood had been wounded after hearing the name Eva. In the last several hours, she'd churned words round her head, words that she'd exchange with the socialite from Paris, who'd always had a natural air of confidence and substantial powers of persuasion–especially when it came to, men.

They navigated down a bustling boulevard, a few blocks from Tamiko's lavish offices. The upscale avenue, home to many department stores, boutiques, restaurants, and coffeehouses illuminated Calla's spirits with its stunning lights, gleaming off towers, where virtually every leading brand on the planet had a home.

Calla glared up the expanse of a seventy-three-story building, its tower disappearing into the night sky. The men patrolled before her in amiable conversation, unaware of her contorted weight of sentiment.

They coasted into a street beneath elevated train tracks, north and south of Yūrakuchō Station. Extending over seven hundred meters, several restaurants stood within the brick arches. They moved into an upscale Teppanyaki restaurant Tamiko had suggested, an anonymous building on a quiet back-street.

Here, Calla would see Eva again. Eva had been their high school, Beacon Academy's own problem child, and once, an adversary on all fronts. Now the owner of part of her father's billion-dollar empire of conglomerates, dealing with everything from luxury goods to wine products, Eva had forked a space on Fortune one hundred's serving plate and recently launched her own international news corporation, Riche Media. The Parisian, who lived in London's glitzy Chelsea, had taken a private flight shortly after Nash had texted her back.

Calla tried to dislodge the weight of anguish that pinned itself to painful memories with Eva. True, the girl had proved herself useful in locating Stan though, her methods had been rather unwelcome and unconventional. *What is she up to?*

They moved to the entrance of the local steakhouse and waited to be seated into the space whose modern entrance contrasted the traditional meal Calla anticipated to have. The contemporary restaurant kept a delicate equilibrium between Japanese and Western styles. Calla's eyes wandered to the all-wood, dim-lit setting circled by several seats along wooden counters, whose centers displayed iron griddles. The frying scent of anything grill-worthy, beef, shrimp, scallops, lobster, chicken, and assorted vegetables tossed in soybean oil wafted their way.

"Have you ever had Teppanyaki?" Nash asked.

Calla shook her head.

"You'll like it," Jack said.

A waiter led them to a high round table in whose center stood three chefs. The cuisine artists chopped, cut, and prepared grilled *wagyu* beef, seafood alongside fried garlic rice, and fixed *miso* soup dishes. The barbecue aromas reminded Calla of her hunger, having not had a genuine meal all day. She'd spent most of the day asleep, trying to counterpart her rhythm with Tokyo time.

They took seats facing the chefs, and Nash ordered. His face relaxed into a smile as he clasped his hands together. "The preparation and presentation of our dinner will take place right here on the heated steel plate."

"Looks like you know the menu inside out," Jack said.

Nash smiled. "You learn to get by after being stationed in Tokyo for more than six months."

Calla's ear caught the clacking movement of stilettos on the wooden floor beneath them. The waft of a luxurious, floral fragrance told her that Eva had found her way to their seats.

Eva. The woman she loved to hate. The woman who'd once thrown herself at Nash challenged her at school, attempted to infringe on her life. The list of offenses was too long to roll through in the twelve seconds it took for the stilettos to settle by their table. Composed, but alert Calla straightened her shoulders as Nash rose, as did Jack.

Calla swiveled on her seat and took in the approach of the elegant Parisian vision. Eva wore a cotton, tweed jacket with a leather trim over a strapless dress of possibly the same make and a pair of expensive satin pumps, adorned with a translucent ankle strap. The pearl necklace around her long neck seemed oversized for Calla's taste, but it sat neatly in line with her auburn locks.

Eva gave Nash and Jack a French peck on the cheek. She noted Nash's bruise over his left eye. "At it again, Nash? How did you get this war wound?"

Nash dipped his head an inch without comment, his face carefully neutral and withdrawn. He seemed to sense Calla's misgivings about the meeting. Calla observed as flawless, manicured hands caressed the spot on Nash's brow. "Dear me, Nash, you need a little peace in your life," Eva said.

Nash removed her hand from his face. "It's nothing." He pulled out a seat for her next to him. "Please, sit. We've just ordered."

Eva slid into her seat and stood abruptly. "Goodness, Calla, I forgot to say hello."

She gave Calla a *bisous,* a peck on both cheeks and took her seat. They exchanged small talk about history and Japanese culture. When their fillet of salmon, grilled shrimp, sirloin steak, with a bed of cabbage, bean sprouts and *shiitake* mushroom arrived, Calla could hold her patience no longer. She pushed her plate away from her. "Eva, you've come a long way. Tell me what information do you have? What did you discuss with my father?"

Eva picked at her food, visibly not a meat fan. "Oh, the usual small chat. Your father is a lovely man."

Calla's expression was a mask of stone. "Don't pretend to know my father."

"I'm sorry, Calla. I only meant that he's such a gentleman."

Calla watched her, contemplating the motives for the well-groomed face.

Jack swallowed hard and shot a glance at Nash's face that gave nothing away.

"I've stayed in touch with Stan. Come on, Calla, I thought the past was done and dusted between us," Eva said.

"It is, Eva. I just want to know why you flew thousands of miles from London. What was so urgent you could not tell us by another means? We have several means of communication in this glorious age of technology, such as a phone."

Jack's body remained immobile, not sure how to react. He glanced from one woman to another.

Eva studied Nash for a few seconds. "Not an easy one, is she, Nash?"

Calla rose, her napkin sliding to the floor. She dipped to retrieve it, and as she rose, picked up her table knife and stroked the steak blade slowly. She aimed the sharp tip toward Eva's face. "Will this conversation require some coercing?"

Eva's horrified face begged for understanding. "*Mon Dieu*! My goodness! I do have information. If you sit, I'll share it."

Nash set a hand on Calla's shoulder. She glanced over at him and took a deep breath before settling back into her seat. Seven months ago, it had been torture to watch Eva throw her affections at Nash, a topic never raised. "Okay, let's hear what you have to say," Calla said.

"Your mother is alive."

Was she lying?

"How do you know?" Jack added.

"I have my sources," Eva said.

"Spill them," Calla probed.

Nash interrupted, his voice soft-spoken but firm. "Eva, if you know where Calla's mother is, it's important you tell us."

"Calla's mother knew Mason very well," Eva said.

"How do you come to that conclusion?" Nash said.

"I spied through Mason's files several months ago. She must be alive. He had a whole dossier on Nicole Cress," Eva explained, her eyes looking away swiftly at the sight of Calla's scowl.

Calla threw her hands in the air. "This is getting us nowhere. I could've told you that." *How can Nash and Jack sit there and listen to this? Why did we let her come here? We have little time left, and Eva is wasting it.*

Calla rose. "I'm going to the ladies' room." She shot Eva a look. "When I get back, I hope your logic has a little more comprehensive detail. Like, why you're really here."

Nash rose and watched after Calla as she scuffed to the far end of the restaurant, crossing tables of entertained diners. When she burst through the grand-mirrored restrooms, her olive cheeks had suffused with blood until they were nearly crimson. She had to face the truth. She'd never forgiven Nash that day in London when she'd witnessed something so tender between him and Eva. The visual felt like poison in her veins.

Calla never gave way to hidden emotions, especially over Eva.

Why was it so hard to forget? To trust. She'd never talked to him about it, and the matter had been flung into the sea, with a lead boulder attached. But now, its weight, however improbable, had come floating to the surface, challenging her equilibrium. *Damn it!* Eva's being out of the picture had made matters easier over the last six months.

Let it go! Then why could she not release the instinct that Eva was hiding something, yet again?

Calla paced back to the table and registered Nash's look of concern.

He drew her close. "You okay?" she nodded and slipped into her seat beside him. "Yeah."

Calla's chair edged over a small bump, possibly a small pebble. As she rose from the seat to remove the interference, her eyes fell on a microchip on the floor. No bigger than a grain of rice, she retrieved the transponder, encased in silicate glass, and examined it. "What's this, Eva?"

Jack took the item from Calla's hand and scrutinized the subdermal implant. "This is a human, microchip implant. Where did you get this?"

Calla turned to Eva. "Eva?"

Eva curled her shoulders over her chest, covering her face with her hand. "It's nothing."

Calla hoisted herself on the chair and moved in toward the socialite, her face inches from her. "Listen, Eva, I'm giving you three seconds. Tell me what this is."

Eva brought a shaky hand to her forehead, letting out an uncontrollable whimper, her face perspiring. "Calla, I can't. He'll kill me!"

"Who?" Nash said.

Eva transported shaky palms to her throat, wheezing for air. She took a sip of cold water. "You don't understand him. He's gone ranting mad!"

The trio around her exchanged perplexed looks before Jack edged forward with intrigue. "I think she means Mason."

"Eva, tell us what this is all about. We can help you," Calla said.

Eva's head shook in uncontrollable jerks, her eyes registering dread as her words spewed in stutters. "I. .. went to see Mason when he was in prison. I owed him a service from months ago. The only way we could settle the matter was if I. .. if I—"

She clutched Nash's sleeve. "Nash, you have to believe me. I didn't want to. He made me. He said I owed him."

Nash raised an eyebrow. "What did he do?"

She shook her head feverishly, and in three seconds, her hands found her throat again.

Calla charged to her side and grasped her arm, raising it so Eva could breathe lighter. "She's having a panic attack."

Eva fell back in Calla's arms, her head limping to one side. Calla delivered five palm knocks between Eva's shoulder blades with the heel of her hand. "Breathe! Eva, breathe. He can't touch you. He's not here."

Eva's eyes trolled into the back of her head. Her hands sagged to her sides before collapsing into Calla, sending them toppling to the wooden floor. Eva's body shuddered for a few seconds.

Then, she was still.

2220 hrs.

Hospitals made Calla queasy. Three paramedics wheeled an injured man through the double doors at the end of the waiting room. The emergency care section of Saint Luke's International Hospital in Tokyo's Chūō district was not busy that night. A young family sat at the opposite end of the waiting room, quietly contemplating while sipping carbonated beverages. The smell of antiseptic and cleanliness resonated in the establishment. She glimpsed up and watched Jack scrutinize the microchip. Eva's one mission. She'd failed Mason, and he would know it soon enough.

Jack fingered the minuscule microchip in his hands as he stood leaning against the concrete divider in the center of the pristine waiting area as few individuals waited for medical results, checkups, treatments, and news that might affect their lives. He raised the microchip against the light. "This subdermal human implant can be embedded in the skin. My guess is Mason intended to use it as a tracking device, or a worse, a detonator."

Calla, who'd sat still listening to him, jerked to her feet and removed the chip from his hands. For several seconds, she rotated the little device in her fingers, before glancing up at his resolute face. "Why would Mason use Eva?"

"I suppose, as she explained, she owed him a favor."

Jack was right. Calla recalled how Eva had made a deal with Mason seven months ago. In exchange for information about Calla, Eva had agreed to deliver a multi-million-dollar deal to Mason through her father's empire, Riche Enterprises, however unconventional the methods. The arrangement had backfired, and Eva's father, Samuel Riche, had walked out on Mason with an unsigned deal. Mason was banking in, even if it meant using someone so vulnerable like Eva. Her journalistic craving for scandalous information was costing her. Just a few doors down the hall, Eva fought for her life, another of Mason's victims.

Calla had insisted Nash stay with Eva in the recovery room. He spoke Japanese, and his ISTF credentials would ease the security check. He could also protect her from any further gimmicks Mason might conjure.

Jack stood leaning back. He checked his tablet as he twirled the device, scrutinizing it every two seconds. "It's also a radio frequency microchip that can extract memories and information."

"That proves that brain messages can be replicated by electrical signals from a silicon chip," she said.

"Any information he can get on your hunt for your mother, helps him know how far you are."

Calla gave him a long pensive glance and rubbed her

moistening hands along her thighs. "We need Eva to wake up, so we can determine how much she knows or has communicated." She took a deep breath. "You can't really blame her. Eva is one of a kind. For years, she's made such poor choices."

"Are you still sore?"

"How can I be? Eva has always been a special one, Jack. At first, I was so angry. I wanted to make her pay."

"Why?"

"Jack. .. I guess it's nothing, just something between her and Nash I can't explain."

"Then let Nash explain. Have you spoken to him about it?"

She shook her head. "I probably should. Eva has never found herself, and all she's trying to do is fill a void left by her father and mother." She glanced up at him. "Much like me."

"At least you know what you want. I doubt Eva does."

"Do I—"

The sound of approaching footsteps approaching made them turn as Nash inched toward them.

A spurt of guilt spiraled through her as he came nearer. "Is she going to be okay, Nash. What did the doctors say?"

Nash nodded slowly, raking a hand through his hair. "She'll make it. The chip implant was embedded close to her neck. Also, Mason poisoned her."

Calla drew her eyebrows together. "He did?"

"Yeah. Before she left London. He figured she'd gain our trust and pass on any information via the chip. The poison would leave her to her fate once he'd got what he needed."

"So she scraped the chip out herself. When?" Calla said.

"Probably the restaurant," Jack said. "She must have felt torn when you were questioning her, and she knew he was listening. So she fingered it out?"

Nash nodded.

"What was she poisoned with Nash?" Calla asked.

"Mercury. The doctors found deposits by the skin where it had been implanted. She's out of harm's way, though. They've isolated the poison, and she's resting now."

Calla lowered her eyes from him. "I'm glad she's all right."

Nash's eyes focused on her face. "Were you okay back there at the restaurant?"

She nodded. "Yes. Why?"

Nash took her arm gently and leaned into her, his head towering a good few inches above her face. "You'd make a fine military intelligence interrogator."

Calla stood motionless. He was watching her reaction. "I—"

"Hey, nothing ever happened between Eva and me."

She watched the seriousness in his eyes. He was telling the truth. He raised her hand to his lips and pressed a lingering kiss on it. "Ever."

Calla dropped her shoulders and managed a half smile as she stroked his hair. "I'm sorry. Eva's in there, fighting for her life, with no fault of her own. She needs our help."

He drew her into an embrace. "Yes, she does. Any progress on the third anagram?"

Calla glanced at Jack. "We've been searching the entire time you've been in there, and we're still at a dead end."

Calla's cell phone rang, and she pulled away from Nash's grasp. She retrieved it from the back of her denim pocket. "Allegra. Hi, yes, we're in Tokyo. .. I know. You spoke to Jack earlier today."

She leaned into the phone. "What's that?"

The strain in Allegra's voice stirred Calla's mood. "Have you found any more intel on your mother's location?"

"No, we had a hiccup here. Mason sent Eva Riche with a deadly message. She's in critical condition in hospital, but will recover."

Calla found she was pressing the receiver closer and closer

against her ear. She placed the phone on speaker so Nash and Jack could hear the conversation. "We found something in Paris that led us to Japan and one of her former colleagues?"

"What was it?" Allegra asked.

"A medieval cloth that matched the first we found in Paris. It's a message. I'm still trying to uncover the third part of her letter to me."

Complete silence took charge of the other end of the line. The trio glanced at each other. Several seconds later, Allegra's voice broke the silence. "Calla, I'm with Veda Westall at the hospital. She woke from her coma and is asking for you."

"How is she? Has her condition improved?"

"I'm sorry, Calla. This is not a good night for you. When can you get back to London? Veda may not have much time."

Calla almost dropped the smartphone. "How much time, Allegra?"

"Just hurry. The government is closing the British arm of ISTF. If Mason is not caught, MI6 will take over. Is Jack there?"

"Yes," Jack said.

Allegra cleared her throat. "Jack, government satellites have been completely overpowered. We're sitting birds and need ISTF special resources now more than ever."

"I isolated one server. We can run on that for about seventy-two hours," Jack said.

"All right. Calla, please hurry."

"I understand, Allegra." She looked at the clock on the phone. It was 10:40 p.m, Tokyo time. She glanced up at Nash. "How soon can we get to London?"

"By morning. We'll have to hire a private jet. I doubt we can get a commercial flight at this hour."

She turned to Jack. "Could you stay with Eva? She'll be delusional when she comes round. We're the only ones who can protect her now."

Jack shot them a knowing look. "Okay. But be careful, both of you."

Calla drew Jack into her arms. "Be safe, Jack."

Stalled for facts, her mind pondered the last piece of the anagram left by her mother. *Who is R-A-M S-K-I-N N-U?*

What did her mother mean by *'a mystery out of ten, a mausoleum of inexplicable men'*?

Two people in her world were in hospital struggling to stay alive because of Mason, and she could not help either. Each way she looked, failure gawked at her. She gripped the phone, her knuckles whitening. "Allegra, I see you in London in the morning."

CHAPTER 20

DAY 8
NATIONAL HOSPITAL FOR NEUROLOGY AND NEUROSURGERY
LONDON, UK
1125 hrs.

"How is she?" Calla paced into the National Hospital for Neurology and Neurosurgery in London, biting at her lips, a dismal shadow veiling her face. The long flight had drained her. But nothing prepared her for the look on Allegra's face when she walked into Veda's hospital room. Allegra stood over Veda's weakening frame in the little private room. She turned her head as she saw Calla approach.

"Thank God, you're here."

Her feet felt heavy by the time she'd stepped to the side of the bed. She watched as Veda breathed steadily, her head facing the grand window that looked out into Queen's Park. A monitoring screen hung above the bed, evaluating Veda's critical condition. Calla knew little about hospital instruments, yet the bleeping from the small screen told her

Veda's state was more life-threatening that Allegra had shared.

Calla stood to one side of the half-raised bed and fixed her eyes on Veda's heaving chest. Her eyes were closed. She rolled her head, moaning gently.

Allegra moved to her side and whispered in Calla's ear. "She's had difficulty keeping medicine down. The doctor told me this morning that her heart is also slowly failing."

Calla shifted her weight uncomfortably from one leg to another as a tear swelled in one eye. She fought it back with a sniffle. "Failing? But she's one of the healthiest people I know, Allegra."

Allegra's hand found Calla's shoulder.

"Whatever Mason did to her in that prison room, destroyed more than we first imagined," said Dr. Risebergl as he approached them.

They turned toward him. Calla slid Veda's hand into hers. "Dr. Risebergl, what's happening to her?"

"She has quite a persistent cough, severe lack of appetite, and a rapid heart rate. That's what the machine up here is monitoring—her heart."

Allegra's phone rang. "I'll take this outside," she said and moved out quietly.

Veda stirred her head. She threw open her eyes and sluggishly found Calla's concerned stare. "Calla. You came."

"Of course." She slid into the chair next to the bed. "How're you keeping?"

Veda shot a weak glance at Dr. Risebergl. "I'm in good hands."

Always an optimist, Veda would not admit how off-color she was from the ashen lines around her eyes, and the dryness of her skin. Her lips and nail beds had turned pale and bluish. Calla gave Veda's hand a gentle squeeze. "I'm here now to take care of you."

"No, Calla." Veda fired a quick glance at the doctor who jotted down notes from her monitor.

"I'll leave you two alone," he said.

Veda's breathing labored as she tried to raise her head. "Calla, I've had the worst nightmares since I went into hospital."

"Shh. .. It's over now."

"No, you don't understand. Mason Laskfell read my mind. I saw my mind communicating words and emotions that I couldn't control."

"Mason can't hurt you any longer."

Veda let out a chesty cough. "I'm ashamed to say I used to indulge in hypnotism as a hobby. That nonsense can really muddle with your mind, or at least it did mine." Her eyes glinted as she spoke. "Calla, I looked into his sick mind."

"Veda, I don't want you to think about it."

"No, Calla, listen, it's important. When he took control of my mind, I tried to hypnotize him in self-defense. That's what got me. He was too strong. And I didn't like what I saw. His mind has no reason, no compassion, and he feels no emotion. There's not an inkling of human empathy in him. It's as if he needs to finish something he started long ago."

Calla gently massaged the lower part of Veda's arm in a circular motion that eased the older woman's nerves. She hated to consider the possibilities. Hypnotism had its side effects, like minds swirling into hyper attention, losing normal judgment, and the increased ability to conjure a whole range of imaginary situations. Had Veda engaged in a battle of the minds? "Veda, Mason's been rumored to be telepathic for years. In fact, many avoided him, afraid he knew their thoughts."

Veda let out a cough. "He's a step ahead of everyone."

Calla folded her arms across her chest. "He's mimicking his mind's chaos and translating it to operating systems."

Veda drew in a profound breath. "You and I know that technology is showing human intelligence a run for its money. He's only obliterating what humanity has raised as a god, and that is the intelligence to do anything with a machine or a byte."

Calla understood. "If he controls minds, he controls systems, basically eliminating individual will on all fronts."

Veda gripped Calla's sleeve and pulled her down to her level. "But he's afraid of something. Something to do with you, Calla, and he thinks you'll find it before he does."

"He wants my mother. But why?"

Veda released her sleeve, her eyes glistening with fear. "I don't know, Calla, but you need to get to her before he does."

"I'm trying, Veda."

"I got your letter, by the way. The one from Colorado."

"I almost didn't send it."

She'd sent the snail mail to Veda the day before she was attacked in Colorado. She pulled her shoulders back, rose, and strolled to the window. "I don't know how to find her. All I have are two pieces of cloth, each no bigger than my palm, with medieval German strokes. None of which make sense. I also have a coded anagram and mysterious, historic riddles she wrote. How do I know they actually lead to something? It could all mean nothing."

"What about your father?"

"You know about him too?"

Veda nodded. "Calla, you're the smartest girl I've ever known. Even when I taught you history at Beacon Academy, you outsmarted many, not only in that private school but your national peers and superiors. You'll figure it out."

"We don't have time. I've two pieces that form part of a larger puzzle."

"If I know you and your mind, you memorized her words.

You used to collect anything related to your parents as if it were gold."

"Yes, I wrote them down when we landed." She fished for a paper from her pockets. "Why did my mother leave this thing to me? I really can't do it. I don't know what she means. And even if I do, no one who knew her can tell me where she is and what she meant by this game of words."

Veda struggled to let her words out. "What does it say?"

Calla turned to face her boss and read the message:

AMENDABLE TILLER
A linguistic victory for one so fair.

AWAIT EMBANK OAT
A model of modernization, a cry from my dwelling charred to the ground.

RAM SKIN NU
A mystery out of ten, a mausoleum on inexplicable men.

"It's the last bit that remains a mystery."

Calla strolled back to her side. "With each part of the riddle, she left a piece of cloth and gibberish written all over it, mixing symbols from across languages and cultures. She left each with a person close to her. My father only knew one. We found the other person in Japan."

"Hmm—"

"We can't unscramble the name of the last person. Nothing came up on government files, public or hidden."

"Maybe, you should unravel the mystery first this time and not the name."

Her mind pondered the words again. *A mystery out of ten, a mausoleum of inexplicable men.*

"Veda, there's a million ancient mysteries that have puzzled the world. It could be anything."

Veda muttered to herself before speaking. "It could be personal to your mother."

"My father claims she was fascinated by history, like me. She studied it and never took anything at anyone's word, always having to verify facts for herself."

"Much like you."

Calla smiled. "It's as if she wanted to be there and experience it herself."

Veda's cough rose to uncontrollable judders. "Don't. .. give up."

Calla sank into the chair. "That's what Nash said. Rest, Veda. You're going to get better. The museum needs you. I need you. I should let you rest."

"You could do my job with your eyes closed. You always could. Now tell me that the frown on your face is caused by Mason and finding your mother, or is there something more? Who is this Nash?"

Calla averted her eyes.

Veda studied her face. "What are you afraid of?"

Her intuition impressed Calla. "There's something I've never told you. Something to do with why I left for a sabbatical. I had to figure something out."

"What? Has it got to do with the letter you sent me?"

"Yes."

Calla wondered if the letter had made sense to Veda. Would she believe anything Calla had to surrender? Veda had sympathized with her at Beacon Academy, and even now, she understood Calla was different.

Veda smiled. "Is this something to do with Nash or your special gifts?"

Calla blushed.

"Huh! I knew it. Must be that athletic one who came to the

museum opening of the 'Zoroastrian Traditions in Persia' exhibition that you curated several months ago. He seemed quite impressed with you."

Veda raised her head and leaned toward Calla. "He has that look in his eyes that says it's real, Calla. You met my husband, John, once. That same look never left his eyes the whole time we were married. Trust yourself. Trust the ones you love, cherish the ones that love you."

Calla wanted to tell her all. She wanted the best advice she could get from an impartial person and from someone who'd mentored her since she was a teenager. "How do I know what I feel is real? It wasn't for my parents. It wasn't for his parents, neither."

"It was for me, Calla." Veda continued. "Only death will ever separate you two–either that or distance may kill both your hearts."

Calla took a deep breath. "What if we are different beings, and come from different places? *Literally*."

"Go on."

Calla took another deep breath. "Seven months ago, Veda, as you know, I found my real father, Stan Cress. I also found out why they had me adopted. It's because I have extraordinary abilities as I wrote to you and an exceptional assignment because of it."

Veda listened intently. Her look edged Calla on.

Phew, she's still with me. Calla felt a prickle of unease stir the small hairs at the nape of her neck as she spoke. "I come from this ludicrous family that can do impossible things like. .. counter gravity." Calla's eyes lit, and she hoisted herself on the edge of the bed, grabbing Veda's hand as if she sought the wisdom of a mother, she'd never had. "I can fight with strength and ability that defies any reason. .. that no woman or man should have."

Her eyes intensified. "I can see through things."

"Calla, that explains much. Things that I wondered about you at Beacon Academy."

"But what am I supposed to do with all of this? I discovered that I belong to. .. that I'm supposed to direct these people, a group of people like me that I don't know and am not sure I like very much."

"Sounds as though somebody believed enough in you to give you such responsibility."

"That's just it. I just have names and broken pieces. " She fingered the paper in her hand. "Like these medieval patches and mother's anagram."

"Calla. I don't care if you come from Jupiter. You were born on this Earth for a purpose on this Earth. There are many laws that govern our world, physics, science, astrology, technology, and so on. I don't think we have all the answers. There's so much we still don't know about our world, its past, its present, and its future. Who's to say that man in his academia is right? Every day, science puzzles man. Nature takes us by surprise, and history mystifies him. We can't explain it all, and maybe, we're not supposed to."

Veda's insistent voice cut slowly through the pulsing in Calla's head. She grasped Calla's hand. "You have free will and choice. The two greatest gifts we have and ones that have been abused many times. Trust in those who walk with you and, most importantly, trust your instincts, no matter what. And don't apologize to anyone for them."

Tears stung Calla's eyes. For the first time in six months, she felt free, not torn between the operatives and what they wanted or what she wanted. Veda, an honorable woman, understood her and her abnormalities, accepting them without resolve.

Veda mopped the tears from Calla's eyes with the edge of her hospital robe. "Now, tell me again. What does your mother's message say?"

Calla wiped her eyes. "A mystery out of ten, a mausoleum of inexplicable men."

"And you say your mother loved history? Hm. .."

Calla nodded.

"Something happened four thousand years ago that still mystifies us today. A mystery found in a basin. Of course!"

"What?"

"Think, Calla, I think we've even had them at the British Museum. It's one of history's ten greatest mysteries."

Calla's eyes widened. "Yes!" Calla said. "The Tarim Basin in China. She must mean the Tarim mummies."

"Don't you see? These ancient people buried their dead, four thousand years ago, in a hot climate and rocky soil that helped keep the mummies' bodies preserved. The bodies should have decomposed hundreds of years ago, but they have not. It's a huge mystery," Veda added.

"My father told me mother went to China often on secret missions, so did Tamiko Watanabe in Tokyo."

"Your mother was a spy?"

"So I've been told. So was my dad."

Veda smiled. "And I thought I led an exciting life."

Calla glanced down at her friend's feeble body. Veda erupted into an irrepressible cough.

Calla seized the glass of cool water on her bedside table. "Veda, I'm sorry. You really need to rest. I'll stay here for a while with you. I'm going to see you through this."

The blue veins in Veda's temples beat wildly as she closed her eyes. Her lips curled into a smile. "Whatever you are, Calla, I've never known anyone with a heart as genuine as yours. It's your true strength. You care intensely about those around you."

Calla relished her friend's kind words. Soon, her soft breathing told Calla she'd drifted into a peaceful sleep. Calla's hand still grasped the gentle woman's right hand as the monitor above recorded a steady heartbeat. Sensing her own travel exhaustion, Calla settled back into the bedside chair and shut her eyes, falling into a slumber of her own.

"Calla?"

A gentle hand nudged her awake. Calla glared up to see Allegra's pained face. "I'm sorry. She's gone."

The monitor above Veda's bed lay still. It had been shut off.

Calla sensed the wild thumping of her own heart. She swallowed the sob that rose in her throat. The person she'd known as a mentor, boss, and friend lay immobile, her hand still intertwined in Calla's.

ST. LUKE'S INTERNATIONAL HOSPITAL
TOKYO, JAPAN
2121 hrs.

HER EYES WERE closed. Above her, a glinting face scrutinized Eva's condition as she slept deeply, in the private ward of the international hospital wing. She'd failed. He had no time for time wasters. Mason had asked her to perform one simple thing. *Imbecile! Like your father, a quitter!*

He'd worn light-colored informal clothes and a set of dark eyeglasses. A routine nurse paced into the room and checked Eva's blood pressure. Mason edged away from the bed and threw her a charming smile. "What's the condition of my daughter?"

The nurse's English was feeble, but she joined a few words. "You must be Mr. Samuel Riche. Eva's father."

Mason nodded.

"She needs to rest now," said the woman in Japanese. "Her body is almost clear of the mercury, I understand from the doctors. Although they're checking to see whether poison was ingested in her lungs."

"But of course," Mason said.

"I'll be outside at my station if you need anything," said the nurse as she cleared several items from Eva's feed tray and sauntered out of the room.

Mason picked up the clipboard next to her bed. The next physician's visit would not be for another hour—m*ore than enough time.*

His eyes traveled to the ventilator next to her sleeping frame as the machine mechanically transported breathable air through her lungs. *Pity you have to go like this. I thought you had it in you, Eva.* He tugged at the tube that traveled to Eva's mouth and nose, its other end attached to the ventilator's oxygen supply. Eva breathed deeply.

He drew a sharp knife from his slacks and sawed at the tubes' edge, his eyes glancing at her as she continued to sleep deeply. The oxygen slowly seeped out of the severed pipe. *You know way too much, and I can't have that, little girl.*

The tube snapped.

Eva remained motionless.

Mason traversed to the door, dragged it open, and peeked out into the hallway. He pushed it shut and locked it from the inside, then turned and watched.

He waited.

Five minutes later, Eva's face paled, and her breathing labored, producing loud gasps and wheezing. She brought her hands to her throat, and her eyes shot open. She glared up, her body heaving before she turned her head and locked eyes with Mason. Her eyes widened as she realized her fate.

"Miss Riche, all you had to do was ask the right questions and be yourself. Your carelessness delays my schedule."

She shook her head in frantic jerks, unable to speak as the machine's windpipe clogged her air passage. She let out an involuntary cough, followed by a gurgling sound.

"It'll be over soon," Mason said softly.

A loud thud sounded on the door behind him. "Eva!"

The pounding continued. *"Eva! C'est moi. C'est papa!"*

Mason moved away from her side, not bothered by the bellowing voice. Eva's father had appeared at the hospital. *Samuel Riche! Moron!*

Mason stood immobile as the oxygen seeped through the end of the severed windpipe. He needed sixty more seconds. More commotion rose at the door, and a loud clamor showed that someone had joined Samuel in the hallway. Mason stood adroit, undeterred by the noise. He strolled to Eva's bluing face and set livid eyes on her. *"Bon nuit, ma petite.* Good night. Sleep comes to those who struggle less."

A gunshot exploded through the room and echoed for seconds in Mason's ears.

Mason's left hand traveled to his leg. A patch of discharging blood stained his light-colored slacks and trickled to the immaculate tiles.

ST. GILES SQUARE, LONDON
1847 hrs.

Nash tugged at his tie, trying feverishly not to feel discouraged. He felt a lump in his throat as he mused on the news about Veda. Calla's loss was his loss. He reached for his travel kit and found his small comb. He groomed his drying hair, sliding it back smoothly, before cloaking on his tuxedo coat. They'd flown in early that morning from Tokyo and with Calla at the hospital; he'd stopped by his London apartment to find a tux. There'd been none. A quick stop on Bond Street had solved that little problem, giving him enough time to reach Allegra's residence, where she'd asked him to come early for the 7:45 P.M. limousine pickup.

He reached for his phone, slid it in the breast pocket, and gawked at the gun on the bed of the guest room Pearl had assigned him to use. It was just a diplomatic function, no need for guns, though he was authorized to carry one into the Embassy reception. On second thought, he reached for it and put it in his tuxedo's shoulder-holster.

Allegra's guest room was nothing short of extraordinary. Her interior decorator had spared no expense for the upper floors, from the chilling champagne at the end of the hand-carved mahogany bed, to the walls of varicolored Venetian plaster, and the rich mingling of Versailles, French-style furniture. He glanced briefly at his reflection in the studded floor-length mirror, as light from a twelve-arm, acrylic chandelier dazzled the virgin wool of his new tux.

He heard a soft knock on the door.

"Come in."

Allegra sidled into the room, an apparition in scarlet. Her flattering frame drifted in a floor-length, *haute couture* gown, embellished with lace and embroidery. Nash tried to hide his surprise at her elegance. Sure, she was touching sixty or sixty-five, yet she knew how to work a gown like a monarch on their wedding day. "Allegra, you look magnificent."

"In this vintage? Wait till you see what I ordered for Calla," she said, taking his hand playfully and twirling under it. "Who says missions need to be boring. I always enjoyed this part of the foreign service."

"I can certainly see that."

Allegra handed him a listening device. He'd requested a

special miniature radio transmitter with a microphone that could record any incriminating material, if necessary. Coercion was not his style, but with only two days left, persuasion with the Chinese ambassador could be necessary.

"Listen, tonight we're ordinary guests at the Chinese Embassy ball. We need to isolate Ambassador Jiang Mah and get his signature on this." She pulled out a document from her sparkling evening clutch. "It won't be easy, right? With the state of current relations with them? Should ambassador Mah refuse to comply, we'll persuade him with your recording and this little baby."

Nash took the document from her hands. "What's this?"

"A little detail British Intelligence has kept an eye on for a few months. It's Mah's, should we say, undiplomatic behavior while on our soil."

Nash eyed the details. "Quite comprehensive."

"If he doesn't comply, I'll need you to help me coax him."

Nash scrutinized the details of ambassador Mah's unofficial dealings. The British government threatened to revoke China's entry into ISTF if he failed to authorize an excavation license for them in the Tarim Basin. The trading chips were details the border police had gathered but failed to act on owing to Mah's immunity status. Mah had trafficked a shipment of sixteen kilos of cocaine, with a street value of $2 million, passed on from Mexico, through the UK, and disguised as shipment resulting from a pharmaceutical trade agreement. He'd authorized other narcotics to be hand-carried into the UK, cushioned in diplomatic bags."

"Isn't ISTF closing?" Nash said.

"Mah doesn't know that, and if we succeed, then no."

Nash set the envelope in his tuxedo pocket next to his cell phone and shook his head slightly. "Whoever said politics was uneventful?"

"You seem to disagree." She took a breath. "Nash, I believe

ISTF can be instrumental in dealing with cybercrimes of the future. ISTF could be the visible side of our operatives. We could get operatives in there to combat the worst cyber crimes of the future, not to mention other international policing that may be necessary. This is where crime is on the rise. It's on every major government's agenda. You know that."

Nash smirked. She was right. "But—"

"Oh, you don't agree," said Allegra lifting her chin.

"Allegra, I let the operatives do what they want. It's when they get too close that they piss me off."

Allegra raised her eyebrow. "This doesn't have to do with Calla and Colorado."

"It does."

"Nash, I like you. I think highly of you, and in my opinion, you're better than a hundred operatives put together, because you have guts. You're fearless and have something in you that stems from more than a man serving his country."

"I'm glad you approve," Nash said, cynicism ringing in his voice.

"Nash, look at me."

He shot her a quizzical look.

She took a deep breath. "I'm sorry I sat by and let Vortigern persuade Calla to leave you. It was against my better judgment. As you see, Calla listened to her heart and told him to stuff it where it hurts."

"Easy, Allegra."

She glanced away from his stare. "I now know better, and I never meant to wound you."

Nash was silent for several seconds. He took a few steps toward her, seized her hand, and raised it to his lips. "Apology accepted."

Her tight lips curled into a smile. "See. I knew I liked you." She turned toward the door. "Is Calla ready? The limo will be here in thirty minutes?"

"I'll check on her."

They strolled out into the majestic hallway, and Allegra ambled down the stairs as Nash continued to Calla's room. When he stepped to the door, it stood slightly ajar. "Cal?"

He knocked three times.

No answer.

He pushed the door open and strolled in. His eyes caught the ball gown she'd laid out to wear next to a Harry Winston, wreath diamond necklace Allegra had loaned Calla for the evening. The vivid, marquise diamonds glimmered in the luminosity of the reset lighting. He let himself dream for a moment as he imagined them around her gazelle-like neck. Nash heard a sound from the bathroom.

Dripping water.

He progressed to the bathroom door. "Cal? It's me."

With no answer from the other side, he poked his head through the door. Calla reclined in a bubble bath, head back, and her tight chin facing the ceiling. Her face held no expression, and her hair spilled out of the tub in a silk curtain that nearly touched the floor tiles. Nash made his way to her, watching as she tried to stifle the sobs that threatened to overwhelm her. "Hey, Cal?"

She dropped her chin, noticing him for the first time as he sank to the soft Persian on the side of the freestanding, roll-top bathtub. Her face was stained with tears, and excruciating emotions as her eyes met his.

He put his hand on her face and set her cheek on his shoulder, unable to imagine the grief she felt. They'd had their first casualty with Mason, and it had struck at their cores. Nash let her grieve in silence as the whirlpool fizzed, quietly massaging her sorrow. She raised her face, and he kissed her chin softly. "Nash. She's gone. I can't believe she's gone," she said, biting her lips to control the sobs.

"I know, beautiful."

Nash was not sure whether she would want to go on. Whatever way she went, was all right with him, whether quitting or going after that moron Laskfell. He let her set her head on his shoulder for several more minutes before she raised it slowly, facing him with rouged eyes. She fared a faint smile from behind teary eyes. "I'm getting your tux wet. Nash, you look exquisite."

He returned her smile. "Still wanna go tonight?"

She nodded. "I need to do this for Veda. Even though I'm exhausted."

"You must be."

"Nash, I'm jetting around the globe chasing a mother I've never met, and the more I dip into my family fund, the more money there is. Who's doing this and why?"

"Why won't you let me take care of you? You don't need to worry about—

"Nash, you've just lost your house."

"There's plenty more where that came from."

"How so?"

"Remind me one day to tell you about some errands I ran in Qatar and Luxembourg."

The comment brought an amused smile to her face.

"Besides, that trust fund in your name has been gathering interest for decades. It's all yours. I think your family was smart in setting it up decades ago," he said.

"I've never felt right touching it. .. until they *really* become family."

"I don't want you thinking about that. I'm here always."

She nodded. "I need to do this for Veda. Could you please hand me a towel?"

Nash shot up and grabbed a towel from the heated handrail. He handed it to her. Calla took the towel from him and draped it around her body. "Let's go get that permit, even if we have to gate crash the Chinese ambassador's little party."

TOKYO, JAPAN
0934 hrs.

The gunshot had been fired inside Eva's room.

Jack surged from the seat he'd taken outside of her room and glared at Samuel Riche, who'd only arrived minutes earlier. "What was that?"

Calla and Nash had left the hospital the night before, and no one had gone in except two authorized physicians and one nurse. He'd seen to the security checks himself. Eva had not awoken once all night the physicians had said.

Jack slid his hand down to the gun in his holster and placed a hand in front of Samuel. "Stand back!"

Samuel Riche reared back and watched Jack pull out his M11 pistol.

Taking a deep breath, Jack edged up against the side of the door and reached for the knob. In one swift movement, he twisted the handle, booted the door and it burst open.

A face he'd hoped never to see again, and there it was scrutinizing him.

Mason!

Jack's lips pressed together in a tight grimace. *Bloody hell!*

Samuel perched behind three security men whom Jack had organized through Tokyo's arm of *Kōanchōsa-chō,* Japan's Public Security Intelligence Agency. They bolted toward the open door behind Jack. Not sure what to make of what he saw, Jack scrutinized a blood train on the floor, snaking from about three meters from the bed toward the door.

Blood caked on the hospital bedclothes. A titanium,

Double Tap.45-caliber pistol–the globe's smallest pistol known to ISTF forces—leveled at him.

Jack calculated as Mason turned the tiny pistol toward Eva's temple. This was not his weapon. Jack had seen Mason's firearms. Aggressive and much too visible. This wasn't it. Eva had fired at Mason and sliced a bullet through his thigh. Jack's quick guess was Mason had succeeded at wrenching the gun out of Eva's frail grip. Her right hand still trembled from the struggle. Barely awake, her ashen face communicated horror, and her elbows pressed tightly into her side.

Jack blinked and directed his aim at Mason. "Hold it right there!"

"One step forward, and you'll be singing a French funeral song."

Jack froze and glared at Eva's terrified face. His pulse pounded loudly in his ears. *Maybe I can aim for his hand. Will I be quick enough?*

Mason's hand hovered over her neck. The bullet would injure both–possibly killing Eva.

The security men hurtled behind him with guns of their own.

"Mason!" Samuel's voice startled Jack from his deliberation. "We can talk about this! Leave my daughter alone!"

"Time to play father, I see. A bit late for that, isn't it, Samuel? Let me see. I think we tried that a few months ago." He dug the steel deeper into her temple. "No, I don't think so."

"There's no way out," Jack said. "You can't get out."

Mason swung to one side and aimed the gun at Jack. The security men stepped back as he slowly drew back the trigger of the progressive barrel. The moment Jack had dreaded since learning to aim a firearm, drew into focus with Mason's perfect aim.

He shut his eyes.

Gunfire exploded in his ears.

Breadths of seconds later, he felt the brutal weight of the four men scuttle for cover on the tiles around his boots.

Jack drew one eye open.

The light had been extinguished by that one gunshot. And with the shades drawn, all Jack could do was squint through blackness. He heard moans and snuffles from the bed. *Is she hit?*

The security guards mumbled in Japanese as they slowly shot to their feet around him. Jack's hand slid to find his smartphone.

He could hear Eva's rapid breathing.

He turned on its brilliant flashlight.

She was alive.

Mason was gone.

2031 hrs

Nash set his ear against his phone. "Masher?"

That was the fourth time the phone had gone silent after an abrupt pickup. Someone was listening in on Masher's phone. *Who?*

He'd tried to reach Masher every few hours after leaving the US Embassy. He clicked off the phone, leaving a brief message about trying to reach his lieutenant friend. His eyes caught an incoming message. *Heck, not again!*

A text message stared at him.

Nash,
I can't let you contact me. Calla's life depends on it.
Don't let her go into China.

Nicole Cress.

Nicole Cress would be no coward. Why would she hide from a daughter she was trying to help? He fingered a swift reply.

Where are you?
Show yourself.

The message would not go through. All he received was a flashing text:

Invalid number

Damn!

He parked his car on a quiet street across from the Mandarin Oriental Hotel with the serenity of Hyde Park on one side and the elegance of Knightsbridge on the other. Stepping out of the BMW, he joined extravagant, Embassy guests arriving at the historic venue, en route to the Opera Ball, a black-tie, fundraising social, hosted by the Chinese ambassador. He'd left Allegra's residence, hoping to get a moment to reach Masher and told Calla he'd wait for her and Allegra at the hotel's entrance.

He fixed his cuff-links and let the evening, October breeze sweep over his clean-shaven face. Would Ambassador Jiang Mah generate any problems for them tonight? They had no time for delays and needed that excavation license signed promptly for an early departure to Beijing. Allegra had tried to see the Chinese diplomat at a less public appointment. However, she'd failed.

Tonight was it.

Nash glanced at his Rolex and proceeded toward the front entrance, where he waited as guests trolled into the luxury hotel, honoring Eastern culture and the unique mélange of the easygoing Edwardian slant harmonized with contemporary luxury. The hotel was one of London's first tall buildings, a redbrick estate, long recognized as one of London's grandest hotels in the flagrant district. He'd been here more than once for work functions with his previous post as a marine and security adviser at the US Embassy in London. Knowing the security prerequisites inside out would work in their favor tonight if needed. If their meeting would be in one of the hotel suites as Allegra had indicated, then security would be better controlled up there for the hosting ambassador and would mean less intrusion.

Then he saw her.

His eyes focused on her silhouette in the carefully constructed ball gown, a one-shoulder, asymmetric, silk-chiffon showing off a line of floral appliqués, embellished with tiny beads. It swept in a breathtaking manner, nipped-in at the bodice for a flawless fit. Nash studied the intricate design Allegra had selected. He admired the classical dress from shoulder to the architectural hemline that sealed the train. His eyes did not leave her for a second as Calla stepped out of the limousine with Allegra.

Lacking self-consciousness as his stare, he waited at the top of the stairs and gawked at her siren appearance as the women made their way to him. Certain his mouth had slacked in approval, he rubbed an eyelid, realizing he'd never seen Calla in evening wear or anything that feminine if he remembered correctly. His eyes failed to turn elsewhere.

Calla reached the top steps where he stood. He held out a hand for both women, taking one on each arm. Allegra's lips curled into a beaming smile. "Are you all right, Nash? Looks like you've been hit by an arrow–an angel's arrow to be exact? It took me a good thirty minutes to persuade her to wear this prime outfit."

Calla tugged at the tight bodice that accentuated her magnificent waistline. “I can hardly breathe.”

Turning to Calla, he whispered in her ear. “Me, too.”

“I’m glad there’s a limousine ride tonight. How do girls walk in these?” Calla said as she showed off her studded leather pumps.

Nash tossed her a cocky smile. “I don’t think you ever do much walking. It’s running I’d be worried about.”

She grinned at him as she slid her arm into his secure grasp, and they advanced behind the line of guests waiting to be greeted by Embassy delegates at the entrance of the palatial ballroom. Minutes later, a Chinese Embassy official in a dark tuxedo, and his female colleague greeted them. “Good evening, Ms. Allegra Driscoll and guests.”

Allegra nodded and extended her hand to him. “Attaché Ning Yuen.”

He bowed. “Ms. Driscoll, you honor us with your presence.”

She returned his half nod. “Attaché Yuen, may I introduce Mr. Nash Shields, a colleague and US representative from the NSA, and this is Miss Calla Cress.”

Yuen dipped his head slightly in greeting. “An honor. Ambassador Mah has requested I take you to his suite, where you’ll conduct your evening’s business. This way, please.”

Allegra shot Nash a quick glance. “Thank you.” She turned to Calla. “Nash and I will go up to the suite. Will you be all right here?”

Calla scanned the room. Nash could tell she wasn’t in the mood for small talk among a group of politicians, opera enthusiasts, and economists–an aristocratic gathering of people she didn’t know. “We won’t be long,” he said.

Assured, Calla nodded and glimpsed into the glamorous ballroom that showcased an opulent feast of rich twenty-four-carat gilding chandeliers and theatrical floor-to-ceiling windows.

"I can entertain the beautiful Calla Cress while you finish your business," said a voice from a watching eye that had stood behind Yuen in observation. "I'm First Secretary Fu Liao."

Liao turned to Calla and raised her hand to his lips. With a verifying look from Allegra, Calla allowed Liao to lead her toward the festivities.

Nash and Allegra tailed the bulky Yuen, his fine iron-gray hair sleeked back with gel. He reminded Nash of the bodyguards he'd often seen around senior dignitaries. This was the military attaché according to Allegra's prep, and presumably, his presence around the ambassador in their discussion would be more of an advisory one. He slid a hand through his tuxedo, to assure himself of his gun's presence–a habit he'd picked up from his marine days and fought uncertainty that came with their silent walk to the elevators.

They ascended to the top floor. Not a word was exchanged among the three. Nash glimpsed over at Allegra. Like him, she noted the silence. She contracted her eyebrows.

As they stepped out into the corridor, Allegra broke the silence. "Is ambassador Mah comfortable with the terms of our ISTF agreement?"

Yuen smirked. The guarded look in his face told Nash he was not fond of the terms stipulated. "Ms. Driscoll," Yuen said, "while ambassador Mah maybe a fan of China joining ISTF, I hold my reservations. ISTF is expensive, demands many resources on our cyber, military, and technology funds, and frankly, I think the organization produces very little results."

"I beg to differ," Allegra said.

"You've not exactly contained the heightened insecurity caused by Laskfell's disappearance, and if I recall, he was the last person in charge of ISTF. Now, he harasses the globe with the same criminal lunacy he was hired to prevent, a romping fugitive."

"The situation is under control," Allegra said.

"Is it? After NASA? Who's next? The Chinese Ministry of State Security? You and I know that nothing is off limits with that man."

"All the more for China to be involved," Nash added.

Yuen shook his head. "If I were the ambassador, I would be cautious."

Nash and Allegra exchanged a grim look. Coercion would be an option. Nash padded the intelligence document he'd discussed with Allegra earlier as they minced to an elaborate door.

Nash peered at the door label.

Imperial Suite

Yuen slid his card through the key reader, and the three sidled into the extravagant space, swathed in traditional and imperial elegance. The suite paraded king-sized beds, elegant side tables, antique desks, and Regency-style furnishings. Two bedrooms led off the primary entertaining area, with ensuite bathrooms attached to each. Nash felt as though he'd stepped back into Edwardian royalty, with only the tasteful cocktail cabinet, crystal chandeliers, the HD Bang and Olufsen plasma TVs, and atmospheric lighting convincing him he was still in contemporary Britain.

"Ambassador Mah?" Yuen said in Mandarin. "I have Allegra Driscoll and Nash Shields for you."

No response.

Yuen shot Nash and Allegra a glance. “Please wait here,” he said as a shadow of alarm touched his face.

He inched his way toward one bedroom. Nash saw him approach the adjoining bathroom and trailed him with light feet.

“Where are you going, Nash?” Allegra said, her voice firm but cautious.

“Be right back,” Nash said.

He continued into the bedroom after Yuen, who’d advanced into the bathroom. When Nash reached the open door, Yuen burst out, waving a firearm. “Quick, call an ambulance! The ambassador’s been shot!”

Nash shuffled past him and barreled into the dimly lit room.

Mah lay face down in a pool of his own blood.

FLIGHT TO LONDON
SAMUEL RICHE’S PRIVATE JET

Jack scrutinized an e-mail from his sister. He didn’t want to get into that now. Not only had he not seen her in five years. E-mail was the only contact, if any, that he’d kept with her. He’d barely had any sleep and now with Eva resting in the back of the plane, attended to by Samuel’s physicians, and out of harm’s way, the tranquility of a billionaire’s private jet was what he needed. Maybe he’d get some shut eye.

How had Mason gotten in, then out of that hospital, let alone the country? How could he have let the thug get away? He’d had one chance in that hospital room, to incapacitate him for good. Mason was using connections and underground methods deeper than the earth’s crust. How had he leached on to the world’s most guarded networks? NASA, the UK government, and what next? How had he maneuvered in and out of borders undetected? He was on every international wanted list, yet he'd appeared in Tokyo, not a hair, nor a thread out of place.

Jack had tried Nash's phone, but it was engaged. He should probably alert him to Mason's most recent jaunt. Unable to sleep, he reclined his seat, sliding into the comfortable leather. That would help. He shut his eyelids for several minutes until his tablet sprang to life, alerting him of a new message.

It can't be. Fiora?

Fiora Kleve was Jack's younger sister, once a contender for Miss Universe, he'd not seen her in five years. She'd been Thaddeus' girl and left him for a loaded jerk in New York, Heres Benassi, an executive vice president at a news channel, shortly before Jack finished his Masters at McGill. The move had torn Thaddeus into shreds, and Jack always thought his childhood friend would never be the same.

He ignored the incoming video call, and when he could no longer dismiss the infuriating blinking light, he scrolled open the video-casting program. Fiora's face glared into the camera, fresh and jovial as it usually was. "Jack?"

"Fiora? How did you get this line? It's a secure government line."

"I have my ways." She paused, glaring at him with eagerness. "How are you, Jack?"

Jack edged up. He wasn't sure what had spiraled the lack of communication, possibly the fact that she'd distanced herself after the breakup. "I'm fine."

"Listen, Jack, I know we've not spoken in a long time, but you are my brother, and I have thought of you often. I felt I could not call because—"

"What do you want, Fiora? Is Heres not giving you enough money?"

"Jack. .. I guess I deserve that." She drew in a deep breath. "I spoke to Tad a few days ago, and naturally, your name came up."

Why would she contact Tad? The bloke was probably still nursing rejection.

Fiora broke the silence. "He told me all the wonderful things you are doing for the UK government and for yourself. All your robotics work and artificial intelligence projects. You were always one for the big time, Jack. To think you used to build your first models out of roadside steel and wire when we were kids in Seychelles. Are you married now?"

"No."

"In love. .. girlfriend?"

"Fiora—"

"Okay. I'm calling you because I have something that may help you. I want to make up for all my mistakes with you, Jack."

"How?"

"Tad told me. Listen, I may not have gone to college like you, but I have instincts. Heres' business usually brings in prominent people for various media functions and interviews. Last night, he asked me to host a dinner for Rupert Kumar, the Indian billionaire."

Jack had not heard that name in months. "What of it—"

"Rupert confided in my husband. I was out of the room, and as I was returning, I overheard a conversation about Mason Laskfell, the international fugitive."

Jack contemplated his next question carefully and let it roll off his tongue in a grunted tone. "What did you hear?"

"Mason has been in touch with Rupert. What for? I'm not sure. But I overheard something about a colleague or person in Mason's circles they kept calling Sage."

The triplet with a sharp arrow that would give Robin-hood a run for his money!

"Heres kept asking how she could come in and help out in some way at the station. Something to do with connecting global media channels. I figured she's a tech whiz who can hack any computer, wire any network. .. you name it, she has the codes, or do you call them algorithms that can unravel the NASA hack. Tad kept telling me about it when we spoke. Jack, he also mentioned that you rescued the UK Space Agency's networks."

How does she know all this? Was she lying? She couldn't. Sage was not only Mason's assassin but his extended brain. She was the one with the codes to break the hack he'd wrestled with for weeks. What if Mason had planned that if he got caught, his jeopardizing efforts would continue with Sage?

"Fiora, be careful. Don't tell anyone what you've told me."

"Jack. .. will it help you? Heres and Rupert continued talking, but I could not follow all of it. All I know is that Laskfell used Sage's intellect to mastermind his hacks. .. Jack, is any of this helpful?"

Jack had stopped listening, and in his mind, he schemed his next move.

Fiora tunneled a hand through her thick waves. "Listen, I wanted to talk to you because Tad told me you're involved with authorities to stop some of the craziness that's been happening at NASA."

"Fiora, don't let your husband know what you've just told me. Mason Laskfell is dangerous, and he'll stop at nothing, even come after you or Heres if he has to."

"What are you going to do, Jack?"

He pinched his lips together. "Get those algorithms."

2123 hrs.

"So, are all curators as exquisite as you?" asked Liao as he leaned toward Calla, his over musky cologne crowding her nostrils.

Calla looked to the door, not enjoying one bit of Liao's exaggerated attempts at charm.

Where are they? What's taking so long?

Stauss's Emperor's Waltz, provided by a hired Austrian orchestra, stopped abruptly. The guests' voices clamored audibly above the silence as an official took to the microphone. "Ladies and gentlemen. I'm sorry to inform you that this evening will be cut short. Although we can't confirm the circumstances, ambassador Mah has been taken ill to the hospital. There's no need for alarm. Please finish your refreshments in an orderly manner and make your way to the rear exits of the room. The building is being evacuated. We apologize for any inconvenience."

Calla scrutinized the movements of the announcer as she left the microphone and joined three other Embassy delegates in hushed conference. Soon one of the men's voices rose frantically, his commands spilling out unsteadily. Calla spoke intermediate Mandarin and understood from the little she could gather that the ambassador would not recover from whatever had happened.

"Well, Miss Cress, I was hoping to know you better." Liao winked. "I'd be happy to escort you to the exit and continue our conversation outside."

What conversation? It had been only thirty minutes of one-sided bragging about the First Secretary's Tai Chi sword collection. Calla tilted her head. "I don't think so. Our inequitable discussion on Chinese art wasn't going anywhere, First Secretary Liao. I'm surprised at how little you know about your country's rich heritage in classic armory. I'll see myself out, thank you."

She gave him a brief nod, swiveled quickly, and turned

her back, leaving him arms folded in a stunned stare. Calla hurried toward the entrance they'd come through and slipped past a frenzied debate between officials and a crowd of security staff who'd made their way into the lobby. Stealing unnoticed, she paced briskly toward the elevators. She had to locate Nash and Allegra. She'd seen them take the elevator. One quick glance at the fortified security around the car doors was enough to alert her there would be no movement. She inched to the fire exit and found the staircase.

Heaving the vintage cloth as she moved, she tugged at the bodice willing it to behave as she charged swiftly up the stairs. *This is why I stick to my jeans.*

She stopped abruptly, ripped the lower part of her train, and slashed a slit in the side, throwing away half of it. With an abrupt glance up the winding staircase, she flung her shoes on the steps and barreled up with better ease as she tore up the floors.

Taking a quick guess at the location of the suites, she headed to the last floors. Once on the topmost level, she stole into the dim corridor and marched several meters past a few suites before halting. A room attendant flung out of a room, her lungs screeching panicked screams. Behind her, a frenzied man in a black-tie leveled an automatic weapon at her face. He shot one glance at Calla, drew the woman into his grasp, and wedged the gun at her temple. "Don't move," he instructed in Mandarin.

"I wouldn't dare," replied Calla. "How about you pick on someone your own size. Like, me."

He bellowed in the woman's ear, asking her to show him the servants' hidden exits.

Calla locked eyes with him. His face, camouflaged with bad shoe polish, revealed that he was of Chinese origin and an amateur at what he'd achieved. Panic oozed from every inch of his posture. He flung the woman to the floor and scudded the length of the hallway away from them.

Calla flashed after him and nearly collided with Nash, who appeared from an adjacent room. He took one look at her, his eyes moving to her mangled dress and bare feet. “Hm...didn't think it would last.”

“Come on, he went this way,” she said as she raced in the direction the man had taken.

At the end of the corridor, the hallway turned abruptly to the right, taking them through another passage congested with distraught hotel staff. They barged past them and reached the end of the second hallway.

The man stood at the end of the corridor, wrestling with an Edwardian sash window. The double-glazed feat of interior architecture refused to comply, and when he saw them approach, he tore out his gun and fired a bullet through the glass. Hoisting himself through the shards, he targeted the gun their way. “Stop!”

Nash had his gun ready, and he inched a step in front of Calla. “It’s a drop to your death or my gun,” Nash said in fluent Mandarin. “What will it be?”

He waved the unsteady pistol in their direction and glanced behind him. “Get back.”

Calla stepped ahead.

Nash held her back.

The man slashed open the rest of the glass, catching a blade that sliced his arm. He yelped in fury and stole out on the ledge.

They pursued as he leaped on the railing that eased his escape to the slated roof. Taking calculated steps, he staggered to the high tiles, balancing his weight against the rafter of the gable and dodged jutting chimney stacks.

“He’s getting away,” Calla said.

"He can't get far," Nash replied and advanced to where the bloodied escapee had stopped.

The man squatted over the ledge of the pitched roof with slopes on all four sides.

Nash balanced his weight and shifted closer to the terrified face. "Why did you shoot the ambassador?"

"He's a disgrace to diplomacy. ISTF will destroy us. That's what the man in prison said. He said if I can stop Mah's romance with Western diplomacy, he'd in return, leave my family alone."

"Who?"

"The mind reader."

"Hey," Nash said. "Can we get off the roof and talk about this? Laskfell can't touch you, and you've nowhere to go."

The man glanced down the dazzling views of Knightsbridge. He was losing blood from his arm and blacking out.

Nash stretched out his hand. "Give me the gun."

The man resisted and raising the weapon above his head, he fired a menacing shot. Sirens of Metropolitan Police cars mingled on the sidewalk below with the mania of uncontrollable evacuated guests, who'd not paid attention to the roof until now.

The man shifted against a chimney stack and glanced down the number of floors.

Nash balanced a meter from him. "Don't do it. Your family needs you."

Calla edged up against Nash, slowly maneuvering forward on her knees. "Laskfell is psychotic. Don't believe a word he says."

A cold draft whisked past them, tossing the man off balance slightly. He slid a foot off the edge and caught the rail in time.

Nash pressed in. "We just want to talk. Let us help you."

The man aimed his gun, apprehension arresting his face. He carried a classic MI6 pistol, possibly a souvenir from Mason. With three bullets fired in the bathroom and one on the roof, he still carried two more rounds that could amass the damage he threatened. He was no professional. And at this close range, Nash didn't want to test the man's shaky aim.

Panicked pedestrians gawked up, restrained by the erected barriers that had appeared below on Knightsbridge Boulevard. The man glanced down again for a second. Losing focus as he peered at the commotion below, Nash knew this was his only chance. He lunged forward and chopped the man's wrist with the flat of his palm. The gun sailed out of the jittery man's hand and flew off the roof.

As the man lost balance, Nash reached for him. In his grasp, the assailant's weakening frame slammed against the side of the roof.

Calla reached for Nash's midriff and heaved the men's combined weights toward her.

Nash pulled back in sync with her. One glance in the man's face revealed volumes. He was hallucinating and panicking more at being caught, than the fall that waited for him below.

When the man's shoulders rose above the roof's level, Calla heaved at his neck muscles, then gripped his torn tuxedo.

The man tore his body from Nash's grip. He swung his legs and kneed Calla's neck. The movement quivered her arms, and her hands released his convulsing frame. Her eyes widened as she perceived the inevitable. Time slowed, and with added concentration, she reached for the belt around his slacks and hurled him above her head.

He landed inches from Nash, who secured his hands behind his back and held him down incapacitated by a wrist grip.

. . .

"He's with Chinese intelligence," said Allegra in the hotel lobby as Nash wrung his aching wrist, realizing he'd taken hold of the man's body for more than a minute. "The police have confirmed he skipped security. The Embassy is not commenting and is still trying to identify him. He's not on any of their databases."

Calla rose from her seat, dusting off what remained of her dress, tainted with soot. "That's because he's on Mason's payroll. Think about it. He shows up just as we are about to get a permit to go into China's Tarim Basin. Mason doesn't want us to find whatever my mother left there for us."

Allegra stood and joined her. "But how did he know? The only people were ourselves and Veda before she—"

Nash pulled off his jacket. "He's following us and getting help."

"Or," Calla said. "He's reading our minds."

CHAPTER 21

DAY 9
SOMEWHERE OVER UZBEKISTAN AIR SPACE...

CALLA LEANED HER head against the window of the Gulf Jet Stream, the ultra-long-range business jet.

"Hey," said Jack, "a penny for your thoughts."

Calla smiled. "Jack, I find it hard to sleep on flights."

"Me, too."

"You were barely on the ground for three hours before we had to board for Beijing."

Jack tilted his head. "I can't imagine someone like you afraid of heights."

"No?"

Jack shook his head and glanced at the back of the longest, most comfortable cabin he'd seen on a private jet. The extraordinary compartment offered wide seats, extensive aisle space, and across seating for meetings or meals, accommodating up to six people.

Nash had claimed a back lounge seat and reclined in its comfort, catching up on some much-needed sleep.

Jack's lips sprouted into a smirk. "Looks like Nash can sleep anywhere."

He sank into the seat next to her. "Are you still thinking about him and Eva?"

Calla rested her head against the glass. "No. Not at all."

"It's to do with Nash, right?"

She nodded, then shook her head slowly.

"You two are my best friends. That makes us closer than most. Can I say something?" he said.

Would she like it? Jack was her confidant, an adviser, and the brother she'd never had. He lowered his voice. "Whatever we find in China, and no matter where your mom is, remember I told you once, family can get weird on you. Sometimes, your friends stick closer."

Calla pushed back a wisp of hair. "Sometimes, I wish we hadn't translated the Hadrius Manuscript and contacted the operatives."

"Oh. .. them. I see." Jack raised an eyebrow. "Why?"

"I don't know if I've ever told you. But remember when Nash and I disappeared for all those months, immediately after we sent Mason to prison."

"How can I forget? You guys left me hanging."

"I'm so sorry, Jack. It wasn't meant to be like that. I was running away from something."

A slight smile, barely perceptible, played on her lips. She glimpsed back at Nash, his frame reclined over the seat, his dark leather jacket over his eyes.

Jack followed her gaze. "Let me guess, does commitment to him scare you?"

"No. I'm afraid for his life. My being with him endangers him, pushes him to the edge, and I can't have that over his life...over *us*." She pored deep into his brown eyes. "And you too, Jack."

"I think we've been doing pretty fine. Let Nash make that

decision. You don't need to worry so much. Look how far we've come."

She contracted her eyebrows. "But the Hadrius asks me to do something I'm not sure I can do."

"What's that?"

"Lead them. Be committed to them, leave my personal life behind and embrace a completely new way of thinking I know nothing about. That's why I want to find my mother. The real reason."

"How can your mother help you with that decision?"

A short laugh rolled from her throat. "She left them and had good reason to. I think I can do the same."

"Why are you so afraid of who you are?"

"Because—"

"Don't you think you can be the person you want and still do these incredible things? From what I know of the operatives, they're there to help and stop thugs like Mason torturing the globe with criminal hacks, and God knows what else. You'd be a great leader."

"I don't want to do it, Jack."

"Why? What is it you want to do?"

"I became a curator so I could be an educator. Enlighten and share my passion with those curious about our world and history. See if there are lessons in history we can take to the future. And somehow escape unscathed."

"Exactly, Calla. And you can do that," he said. I admire your strength, intelligence, and knack for the world's historical mysteries. You're stronger than you think, and I don't mean physical. I know you could kick my butt any day. I meant that. .. you'll find you need Nash just as much as he needs you. Please do me a favor and be straight with him. He's the kinda guy you can do that with."

"But Allegra and this Vortigern told me—"

"Since when does Emperor Caesar dictate to Calla? No one

has ever told you what to do. Who's Vortigern to say anyway?"

Jack was doing it again, brightening her mood at the right time. She held back an amused chuckle. "He's like the godfather of the operatives. The CEO and the guru, who keeps them in their place and masterminds their strategies."

"Sounds as though he may be out of a job. Have you thought about that?"

This time, she couldn't contain the laughter brimming on her lips. "When I met him and discovered that Allegra was an operative, they told me that I couldn't be close to anyone who wasn't. That's why they tried to erase yours and Nash's memories. You're the two closest people to me."

Jack thought for a moment. "You're right, that wasn't cool. But without you, we can't beat the living daylights out of Mason and those who'll come after him. You understand the mindset of the operatives and average people and can bridge the way the two minds work. That's why you need to embrace who you fully are. Don't worry about Nash or me, for that matter. We're inches behind you. Always."

"Even with the continuous risk to your lives?"

"We make our beds, and we'll sleep in them too."

Calla leaned on him, his boyish grin widening. "Jack, the operatives toasted Nash's house."

"Nash has a house?"

"Had."

Jack whistled.

"I know," Calla said. "The man has roots after all the traveling he did as a kid. I was impressed and a great hideout it was too."

"Yeah, Nash has his surprises. .. all good ones though in my experience. Was this house in Colorado?"

She nodded. "In the Rockies." Her voice suddenly pitched low. "Jack, I don't know what these operatives are capable of.

How far they'll go to make sure I'm theirs. For crying out loud, they kidnapped me."

"Yes, but if you lead them, you could change all that. Couldn't you clean house? Change the rules. That's what bosses do. You're a smart cookie. Right some wrong." He drew in a breath. "Besides, Nash and I would never let anything happen to you. It does not matter how super equipped or capable they are."

And he meant it. Calla set a hand on his thigh and glared out the window, watching the endless view into nothingness. "Thank you, Jack."

"You're welcome. Have you told Nash of your doubts? Your fears and struggles?"

She shook her head. "I tried. There's also something he so desperately wants, and I can't give it to him. I tried to tell him, but that's when this operative Lascar barged in and nearly sliced our heads off."

Jack leaned in. "Calla, I've known Nash a long time. He's trustworthy and the most genuine person I know. He'd take any secret to the grave if you asked him to."

"He would. .. wouldn't he?"

"I wouldn't worry about us or what the bloody operatives say. Kick some ass, Cal. We believe in you. Please be upfront with Nash. .. promise me that. That man couldn't live with himself if anything happened to you. I've seen women throw themselves at him, and he turns them down one after another, even before he met you. As if he were looking for you all his life. He's never been the same since you nearly sliced his jaw with that ski. You're on a pedestal of your own. So unless you don't love him. .. then tell him."

"Vortigern says we're such different breeds—"

"I don't want to hear that name again? Nash and you are alive now, at this time, and have living emotions and intelligence within you. No one can tell you how to live your lives." He faked a punch on her shoulder. "I know you'll tell him. .. incidentally, are you afraid of meeting your mother?"

She remained motionless. "No, I just want answers."

"Let's look at the last piece of the anagram again."

They read it on the tablet where Calla had transcribed it:

RAM SKIN NU

A mystery out of ten, a mausoleum of inexplicable men.

"Let me see that," Jack said, taking the tablet in his hands and scrolling to an application. After several scrambles through the possibilities, he raised his head. "Look here. I think we seek a certain KASMIR XUN. His or her credentials cross-check with a secret service mission thirty-one years back that Nicole Cress led in Kazakhstan. One thing about chasing hackers is that you begin to think like one. I just hacked into an old MI6 archive. It's taken me five months to crack, and here we go."

Calla sighed and gave him a peck on the cheek. "Jack. You are my star."

"Not sure about that." He took one glance at the back of the plane and smirked. "Naa. .. I think you mean that guy over there."

"One more thing, Jack."

"What's that?"

"One thing that will give me closure is when I look my mother in her eyes and figure out how she could leave her newborn baby behind. Her own flesh and blood. Jack, that's what really scares me about Nash and me. I'm so afraid of ever doing something like that to my own flesh."

URUMIQI MUSEUM, XINJIANG, CHINA

1021 hrs.

"He said he would meet us here." Calla moved around the Silk Road exhibition at the Urumqi's, Xinjiang Autonomous Region Museum. It was her first time in China and her first time at the famed building. The collections, boasting over fifty thousand items, captivated her. In Xibei Lu, in Urumqi City, the Xinjiang regional museum was larger than most, a center for the collection and study of cultural relics uncovered in the region–and home to some of the area's most well known and controversial artifacts–the Tarim Basin mummies.

It was one of the most modern buildings Calla had seen in the city on the drive from the airport. The museum displayed local culture, a taste of traditional costumes, religion, marriage customs, and festivals. Built in a semi-modern style incorporating traditional architecture, museum architects had derived inspiration from the region's ethnic subgroups, especially *the Uyghurs,* a Turkic ethnic group living in Eastern and Central Asia.

The trio drifted under the thirty-meter-high dome, the heart of the museum's entrance, and gravitated to the first floor. Honghui Zhou, the head museum curator, was to meet them at the entrance, near one of the major collections of the museum, objects associated with the Great Silk Road. The section amassed diverse, silk clothing, exported overseas in the Middle Ages, and artifacts found on various caravan routes, once crossing as far as Eastern Turkestan.

"Some of these collections seem new," Calla said.

"It's not as big as I imagined," Nash said. "Intriguing, though."

A tour guide directed a group of political dignitaries through the gallery entrance, and the three companions glanced past them, hoping to locate Honghui–whose picture they'd scanned on the museum website. Jack leaned against the far wall and glimpsed at a displayed traditional costume. "How does one move around in that?"

"With difficulty," a voice boomed behind them.

"Mr. Honghui Zhou," Calla said.

"I take it you're my guests from London."

Calla extended a hand. "Thanks for agreeing to meet us. I hope the haste with which I contacted you didn't disrupt your schedule."

"Not at all, curator Cress. I'm intrigued by your interest in Chinese mummies and ancient corpses. They're the highlight of the museum. Do you know much about them?"

"Quite," she said.

"Your field is more Roman and Byzantium collections."

"I make it a point to gain a well-rounded knowledge of history–all history."

"So, what can you tell me about the mummies?" Honghui asked.

"They're associated with much scientific speculation. It's believed they all belong to the Loulan Kingdom, extinct in the first millennium," Calla said.

Nash joined in, with his background in historical studies sparking his interest in the conversation. "They were preserved in the ruins of the cities in the Taklamakan Desert—"

"Of the ten mummies displayed, the central focus in the collection is the 'Loulan Princess'–the mummy of a four-thousand-year-old woman, whose facial features are strikingly European," added Calla.

"Hm. .. did you write the booklet?" Honghui asked. "Why don't we start at the beginning? I'll take you to the mummy room," Honghui said. "But first, have a quick look around the Silk Room."

Nash's phone rang, and he stepped to one side of the long gallery.

. . .

Calla's heart sprang with anticipation, eager not only to view the mummies for the first time but to know what had interested her mother in this place.

"Miss Cress, I hope your trip here was not in vain," Honghui said as they left the Silk Room moments later.

"Why's that?" Calla said, a puzzled look crossing her face.

"The mummies are not here."

"I'm certain they're in this museum."

"Normally, yes. But not today. They're en route to California as we speak."

1025 hrs.

"Shields, if you can, load up your videoconferencing app, do so now."

Colton's voice was strained. Nash pressed his cell phone against his ear in a quiet corner at the end of the Urumqi Museum. He flanked his back against the wall. His CIA contact rarely panicked and rarely called. This was important. He shot a quick glance at Calla and Jack, who meandered the extended, Silk Road exhibit as they waited to be directed by the Honghui toward the mummies.

He shuffled to the other side, pacing the gallery on the first floor, marked by a long corridor that made him feel like he was walking back across the sands of time. He proceeded past countless artifacts unearthed over time. Nash pressed into Colton's uptight voice. "Why?"

"It's about Masher."

Why would Colton call him in such urgency?

Nash had still not tracked down Colonel Lieutenant

Masher. At the end of the exhibit hall, he searched around for a quieter room. On the left side of the first floor, he eyed a quieter exhibit detailing the lifestyles, clothing, instruments, and customs of each of Xinjiang's twelve ethnic minorities. He cowered behind the replicas of a courtyard home, displays of hats, multiple instruments, and traditional Uyghur clothing.

Once positioned, he fired up his electronic tablet. Within seconds, he had linked to a secure 4G network and dialed into the CIA's locked network.

"Shields? Where are you?" Colton said.

"China."

"I've some rather disturbing news. I've just stepped out of a task force meeting investigating lieutenant Masher."

Nash's heart slumped. "Why, Colton? You retired months ago."

"They've hauled me in."

"Because you served with Masher and know him."

"Right."

This is serious. What have they got on Masher?

"Why's he being investigated?" Nash asked.

"He has information relating to Project HORIZON–you know the operatives and supposedly on Mason."

"Have you see Masher? Is he okay?" Nash said.

"He's at Langley *and* not talking."

Masher was safeguarding the contents of his report. Project HORIZON, the operative report Nash had churned around his mind for months. The more he knew, the more he felt he couldn't complete it for Calla's sake.

"Nash. In the past, we've dealt with Stan, and he told us much about the operatives."

"You know everything I know."

"CIA thinks Masher knows more, especially about their weak points, their technology vulnerabilities. They believe

Mason is not working alone, that somehow he's working with them."

Nash thought back to the day he escorted Mason to prison and the deal they sealed. He would protect Mason's mother as best he could in that psychiatric prison ward if Mason unearthed the operatives' weaknesses. Through coercion of the criminal, he'd rather not like to remember, he'd unearthed their vulnerability and the one thing that made Calla defenseless.

"We need to have it?" Colton's persuasive voice broke his train of thoughts.

"What's that?"

"We need any information Masher has on the operatives that he's not surrendering."

Masher knows nothing! The man's the most honorable lieutenant in the US defense system, and would never betray his country. Masher was not telling on him.

Nash's hand quivered at the thought that his friend was guarding his secret. He had to switch the tablet to the other hand before he could continue. "How do they know Maser has information?"

"They know he talked to Stan Cress, and they searched his office in the Embassy in London."

"Did they find anything?"

"Nothing, that's why they took him in."

"Why are we so afraid of the operatives, Colton?"

"You sound sympathetic."

"From what we know from Stan, our technology centers could use a makeover with what they know."

Nash's thoughts fell on the memory stick in his backpack.

Colton looked around the room and leaned in closer on the screen. "Nash, what's this all about? Have you finished your report on Project HORIZON? What does Masher know?"

Nothing!

"Listen, Nash, I helped you once. What can you give me on this? I know Masher, and you are close, and that's one reason you took that marine job in London. The boys here will stop at nothing if they feel what Masher has disarms Laskfell's hacks. They're cross-examining Masher and might use force, now that Mason is MIA. The US was hoping to have Mason extradited here for his worm that ate the stock market seven years ago, and now NASA."

Nash pondered for several seconds. If he gave Colton anything on his report, a discussion on Mason and the operatives would endanger Calla. She would be the next one they would investigate. The operatives were getting on his nerves–one minute fighting with the good guys and one minute chasing a mandate of their own. He couldn't give away what he had discussed with Mason, what he was learning about the operatives, and what the report on the memory stick disclosed.

No.

Calla's life depended on it. And for once, he reverted to a decision he'd made the day he'd known he could not live without her. Family came first. She was his family–whether she liked it or not. Could Masher withstand the interrogation? Was he fair to Masher? He didn't know. Nash wasn't so familiar with CIA interrogation methods. He imagined though that they would not be pleasant for his old friend. He'd heard of Masher withstanding Southeastern Asia interrogation methods as a Vietnam POW.

"Shields?"

"Colton. I don't have any information to give you my investigation on the operatives continues."

The next words broke his spirit more than anything he'd ever known. "I'm not familiar with any information Masher may have."

—

MUMMIES ROOM
SECOND FLOOR, URUMIQI MUSEUM
1034 hrs.

Calla's heart sank to her belly. "But on the phone, I understood we would get a chance to see the Tarim mummies."

"The mummies are not here." Honghui glanced around to see if he were being overheard. He took Calla's arm and led the group to a quieter location within the museum gallery. "I really shouldn't be telling you this. But I can get you a sneak peek."

Nash joined the intense discussion. "You just said the mummies are not here. I thought you said they're on their way to America?"

Honghui glanced at him. He was a good foot and a half shorter than Nash and shifted away from the taller man. "The mummies are in holding, 3250 kilometers from here, as the paperwork is carried out. They're in a container at Tianjin seaport, leaving tomorrow night."

"That's like a day and a half's drive," Jack said. "We don't have time."

Calla glanced at Nash. "Let's take Allegra's jet. It has not left yet."

Honghui nodded. "I can take you there and give you thirty minutes to view them and do what you need to do."

"Why are you doing this, Honghui?" Calla asked.

"I owe you and Veda many favors. Without that training I took in London with you, I would not have this job."

Calla's eyes lit, thankful she had not come all the way to China for nothing. She hardly remembered Honghui at that workshop they'd conducted at the International Conference of

Museum Curators about a year ago in London. She may have also been introduced to him at another occasion. Was that his only intent? Calla couldn't delve into his motives. They needed to see those mummies and gain clues about her mother's whereabouts. Calla raised her chin. "I'll alert the pilot."

"What's your interest in the Tarim mummies, besides their lack of Chinese features?" queried Honghui as he slid a scheming hand on her arm. "Somehow, I feel this expedition is not business related."

Calla glanced at him. She'd read about him on the plane from London and heard the rumors about his very public, personal life. A gruesome divorce after a scandalous affair with a politician's daughter. Quite the womanizer he was. Someone to keep at arm's length. She smirked briefly and removed his hand from her sleeve. "No, it's purely business."

"Okay, then we can take my car to the airport."

Close to an hour later, they boarded the private jet and settled for a six-hour journey to Tianjin. Once off the plane, they were met by a driver who drove them to Tianjin seaport and a secluded section containing hundreds of containers. Honghui spoke with two security men, flashing his credentials and the excavation permit from the London Chinese Embassy, the Chargés d'Affaires had signed on behalf of the ambassador. After a heated debate over an exchange of favors, Honghui handed the man foreign banknotes, a combination of euros and pounds sterling he'd coerced from them.

"Is that how they conduct museum business here?" Nash said to Calla as they observed the exchange.

"Now it is," she said.

They stood watching a few meters away from the bartered exchange.

Jack leaned into his companions. "That's a bribe if I know one. For now, as long as we are set to see those mummies, I don't want to know the terms."

"I'll keep watch," Nash said.

Honghui moved toward them. "This way."

He guided them to a red, forty-foot, transportation container and climbed the stepladder. At the entrance, he punched in six digits that dragged the sealer that secured the metal box to one side. Honghui handed each a flashlight, and they proceeded within the tight, climate-controlled spaces. An acrid smell, stole past them as they carefully maneuvered the sealed cases and freight boxes.

Honghui studied Calla's face in the fierce glow of the high-energy flashlights. "Listen, Calla, ten minutes tops. The box will be hauled in the ship in thirty minutes. I just paid for a thirty-two-hour delay."

Calla pursed her lips. "Okay."

Honghui gripped her arm. This was getting to be a habit with him. Her eyes traveled down at his inappropriate hold of her. *I could wring your neck.*

Within moments, as Jack and Nash minced to the end of the container, Honghui's hand rose to her upper arm, and he caressed her shoulder. She seized his hand and, with a violent warning, thrust it to one side. "One more move like that and bribes won't be the only favors you'll pay for. Try hospital."

The force knocked Honghui to the ground and raised an eyebrow from her companions. As Honghui writhed on the ground, she set her shoe on his wrist. "Honghui, you should really be ashamed. As if a public divorce weren't enough. Be glad they let you keep your job."

Honghui's astounded eyes studied her, aghast at her force and strength.

Nash stepped back to where she stood. "Friend or foe, Cal?"

"If he stays on the ground till we're done, friend. One move before I'm through, foe."

Nash shook his head, amused. "I wouldn't mess with her if I were you."

"Now," said Calla. "If you wish to fulfill your end of the bargain, I'm all ears. Otherwise you may need a hospital trip before you return to work."

She put a hand out and helped him up. "Now, I assume these mummies came from a certain precise location in the Tarim Basin," said Calla, setting a warning glare into his stunned face.

"I can get you a map, or let's say a coordinate. It's an app we use at the museum when we communicate with excavators in the Taklamakan Desert and the Tarim Basin. But you need permission to even excavate there."

"We're not excavating."

"Nevertheless, I think you still need permission and possibly an escort. Let me make a phone call and see what I can do."

—

1717 hrs.

The metallic stench in the forty-foot transport container churned Calla's stomach, making her insides queasy. Its claustrophobic sensation filled her empty lungs as she focused on a glass-encased box.

She examined the case with the lifelike Tarim mummy, a male, defunct body with his intricate clothing and faint eyelashes covering his sunken eye holes. Her flashlight dazzled into the four-thousand-year-old face. With distinct, non-Asian features, in the morbidity of the Chinese transport container, he was perfectly preserved. Even after the passing of thousands of years, the red-haired mummy with Caucasian features rested in serenity. With recessed eyes, shut like a Buddha in meditation, he wore a black-felt, conical hat with a level brim. The mummy next to him glared back at her, his gape descending into the depths of her being.

"Give me a clue, my friend," she whispered.

"Is it here?" Jack said.

"That's what we need to figure out. I don't know why my mother chose these mummies. We've got to examine them carefully. They are our only lead," Calla said, her voice echoing off the iron walls.

"What if there's nothing here?" Jack said.

"Then, we go to where they were found in the Tarim Basin."

Honghui Zhou returned and observed Calla from a few meters away, with his back against the uneven façade. "Do you have what you need?" He checked his watch. "Your time's up."

Calla moved with caution and turned to Jack as he handled a high-speed, satellite tracker.

"Is the emergency communications pod up and running now?"

"Give me a second," he said. "How can we fight a worm on global networks when our own gadgets are the first targets."

"We have to, Jack. If there's nothing here with these mummies, we must go to the heart of the desert, and we can't do that without satellite link up."

Jack shifted from his uncomfortable position between two stacks of freight, shipping boxes. "I can't guarantee that. The geospatial positioning in this fly zone is messed up."

"How many hours do we have on the current battery?" Calla said.

"Less than one."

"Not good. We'll need more than that to get to the exact spot in Xinjiang, where these mummies were found."

Aching with fatigue, he shot her a long glare. "I'm trying, Cal. She's not responding."

Honghui's eyes were on Calla's pinched face. A glacier of anxiety settled over her. She ignored him and set a hand on Jack's shoulder. "We're headed out to a very deserted area. The north of Tibet on the eastern side of the Himalayas. The desert is extremely dry as the bones on this mummy."

Jack smirked. "I wouldn't expect anything different on a trip with you. I gave up comfort when I met you."

Nash stepped into the already crowded space and proceeded to the mummy case where Calla stood. "Not much of a looker. I take it this one is not hiding clues."

Calla shrunk from the fervent gray of his scrutinizing eyes. She cast him a half-smile. "They're incredibly well-preserved, but I doubt anything could fit between his decomposed skin and desiccated hunting gear."

Nash maneuvered over to the next displayed corpse, dodging custom-designed cases of exhibition treasures. He slid his hand across the adjacent glass case. "The Beauty of Xiaohe."

Calla glanced at the intricate, wooden pins, fixed atop the female mummy Nash was referring to and sidled over to the pristine case. "I don't understand why my mother picked these mummies? They're quite controversial and have mystified the curator world for years. The fact that some of them were blond with blue eyes says they could've been Westerners that had settled in what is now Xinjiang."

Honghui raised an eyebrow. "Their origins are debatable."

Calla peered at him for all of two seconds, attempting to avoid a dispute in the iron tank. "The Tarim mummies were, at least in part, Caucasians. We'll just leave it at that."

For the first time in ten minutes, Jack tore his eyes off his electronic device and sailed over to where Nash stood. "Let me see that."

"Hey, not so close. The private tour is over. Time's up!" Honghui said. "Listen, Calla, I'm doing your boss at the British Museum a favor by letting you in here. Have you found what you need? I have to box these mummies up for departure. The boat leaves in an hour."

Calla couldn't tell if she liked the man or not. "Of course. We're done here."

"My obligation is now paid. No more favors."

"Favors?" Nash said.

"Calla authenticated some of our most valuable collections at the Urumqi Museum, together with Veda Westall, her boss. I'm just returning a favor. It was my job, not theirs. Now, if what you're looking for is not here, you must leave."

Jack set a hand on Nash's shoulder, and they gravitated toward the entrance. They lunged off the container onto the shipping park and took in the expansive space of the busy dock, that assembled an array of shipping vessels. Their ears caught the hiss of prepped steamers as they cued up for departure from the largest seaport in China. A few popular cruise vessels docked as crews, and passengers made final leave preparations in the early hours of the October day.

"She okay in there?" Jack said.

Nash caught Calla's eye. "Yeah, she is."

She switched off the flashlights and handed it back to Honghui. "I take it you got my map?"

Honghui smirked. "This way."

They progressed to the door. Honghui pulled out his phone and paced to the edge of the container. He disappeared for several minutes before returning with a piece of paper in his grubby hands. "Our sources say that this is the exact spot. I've sent the digital file to Jack's phone, as you requested.

Now I've never been there myself, but..." He eyed Nash and Jack with a smirk. "You have two solid guys here, and I've asked our best archeologists and a couple of military men to go with you."

"We don't need company," Calla said.

Honghui stroked his chin and leaned forward as if to touch her shoulder. "You're in China. We have our regulations." His accented English was impeccable, British, mélanged with eastern pronunciation, and to the point. "The area stays as it was found. Nothing is to go missing. You get the drift."

Calla didn't care for the spiteful comments. For now, she would agree to his terms. "We're not treasure seekers."

"Are the Tarim mummies all you have to go on? Your mother must have left more information," Honghui said.

She gave him an alert gaze. "How do you know about her?"

"Wild guess."

Calla squinted and eye. "And their place of origin."

"Not much is it?"

Calla itched to escape Honghui's perturbing glare and proceeded to the exit. She leaped off the container onto the concrete, where her companions waited.

Honghui followed. "It's a long journey to Urumqi and quite a strenuous hike through the desert."

She shot Nash and Jack a knowing look. "We'll manage."

CHAPTER 22

DAY 10

JACK, NASH, AND CALLA jumped into a Toyota Tacoma truck and zipped to the airport, where they boarded a Gulfstream G150 jet that flew them to Urumqi, the capital of Xinjiang in Northern China. As per Honghui's arrangements, two frontier defensemen, clad in infrared camouflage uniforms, and a couple of resident archaeologists met them outside the Urumqi Museum. The men guided them to a military truck.

Hours later, on the back of the armored vehicle, Calla awoke, her head thumping the side of the off-road vehicle. They bore down the southern route of the Silk Road, the historical, international trade-route between China and the Mediterranean, whose arid nature had formed a vast wasteland in the autonomous region in northwest China.

She tugged at her thermal parka and adjusted her winter hat as they crossed into the Taklamakan Desert. Combative winds made their way through the back of the vehicle with fierce resolve. Calla glanced back along the road they had taken, observing the vast desert. No other vehicles lumbered the deserted climb. The transparent canopy above them flapped in the trail wind, their only shelter against Arctic gusts. Soon, the truck revved up a steep sand dune, on the southern route to Tarim that ran from Kashgar to Dunhuang.

Crossing the 'Sea of Death', as it was locally known, the place barely produced enough water for vegetation among its harsh wastelands. It was a risk she'd taken without much thought. *This place is a death trap. What on Earth was my mother doing here?*

This wasn't how Calla had envisaged the trip. Certainly not venturing deeper into nothingness.

And for what? A mother who had abandoned her at birth without a second glance.

When the Toyota ground its tires up the dunes to Hotan, nearing the citadel at Mazar Tagh, doubts began to creep into Calla's head. She leaned into Nash's shoulder, who sat on her left and studied the Hotan cross-desert highway, west across the Hotan River. Off a ruined hill fort, the site dated from the time of the Tibetan Empire. It meandered deeper into the nucleus of the Taklamakan Desert, the world's second-largest shifting-sand wilderness. The Toyota turned in to the interior of the desert basin where more mobile sand dunes dusted the plains, largely devoid of vegetation.

Nash whispered in her ear, unease lining his features. "Don't like this. We've been on the road longer than planned."

She moistened her dry lips. "We can't stop now. My mother's life may depend on it."

Nash's head backed up against the truck's edge, his eyes firmly on the two military men. "Your call, Cal. Stay close."

Calla questioned the distrust in his eyes, in particular, as they fell on the two *Tai Chi* swords the men carried. Was this typical of the frontier-defense army Honghui had organized to chaperon them? Nash was pondering the same thing. Had she dismissed the weapons altogether in their haste? Though reserved in demeanor, Calla wondered about their escort, especially the taller one with his angular build and slanted brown eyes that blazed at her like two amber gems.

The second man, short and stocky, gave her the impression he was physically capable of slicing any attacker in two, from the way he transported his weapon. He too gawked at her in silence, caressing the brass-handle in his hands, as he chewed a disdainful brand of tobacco. The two archaeologists had taken front passenger seats. One dozed with his head bouncing on the other's shoulder as the truck jolted, maneuvering the rutted roads.

Calla's face grimaced. Her eyes wandered to Jack, whose satellite tracker still failed to pick up a secure British government satellite for most of the trip. Their expedition depended on reliable communications systems. Calla embraced the truth. They had no network signal reception. At the foot of their climb, Calla had detected the mixture of stone and sand along the highway, hardly a place for life, human or otherwise. They could be out of communication with anyone who knew them. Their fates rested with the leniency, or not, of the silent men in the truck.

Rigidness lined her brow. "Nash?"

"Yes?"

"There's no sign of civilization. I haven't seen a town, truck, cattle, or a camel for the last two hours. Not even a riffraff shop or temple."

His eyes lingered on the swords. "Thinking the same thing here."

She edged into him, the cold metal on the side of the truck seeping through her skin as they hunched in the rear of the truck. A swarm of zone-tailed hawks squawked overhead in search of prey crossing the sterile expanse. How long? Had they been too quick to accept Honghui's terms? Nash's face set off a warning glare as he peered through the torn canopy. "Damn it!"

Calla lifted her head and squinted at the approaching menace of nature's force. Having never experienced one, the veiling dust that headed their way, dropped a weight in her gut. "A sandstorm."

Nash's eyes narrowed, focusing on a cacophony thudding behind him. A dozen military men veered up the dune on horseback, the hooves of their beasts trudging the sand. The cloud dust brewed meters from them, shrouding fog as it gathered dust and airborne particles that assailed their skin. As if nature's reprimand was not menacing enough, Calla's instincts told her to glimpse ahead at the larger military man. His unwavering face clung to her with irate eyes that narrowed into her soul.

Nash leaned into Jack, his tone low. "Any luck with the satellite, Jack? Can you pick up our location? The storm might throw us off course."

Jack shook his head. "I don't get it. The GPS tracking system and signals are all acting out of sync."

"I saw this in the Sahara two years ago. We need that satellite link, Jack." Nash said.

"I can't do anything." Jack's voice was barely audible from the swirling howls of the growing dust cloud. "The battery is dying out. The compass says we're off course."

Nash was on his feet, his head touching the canopy. "Let me see that."

Jack handed him the tracker. As he reached for it, the vehicle came to an abrupt halt, its tires grinding the sand and jolting the three friends forward. Calla raised her head from where it had hit the metal side of the truck. The Toyota perched itself on the edge of a steep, rocky slope. The blast of blistering, sandy air made any visibility close to impossible as the wind picked up again.

"Let's draw the canopy," Jack said.

"Says who? Up!" the first military man bellowed at them. "We'll take all those tablets, phones, and any piece of wire on you that dares uses a byte or link to a satellite."

"No, you won't," Calla said.

His dagger edged to her throat. "Let's see how well you handle diplomatic relations in China."

TARIM DESERT, NORTHERN CHINA

They turned toward the severe voice. A Tai Chi sword, its shimmering blade glistening in the dimming light of the car's taillights, stood between Calla and the tall man. He pointed the tip of the blade under her chin. Any movement and the cutting edge would sliver her skin. She drew a deep breath and edged back against Nash. The swordsman's condescending tone shook her nerves. "So, you want to awaken the ghosts that live around here."

"You're superstitious," said Calla in Mandarin. "You've got it wrong, friend. As we told Honghui, we're not here to disrespect the archaeological site."

"Save it!"

"I just need to find a coordinate and a man my mother knew."

The man edged the sword tighter against her jaw, piercing her olive skin slightly. Drops of seeping blood dripped on her all-weather parka. Her eyes progressed down to where the blood had trickled.

"Liar!" said the swordsman, his demeanor unyielding. "For

years, the Western world had sought to change our history, claiming they brought civilization to the East. Isn't that what you Western curators teach? We're not going to let that happen."

Her braced breathing intensified as the blade tunneled a little deeper. His putrid breath filled her nostrils.

"That's enough. Put that down." Nash's commanding Mandarin startled Calla and awakened her resolve. He set a firm grip on the man's bulging wrist.

The attacker resisted Nash's sharp wrist pull and edged his ancient weapon closer against Calla's skin. "Aren't you the American? You want to steal secrets for your government. Maybe look at our reserves of petroleum and natural gas in this area." His nostrils flared. "Or do you want to spy on our nuclear testing facilities? Get off the truck, all of you!"

His military partner carved toward them as Nash, Calla, and Jack hurtled off the truck, barely able to see ahead of them. The heart of the sandstorm matured meters away. Within minutes, their visibility would dissolve altogether. As the whirling dust maneuvered toward them, Calla staggered to her feet, barely able to visualize the attackers in the dancing dust. She made every effort to remain unruffled.

With feet shoulder-wide, the first man lengthened his dagger and pitched it in front of her.

Calla dodged back, crashed into Jack's firm chest, and landed on the heaping sand.

Nash studied their opponent's movements, ready to launch a preemptive strike with his bare fists. He suddenly drew the second man's weapon and clashed swords with the first attacker. They struggled blade to blade until Nash drove him back with a sidekick to the waist.

He recoiled to the ground.

Calla and Jack pulled themselves upright. When the first

attacker engaged a second strike with the blade, swift and gazelle-like, Nash dove in front of them for a block.

The blade slit a cut in his arm, and the pain made him lose focus for a few seconds. Determined to mince their assailant, he cut across the sand and engaged a roundhouse kick in the man's diaphragm.

The jolt propelled the military giant off his feet, and he crashed into a sand heap that had gathered at the automobile's rear tire. His companion retrieved his discarded Tai Chi and thrust it ready, driving toward Nash. The man suddenly shifted and extended his weapon, with its tip threatening to slice Jack and Calla's midriffs.

Jack kept Calla back with his extended hand in front of her. With no clear warning, he shot forward and administered a sidekick that sent the sword attacker colliding into his fallen companion who'd gone unconscious.

"Listen," said Nash in Mandarin, with his sword in an *en garde* position. "As she said, we're just looking for harmless information."

The second man barged ahead, with his sword drawn-out.

Nash blocked him with the flat of the blade as Jack tripped him to the ground.

He jetted up. Nash moved back, measured twice, his poise confident and geared. He cut once, clanging swords in the swarming dust before thrusting the attacker to the ground.

Calla's adrenaline rose, fearing for their lives. A determined instinct to save them nudged her. Her operative mind churned the scene in front of her. *This had to end. They can't fight in the sandstorm. We'll all be buried.*

"This ground is consecrated," said the injured military man as he wiped his bleeding lip. His voice was swallowed by the howls of the wind as he pointed to the edge of the towering sand dune. "We don't need Westerners disturbing our history."

The former military man regained consciousness and drew a gun from his military attire. With the two men, now feet wide apart, ready to slug every weapon in their possession at them, Calla knew she had to draw on greater strength. The men marched forward as the sand blizzard slashed their faces, blinding their eyes as it advanced.

Calla's feet trudged through the resilient sand, sandwiched between Nash in the front and Jack in the back. "I'm sure we can talk about this?" she said.

"You'd think?" the second man said.

Jack gripped Calla's shoulder. "There's no more foot room. We're up against the edge."

Calla turned back and saw the vast drop of the dune's border.

The three stood with their feet, losing grip in the sand. Nash and Calla exchanged a knowing look. She took a deep breath, slung round slicing her foot under the legs of their assailants. The motion left a small cut in her wrist as it deflected off a blade.

The assailants thudded to the ground, swallowing a gust of sand. Still clasping onto their weapons, both attackers sprang to their feet with the acrobatics of trained fighters. They thrust forward.

The wind made it difficult for any of them to stand with stability, and as the cloud engulfed them, they found themselves back to back surrounded by the two swordsmen who were joined by the driver and the archaeologists. With her back against those of her companions, Calla whispered. "Trust me."

With one, swift movement, she linked arms with Jack and Nash.

The archaeologists clutched shotguns.

A bullet zipped by Jack's leg.

Calla scrutinized the attackers, then the drop behind her. It must've been several hundred feet. A sharp drop to the base of God knows what and probably littered with thorns, rocks, and if they were unlucky, quicksand. Her eyes blinked in the force of nature's violent onslaught. She closed her eyes, and with arms interconnected with Nash and Jack, she heaved the men with her into a swift jump over the torturous edge of the jagged cliff.

They caved a fast dive into the bowl of land ringed by the Kunlun Mountains to the southwest, the Tibet Plateau to the southeast, and the Tien Shan ridges to the north.

The Sea of Death.

CHAPTER 23

DAY 11
EASTERN SIDE OF THE TAKLAMAKAN DESERT

MASON EXAMINED THE ENERGY panel. With a *shinobi* veil shielding his face, Ridge stood a few feet to his left, surveying his every move. To his other side, Rupert Kumar stood by adjusting the panel to capture the best of the afternoon light. The billionaire from Agra had paid a stocky sum for the New Energy base and corrupted as many Chinese officials as his billions could fetch to stamp the base in the Eastern region of the Taklamakan Desert. Under his newly established site, vast expanses of resources were buried, and Kumar's acquisitive eyes were set on groundwater, oil, and gas.

It had been part of an agreement Mason had signed with Kumar several months back as head of ISTF. He'd used his influences in China's interior ministry and allowed Kumar access to the best natural-energy scientists for an environmental establishment. Kumar owed him no favors. When told by Sage, the idiot in London had shot the ambassador, failed to escape, and that Cress's next destination was the Tarim, he'd had no option but to make the journey himself to the shifting-sand desert.

Anything she had on Nicole Cress at this point was like gilded gems. The woman had altered his childhood and his perception of women altogether.

Several solar panel workers stood in Chinese military attire cross-examining a new arrival of plates. The uniform was there to raise no eyebrows. They also tested the base's biologically-friendly energy procedures that enabled the purification of water, illumination of the tents, and the old military base, plus the powering of solar energy that allowed the use of other technologies in the camp.

Though Kumar was keen on environmentally-friendly practices, little around his camp showed the forefront of good conservation practices, from the generator system and Jeeps that belched fumes with each excursion they took across the desert dunes. Even though Kumar owned every inch of the energy camp, to the outside, it was Chinese property. A diplomatic feat Mason had managed himself, nine months ago.

Rows of panels lined the otherwise expansive base—one large solar array installation. Kumar was going to make a fortune shipping energy and gas to the remote parts of the Earth. On his list were not such obvious places like Mexico, Cambodia, and Namibia, and what better place to test his extracted reserves than the unforgiving desert.

"It's genius," Kumar said. "And it's creating billions for me."

I'm sure.

His wide snicker always made Mason weary–not sure why. The man was close to a head shorter than he was, and as frail as a household pest, with a grin that could make any dental company proud of the products he used.

They stood at the farthest level of the New Energy base on

the edge of the camp, bordering a plain that led to continuous sand dunes, some close to 300-feet high. He examined the windbreak belts around the camp and stroked an itch around his silver-streak hair. Mason removed the army cap. The sun was dying anyway, and he sensed a nutty taste in his mouth from the questionable afternoon meal that had been served.

He spat on the ground and patrolled around the two sample panels, his feet picking up the dusty sand. "Kumar, I want to buy back this business from you."

Kumar raised an eyebrow and halted his examination of the solar panels. He leaned back and sipped from a steaming teacup before erupting into a roar of laughter. "Mason, I've agreed for you to use my station here to conduct whatever business you want. I've turned an eye from the authorities who want you so bad they can't think straight. I know you're a wanted man, and I could fetch a ransom from any Western government for your incarceration. Money I have. What I want to know is, what do you want with my new energy base?"

TARIM BASIN, 0712 hrs.

The rough ground under her feet cracked for lack of moisture as Calla held onto a protruding segment of the eroding desert rock she'd barely gripped on the way down. They had descended in an arm lock, and it had taken every exertion of will and strength to control the motion of their combined weights. Visibility challenged them on all fronts in the dim morning hours, as the sandstorm settled over the chasm. Yet a slight wind-sculpted sand piles in a variety of shapes beneath them. It whistled past them and sent sand streaming down the steeper side of the cliff.

She'd supported the men's weight for all of two and a half

minutes until they'd each secured a hold on the ginger-colored, rock-varnish that coated the exposed pillar surface of the canyon cliff. Her shoulder muscles had held out for several minutes, and her pasty fingers ached from supporting weight three times her size. The only act she could conjure to save her friends from the onslaught had been to take that plummet and depend on defying gravity with a confidence Paris's training with Nash that sparked.

She glimpsed out into the waterless death trap, then above for the threat of tumbling rocks, as they each secured a spot in a cove of the rock cliff. Caught halfway between a deathly drop and firing guns above them. Calla wondered how long they'd be able to cower from nature and the Chinese army's menace. Soon, the firing halted, and they heard the grinding of truck tires as the van sped off without them.

With no transportation, it would probably take three days for any search or rescue to reach them.

First things, first. She glimpsed down first at Jack. "Hey pal, you okay down there?"

Jack coughed as he balanced under a drooping, giant-rock fragment, his voice hoarse but jovial. "Next time, remind me to get a parachute if we go diving off a bloody desert cliff."

She glimpsed to her other side. "Nash? Soldier, are you okay?"

Nash forced a nervous laugh. He's footing seemed more secure than Jack's. "Okay, beautiful. How are we getting off this cliff?" He glimpsed down the torturous drop to plains of pebble and salt flats, punctuated by craggy desert pavements, possibly another fifty feet before they'd be on the ground.

"I didn't think that far," Calla said. "Nash, do you still carry that climbing rope in your travel pack?"

Nash balanced his weight on the small wedge of rock and reached for his backpack before drawing out a low-stretch rope.

"How long is it?" Calla said.

"About. .. fifty meters."

"That should do it."

"What do you have in mind?" Jack asked, his cough intensifying.

"I'm making this up as I go," Calla replied.

"Here," Nash said, tossing the rope up at her.

Calla grasped the high-quality, untreated rope and flung it around a secure boulder to their right. Her aim was accurate and sure. Leaning back against the rough surface, keeping the center of her gravity balanced, she secured a follow-through knot around it. With the other end, lacking a harness, she wrapped the rope around her waist and began a controlled descent down the rock face until her feet touched the thirsty ground. She released herself from the knot and angled the rope toward Nash, who took hold of its taut grip.

Nash pitched it to Jack, who stretched for it and lost his footing. He slid down several feet before tangling in the suspended cord's loosened stance.

With the rope taut around his chest, Nash slid down the rope, gripping his boots on the rock's edge for support until he seized Jack by the waist.

Calla held the rope until Nash had a strong grip of its tautness, and with the expertise of a rock climber, Nash rappelled off on one strand of rope, using Jack's incapacitated weight on the other strand for counterbalance. As Nash slid down the taut rope bringing Jack with him, Calla could not help wondering whether Jack was all right. Once on the ground next to her, Calla glanced down at Jack.

He was not moving.

—

"Jack!" Calla said.

Jack didn't respond. They released him from the ropes, and she glanced up at Nash.

"What do we do?" Calla said as she looked ahead of them.

Morning light began to hit the inland basin. Calla searched the printed map Honghui had given them for any clues. She scanned the landing that overlooked the heart of the Taklamakan Desert bordered by mountains, the Gobi, and oases. "Nash, he's really hurt."

He checked Jack's pulse. "He's breathing steadily, but we need to get him medical attention. The rope caught his chest, probably crushed the wind out of him, and he's sprained his ankle."

"I know what that's like," Calla said, cringing at the thought of the pain Jack must have endured in his slip.

Nash searched his backpack for an instant travel icepack he always took on field assignments. The pack provided immediate cold without refrigeration as it rested on Jack's now exposed ankle. He helped him ingest a couple of painkillers before elevating Jack's arm around his neck and hoisted his semiconscious body for support.

Calla stared at the cell phone for a moment in unbelief. "Our GPS is out, and I have no cell reception. Without a tracking system, how do we know which way to go?"

Nash glanced over at the high mountains in the distance, then round the valley of the large sedimentary basin. "We need to head for the military bases. I once saw a CIA file locating three nuclear bases near here. That's why those men on the truck were so nervous."

"You sure?"

"Yeah, the basin has tons of oil and natural gas resources, making up about one-sixth of China's total energy supply."

"It won't be safe for us there," she said.

"We've no choice."

Calla stood erect and glared down at Jack's swollen ankle,

duct-taped with the icepack. What advantage were any of her abilities now? They were ineffective against hunger, thirst, further sandstorms, flash flooding, and God knows what else. They started a march with Nash supporting Jack.

After an hour's trudge over sand dunes, they came to the Tarim River. The liquefied water from glaciers carried much sand, mingling with shrub like vegetation and stunted trees. Jack coughed and opened an eye. The painkillers had helped, but without transportation and nourishment, Calla feared they were at the mercy of the Basin's terror.

Who was this Kasmir Xun? A man, a woman? Did they live in this desolate place as Nicole's note had hinted at? Was Kasmir still alive? In all honesty, she'd assumed he was a curator for the mummies or at least dealt with them. But as they stood deserted, possibly miles from the buried cemetery where the mummies were found, any hope of finding him or her had blown off with the sandstorm.

Calla cupped some frigid water in her hands and threw it in her face. She glanced over at Nash, as he checked Jack's wound. "How are you holding up, Jack?"

"I'll live."

Calla was moved by Jack's positive attitude. She dipped to fill a water bottle from Nash's pack they'd emptied an hour ago, when a face stared at her, reflecting in the water below. "I wouldn't drink that if I were you?" said a gruff male voice in Mandarin.

Calla shot round.

Her stalker had two silent companions with him. He tossed a leather water satchel at their feet.

Calla stared up at him riveted. Where had the little man come from? He wore ethnic clothing, similar to those of the ancient *Uyghurs,* a gown fastened with a long scarf around the waist. He looked Indo-European and beamed a smile from ear to ear. "Goodness, you're the spitting image of your mother. I never thought you'd survived."

"Kasmir?"

1830 hrs.

It's none of your business. Mason refused to delve into his intentions. The sheer fact that he needed a place so remote like this desert to rid himself of the three most bothersome people in his life itched his skin. No one would find them here. No one would search in this remote place. But. .. governing much of the globe's natural resource bases would convene well with his strategies for next week.

"Leave that to me. I never discuss my affairs, Rupert."

Kumar steadied the panel and streaked his sweaty brow. "Well, then my answer is, no."

He signaled to two base workers to carry on adjusting the panels and led Mason to a nearby tent. They took shelter under a canopy from the fading sun as Kumar poured himself hot water with green tea in a long glass. "Care for some?"

Mason shook his head.

"I can't sell you this base. This is the best business I've had in a while. It's the future. Oil and resources may dwindle, but so long as the Earth keeps revolving, the sun is truly god."

Mason turned his head as Ridge approached. His eyes narrowed.

The triplet whispered in his ears.

"I said no injuries," Mason said.

Ridge's stone face glared at him. "There were none."

Mason peered into the beady, black eyes of the over-muscled triplet, the most callous of the three. He was proud of his work. The man had delivered. This combination of human and scientific strength was the future of relinquishing his kind–the operatives. Not even Cress stood a chance. He shot up and glared into Ridge's granite-like face. "Good. But she should be dead and those two with her as well. Looks like I'll need to do it myself!"

Ridge took a step back. Mason understood that though the assassin could annihilate him with his bare hands, his will forbade him. "They'll be here at the base soon. The Chinese military is escorting them."

Cress was now his. With no communication to the civilized world, and possibly out of resources, she was at his mercy. This moment had been mediated in Belmarsh Prison more than any other–the day. He'd do it over again.

What would be the perfect end to the offspring of the insolent Nicole Cress, a woman with more nerve than that husband of hers and Mason's mother put together? Cress junior reminded him of himself. And if he was right, her resolve was as determined as his.

Ridge stepped away, attentive to the telepathic gape that could bend him into submission.

Kumar peered into the two men who towered above him. "Mason, your welcome is up tomorrow. I want you and your thugs off my property by dawn."

Kasmir put his right hand in the middle of his chest, then leaned forward in a customary greeting. "I saw you being harassed by the gun and sword idiots up there. We came looking for you but lost you about two hours ago in the sandstorm. Come, looks like your friend may need attention."

Kasmir piled them on the three camels they had with them, and they rode to the Kizil Caves, a set of Buddhist rock-cut caves near Kizil township. The caves stood in the cliffs of Querdagh Mountain in two forms, living quarters for monks and meditation houses.

Calla jumped off the camel and faced the entrance of the caves.

"This is the commercial hub of the ancient Silk Road. I've lived here all my life and help preserve this third-century, Buddhist cave," Kasmir said.

She turned to him. "When my mother's note indicated the Tarim and the mummies, I imagined you'd be a curator in an actual museum and not the Kizil Caves. It makes sense now. I don't know why I didn't think of it."

Kasmir and his seven-member family lived in modest apartments at the back of the caves. "There's so much work involved in the preservation of this site," Kasmir said as he led them into his unassuming living room.

An elderly woman attended to Jack's wounds using a natural combination of a tonic water bath and a few drops of grapefruit, essential oil.

"I didn't know that traditions continue here much like they were thousands of years ago," Calla said.

"We continue in the ways of our ancestors. We grow rice and grain, grapes, pomegranates, plums, pears, peaches, and almonds. That's how we make a living. The ground is rich in minerals and kind to us. The air here is fresh and healthy for us."

Nash leaned forward. "But you were with MI6."

"Only temporarily. .. helping with nuclear and economic relations."

"Undercover?" Nash said.

"It was a long time ago, and only briefly. I did it to fight for the preservation of our culture."

A small boy handed the guests a spread of citrus fruits, green and red peppers, and melons. The trio had been cloaked with embroidered clothing to keep away the wintry winds. Kasmir disappeared for several minutes to the back of the house and returned with a wrapped bundle. "Calla, here is something that Nicole gave me for you. I'm not sure what it is and have never opened it."

"You never wanted to know?" Calla asked.

"No. I trusted her, she trusted me."

Calla took the bundle and opened it. Her eyes caught a printed cloth resembling the other two. She placed them all together, and the three cloths formed a complete five-by-five-inch piece of manuscript of medieval gibberish.

"What is it?" asked Kasmir.

"That's what I need to figure out. She left me three, and here they are. But they don't make sense to me."

Calla, Nash, and Jack mounted a Toyota Jeep Kasmir hired for them, armed with a local-global positioning unit and food supplies. "It's a few years old, but should get you to Urumqi."

"Thanks, Kasmir."

He gripped her hand as she mounted the Jeep. "And if you find Nicole, forgive her. She did the best she could with what was in front of her. It wasn't an easy decision for her."

Calla nodded their thanks as Nash started the Jeep down the dusty road, and they braced themselves for a ten-hour journey. They proceeded along the stretch of road for two kilometers west of the Kizil until they reentered the desert road to Urumqi.

As they stared ahead at the bare road, a shot fired through the air.

Nash shuddered the Jeep to a halt. Without warning, men on horseback surrounded their vehicle, dressed in indistinguishable, military uniforms carrying a plethora of firearms. The front man rode before the others and jumped off his horse, gravitating to the driver's side, his gun pointing at Nash. "Step out of the car."

He spoke with a British accent.

"Why?" Nash asked with stern confidence.

"You're trespassing on protected ground."

"Says who?" Nash insisted.

The man slapped a piece of paper up against the windshield they guessed was a warrant. "Says the law of Xinjiang."

Calla glimpsed out the passenger window of the Toyota. Four military vehicles caught up and blocked their path—front and back.

CHAPTER 24

1901 hrs.

I*mbecile!* DID KUMAR think measly armed men would throw him off the base camp? He couldn't rely on fools. It did not matter any longer. In a few hours, they'd all be gone.

Cress was on her way.

He cursed under his breath. *No offspring of Nicole Cress's going to ruin me.*

With a sure hand on the steering wheel of technology systems, Cress would not be able to stand; however aptly, she'd reversed his hacks in London six months ago. Mason's fingers twitched as he gnawed on his thoughts. Nicole Cress was badgering around. The world was unstable, and only when he gained full control of the operatives' resources, could he defend the innocent–his way.

Innocents like my mother.

He had to stay focused. The only way he could steady the off-balance network systems had endured over the years, was to rebalance everything. Like the twenty-five network vulnerabilities at US power plants, the hacking attack on three

South Korean broadcasters and two banks. How about the Pental-Marsh department store attack, which was installed from an insecure Wi-Fi network in one of the company's shops? More than sixty-five million people had their credit card details stolen, or was the figure closer to a hundred million?

He could seize control of all these facilities' servers and balance them. Protect them.

Cress's last interference to his software had created technological disharmony. It was time for that ageless proverb. *An eye for an eye. That creates balance!*

His thoughts traveled to the woman trapped in that little cell in Texas. His feeble mother.

Remember her in magnificence, or it will make you weak!

He'd finally found the answer to that little problem. But he had to be careful; Cress was perceptive, much like him.

Mason cranked his hands and stepped out into the daylight, halting at an approaching phantom across the horizon. For a minute, he thought he'd seen her.

Nicole Cress?

1816 hrs.

"You're trespassing!" Sage's brash voice punctured their ears. Calla never imagined she would see the red-haired, Santorini archer again.

She stood broad-shouldered, the last born of the metamorphosed triplets, in a bodysuit too snug for desert hiking. Her arrow was marked at Calla's middle. Behind Sage, approximately ten men in four-wheel-drive, desert Jeeps aimed accurately leveled firearms.

Ridge, the tall, watchful ninja, harboring a complex form of martial arts, who'd snatched her backpack in Akihabara market, bore into Calla with raged eyes that seemed to permanently slope his bushy eyebrows. New confidence brimmed from the shinobi, possibly because ten more like him gathered around him. How could she tell? Perhaps Mason, had concocted them all? Worse, they slithered like androids telepathized by his authority.

She stepped out of the Jeep, renewed strength coiling in her muscles. Nash shuffled out of the Jeep and bucked by her side taking her hand as his narrowed eyes contemplated the schemes brewing in her mind. "No, Calla," he muttered. "There's got to be more. These soldiers may not be normal."

Nash was right. They'd been foisted, and the trio was clearly outnumbered.

"We're not trespassing," Nash said. He slowly drew out the slip from the Chinese Embassy and the local excavation permit Honghui had arranged. "This gives us ample permission to be here."

Sage raised her bow and sizzled a furious arrow through the sheets of paper, pinning them in the cracked ground.

The enraged arrow missed Nash's hand by mere centimeters. "This discussion is over. Let's move," Sage belted.

Calla and Nash stood immobile.

Calla contemplated their options. The desert was vast, and they'd never outrun these thugs in a desert that extended six-hundred miles from west to east.

She eyed Jack back in the Jeep. A hoodlum traversed to his side and plowed him out of the backseat, hurtling him toward them. Jack limped along with them as they were marched toward the camouflage vehicles, guns in their backs, and enough arrows from Sage's bow to pin a dozen tails on any donkey.

Calla caught the tiny movement of the muscles at the

corner of Nash's jaw. He leaned into her and whispered. "There's an undercover military base not too far from here. It was on the satellite before we were ambushed."

Jack tried to ignore the strange aching in his ankle as he leaned into them. "It's the one the Soviet government helped build in the sixties. It was kept to monitor new energy resources here."

The cold tip of a gun's barrel dented in Calla's shoulder. "Move!" commanded an armed criminal.

Jack ignored the harsh requests, probably getting used to it by now and leaned into Nash. "Do you think we can get communication over there? I think India may have been involved with that Soviet base. Any idea what diplomatic relations are like with them?"

"We need to reach Allegra. But even if we can jump these thugs, how do we get there? And the question is which side will they be on?" Calla said.

Nash rubbed a palm on his tight jaw. "Plus, we don't know who's running it now."

He squinted in the fading sun. "We need to find a way to get there. After the Cold War, Russia looked for ways to sell the base off, and my take is the Chinese government reclaimed it."

Calla raised her eyebrows, scrutinizing several sheets of solar panels in the back of one Jeep. "Let's just hope they are not headed there first."

By the time the sun set on the wasteland, the Jeeps and horses accelerated into a large compound, sandwiched on a plain between two desert mountains. A technology oasis in the middle of the desert, set on a span of land that could have measured close to five-hundred acres.

A rusty smell hung in the air as Calla observed a legion of

solar panels that traveled as far as she could squint. Hemmed in by the unforgiving desert on expansive acreage, they stretched across a desert flanked by high mountain ranges.

"Home sweet home," Sage called as she dropped the back tail of the Jeep's trunk. "Let's go!"

Calla tilted her head. "Is that what you call it? That would explain your outlandish hospitality."

Sage, and with the towering Rajput in tow, trooped them into a two leveled building, mostly cast out of containers, whose sides had been wedged with glass panels to admit sunlight. Once inside, Calla bore a cold breeze drifting through her body-armor shirt Nash had insisted they pack for the desert. Bulletproof on both sides, custom had warned her that should she ever glare into the eyes of the criminal who's refused to expire, she would have advantage.

It was a smell that had graced her nostrils one too many times–expensive cologne so greasy it could sizzle a pan of stir-fry.

Her eyes glanced up.

Mason glared at her. She'd only hoped to see him behind a grate of bars.

Mason retracted and hustled to prepare a welcome that would greet Cress, a microchip, he could dislodge in her, safely nestled on a trigger in his hands. After he was done with her mind, she would be useless. He peered out the base window again and caught a glimpse of the trio. It was not Nicole.

The daughter will do for now.

She trekked over the fractured desert ground as an evening wind shrilled around them. Mason moved to the front of the building, twirling the silicon ship in his hand. *Just a few more hours.*

Sage and her brothers funneled the trio into the base's main entrance. Mason suddenly felt warm. Had a breeze swept in? He clenched his jaw. He needed to look into her eyes and read what lay behind that knowledgeable mind. Operative or not, he knew how to get around her protected concentration, a detail the operatives had overlooked.

Calla stepped into the light. Her eyes bore into his depth, cold as frost. She swallowed hard, trying to control the urge to be sick.

The marine was no different—dry heaving coming from his throat and the other one, the ingenious mathematician and technology schemer. The last time he'd dealt with Kleve, he'd created a bugging device using computing techniques that could gnaw at any security network. Jack would have been a good confederate in his little ring of programmers.

Jack eyed Mason with a growing scowl on his face.

He has his limits too. Sage will see to it.

Mason took a step toward Calla. "You've finally seen it fit to have a conversation with me."

Her lips warped into a snarl. "You belong in a penitentiary."

"Prison is for criminals. I'm not a criminal."

Nash took a step toward him, averting his eyes–his six-foot-three frame on-par with Mason. "What do you want this time?"

"I have a proposal for you." Mason turned his attention to Calla. "It's about your mother."

She glimpsed over at Nash as he took a deep breath, visibly failing to relax. "The last time you discussed my mother, we ended up in a smoke bomb. No, thank you," she said.

She stirred closer.

That's it. Come nearer, my girl. Mason scrutinized her emerald eyes for several seconds. "It's entirely up to you. I've devised a methodology–a network that connects the globe in one secure grid system. One, that's impenetrable."

"We're not fooled, Mason. You've been wreaking havoc on security systems since you entered Belmarsh," Calla said.

"Oh, that. That's just to prepare for the finale."

"What do you have in mind?" Jack said.

"Technology that involves a new level of encryption that reverses the engineering mechanisms through which most hacking is done."

"Impossible," Jack said. "Every system, at one time or another, reveals its vulnerabilities."

"Exactly," added Sage, her voice commanding and sensual. "Our system deciphers codes it would take ages to decrypt, even in today's so-called advanced computing age."

Mason folded his arms across his chest. "My proposal to you and those who come on board with me is one; to provide the world with an impenetrable, hack resistant network that governments, corporations, and groups could buy from me and in return, they obtain an international manager for safe signals intelligence with my people on the watch, protecting them. .. really from nothing. But if they need assurance, I'm there."

"You mean sell your network soul to the cyber devil," Calla said.

"Hm...stop giving me ideas," Mason said. He turned to Nash. "Shields, think of it this way. It will be the NSA for the globe with the added benefit of supreme, network security at my affordable prices and cooperation. "

"And bring global networks to their knees unless they pay for your hacking assistance. I don't think so."

Mason studied Nash. One of three men he'd encountered

who could clash bullets midair. It was extremely difficult to hit a bullet or arrow midair, to the point of impossible. A skill many had trained at in ISTF, and many had failed. But this one man, call it concentrated skill in weaponry and combat, he could. The key was to wait until the bullet reached the top of its trajectory and fire when the force of air resistance equaled the force of gravity. Shields was not only a skilled shooter, but he also had brains and Mason longed to get him in his telepathic chair, if only he could get him there before the marine's gun went off.

Shields had been one of three men out of ten who'd been selected to train in the special skill at ISTF. Only three could time the precision of a fired bullet, based on a combination of body language from the attacker and the type of gun.

Mason drew in a sharp sniff. "That's persuasion I'll throw in. I may even use the NASA gimmick as a bartering chip. Sad to see that my methods are unconventional."

"You want to be a networked, intelligence provider, just on the wrong side of the law," Nash said.

Calla squinted, moving her gaze from Mason's grueling stare.

Mason took a deep breath. *She's stronger than I thought. That was not easy. I couldn't even move one memory or read one emotion.*

Jack edged closer. "How exactly do you propose on creating this genius, hack resistant network?"

"Ah, the tech expert! You and Sage could be the world's leading innovators. I'm afraid I can't reveal all my cards. Not just yet. My gift to the world is signals acumen. Why stop me from making global networks safer?"

Calla straightened her shoulders. "No, thank you, I prefer a joint approach."

"Like ISTF? Five governments failing to make any cohesive decisions? By the way, I thought you may disagree, so here's the real catch."

She caught his eye. "Aye, there's the rub."

"I have a little favor I need, Cress. I may reconsider if you hand over the whereabouts of your mother dead or alive. Ridge says she left you a message. That woman was no fool. She took something long ago that belonged to me, and I need it back."

"What's that?"

"That's my affair. This way, please."

They entered a darkened room that housed a few monitors. Mason pointed to the first monitor. "In eight hours, ninety percent of corporate networks will be synced to mine, and not a soul will know that they're being watched and manipulated. Every little piece of technology they use that requires a network avenue will be entirely at my disposal and control. The servers and satellites necessary are in place."

"You must have taken decades to contract such a scheme," said Jack.

"Exactly. Here's my deal." His eyes caught Calla's. "Perhaps it's more like blackmail."

Mason switched on a monitor.

Calla's eyes traveled to a figure moving on the screen in oblivion. "Father?"

Stan sat reading in his study in the Cotswolds.

"There's Stan Cress in his retirement manor unaware that his surveillance camera is in my control." He shook his head. "Stan was once a promising secret service agent. I take it this is your father." He grazed her shoulder with his thick palm, setting off an enraged glower from Nash. "Give me all the information your mother left you. I'll find her dead or alive, or your father's lovely manor will not only burn this time, but it will also sizzle."

Mason's lips curled into a smirk as he faced Nash. "I take it you have some experience with that."

"So what will it be? Your father or your mother?"

2310 hrs.

Nash clenched his hands, grasping the metal grills of the cell. He imagined once it was as a panel storage room at the far end of the energy base camp. Ridge had escorted them into the stale space holding two beds, a stack high of solar energy panels, and a sink. He glimpsed through the metal grate, looking both ways. The room used to be an old prison, possibly used when the Soviets created it. Tamper-proof storage like rooms lined both sides of the walkway.

Nash studied the floor where a heavy iron ring dented the cement about a meter from where he stood. Possibly used for prisoner punishment, or worse, solitary confinement. Calla sat on the edge of a drop-down bed, her head supported on her knees with her hands.

He made his way toward her. "Hey, beautiful, snap out of it. We've with been through worse."

Jack sat idly on the stone slab opposite them. Mold and mildew crept past their nostrils, begging one to wonder how the base remained moist in a parched desert. Without a window or any sort of fresh air, Nash worried the stench might get to them.

"Could someone please tell me how we always get ourselves in such binds?" Jack said, grinning at his nonreceptive cell phone. "The last time we were this intimate, was in a similar cell in Rome."

Nash set a hand on Calla's knee. "We'll be out of here soon."

"Mason is keen on playing god," Jack said.

Sudden anger lit in Calla's eyes. "He can't."

"Think of it," Jack said, as sweat prickled his scalp. "If any government or corporation fails to cooperate with him, they risk network infection."

Nash drew in a sharp breath. "You mean he'll hack their networks anyway?"

"Exactly," replied Jack. "That's what the NASA hacks, and those of the British Parliament have been about. He's demonstrated that he is capable."

Nash rose digging his hands into his hair. "Then, global networks are at a standstill."

Calla peered from one friend to another. "The only way anyone can stay secure and resist him is to stop using a cell phone, tablet, company network, a flight, e-mail or even a Wi-Fi system. .."

Nash took a seat next to her on the rough blanket beneath them. "Essentially, anything related to a network."

Calla breathed hard. Her usually lively eyes sparkled with weariness. "The choice will be to discard every item of technology we use or cower under Mason's radar. Think about it. Everything uses technology and a network. Even the food we eat." She shot up and slammed a fist in her palm. "We can't let that happen. That would mean rewriting history, going back to the drawing boards, and starting a new Internet, a new world. I became a curator to explain history and take us into the future, not to destroy it. Which is what will happen, either way, we go?"

"That's right, Cal," Nash said. "We can't let him take the network world hostage and risk redrafting a major part of history. The idea of data communications between computers began in the late sixties and early seventies. Researchers began progressing ways of connecting computers and exchanging information. If those network avenues are compromised, then so is network history. We would have to start again, or. .." He glimpsed at Jack. "Hack his software like we did last time."

Jack scratched his head. "Last time, we broke into his manor and found his logarithms. This time he has them bolted securely with the bionic witch, Sage."

"And his brain," Calla said.

Nash studied the low hanging bulb above them, before turning to the caged door that imprisoned them. The best way out was by deactivating the lock on the metal grill. He shot up and drifted to the grated door and tugged the iron before turning to Calla. She could break it with her bare hands. He was certain of it, with those same genes that had opposed gravity. Her head drifted back into her palm, with her elbows balancing on her knees. Had she given up? Their time had been marked for dawn–only six hours away. By then, she'd have to surrender all she knew about her mother, the little information she had.

Nothing.

Nash leaned his back into the solid grate grills and studied her. She raised her head back, eyes swollen with anguish, confusion, and struggle written on her face. He managed a weak smile. "Calla, you can break that lock."

Jack set his back against the far wall, the whites of his eyes flashing. He was thinking the same thing.

Nash strode to where she sat and dipped to his knees in front of her. He shifted a lock of hair from her eyes. "Cal, he took my gun, we have nothing but you now."

"Even if I did, Nash. Then what? Sprint through the desert without supplies, water, or communication. We're in the middle the second largest, bloody desert in the world."

"We can't give up now." He glanced over at Jack. "There's a way, and we can find it–together."

He longed to get closer to her. To encourage the closeness that had escalated when they were alone in Colorado and most recently in Paris, but he knew from experience that he could lose her that way. Helping Calla reach her potential had made him lose sleep. She could outsmart Mason. He knew it. But she had to want to.

Calla weighed him with a critical squint. "We have no time. What if—"

"No, Cal," Jack said. "We don't entertain bullies. Come on, you learned that at Beacon Academy."

Jack shot up and paced the little cell. "There must be some way to reverse the worm and break into that brain of his."

Calla pulled out the three shreds of medieval cloths and unrolled them. "My father is alive. I don't know if my mother is. Doesn't it make sense to save the one who is?"

Both stood speechless. Jack spoke first. "I don't know what the correct choice is, but without your mother, Mason cannot instigate his scheme. I feel it. Almost as if he needs her."

"He must have some personal vendetta with her. Something she did to him," Nash added.

Calla peered into the glares. "I promised my father that if Nicole is alive, things would be restored between them, that he could finally have closure with her."

Nash's chest caved in. H*ow does one make such a decision?*

Regardless of how he felt about his father, it was highly unlikely he could choose between his own parents. No one should have to face such a choice.

"How does anyone choose between two parents, Nash?"

She had read his mind.

He could do nothing for her.

CHAPTER 25

DAY 12
THREE MINUTES BEFORE DAWN

NASH'S EYES SHOT open. The blast of an explosion shattered throughout the cell, jerking him forward. He plummeted off the little bed, his head hammering the floor. His eyes drifted to the front of the cell.

Jack stood glimpsing through the grill.

"That's not a manufacturing mishap. Someone has detonated an explosive. It sounded like a grenade, an impact one," Nash said.

Calla jerked herself off the bed and joined them by the wrought iron. The explosion had woken them, and as Nash peered through the gate, his eye caught sight of pieces of metal from the outer casing of the grenade that had sailed outward at immense speed. Someone had embedded the grenade in the wall opposite them.

Whoever it was had to be close and had possibly missed his target.

Us.

Soon sirens overwhelmed the complex. Thundering

footsteps signaled that the place was being evacuated. Nash swore under his breath. They were barred in a cell none would remember to evacuate.

He raised his hands looking for grip and located an iron bar, part of the piping that ran above the cell. He set his hands on it and hoisted himself up, setting his boots against the rigidness of the metal grate. In one heave, he bent his knees, drove off, and slammed the grate with a loud thud.

The steel bars rattled, and dust broke away from the hinges.

Jack did likewise, placing his hands next to Nash's on the piping. Both men booted the rail several times in accord until the left casting cracked the door's hinges.

"We're on our way," Jack said, a beaming grin forming on his lips.

They raised their hands again, bracing themselves for another thwack when Jack peered to the far right. Calla had joined them.

She gripped the pipe and pulled herself up. Together they slammed the iron gate to the ground. They scuttled out into the cemented corridor. A screaming alarm blared, and gray smoke slinked through the passageways, challenging visibility. Workers charged from their quarters, some armed some not.

Jack raised his satellite phone up and shook it several times until he latched on to a signal.

It disappeared.

He tore open the back casing of the phone and rewired the circuit board–and the conversion chips that translated the incoming signal. "Huh, she's up." He showed it to Nash. "Got those long and latitude coordinates? How far do you think it is to that US base from here?"

"There's a US base here?" Calla asked.

Nash smirked. "There's always a US base."

He seized the phone and fingered in the coordinates. "It's

about twenty miles from here. Let's see whether we can grab a Jeep."

The trio turned the corner at the end of the passage, spurting past masked soldiers, who paid them no regard.

Startling motion drew Nash's eye. *That face.*

The barrel of a sniper's gun was aimed at their faces. He was attired in sand-colored, desert camouflage, combat pants, below a body cover vest. Behind him, three other men caught up in similar attire.

"Looks like we got here in time," said the man grinning at Nash.

He remembered that grin. Frankly, he would've rather ran into Mason Laskfell.

"How's that house of yours?" the sniper said—the same marksman who'd carbonized his house in Colorado.

0619 hrs.

Mason shot through the rubble. He'd fallen out of his bed.

He checked his watch. *It was time.*

He peered out the small box window before stepping into the hallway outside his quarters. The energy base had transformed into an uncontrollable evacuation, with damaged solar panels, drills, and office equipment littering most passageways.

Bugger! His detonator set at Stan's manor had been damaged in the explosion. He stared at the unresponsive cell phone. There was no way he could now barter for information about Nicole.

He heard the sirens and the shouts of escapees as their boots thundered in every direction.

Sage burst into his path and tossed him a bulletproof vest, a hardhat, and some keys. "It's time. Let's go."

He set the bulletproof vest over his head. "Is everything ready?"

"Yes, the Jeep to the airstrip is outside. This place will be torched to the ground in exactly ten minutes."

He moved with sudden speed toward the fire exit.

Sage scuttled after him.

"Anything from Cress?" he asked.

"They've gone, the cell is empty."

He would have to find Nicole another way. Her trail was widening. Pure and guileless. Giving Cress that ultimatum meant she'd not try anything foolish.

Cress could not choose. He'd predicted her intentions and was right. He was always right. He had made the rules, and now he was going to break them. That's the way to keep in control of signals intelligence. The world needed minds like his to sustain it. If this worked, he'd soon reunite with that fool, so blinded by jealousy he'd go this far.

It wasn't his headache.

CHAPTER 26

0725 hrs.

NASH BLINKED TWICE. The operative had surfaced from thin air. Had he caused the explosion breaking them out of Mason's cell? He'd deal with him and keep Calla as far from him as possible.

The operative peered through explosive smoke at the end of an abandoned passageway that lined the south wing of the energy base. Water gushed down the corridor escaping a burst pipe and spurted at their feet,

"Let's go!" Lascar's voice reminded Nash of a sergeant major he'd once known in the marines. Brash and overconfident, it echoed through the emptying halls.

Calla set a hand on Lascar's arm as he approached them. "Lascar? How?"

"Questions later. We need to move."

Nash scrutinized the operative's covert procedures as Lascar set an explosive on the far wall to their left. "Stand back!"

The explosive blasted a hole through the cement, pitching rubble in their path.

"This way," commanded Lascar.

Nash knew it was the same operative that had abducted Calla in Almont. He leaned into her side. "You know him, Cal?"

"I'll explain later," she said.

"And I'll follow gladly," Jack said.

They slithered past a security gate at the end of a second corridor.

"Where do you think you're going?"

Kane's sharp voice pierced the commotion, shoulders broad and eyes piercing the crowd.

Lascar raised a smooth firearm. The silver safety grip stretched into a thin chassis and exploded three rounds at him.

Kane slumped to the concrete like an unbalanced domino.

Nash scrutinized the miniature shells that had sizzled from the barrel. He'd never seen anything similar.

The group bolted past the Rajput warrior, and Lascar led them to a low opening he'd blasted through a wall to the base's exterior. He motioned to them in sign language, commanding them to crawl through the rest of the way.

Jack slid through first, followed by Calla. Nash stopped before crouching and glared at Lascar. "Who are you?" he said.

"Someone you'll never be, even to her."

A gunshot fired behind them, and both men zipped their heads around. Kane, undeterred set himself charging after them.

Nash ignored Lascar's nudge at a brawl. The operative with the explosives would have to be dealt with later. He crawled through the grim tunnel after Calla. After slinking on the chilled cement for close to three minutes, they surfaced outside on a sand hill as morning light began to flood the wasteland.

"Where to, Lascar?" Calla asked once the group had surfaced.

Lascar seized Calla's hand. "Follow me."

Nash's lips pressed tightly as the group trudged through taxing sand, charging away from the energy base and toward a deserted road.

Blazing headlights blinded their path, and a heavy truck accelerated through dawn's fog on the dark road. Lascar's advances with Calla were seeping deep under Nash's skin. Where had he been when Calla needed help in Uganda seven months ago? In Rome? Goodness, the last three years?

They charged toward the truck and saw Allegra hurtle out of the driver's seat. An army camouflage cap shielded part of her face, her long braids pulled back in a neat plait. "Thank goodness you're alive. This way was easier than negotiating diplomatic terms. We need to get you safely across the border. China has revoked ISTF's terms and anything connected to us. They'll be waiting for you if you head toward Beijing."

They hustled into the van, and Allegra sped the truck down toward Pakistan.

With no words exchanged, hours later, she nosed the vehicle up to the border barrier between China and Pakistan, at the Khunjerab Pass, positioned on the northern border of Pakistan's Gilgit-Baltistan, Hunza and Nagar districts, on the southwest border of the Xinjiang region.

The truck came to a shuddered halt at the border police station, and an officer stopped and spoke to Allegra. "A British truck in China? I would expect more judicious means, Allegra."

Allegra eyed the checkpoint soldier and revved her gears for Pakistan before howling out the window. "You know me."

"Okay, move. I never saw you here."

Allegra winked at him. "Thanks."

When they reached Gilgit-Baltistan, they jumped off the truck to rest. Nash helped Calla down from the backside of the truck as Allegra tossed them some water bottles. Calla turned to Lascar. "I don't know what we would have done without you."

Lascar inched forward. "Doesn't look like you were doing much, even with the so-called qualified help you had here."

Jack moved toward Nash and set a hand on his shoulder. Nash was ready to speak, but on second thought, he turned his back to Lascar.

"I'm talking to you, marine!" Lascar said.

Nash swiveled around slowly. "You're out of line."

"Says who? The tough guy who ran out of options?"

Anger welled up through Nash's veins, his internal response challenging to bolt one straight punch into the operative's jaw. He clenched his fist and dragged in a sharp breath before turning his back to Lascar a second time.

Lascar zipped him round with a violent grip on his shoulder. Nash lost balance for a few seconds before thrusting his frame in front of Lascar. Eye to eye and inches from each other, the men sized each other, each scrutinizing the other.

Fury rose to Lascar's lips. He swore and launched himself at Nash, grabbing him by the collar with both hands. Lascar twisted his knuckles inward against Nash's neck, aiming for a choke.

Nash slid under Lascar's arm and forced a hand to the crook of Lascar's elbow and knocked it, downing his wrists until Lascar lost balance and plummeted to the dirt.

Lascar wiped his mouth, shot up, and drew his pistol.

"Enough," Calla said, fury rising to her lips as she broke up the two men. "We're wasting time. Can we leave the mannish parade in the desert and get out of here?"

A spurt of rage spiraled in Lascar's eyes, and he edged

away. "How can you trust someone who keeps things from you?"

Allegra minced toward the men and raised her hand. "That's enough, Lascar!"

Lascar's stare remained livid, not once leaving Nash's infuriated face.

"What're you talking about, Lascar?" Calla turned her attention to Nash. "What's going on here?"

Lascar stepped forward. "Looks like your marine here made a deal with the devil. We're all hunting Mason and Nash has had the answers all along, not to mention the most crucial thing we need to bring Mason down. I wouldn't be surprised if he lets us walk right back into Mason's mind games."

"That's loaded, Lascar," Calla said. She turned to Nash. "What's really going on here?"

"Don't listen to him," Nash said, sensing the back of his neck prickle. "Desert sand must have clogged his vision and stimulated his ego."

"Not so fast, marine!" Lascar shot Calla a glance. "Nash's been in touch with your mother for more than fifteen months. Why do you think he knows so much about the operatives and Mason Laskfell? How did he know enough about Mason to silence him in prison? He probably helped him escape."

Nash threw a violent punch into Lascar's jaw. However, much his knuckles hurt, it felt damn good to set the operative straight.

Launching another brawl, Lascar threw a fist that hit Nash in the shoulder joint and set him back.

Nash made a visible effort to pull himself together. He rose from where he'd fallen and moved to the side of the road, shaking with impotent rage.

Calla moved quietly behind him. "Nash, what's he saying? Is it true?"

He raised his eyes slowly toward her. "Yes. It is."

—

"I swear, Calla, I don't know where she is," Nash said.

She pulled away, haughtily from his grasp. "Why didn't you tell me, Nash? Does my father know?"

"No. She sends me messages in this discreet way. She found me. I don't know how and her one request was not to tell you because it would endanger you. .. and Stan."

"But, Nash—"

He could not bear to see the tear surfacing in her right eye. Was she right? But, he'd had to keep Nicole's wishes. Otherwise, he would have lost contact with her.

He remembered the meeting well in a mall in Boston, fifteen months ago. The night before, he'd been working late into the night at his hotel, cleaning up some old files, when without warning, his computer went into encryption mode. It was a virus and a strong one. The NSA could beat any type of encryption. Perhaps he could grab text and work around the encryption. After several attempts, it was clear the hacker had a message for him.

It unraveled itself on his screen.

Nash Shields
NSA Employment number 27130-1084

He wrote a response.

Who's this?

The answer came:

Nicole Cress… Calla's mother.

After several exchanges with the woman calling herself Nicole Cress, Nash was still doubtful, until she shared her former MI6 number and details about Calla's adoption.

Still, he had to be sure. He wanted a face-to-face meeting.

The place they were to meet was Fanueil Hall, in downtown Boston, steps away from the Atlantic, a shopping meeting point of locally loved and nationally known shops, congested, most of the time with shoppers indulging in worldwide cuisine as cobblestone promenades were graced with musicians.

A public, loud and vibrant place.

They were to meet on opposite balconies on one of the main shopping walkaways, where Nicole had left an earpiece under a plant.

When Nash arrived, a lone woman in all black with dark glasses and headgear, making her downright unrecognizable, stood on the balcony opposite him. So began a conversation. It had lasted three minutes and twenty seconds. Nash failed to trace her after she'd spoken, then disappeared through the crowds. There'd been one agreement. She would contact him and only via an encrypted website whose web address she sent to his tablet.

The woman knew her technology, and he'd left knowing undoubtedly it had been Nicole Cress, though he'd failed to see her face. She'd been a step ahead of him each time, a real MI6 agent.

That's why he hadn't trusted the incoming calls on his cell phone. It had never been part of the agreement.

He reached for Calla again and drew her away from the others, sensing an awkward response, deep in her. She was slipping away. His lips trembled as he spoke. "It's the truth. I have never lied to you."

Two lone tears appeared beneath her lashes. "How could you not tell me?"

"I couldn't beautiful. She would have broken all contact. She told me specifically not to say anything to you. She said it would have endangered yours and her life. I had to protect you, Calla. I can't help it. I've always felt the need to keep you safe."

"But Nash, we're supposed to have trust and a connection that neither my past nor yours could ever contaminate. Our parents lived in lies. We're different, Nash."

"We do. .. and we still are. Please, Cal," he said in a strangled gasp. "I didn't lie to you—"

His face was naked with anguish; he brought a shaky hand to his face to mop away his own tearing anguish. "Believe me. I'm sorry, maybe I should have told you. I don't know. I just love you so much, and I was trying to protect you—"

A guarded look surfaced in her eyes.

Jack approached them and set a gentle hand on Calla's shoulder. "Cal, Nash would never do anything to harm you."

She moved away from his embrace.

Nash drew her in his arms. "Cal, please."

For a few seconds, her red-rimmed eyes welled with emotion. She suddenly raised her head. "Don't, Nash." She drew back with a shudder, slithering away from him. "All my life, people supposed to protect me, love, and be there for me have lied to me. My mother, my father, Mila. .. and now. .. you."

Nash's eyes clouded with hazy sadness. He couldn't believe her words. He never thought she would see it that way.

Betrayal.

He thought he'd been protecting her by keeping the

madness of her past, her illogical family, and the operatives from her.

She was right. How different had he been to those close to her? Those who'd let her down. Whatever he said now wouldn't matter any longer. He'd lost her.

Lascar began to walk briskly, threading his way purposefully toward them. "I tried to warn you, Calla." He glanced at Allegra. "We all did."

Allegra cleared her throat as guilt settled in her voice. "Calla, please, some of this is my fault. Listen to Nash—"

Calla took a step from Nash. "I've heard enough."

Lascar gripped her upper arm. "We need to get moving."

"Nash. .. I need to be away from you now.. ." Calla said.

Had he heard the words, right? He reached over and touched her wet cheek.

She drew away. "Don't. Please don't touch me. .. I don't need you to help me anymore."

Jack intervened. "Cal, you don't mean that. .."

Nash ran his hands through his wet hair. He'd barely noticed the rain that had started a slow descent over the descending hills. It was over for her. He knew it, just the way she'd said 'touch'. All he saw was his mother walking out on his father. He'd failed her like his father had let down his mother with lies.

It was the Shields family nightmare. .. again. Though he mustered the courage to speak up, his words fluttered out in a shaky tone. "Calla, I'm sorry. I'm so sorry I failed you."

This time, Lascar gripped Calla's hand and slowly led her to the truck.

Jack's face drew tight with fatigue and concern. Two deep lines of worry appeared between his eyes, as he nudged a deadened Nash. "Come on, man. Snap out of it! We always come out of the worst binds. This is just one of them. Don't let her go like this. .."

Calla stepped into the truck with Allegra and Lascar. She glanced once at them before settling in the army truck as Allegra leaned forward, hunched slightly over the steering wheel ready to start the vehicle. She engaged the gear. "Guys, are you coming?"

Nash could not bring himself to look at her. *She does not want me to.*

Jack shot a glance at Nash. "Nash, come on. .. we'll work it out, mate," he said with a distinct note of apprehension.

Nash failed to budge. With numb stillness, rain beat on his face, jacket, and arms. Jack stood by his side, dumbfounded that he'd been brought to the instant of choosing between his two best friends. Right now, one needed him more than the other. As they stood on a deserted road, Jack raised his chin toward Allegra, a glazed look of despair beginning to spread over her face. "No. We'll find our way from here."

Allegra leaned forward and started the ignition. "Please, come with us. We need to leave now."

Nash shook his head, slowly unable to glance at her.

The truck began a slow descent down the slope farther into Pakistan.

Several minutes later, as he stared after it, Jack ran a hand through his dreds. "How on earth are we going to get out of here?"

CHAPTER 27

ISLAMABAD, PAKISTAN
0957 hrs.

THAT WAS EASY enough. Mason struggled his way to the plane. "Go!" he shouted at the pilot.

The pilot nodded.

Sage jumped in after him as Mason glared down at his injury from Japan. It had started to ache, having not had proper medical attention. He'd only needed three seconds.

He'd barely made it out alive of St. Peters Hospital with the security Shields had instigated. He'd extinguished the lights with one shot at the switch and stolen past terrified attackers with speed he didn't know he still had. He managed to get the help of three greedy guards who'd cowered to the floor with Jack. They'd given him the escape passage only twenty minutes earlier, and his pockets were now lighter. Money was never a problem. .. why should it be now? Twenty-thousand pounds sterling was all it took.

He'd needed to get out of there fast. How he did it, he didn't care.

And now, Stan or Nicole, it didn't matter.

Cress had failed to decide. Or had she been saved by the blast?

All he needed was those damn notes. The idiot would get them for him. The man had been avaricious enough when he came to him, mumbling unintelligible threats about Shields.

What did he care? Shields was no operative, granted he knew much about them, and he could fight in a ring with the best of them. But what did he care what Lascar's misgivings were about Nash? That made it easier for him.

Lascar was driven by jealousy. What was it about that Cress girl that tore both men apart? He remembered the pain he'd seen in the operative when he came to him to bare his soul. The first time he'd cracked an operative's brain activity, which would make Cress easier to handle.

Mason had never had much time for the tender side of human sentiment.

Things were set in motion.

Lascar knew what to do.

HUNZA, NEAR CHINA-PAKISTAN BORDER

Jack peered at him quietly as Nash watched the truck depart. It slugged the mud as the trickle that had started settled into a mountain downpour that beat over their heads. Nash's hair was wet throughout, his mountain boots moist, his jacket soaked through. He stood on the road for several minutes without moving.

"Nash, I'm so sorry. She didn't mean it."

Nash turned to face Jack, his face expressionless. The last ten minutes had scarred him deeper than any knife wound. "Yes, she did."

. . .

Jack scratched his head. Granted, Calla had searched for her mother all her adult life. He knew that from the moment he'd met her. Nash had not once surrendered any knowledge of his communication. Nicole hadn't wished it, because it was not safe for Calla to know where she was. Nash had only tried to protect them. *Shouldn't that be commended? I mean, the guy's a man of his word. That's a rarity these days.*

Jack didn't understand the opposite sex at all, especially the smart ones.

The connection his two best friends had was something he one day desired to find. Who was this Lascar anyway?

Nash shrugged out of his jacket and wrung out the rain. Jack noticed that though the temperature was low, Nash didn't feel the cold as he slung the coat over his shoulder.

Jack retrieved his phone. "We're not far from Hunza."

"How many miles?"

"About five."

"We can walk that."

"Nash, are you really giving up on her? What about—"

"She doesn't want me. I can't change that," Nash said, shrugging.

"I don't believe that. I've known her for a long time. Nash, she may have all the pieces left to her by her mother, but she still needs to figure out what they mean and, most importantly, where she is. She can't do that without you."

"Looks like she's going to—"

"We need to help her."

"Calla's decided she doesn't need our help. Let's get to Hunza and rent a Jeep that will take us to Islamabad. That will be the easiest route home."

"Home?"

"Where's home, Nash? You yourself have said home is where people you care about are. Calla is out there with frankly a very questionable guy, and you've been on this journey with her since it began. Don't give up on her, Nash. I know it'll kill you—"

Nash threw his hands in the air. She doesn't need my help."

"You know she needs us. This Lascar guy may be an operative with muscle to match a bull and bitter breath to go with it, but he lacks one thing. .." Jack edged closer. "He doesn't have your belief in her, your determination, and guts! All the things that Calla needs right now, and you're the only one who can give them to her. None of these other people have ever given her that, or are capable of it."

Nash started walking in the direction of Hunza. "Let's go."

"I've never known you to give up, Nash. If not for Calla, do it for you! Prove to yourself that you're right, that your instincts about people are never wrong! That's one of the first things I noticed about you. You can read people a mile away. And I know you know something's not right!"

Was he convincing himself? Nash wasn't one to give up. Whatever he decided, Jack purposed that he'd stand by Nash.

He needed to.

"Calla's with people who *want* her most," Nash said.

Jack's face angered. "Bull! But they're not the ones who she needs most."

ISLAMABAD AIRPORT

"You made the right choice."

Calla glanced over at Lascar, who buckled his seat belt next to her in the first class compartment of British Airways flight en route to London. She stretched her legs. She'd not spoken a word to either Allegra or Lascar on the long ride to

Rawalpindi, avoiding them as best she could when they chartered a flight from there to Islamabad.

Her head hurt. She'd taken an aspirin from Lascar to counter the pain and slept most of the trip. She would find her mother, didn't need anyone–never had in her twenty-eight years. She'd managed without anyone–for the most part. Her father, she could forgive. He'd had no knowledge of where her mother was and didn't know that Nicole was contacting Nash. Stan was family and those you couldn't choose.

But Nash was her... She could not find the words. It was as if Nash were part of her soul. *A silent hero—dependable... a liar!*

No, that he's not.

But he'd keep an important piece of the puzzle from her.

Had Allegra and Vortigern been right all along?

The plane chortled its engines, and soon they were airborne. As they took height, Calla tried to put the past day's events in perspective. Her eyelids weighed down with fatigue, and she drifted into a deep sleep. She shut her eyes as the plane made its way through the clouds and what looked like a smooth ride ahead.

CHAPTER 28

DAY 13

A HAND NUDGED HER shoulder. "Get up!"

Calla shot her eyes open. A face she knew all too well and hoped she would never see again stared directly into her eyes. Her hands were tied with steel cords. She wrung them, and a scorching sensation distressed the skin around them.

"Refrain from movement, or those hands will be charred."

"Mason."

Calla glimpsed around her. She was still on the airplane. It had landed and was completely deserted. She peered to the seat where Allegra had been.

Empty.

"I've taken care of her," she heard a man's hoarse voice say.

She shot a glimpse behind. "Lascar? What's going on?"

Mason frowned. "I'm glad your memory serves you well even with the drug he slipped you at the start of the flight."

Her eyes narrowed into Lascar. "You're starting to make this a habit."

Lascar moved closer to where Mason sat on the edge of the aisle seat across from her. Her head pushed back, eyes burning into him. "Where's Allegra?"

Lascar snickered. "You should've listened to your marine back there. If he's still alive."

She studied him for two seconds and, in one swift instant, swung her leg and caught Lascar's jaw. She sprang to her feet and landed centimeters from Mason.

He remained seated, watching with assured calm. Blood seeped from Lascar's jaw and trickled onto his shirt.

Lascar leaped up, attempting to strike back. Mason held out an outstretched hand. "Enough." He pulled a gun to Calla's head. "Now, Cress, you'll come quietly, or this gun may accidentally go off."

Calla remained still, her lungs heaving in her chest.

Within minutes, Mason marched her off the plane, his gun edging into her shoulder blades, with Lascar tailing behind. The warm climate was a contradiction to the weather she'd left in the Pakistani mountains. A warm gusty wind slapped her arms and legs as she descended onto the asphalt, hands restrained to her front.

Mason steered her toward a waiting dark Land Cruiser.

She took a glimpse at her new destination. Before her head was shoved into the backseat, the distant, Andalusia mountain ranges that had greeted her on the tarmac, told her she was in Spain.

—

ON THE ROAD TO ISLAMABAD

Jack read no response from Nash's face, as he edged his back in the leather of the front passenger seat of the Land Cruiser he'd rented for them. It was the quietest he'd ever seen Nash.

"You in a hurry, buddy?" Jack said.

The bleary road ahead was barren of traffic. Seventy-mph winds clouted their windshield as Nash churned the engine into fifth gear. The cruiser made its way on the damp road as they left the mountain paradise to Rawalpindi in the late morning, where they'd catch a flight to Islamabad. The region frequently experienced mudslides, and deep ravines could be spotted in range.

Nash remained silent. He'd contacted the US Embassy in Islamabad an hour ago, and they'd arranged their travel back to London after a minor debrief on Mason Laskfell's latest attempts. The moron had probably exploded a major energy plant in the North West of China, on the US's intelligence watch list.

Something told Jack that London would not be Nash's end destination.

The tablet responded to a secret British Intelligence signal.

"It's the only uncompromized link I have left."

Nash didn't respond but kept his eyes ahead as the sunset rays glared on the wet downhill road.

"Do you want to talk about it?" Jack said.

Nash stared ahead at the deserted road. "No."

Jack set his head down and found his videoconferencing application. He'd remembered something that Stan had once told him about MI6 intelligence procedures of the 1960s, and how they used to intercept signals. The secret service had used shortwave radio stations, characterized by unusual broadcasts, often created by artificially generated voices reciting streams of numbers, words, letters, tunes or better known as the Morse code. Mason had perfected this method of transmitting text information as a series of on-off tones, lights, or clicks openly understood by a skilled listener. The code Mason was using was new. A similar method, only he was not interpreting the basic Latin alphabet to intercept their communications. He was encrypting sophisticated, computing language.

If Jack could speak to Stan, then maybe he could get some ideas on how MI6 had used it, if they would admit that they did. He could reprogram it.

He dialed Stan's videoconference number, and his tablet captured indistinct images before Stan's living room drew into focus. The connection was pathetic but would do. Stan stood to the corner of the room, staring out the window. He'd left his computer on. He turned when he heard the system on his den table dial. It raised a curious look from his face. Stan strolled to the computer, shoulders drooped, with a slow, unsteady step and hit a button on his computer. "Jack?"

"Hey."

"Is everything okay? Is Calla with you?"

Jack wasn't sure the best way to answer that question. "She's with Allegra."

"And Nash?"

"He's here with me. We're in Pakistan."

"That doesn't sound right. What's going on?"

Nash's mouth was tight and grim as Jack shot him a glance. "Maybe another time Stan. Calla's fine."

"I should've come with you. I won't forgive myself if anything happens to her."

"Listen, the only way you can help Calla now it by giving us any information about her mother's location."

"I don't know where she is, Jack, or if she's alive."

Jack shot a purposeful look at Nash. "Oh, she's alive."

"How? Where?" Stan said.

"We're not sure yet."

Stan frowned in concentration. "What can I do?"

"Stan, several months ago you mentioned that Secret Security Service used a numbers station called 'Carman's Whistle', a line of communication through which spies securely received encrypted messages at specific times and could, therefore, isolate the Services' mainframe computers from contamination with the intelligence they received if necessary."

"It was a shortwave, radio communication spies used. It used higher frequencies for greater range. There were many other uses, like delivering encrypted messages to overseas agents. I received the broadcasts many times, and they saved my life," Stan said.

"I wonder whether Mason is using the same method to communicate with his hackers and stay one step ahead of us. You don't, by any chance, have details of those logarithms. It may help us intercept his messages and find his broadcasting hideout. "

"Whoa! Jack, that was ions ago. I don't see how those programs could help with today's technology and at the rate at which Mason is eating up cyberspace."

"It's not the technology I need, it's the principle. He's probably using the same method, only with a new code, which I need to figure out. That's how he's getting to global technology systems before we can bat an eye."

Stan's face hardened. "Even if I could, Jack, such information would be classified and filed. We would need someone in authority to reopen them for us, surrender the classified location of the original broadcast location, or get ISTF to do it—"

The screen went black.

"Stan?"

"What is it?" Nash asked.

"He's gone."

Jack attempted a redial.

The connection failed to respond.

1327 hrs.

Calla glimpsed at the white arches. The sequence of crisp curvatures of Seville airport welcomed her calculating mind. She gawked at the clouds above, threatening rain, although temperatures looked moderately warm.

Mason shoved her into a chrome Land Cruiser and watched her for a moment. "Comfortable, Cress?" He slumped into the seat next to her with Lascar and the driver sitting up at the front.

She scrutinized his intense eyes. "What do you want this time, Mason? Didn't prison agree with you?" Her voice was curiously flat as she spoke.

His eyes narrowed. "You're my latest and probably last project, Cress. If I can crack you, I can crack anything."

She squirmed beneath the steel grip on her wrists and felt a corresponding lessening of pressure from the thin restraining cuffs. "I'm flattered, Mason. I'll make sure I give you the challenge you've so anticipated."

She tugged at the cuffs. Their grip on her wrist tightened, and pain shot through to her shoulder.

"I wouldn't fight those if I were you. Don't get me wrong, I'm sure you could snap them in half. But bear in mind, the inner sides of those cuffs are lined with miniature needles that will shoot a powerful hallucinating deliriant up your bloodstream if they pierce your skin beyond a centimeter. This means you can afford little movement unless you wish to sing all your secrets to me." He checked his watch. "In ten seconds."

Calla glanced down at the modern steel cuffs. A small red

light beeped on the outer ring, a motion detection sensor, guaranteeing she couldn't go anywhere without Mason's knowledge. Calla couldn't help wondering why Mason hadn't killed her. What now? He'd accelerated his program to manipulate any global computer connected to the Internet. Had he used the same gimmicks to increase his telepathic mind to hypnotism?

Calla was not sure how it worked. She couldn't look him in the eyes. That was as far as her knowledge in hypnotism went. Hallucination was another thing. She wouldn't be able to tell the difference between reality and the imaginary. Her hand bent painfully at the wrist. "You're one sick criminal, Mason."

Lascar glimpsed back. "Hey! You promised not to hurt her. She's just an experiment."

Mason broke into braying laughter as Calla contemplated. Mason would keep no such promise.

Within the hour, the car nosed into a parking lot outside a villa in Seville's old quarter of Barrio Alfalfa. The large Andalusian mill house was set in mature gardens of oranges, lemons, palm, and olive trees surrounded by open countryside. Ridge joined them on the cobbled lot and jumped into the Rover, and they continued on a heated drive toward the Andalusian Mountains. Soon the Cruiser entered a private gated community in the agrarian mountain countryside, positioned on the fringes of the village of Benahavís.

With her wrists still imprisoned in a set of deadly cuffs, Mason marched Calla into the villa, a converted seventeenth-century *casa* that seemed meticulously restored and converted into a private home. Built in the conventional Andalusian white village style, its architecture merged many modern characteristics.

They traipsed past expansive living rooms. Oversized

windows allowed in a steady, Mediterranean breeze, and Mason's style had spared no luxury with the indoor fixtures—the interior design being fashioned closer to Italian Renaissance.

A robust, middle-aged woman, displaying several degrees of masculinity met them in the hallway. "Everything's ready, sir."

"Good, then by all means, let's begin."

Had it not been for the acidic ache around the cuffs, Calla longed to scuffle herself free, slam a fist in Mason's chest, and a knee in Lascar's groin. The steel didn't look any more resilient than the double-glazed windowpanes of the Shard skyscraper that she'd tossed her fists through once to rescue Nash. The more she grappled with her wrists, the worse the agony that filled her hands with a vicious sting. "What do you intend to do with me?"

"All in good time. First, I would like to offer my hospitality," Mason said.

"I don't wish to be entertained by you."

Mason glared at her. "Stubborn as your mother. Let's see if you can sustain my investigations longer than she did."

Calla's face went taut with anger. Mason had more than once referred to injuring her parents. He'd first threatened her with the topic at Murchison Falls in Uganda, and now he'd done it again.

Mason jetted her toward a rooftop garden, three floors up, overlooking a miniature canyon. With no warning, he jostled her violently into a lounge chair. "Try to relax."

Lascar took a seat across from where Mason perched over her in the roof garden. Mason shot Lascar a perturbed glare. "You leave now!"

Lascar's eyebrows drew together in an angry frown before he rose and ambled to the door that led back to the lower floors of the house.

. . .

"Calla Cress. A very promising operative. The one who's to take on the mandate. I've heard it mentioned that you and I aren't so different."

"I'm nothing like you."

"You and I have the same genes. The same *operative* genes. We both know what we want. We're both distrustful of people. We both don't trust those closest to us, and we both have very ambitious women for mothers."

"What makes you think you know my mother?"

"I know you're every bit like her—untiring, strong, and will let no man rule or tame you."

Calla writhed at her wrists. "Take these things off before I shrink your neck to their size and use them as a mutt collar."

Mason flung his head back in a roar of laughter. "You've always had it in you. Don't be sure about that. The last time we met in such a state, I didn't make myself clear. This time, there won't be much conversation between us."

Mason regarded her with a knowing severity.

She gazed away. Yet something stouter than her will made her face him. Perhaps it was curiosity. Perhaps it was interest. Calla wasn't certain. All she felt was an alluring force and pull as his voice took on soothing subtlety. His words comforted her mind.

How?

She took on an amplified state of focus and concentration, able to deliberate intensely on a particular thought or memory. Her eyes drifted. It was not sleep. It felt like freedom—as if she had no individual will.

She didn't desire one.

Calla stopped resisting.

CHAPTER 29

When Calla's eyes shut, she wanted to fight —to break free, but her mind repelled.

She could hear Mason's words. Something was wrong. Mason didn't use belligerent words. In fact, he'd become inaudible to her, as if a voice in her spoke louder.

No! Wake up, Calla!

The voice was in her head, but where was it coming from?

It sounds like, like...like...

Nash.

Calla forced her eyes open. She blinked twice, sensing an urge in her mind to resist. Mason twitched as if by some accident he'd registered strength from her active mind he'd not expected. He'd turned his back to her as he paced the quiet garden roof with his hands behind his back.

She spotted his gun in his back pocket. Calla dragged in a deep breath and recalled what had always reignited the strength she was born with. If she believed in herself and gathered strength from the conviction of those who believed in her, she would be unrelenting.

Mason shot round and with one stride her way, moved his hand to her throat as she attempted to move. She lunged forward and swung her leg across his jaw, a jolt that tossed him staggering until his back was to the ground.

Calla shot up, and with both feet on either side of his neck, she brought them together until his air supply began to diminish.

His body writhed under hers.

In one able instant, she stole a quick breath and tugged at the cuffs. She'd have to bear the sting of a thousand needles and the deadly deliriant, but perhaps for a few seconds. She'd rather face potential sleepwalking, a blackout state, or even a psychotic episode before she'd let him manipulate her mind—the only one she had.

She held her breath and broke the steel cuffs free, barely noticing the sting of the microscopic needles as they shot venom in her bloodstream. With freed hands and an incapacitated, six-foot thug at her feet, she glanced around for her exit. Her eyes fell on Mason's shirt pocket and studied a bulge the size of a child's crayon. She reached down his shirt pocket, as his agony threatened to have him heaving, and pulled out a small bottle.

Calla sent one more blinding blow across his face and gulped the contents of a bottle. "You're a very thorough man. You didn't know whether the deliriant would work. So this is what I would've done, as one who thinks like you. I would have carried an antidote!"

She scuttled to the open door through which Lascar had departed earlier and set off at a run down the stone stairs. Her race down the steps brought her lurching into a charging woman—the same woman who'd greeted her earlier and had heard Mason refer to as Mrs. Hawke.

Hawke drew a firearm and held it with both hands. She

backed Calla up the stairs again with its barrel, almost touching her face.

Calla slid under Hawke's gun and grabbed the back of her head. She shifted out of the line of attack, before driving her foot into Hawke's knee, a jolt that sent the heavy woman toppling on the stairs.

Hawke's falling body nearly bowled Lascar as he sailed Calla's way.

Calla charged up until she was back on the roof.

With Mason shambling to his feet and Lascar making a dash for her, Calla raced to the edge of the garden and stared down one corner of the roof. Whereas three ends of the garden looked into the extensive grounds, the side Calla stood perched on overlooked the cliffs of the hundred-meter canyon. About two-hundred feet away from the roof, she saw a bridge spanning the canyon.

Could she do it?

"How many times do we have to do this, Cress!"

Mason stood unrelenting, his frame clumping toward her. Her hands crawled behind her and gripped the roughness of the garden's edge. She got a grip of the stone and pulled herself across the roof border, leaping backward on the ledge. Hunching on her knees, she took one peek down at the decline. Ridge and Kane waited at the foot of Mason's canyon villa.

If she shot down, she'd have to contend with them, or stay and combat with the two opponents in front of her.

She closed her eyes, ready to hurdle.

—

Calla pressed her hand against her heart, feeling its irregular speed and steadied herself for a leap into the abyss of further struggle. Her feet balanced over the perimeter of the stone wall, overlooking the canyon. She glimpsed at a road off the property, which tunneled through a shoulder of the valley, leading to flatter terrain.

She would control a smooth landing. As her mind contorted her next move, her ears caught the sound of a helicopter above her. Its assertive blades fanned her hair with its blizzard force and the impeccable shrubbery that stood beneath its gust.

An air-assault rescuer, roped down, deploying himself from the open aircraft. Dark suited, he slid on the braided rope above her and seized her with a tight grip around the waist. The chopper's blades above nearly made her lose her stability, with the wind from its rotating propellers vacillating her hair at uncontrollable speeds. Calla squinted, her eyes peering up at the chopper. The suited man hung, suspended from the aircraft with a rope to his shoulder harness. His eyes were covered with interchangeable, ballistic goggles, worn over a dark headgear hood, making it impossible to identify him. Still, he remained on mission and brought her body to his as her eyes streamed, weeping with torrid winds that tore at her face.

The rescuer signaled to his counterparts above him. The helicopter took lift, and they sored over the edge. The chopper's acceleration caused a jolt that sent it off to one side for split a second.

It steadied.

Calla forced a glimpse down at Mason and Lascar, who could barely stand under the helicopter's force. As the aircraft knifed off the property, Calla felt her heart pound against the stranger's strong grasp. She had no choice but to hold on to his sturdy shoulders as the chopper took flight.

Calla glanced down as Lascar attempted to fire his gun, but his spit of gunfire failed to reach them. A drowsy Mason rose rubbing his head. He, too, grabbed his gun and fired.

The aircraft hovered over the main villa and soon sailed westward. The man's arms tightened around her midriff. Calla could barely breathe with his tight grip. She gasped for air as the helicopter steadied, racing across the Andalusian landscape.

The rescuer tugged at the rope signaling to a second suited associate in the helicopter. It was an indication for his partner to hoist them up. The rope began a steady ascent toward the aircraft. Once on the floor level of the craft, the second air-assault fighter grasped Calla's arm and hauled her into the chopper. Her legs lifted to the helicopter floor, and soon, he heaved her capturer into the cabin and slammed the doors shut.

Calla and the suited man took seats opposite each other. He kept his gear on, and for a second she couldn't distinguish the two. They were both clothed in midnight-blue attire, with Blackhawk tactical vests, black gloves, knee pads, elbow pads, drop holsters, and spare ammunition pouches. The second man removed his headgear. "Hey there, Cal. I'm Reiner. Welcome aboard."

Calla's lips were drying. "Hi..."

His accomplice remained silent and turned his gaze toward the window.

Calla glanced over her shoulder at the pilot with the controls.

"Good to have you with us, ma'am." Though suited in black like the other marines, with a helmet and radio controls, Calla could pick that voice from a crowd. Jack's blithe face smirked back at her. She forced a weary smile, turned, and leaned back into the seat of the aircraft. Safely buckled in a chopper among friends, she stole a look at the man across who'd saved her life.

Nash's face was still masked. It had to be him. His

behavior was difficult to read. He'd come back, despite how she'd treated him.

Calla felt a lump rise to her throat. How senseless had she been?

She bit her lip. What would she say to him? She wanted to look into those gray eyes that she knew so well. Calla could not think straight. She couldn't see his face but knew it was pain he was covering with his visor mask.

Nash moved his gloved hand to his chin and still said nothing.

The chopper's rotating blades made it nearly impossible to communicate. The aircraft soared above Mirabella as it left Seville behind. It ascended, taking the route to the south tip of the Iberian Peninsula around its eastern coastline. Within minutes, they flew over the Bay of Algeciras, across from Gibraltar, with a gleaming view to the sea's narrow strait that connected the Atlantic Ocean to the Mediterranean Sea and separated Spain from Morocco—visible from the full-length window of the helicopter.

She pulled her eyes away from the ocean scenery, and back toward Nash, her palms perspiring with each minute that flew by. Calla needed to do this right. Out of duty, he'd forgive her, but would he still hold her in that intimate place that only they'd shared. How much rejection could a man take? How deep had she hurt him?

The chopper circled to the right. They weren't going to land in Algeciras, which only meant one thing. They were headed for Gibraltar, and to accomplish that feat, the pilot had to have the highest clearing for flying into the no-fly-zone.

On the most southern points of the Spanish mainland, Gibraltar peered at her with its predominantly smooth, sandy-strewn rocky beaches on the western coastline.

Less than a half hour later, the chopper touched down on the grounds of a large country villa.

"We're here," Jack said.

Calla glanced out the window at the waterfront estate that gave way to sweeping views across a pristine bay. The Mediterranean façade, whose brilliant architectural detailing of coral cast stone, attractive cypress, and Baroque ironwork made Calla wonder about what sort of place they'd landed.

The front entry was spacious. Two regal *porte-cocheres*, more like carriage porches, sheltered the motor court and a three-car garage. As if reading her thoughts, Jack removed his helmet and goggles, his lips curled into a smile. "We're at an ISTF safe house, courtesy of the British government."

Calla gave him a knowing nod. Reiner and Nash unbuckled their restraints and rose to descend from the aircraft.

Calla did likewise.

Was he going to walk away without a word?

Jack turned the motors off and peered her way. "Good to have you back." He glanced at Nash, who'd yet to move off the chopper. "I'll leave you two alone for a minute."

Jack stepped off the aircraft and strode with Reiner toward the house.

For several seconds, neither said a word.

Nash removed his black Kevlar helmet and gloves, and set his palms over his knees. His face registered no emotion.

"Nash, I'm sorry," Calla said.

She waited for a response, her throat fighting back a choke.

Nash cleared his throat.

Calla continued. "I'm sorry I doubted you, Nash. I was wrong."

He rose and settled in a seat next to her. His hand slowly moved to her cheek as tears trembled on her eyelids. With a soft sigh, he first kissed the tip of her nose, then her eyes. Finally, he satisfyingly kissed her soft lips. Then pulled back.

"No, I'm sorry. I should have told you about your mother. I don't know why I didn't."

His face changed suddenly. "Calla, I may have withheld information from you, but only because your mother asked me to, just like you asked me to take you to Colorado without telling a soul."

"I know, Nash. You always keep your word."

"You didn't wait for me to explain. I don't think we can keep going on like this."

"What do you mean?"

"I'm going to do the most difficult thing I've ever done, Cal. I'm going to give you one less complication. Being with me interferes with your life, your choices, and I don't want to be the one who screws with the decisions ahead of you."

Alarm filled Calla's eyes. "What're you saying?"

"I have to leave you to be who you are."

"Nash, no.. . Please, I can't do this without you."

"You can."

"But you said we should not give up."

"I'm not giving up on you, beautiful. I'm releasing you."

"I don't want to be free of you, Nash."

She set a hand on his chest. I—"

He kissed her wet eyes. "Make me proud, Cal. I know you will."

They heard footsteps near the chopper as Jack returned. "We just got intel on Mason. We need to move."

Nash nodded slowly to Jack and diverted his eyes back to Calla. "Jack. This is where the road ends for me. I promised to help get Calla back. Reiner in there is a good marine and will take over from where I left."

"You can't be serious, Nash."

Nash stepped off the chopper and set his feet on the parched lawn. "You guys will do it. You'll finish Mason off."

Had she heard him, right? Was he leaving? Calla stood

motionless on the lawn, as Nash careered to the pilot's seat. He buckled himself in before cackling the engine.

She couldn't find the words.

The blades started rotating, and Jack pulled Calla back from the onslaught of gust wind. Nash took one look at Calla before placing his headpiece and goggles on.

Nash, please don't go. Before she could let the words out, the chopper ascended. Calla's throat dried, completely choking back words and emotions she'd failed to voice.

She fixed her eyes on the flying beast. And in minutes, it disappeared over the rock-strewn cliff.

The wind whistled from the Alboran Sea, slapping her skin. Calla turned to Jack. "He's gone. I didn't know what to think about the information he had about my mother."

"It wasn't your mother who sent him those text messages. Nash may have gotten a call from someone claiming to be your mother, but it wasn't her. I checked the signals myself. We both think Lascar sent those text messages. Your mother communicated with Nash by a website and an e-mail address that changed every day."

"Why didn't he tell me?"

"He tried, C."

"He did, didn't he, Jack?" She raised her chin with a cool stare in his direction. "Will he ever come back?"

"I've never seen him so upset *but,* I've never known him to quit any mission."

She slumped to the ground, a sharp pain filling her gut. "We can't do this without him."

Nash was gone.

"I'm torn, Calla. I can't see you both like this."

She bit her lip. She'd never told Nash the most important words he needed to hear.

Jack and Calla strode toward the villa in silence and sauntered through ornate doors. Wrought iron detailing adorned the entire door frame. As they advanced through the entrance, Calla glanced up the two-story ceiling with its false finished dome and impressive chandeliers. Each space of the large interior incorporated opulent finishes and displayed exceptional attention to detail. Custom cabinetry, woodwork, and furniture flowed throughout, while the exceptional use of granites, marbles, and onyx complimented each surface in the main rooms.

"What's this place?" Calla asked, losing her orientation in the surroundings for a minute.

Jack strolled to the far end of the hall and pushed the doors open to a vast reception room, with a grand piano by the window looking out to the villa grounds. "An ISTF base, authorized by Allegra herself. She's inside. Your father is here too."

Allegra! Calla had almost forgotten. She had been on the airplane with her on leaving Islamabad.

Jack saw the alarm in her face. "She's okay. Mason and Lascar drugged her on the plane, persuaded officials with much money to haul her off. When she came to in a business lounge at the airport, she alerted us before we left Islamabad."

"You came straight here to get me. How did you know where Mason was heading?"

"Your phone was still on you. Remember, I put a tracking device on it." He snickered. "I always know where you are—most times."

Calla approached Jack. "I owe you an apology too, Jack. I'm sorry."

"Apology accepted on the grounds that I see what you do best. Do you still have your mother's patches?"

Calla nodded and padded her undervest.

"Good, because the only way we can reverse the coordinates to Mason's hack program is if your mother gives them to us. At least that's what Allegra believes."

"What makes Allegra so sure?"

"Calla, we need to find out exactly how much your mother knew Mason. What she knows can help us greatly here before the other defense systems of the member governments go bust as well."

Calla felt around her pockets and found the undergarment pouch, a safe place she'd carved out for her treasures. "They're here."

Jack interjected, taking a seat on the sofa. "We need to find your mother within the next forty-eight hours, or Mason sets his computers in motion."

Calla spread the strips of ancient cloths on the large coffee table and observed the perplexing symbols. She turned them around several times. "I wish I could figure it out, but I've searched my mind completely. I don't get what this is, what she was trying to say to me."

"That's because your mother was a genius," a voice behind said.

She turned around.

Stan stood, arms folded in the arched doorway. "Father?"

"You had me so worried, Calla. And from now on, I'm coming with you."

"So, you're not afraid to face her." She drew him into a hug. "Thank you."

"After that moron torched my house, with me barely able to get out, I had to teach him a lesson. He's messed with my family one too many times."

"Mason's turning this into a habit," Jack said.

"I'm sorry, dad, about your house," Calla said.

"I'm alive, you are too, now let's find Nicole."

They settled back around the coffee table. Stan tilted his head to one side. "This must've been something that meant much to Nicole. It's like an excerpt from her diary and really personal to her. Having lived many identities as a services' agent, she must have wanted something no one could associate with that life," Stan said.

Stan's lime eyes narrowed furiously. In one unforeseen movement, he rose and glided toward the window. He stood frozen before it for several seconds and smacked his fist through the pane. As if not sensing the sting from the shattered glass, he left his bloodied arm in the bed of spiked glass.

Calla hurried to his side. A bloody welt had opened above his knuckles. As it bled, Calla pulled a napkin from a nearby dining table and gently eased his fist from the glass spikes. "Father, you need to release it. Whatever you know can help us."

"No, Calla, I'm not going back to that place. That night when we left you at the orphanage. That's when this madness started. If I hadn't left you, she would've never left me."

"That's not true. You yourself said that you both agreed. We can't change what's in the past, but we can change the future. Starting now."

Jack swaggered across the room. "Stan, you may have let Nicole down, but she let you down too. If you don't help us with this, then you've lost her forever," Jack said.

"And never know closure," Calla added." By helping us find her, you help so many people."

"All right," Stan said. "Your mother took something from Mason. Codes of some sort, or perhaps coordinates that could reveal the location of his hideout. The week before we left you at the orphanage, she'd discovered that he may have started this technology hack the minute the Internet began."

Stan's fist eased under Calla's confident touch. He held back a deep pain stemming from his agonized arm. "We need to get to Eisenach. In Germany."

"Eisa. .. what? Why?" Jack asked.

"I get it. I thought of this, but it seemed incomprehensible at the time," Calla said before she strode back to the table and set her hands on the patches. "When you piece these together, this way round," she rotated the documents, "they make up a bar of music."

Calla studied her father's face, enlightened that she had almost read his mind.

"I do not hear any music, Cal. Enlighten me," Jack said.

Calla hoisted herself on the edge of the seat. "This bar of music forms a copy of an old score. At first, I was trying to decipher words, hieroglyphics, and I ignored one of the world's most obvious forms of symbols—music notes. Look, here they're scribbled in such a hurry and not in sync. That's what makes it look like gibberish. One has to know how to chord them together, forgive the pun. Come."

She ambled to the old piano and leaned over the tired keys. "I've not played since I left school, but listen to this."

Bars of arpeggios seeped from the tired instrument. "It's Bach," Calla said.

"Okay, enlighten the few of us who've never crammed a note of music."

"It's the last movement of the cantata *Herz und Mund und Tat und Leben,* the 'Heart and Mouth and Deed and Life', or better known as *'Jesu Joy of Man's Desiring,"* Stan said. "Your mother used to play that piece repeatedly when she learned she was pregnant with you."

Stan moved to the piano. His fingers ran over some notes and joined her in a series of melodic cascades on the keys. He took a seat next to her. In a symphony of harmony that filled the old villa with the absorbing sound of Bach, father and daughter complemented each other's playing.

Jack watched the reunion. Harmony and melody finally at ease and rest with each other. Calla stopped mid-stanza and turned to Jack. "There's a radical aspect inherent in Bach's work. He was as much what we would call a modern rocker and a classical composer. He probably helped encourage the rationale in academics that mathematics and music share."

"Eisenach is Bach's home," Stan added, setting the hood over the piano keys. "Music theorists used mathematics to understand melody. Your mother took inspiration from the composition as a cryptanalyst, codebreaker, and code writer. She always played Bach, Calla."

Jack rubbed his chin. "So you're saying perhaps the codes we need are linked to Bach's music—"

"Or," Calla added. "Bach's hometown has clues to her whereabouts. Whatever it is, we need to find out, in Eisenach."

"Calla's right," Stan surrendered. "When we left you at the orphanage, Nicole must have gone there. It makes sense to me now. Bach always soothed her. It must've been a way of dealing with her loss of you. But maybe there was more to it."

CHAPTER 30

DAY 14
HOUSE OF LORDS CHAMBER
PALACE OF WESTMINSTER, LONDON

ALLEGRA TWIDDLED HER thumbs as she waited for the House of Commons' debate on cybersecurity to begin. She eyed Baroness Worthington, chairperson of the House of Lords' Constitution Committee, about to open the debate. To her right sat Lord Berkshire, who would respond for the government. Though still a classified organization to the public and members present, the debate would determine funding for ISTF, conveniently hidden in the cyber technology research budget.

If the debate went against the government, ISTF would be written off as threatened by the PM. If only they could find some non-incriminating way to prove the strides ISTF and the operatives had taken to prevent global cyber havoc. The PM was stubborn. Too sacred for his party's unity, he would go with majority vote, and it wasn't looking good.

Lady Baroness stood to open the debate, her fingers filing through a thirty-page report. As she took the podium, her aid sidled to her with an open laptop. She grazed her fingers over the keys and glanced at the room of eager listeners.

The House of Lords, the upper house of the UK parliament, was made of 750 members, called 'Peers' whose duties were to scrutinize bills approved by the lower house—the House of Commons.

Allegra's bill was in the eager hands of Baroness Worthington. They could debate the cyber research budget or reject it altogether, which would give Mason free rein in cyberspace with his latest worm. The baroness keyed a few items on her laptop and glared at the expectant participants. She'd chosen to project her presentation on the back wall.

The screen fired up, then flashed gibberish, programming language, seconds later. The baroness' confused gaze met the audience's, and she turned to her aid, who shrugged. With no warning, one by one, members drew their cell phones out of pockets and purses when a shrill of rings wailed through the room in unison.

Allegra drew in a deep breath. "He has the government where he wants it."

Several security guards rushed in, aiming to calm the disarray of traumatized participants. The shrill prevailed for close to sixty seconds.

In one sudden moment, the shrill of rings halted. A silence of confusion gripped the room before Allegra shot up and moved toward the Prime Minister, who sat with his aids, confounded like the rest of the participants. "That's a warning from Mason," Allegra said. "You'd better support ISTF, or let this confusion prevail on your watch. I wonder which will be worse, failure to contain a sustained cyber-attack and the ability of everything from armed forces and UKSA to operate effectively or. .. failure at reelection."

The PM's mouth slackened. "What are you saying?"

She narrowed in his space. "I'm saying that our systems

are fatally compromised due to their dependence on information and communication technology. Now let me get on with my job."

Calla stood in front of *Bachhaus*, the first museum in the world dedicated to Johann Sebastian Bach. She scrutinized the five-hundred-year-old, half-timbered house—mistakenly identified as Bach's birth house in the middle of the nineteenth-century. She squeezed Stan's hand as they proceeded inside the yellow thatched building that used to be the living quarters.

They ambled past historic furniture, artwork, musical instruments, and household artifacts. Calla gravitated toward the music instruments' hall, where a concert of four violinists and a cellist was in session. They took their seats at the back of the room as the wooded instruments filled the hall with newer renditions of Bach's loved pieces. Calla observed as tourists relished the music. She narrowed her gaze, focusing on which of the four violinists was Frau Faust—the woman she'd spoken to on the phone.

When the concert adjourned, the musicians rose for a bow. Calla shot up and paced toward the quartet with her father and Jack. "Frau Faust?"

A woman of pale skin, hazel eyes, and shoulder-length, black hair smiled and stretched her hand for a firm shake. "You must be Frau Cress. Let me pack up my violin, and I'll be with you."

Calla turned toward the door to wait at the entrance of the hall for Frau Faust. Within ten minutes, the woman reappeared sporting a navy-blue blazer and a tweed skirt, having changed from her period costume.

"This way," Frau Faust said, her English sprinkled with a hint of German intonation.

"Thank you for your time," Calla began

"A pleasure, Miss Cress. I read your online British Museum resume. I worked with Veda Westall. She helped brainstorm for museum presentation ideas here, giving our work here a more international profile. I'm so sorry to hear about Ms. Westall. She was a brilliant curator."

"Thank you," Calla said.

They passed a series of rooms housing collections of musical instruments, presented to reflect the era of Johann Sebastian. Frau Faust observed as her guest admired the surroundings. "We've close to four-hundred instruments, about one-fourth of them originating from the sixteenth to the eighteenth centuries. If we have time, I'd be glad to show you—"

"That's just it, Frau Faust," Calla said. "We have no time. I wanted to come in person. This is my father, Stan Cress, and my colleague, Jack Kleve. We work with British Intelligence and are looking for someone that you might know. According to the employee records of the museum, I understand that a certain woman called Annelie worked here."

A flicker of apprehension coursed through Frau Faust's eyes, probably bewildered they had access to such classified information. "You mean Nicole Cress."

"How do you know that name?" Jack asked.

The woman glared from one mesmerized face to another. "She's my sister."

Calla stared blankly with her mouth open and turned to Stan. "Did my mother have a sister?"

Stan stepped forward, his eyebrows pinched in confusion. "Nicole never mentioned having a sister."

"I guess she wouldn't." Frau Faust observed Stan's surprised look. "Especially when you two met when working for MI6. It wasn't protocol. Nicole's job, as you know, didn't take well to family. Secrecy was her way of protecting me from her work."

Calla took Frau Faust's hand and merely stared, tongue-tied.

"Please, come with me," Frau Faust said. "I can take you to Nicole's private apartment. She bought the place about thirty years ago. It's secure there, and we can talk."

As they strolled into the sunlight, Calla's expectation grew, and she pulled out the patches of music. "Frau Faust."

"Please, call me Elise."

"Elise, can you think of why my mother would send these to me."

Elise passed her hands over the patches as they walked. For several minutes, she fingered the items without a word. "Do you know what these are?"

Calla shook her head.

Stan caught Elise's eyes. "It looks like a manuscript of music. From a seventeenth-century scrapbook from the looks of it. Probably scribbled by a copyist or a live in apprentice of a professional composer."

"If placed together, it makes up Bach's *Herz und Mund und Tat und Leben,* right?" Calla said.

"Yes, but do you know what these words below the symbols say?" Elise asked.

"I focused more on modern German," Calla added.

"How much do you know about Bach and his life?"

Calla shook her head. "Not much."

"This here is a signature. The copyist. Yours and my ancestor worked for Bach when he was penning the original notes of the suite. The copyist made a mistake, so this patch was used to practice the inscription. The copyist kept this as a souvenir of his work with the master. It was found several years after his death in an old trunk in our family home."

"So, that's how Nicole came to have it?" Stan said.

"It's the reason I'm here and feel I have a personal connection to this place," Elise said.

"Nicole never mentioned her lineage back to Germany. When we met, we said little about our past. Eventually, when she was pregnant with Calla, I had to tell her about the Hadrius mandate on the Cress's family line," Stan added.

Elise pushed back a wisp of hair. "This came from a private collection of memories. Your mother inherited this through her grandmother."

"Why would she mar it by cutting it up?" Calla said.

"It's her way of saying the three pieces belonged together and that they told a complete story," Elise said.

They strolled to the back of the building, then on Frauenberg Strasse, a stretch of boulevard that overlooked the museum. After turning in to a small adjoining street, Elise directed them up a staircase that led into an apartment building whose fragments of original Baroque architecture were still visible. Elise keyed the door and led them into the building. They clambered two flights of narrow stairs before she pushed open a front door to a large studio apartment. Spacious, with cleanliness and a contemporary feel, it housed several rustic antique pieces in its décor.

The living space opened on to a fully equipped kitchenette. A queen-sized bed adorned the far corner of the room. Clean, the apartment showed no signs of having been lived in for years. Calla moved toward the bed, scrutinizing the watercolors on the far wall. Her eyes fell to a small artist station near the dining table. A small photograph frame lay on the mantle above a dated fireplace.

Stan eased toward the frame and ran his hands along the silver edges of the picture of a baby. "Calla."

She turned to him, his face unreadable. The words had left his lips more audibly than he'd perhaps wished. Calla took the picture frame from his hands—the only baby picture of herself she'd ever seen.

Calla rubbed her hand across her eyes.

"That's you, taken a few days after you were born," Elise said. Jack moved his head slightly to establish perspective, as Calla studied the black-and-white image of a baby with dark, straight hair and a pinched nose who lay sleeping in a woman's arms. He placed an arm around her shoulders. "You all right, C?"

"Yeah."

Jack took the picture and studied it. "She must have thought of you all these years. Tell me, Elise. Where's Nicole?"

A look of horror fell on the thin woman's face. "I was hoping you could tell me?"

Calla grabbed Jack's arm. "What?"

"Nicole disappeared about five years ago, and I've not seen her since. She left me this note."

Elise paced to a nearby drawer and pulled out a letter scribbled on lined paper.

Dear Elise,

You've always known there is much about my life I can't disclose, and in all those years, I've always asked you to trust me. This is one of them.

I have to leave. If only to protect you from the madness of my existence. My work is too dangerous to disclose. I have to leave

before I can endanger your life. I promise to return one day. .. when it's safe."
N

Elise sank into a seat by the bed. "Your phone call yesterday was the first mention of Nicole since she disappeared. When you used her German cover name 'Annelie', I knew you had to be close to her. She always said one day, her daughter would come looking for her, and if so, I should help. It took one look at your picture on the British Museum website to see the resemblance between you two."

Elise's gaze remained meditative, possibly colored with memory. "I was so hoping you might know where she is."

CHAPTER 31

"I'M SORRY, CALLA," Jack said, thinking of the conversation he'd had with Nash that morning. He'd not told Calla about it, not wanting to upset her. They needed Nash.

Nash's intelligence into his communication with Nicole for more than fifteen months, was critical. He shoved his hands in his denim pockets. A chill from the unheated room caressed his bare arms, and he slid on his leather jacket.

Nicole had been careful. The e-mails came to Nash's NSA account, encrypted with a link to the various websites through which they communicated. At first, Nash thought it was a hoax, especially seeing that it wasn't too long after he'd met Stan. But his instincts had told him if the woman were sincere, she'd know much about Calla, especially before Calla came to the orphanage.

Jack recalled Nash saying in a conversation with Nicole, she'd not only given him Calla's adoption details, the orphanage but details concerning her relation to Stan. Still, Nash hadn't been convinced until the day Nicole had said she would meet him in Boston. From that day, the woman used an encrypted e-mail address that changed every three hours. Nash never knew how she'd found him.

Calla's eyes shifted to Jack. "If Nicole was in touch with Nash in the last fifteen months, then she must be alive, and Mason must know it. Her life is in danger."

"We'll find her." Jack reached for his electronic tablet from his backpack and scrolled through two applications. "Here. This was her last communication with Nash. I asked Nash to send me the information. It was about four months ago, I think." Jack showed her the e-mail on his tablet. "I will try to break into the server from which this was sent and verify that. The encryption is difficult to break."

Jack took the tablet and sent the e-mail to his laptop. "This may take a while."

Stan walked away. Calla crossed to where he stood, staring at Nicole's artwork.

"She stopped painting when we were married. She was happy here," Stan said.

Calla scrutinized his downcast face. "Father?"

"I can't believe she was here the entire time."

Calla stared around her carefully. "This must be strange for you." She took a deep breath.

Jack reentered the room. "Got it! In all of the communication with Nash, Nicole never signed her identity as A-M-H."

"What's that?" Calla asked.

"A code she set up," Stan said, looking at his daughter. "Every agent had a code."

He studied her face. "Nash has done more than I can ever repay for my family. I wish I had the same amount of courage and resolve. Why isn't he here?"

She bit her lip and avoided the topic altogether. "You were brave when your family was threatened. What man wouldn't have done what you did? Is there no other clue you can think of. What is A-M-H?"

"Believe me, Danielle's name was the best I could do. The more I discover with you guys, the more I realize she kept many secrets from me. "

"People change over the years, Stan," Jack said.

"Why?" Stan said, glaring at Calla.

How could she answer him with any wisdom, when she couldn't even understand her emotions with Nash?

"She left me, too," Calla said.

"That night, when we left the orphanage, Nicole was tormented with such guilt, confusion, and anger all directed at me, I suppose. But we knew there'd be no other way for you. We had to distance ourselves from you if you were to be safe from the operatives and when the CIA offered to help, then Nash, well—"

Calla set a hand on his shoulder. "From where I'm looking, you did the best you could with the information and choices you had."

Calla gaped at his hand and smirked. She knew Stan was not convinced as she crossed to the wall overlooking the busy Platz. She stopped suddenly. "Wait a minute.. . "

Jack and Stan's astounded eyes met hers as she advanced to where Jack sat. "Let me see that last e-mail that my mother sent to Nash."

Jack handed her the laptop. She reread the e-mail.

"This e-mail is three days old, not four months as it says 10.07 when decrypted with your program, Jack, July tenth. It's actually 07.10— October seventh." She was thinking British, not American."

"Where are you going with this?" Jack asked.

"The e-mail you showed me says in the subject line: '*On this day. It began. Her Majesty's anger blossomed*'. Why?"

Jack's face was a curtain of confusion. "And—"

"She was asking Nash to look up something that happened on that day."

CHAPTER 32

"ON OCTOBER SEVENTH, in 1940, Buckingham Palace was hit by a German bomb. That's when a special arm of the Secret Intelligence Service was born, so they could delve deeper into intercepting enemy intelligence," Stan said.

Her stride confident, Elise reappeared into the room with a pot of coffee and traversed to the other end of the apartment. She found a volume on British History. "Nicole kept many work memoirs here. I may know what you're after. Ah, here it is." She tossed a volume to Calla.

"I don't believe it," Stan said, shooting up. "Don't tell me she was part of that."

Calla stared at the volume:

THE UNKNOWN HISTORY OF THE BRITISH SECRET SERVICE
By Charles Berkingstone
Former, MI6 Agent

Jack advanced with determined steps. "Part of what?"

"The theory many of us thought heightened intelligence into all foreign communications. According to the rumor, the bureau responsible for interception and decryption of foreign communications was given the ultimate go ahead. Spy without conviction—or morals."

"They wrote a memo detailing how to sniff out moles and how to send messages to agents in the field and the blueprint for what is now referred to as number stations."

"This must be it," Jack said.

Calla swept her audience with a piercing glance. "Number stations?"

Stan sighed. "At first, it seemed like another method of gathering information to avert dangers to state security."

Jack's eyebrows knit. "It's not?"

Calla took the volume off the shelf. "What's she telling us? This is just a copy of the volume she mentions in the e-mail."

Stan moved closer. "Open it."

She pulled open the cover of the book and found the first page. "There's nothing here, father."

Stan took the volume from her hands. "I need a knife."

Jack pulled out his Swiss Army knife.

Stan took it and worked at the edges of the tired volume. The knife pierced the border of the thick, leather edges, slicing off the glued page. The group clustered around him as he pulled at the front cover.

Calla's eyes fell on a two-toned document beneath. "It's a blueprint of some sort."

Stan moved the worn book around in his hands. "It's a blueprint to the broadcast location of an underground, numbers station. They were used after the war to transmit covert messages to spies and later used as hideouts to spy on cybercriminal activity in the early years of the Internet. I thought she had abandoned that project." He looked up at the staring faces. "I think she has been developing a plan to infiltrate cryptographic criminality from day one. This location of the broadcasts was secret and, to my understanding, closed at the end of the nineties." He sighed. "Not once did I imagine she was part of it."

Jack intervened. "Perhaps, that's what she took from Mason. In the early days of the Internet, the NSA thought of building similar pods as they called them. She must've thought there would always be a threat and aimed to be one step ahead."

Calla straightened her shoulders to relieve an ache. "That's probably why she contacted Nash? Nash would have been able to gain inside intelligence on such operations. But do you think this place is still running, father?"

Stan paced the room, his fingers rubbing his nose. "Those places were built as independent communes and were to house the many clandestine people who worked there, their families if need be. They were fully equipped with lodgings, technology rooms, broadcast equipment—you name it, in case the broadcasters needed to be there on long assignments."

Calla watched him stride toward the doorway, expecting him to turn, but he didn't. "ISTF must've taken these places over after the Government Communications Headquarters, known to you as the GCHQ, refused to fund them."

"But, where are they?" Elise asked.

"They were scattered across the US, Europe, and the UK. But now, the problem we have is the government destroyed them after the Cold War. Spy houses, as they were known, gained a bad reputation after British spies got too close to information the Russians didn't want them to have. They'd hacked into cyber communication related to a diplomatic plan between Russia and India." Stan eyed them one by one. "I seriously doubt they exist now."

ST. GILES SQUARE, ALLEGRA'S RESIDENCE
0912 hrs.

"Allegra?"

Calla proceeded through the front door of the St. Giles residence. She'd attempted to reach Allegra all morning. "Allegra we're back—"

Movement drew her eyes as Taiven appeared from behind the den door. "Calla."

She took a step back when he approached. "Taiven?"

Another man appeared from around the corner.

"Prime Minister.. .?"

Taiven crept out of the room and closed the door silently. Stunned at the appearance of an army of security from 10 Downing Street, Calla's mouth dipped in puzzlement. "Now you're someone I wasn't expecting to see," she told the calm man that appeared before her. He was short, with an elegant build—a wily gentleman with deep-set eyes. Three police bodyguards took position in three corners of the room.

"Miss Calla Cress. I was wondering when I would get a chance to meet you. I was hoping you could tell us where Allegra is."

She peered behind the PM, catching a glimpse of Taiven's peeking face, concealed behind the shadows of the den door. "Isn't she here?"

"This is just an impromptu appearance. This wasn't a scheduled call."

Couldn't they see him? The bodyguards stared on blankly as if Taiven's presence was oblivious to them.

"Come with me, I think it's about time we had a chat," the PM said, walking right past Taiven, leading her to Allegra's den.

Taiven nodded and stepped back—a sleuth among the shadows. Was he only visible to her?

"Now, Miss Cress, I haven't been as open with Allegra as I should have. You see, I've been sitting on a decision for some time."

"What decision is that?"

He took a seat in one of the lush sofas. "I wanted to recommend the closure of ISTF. After all, we have the Security Intelligence Service. But ISTF accomplishes one thing for me. It can go beyond what the SIS can't. Its technology budget is replenished year after year by interested donors, allowing our engineers to advance faster than typical governments can."

Must be secret funding from the operatives.

He continued. "There's a list of private donors who believe in this organization. Most of them, anonymous."

Bingo! "I see."

"I know you had the largest hand in stopping Laskfell gimmicks last time, and the team believes in you. So maybe I should reconsider closing ISTF."

"What're you getting at Prime Minister?"

"A file has come to my attention from the Americans. Now it's incomplete. From what I understand, it's been an investigation they've had going on for a while into a certain group they are calling *the operatives*, who seem to be a global underground movement."

"Where's this going, Prime Minister?"

"Allegra can't lead ISTF forever and if the operatives are a threat to us, or not. .." He shrugged. "I don't understand them, but maybe you can."

"You seem to know more than I do about the operatives."

"Yes and more so from what the NSA has been analyzing for the last several years. According to this intelligence the NSA intercepted, some of their communications systems I hear are many years ahead. Pending a final report on them, I think we need to up our game, and ISTF is in a position to do so."

"What exactly do you want done with the operatives?"

He grinned and straightened his shoulders. "Should we continue to face a threat from a cyber, technological group like this whose motives we don't understand, I want to be prepared? I'm considering keeping ISTF open for this purpose and on one condition."

Her eyes narrowed. "What's that?"

"You'll take over when Allegra retires in about a year's time, and you'll make it your duty to truce with the operatives if that's what we need. I want to get in bed with these scientific and technological minds before the Americans, or any nation for that matter. For once, we could have the upper hand."

"But the Americans are part of ISTF."

"Yes, but at my recommendation, you could lead it for us."

She wasn't sure how much the Prime Minister knew. How much did he *really* know about the operatives? What was this report? Nash had begun to tell her about some of this intelligence NSA had gathered.

Calla slumped into the seat next to him. Is this something she would do? "I'm sorry, Prime Minister, but what would make me qualified for such a job? I'm just a museum curator."

He tossed a file on the desk. "This is your ISTF file. There's no one in ISTF more qualified than you. Operatives understand our history, our weaknesses, and use them against us. I'm also aware from the Security Intelligence Service files that your parents were MI6 agents, and that your father, a possible operative himself, is versed in operative behaviors."

How does he know that?

"Nothing slips by me, Miss Cress." He stood. "I guarantee you the full backing of my administration. Do this, get Mason the same way you got him once, then let's talk. I don't need your decision now."

The Prime Minister strode out of the room and was escorted into his waiting car by his guards. Calla moved to the porch, her eyes following the government charade until it cornered off the square before reentering the building. She shut the door behind her and drew in a sharp breath.

Had Taiven been there? Had he witnessed the conversation, or had that been her imagination? She'd never understood the operative.

What was she going to do with this now?

CHAPTER 33

DAY 15
FORMER ROYAL AIR FORCE BASE
PLATRES WOODS, CYPRUS
0600 hrs.

THE AIR REEKED of staleness, an impression of fall arriving on the southern slopes of the Troodos Mountains, twenty-five kilometers from Limassol, Cyprus. On the edge of a small residential settlement of mainly shepherds and vine growers, downhill from the main town-center, Calla and her special weapons and tactics team waited. The cool ground under her felt moist as the group waited. Above them, dark clouds warned of possible precipitation, and though the air was still, the gushing pour from the Kalidonia Waterfalls, only several hundred feet away, filled the air with the only whispers of movement.

Calla pulled binoculars over her eyes. "The entrance is covered by a camouflaged trapdoor. Jack, do you have those door codes I sent you to get into that facility? Security Services spilled the beans on the number stations, thanks to a little encounter I had with the PM. They say we can manipulate them remotely."

Jack leaned into her side. "Is he really here? How would Mason get in?"

"The same way he has gone past immigration radars undetected. He used to head ISTF. He has enough people working with him than I care to count," Calla said.

"If Nicole is here, Mason is not far," Stan said, crouching next to Calla.

Jack channeled his tablet and fingered in the coordinates on the Service's secure server. Ten operatives had escorted them to Platres, and another ten waited in Limassol. Jack pointed out the base's entry points on the tablet. A couple of mossy, concrete buildings where the base once stood and a few depressions in the ground signaled that dispatched units used them as observation posts, or to store ammunition and technologies.

The blueprint the Prime Minister had provided Calla was accurate so far. She'd agreed to his terms on condition he gives them everything he knew about the number stations the government had tried to conceal for decades, and that he allow the operatives and ISTF agents to work together. According to the Prime Minister's informants, one number station's signal was still active and presumably in use secretly. However, after MI6's investigation, it was the only one operating without their knowledge. The sheer stillness and rundown nature of the base begged one to debate the fact.

Uninhabited, the trails leading to the base had afforded them a good ten minutes as they tore through shrubberies, thorns, and rubble. The base stood at the apex of a wooded hill.

Calla raised a silent signal, and the group filtered to the entrance—a barred manhole cover. Jack keyed in eight digits on the small control panel concealed within a nearby dead tree set in concrete. Above the tree, rose an antenna wire, concealed in the moldy bark—a feature most auxiliary unit sites had used according to the Prime Minister's office.

The manhole cover slid open, unlocking the hatch whose original mechanism was set with a counterweight, incorporating an obscured mechanism for opening it from the outside. Jack had been informed that all openings were now digitally controlled, having been reworked in the 1980s.

The armed troops funneled through the opening, entering through the hatch and proceeded down a dimly lit tunnel. At the end of the passageway, they advanced down a ladder constructed out of an old piece of estate fencing. At the bottom of the ladder, they spotted a blast wall, a high-integrity, fully-welded gas-tight system, manufactured from profiled steel to protect against blasts and explosions.

Calla studied the walls, clearly housed with impact and heat resistant qualities. She spotted a narrow opening to the left. Calla stood to one side and Reiner on the other. Calla's dark clothing and headgear felt heavy. She preferred using the operatives' light, combat clothing. However, she needed to blend in. Mason had to be ambushed by one unit. No one would be isolated as a target.

Calla signaled to Jack to release the door. Maneuvering the tablet's program, he keyed in the coordinates that slid the entry open.

Nothing within the exterior of the base gave way that it was a high-profile technology unit, given its interiors and compounds, rusted with grime, soot, and water damage, which run down most of the deteriorating walls.

Is this where Nicole was operating to frustrate Mason?

Once inside, Calla glimpsed back toward the hatch and the other blast walls, as her teams filed in. The section of the establishment was state-of-the-art and had been kitted with standard fittings, though somewhat eighties looking.

No one was about.

Silence gripped the halls.

The first room down the passageway was a tech-control room, with a long, arched desk on which seven monitors stood, facing a wall of beamed, global cyber activity. Deserted and quiet, the wiring told her that the technology was anything but primitive.

To one side of the room was a chemical toilet that was behind the doorway on the left. Calla, Jack and Stan, along with two operatives, filed into a second room, a kitchen with a cooking stove. The numbers station had been designed to drain itself of any water finding its way through possible entry points. The water flowed down a channel in the center of the floor and ebbed out of the base through escape tunnels made from corrugated iron.

Calla spotted a maneuvering eye camera on the far wall of the main hall. Someone had to be on the other side of that camera. She peered toward the escape tunnel where a second door stood.

Low audible voices came from within its walls.

They heard a gunshot blasting through the silence. It came from the closed room. The teams retreated and found cover on the floors along the gangway walls.

Calla raised her head. "I'm going in."

Stan, Jack, and three operatives joined her.

"Wait for my signal," she whispered.

They snaked around to one corner of the door. Jack found the camera's internal protocol position and hacked it, beaming an image from the other side of the door onto his tablet. They could see motion and movement but failed to make out the faces, or the number of people within.

Jack backed away from the door and signaled to Calla to join him. He whispered. "The signal is really strong here."

Voices caught Calla's ear—ones she recognized. They waited until the hubbub died down, and when her eyes met, Jack's they told him to key in the code to open the door.

It remained jarred.

The code had failed.

Silence.

Drawing a deep breath, she eyed each team member and jolted a boot against the steel that threw the door off its hinges. Her eyes traveled to a recliner chair, resembling a dental chair, where Mason held a woman by the hair.

She was strapped in, and agony gripped her rouged face.

0707 hrs.

For a minute, a huge air bubble settled in Calla's throat as her eyes met those of the woman she knew was her mother.

Calla felt like she was staring into the face of her future. Though some had said it, not until this moment did she really perceive what they meant. Her mother was a mature version of her—frosting, hip-length ebony hair, olive skin tones, emerald eyes, and restrained athletic legs that could beat any opponent into shape.

Calla felt a shiver run across her shoulders as she made a movement toward her confined mother, whose captor arched above her with a medical instrument that resembled a dart she couldn't identify.

Nicole's head rotated to one side as she saw her grown daughter for the first time. Previous struggle with Mason showed in her angered face, as her moist hair covered half her cheeks. Even then, her proud eyes greeted Calla with confidence.

Calla spoke steadily, her eyes mined into Mason's. "Hands off, Mason."

Mason rotated the small dart in his hands, with a snicker from hell playing on his lips. "Make me."

Tears of anguish streamed from Nicole's face. She shifted her eyes slightly toward her aggressor—her mouth gagged. The gulp that leaped from her mouth was inaudible when they fell on Stan's face.

As Stan filed to Calla's side, his elbows wide from his body, chest thrust out, Calla could have sworn he would have pounced on Mason there and then if Nicole hadn't been in a vulnerable position.

Calla's eyes traveled to the far corner of the room, which she'd now identified as the main living space of the numbers station. On a medical bed, surrounded by equipment, a second elderly woman of robust build rested, her head jerking from side to side. Her dark graying mane fell on the white pillows beneath her head. Clothed in street attire, Calla guessed she'd once been a fighting woman.

Mason held a hand to Nicole's neck and crushed his thick fingers into her skin.

She shrieked in choking pain and kicked with her feet.

Mason shot Calla and Stan a look. "I found her before you did. Nicole left my house years ago with a threat. Little did I know it was literal. This was the last place your Nicole here, and my mother there decided they would destroy the Hadrius Manuscript. Here is where they planned most of those MI6 missions. Here is where their friendship began, and tragically ended. It finally made sense and took me some searching through mother's confiscated belongings when she was arrested, and thanks to ISTF, I found this location."

Calla took a deep breath, trying to steady her anger. "Release the women."

"But why? Nicole brought your mother here three days ago to keep her from me."

"Perhaps to save her from the same fate you're about to face," Stan said.

"Always a smart one, aren't you, Cress. Oh, forgive my impoliteness, but let me introduce you properly. I don't think you've met since birth. Meet your mother."

Stan inched closer his gun leveled at Mason. Kane and Ridge appeared through two stand posts at the ends of the room and seethed into their beings with indignation. Soon a band of five armed men shuffled into the room behind them.

Mason's hand tightened around Nicole's neck. "One move and this needle goes in. I've perfected my deliriant Cress, so don't try me. All of you out! This discussion is between the Cresses and me."

Calla nodded to the operatives and Jack.

Jack held onto to her hand and swallowed, trying not to reveal her annoyance at Mason, but when he saw Mason's hand tighten around Nicole's exposed neck, he obliged.

Mason called to his men behind him. "That means you, too!"

They filed out with Ridge and Kane tailing at the end.

Stan remained side by side with Calla, his gun still pointed accurately at Mason's grinning face.

Mason groaned a deep maddening sigh. "I never thought I would see the day when I'd have the Cresses in one room." His eyes fell on Calla. "Looks like I have what I came for, I can't say the same for you, though."

———

0715 hrs.

Jack filed out back through the passageway with the other operatives. The door closed abruptly behind them. Hindered on the other side, he had no way of knowing what was going on behind the door where Calla was trapped with a psychopath.

He hadn't left the room though without spying at the technology, especially the terminal that stood near the recliner bed. That was Nicole's terminal. She must have been very close to disarming Mason's hack as she kept an eye on his incapacitated mother.

His fingers danced over his tablet, trying to hack into the room. Perhaps he could log into that computer remotely and reverse the hack now with how far she'd advanced.

Jack slid away from the group undetected as Kane and Ridge cornered the others. Crouching down to the concrete floor, he keyed in the coordinates for a sophisticated hack, he'd created. He dug through code, looking for exploitable ciphers in the networks of the base.

His ears caught struggles behind him. The operatives were taking on Ridge and Kane.

Hurry!

He just about had it. *Maybe? Could this work?*

His tablet located the IP address for the computer in the room they'd just exited. It was logged onto hidden MI6 servers. Jack attempted several computing combinations he'd spent the last twenty-four-hours working on. *One of them has to be it!*

Nicole's screen showed up on his tablet, and he found the program she was working on. She'd managed to fill several characters into a twelve-space bar. *This is it! She had him!*

Jack pounded at the tablet, trying more code combinations. From the screen, Nicole's counter indicated Mason had one hour left on his system.

In one hour, his hack would be irreversible. Jack knew it. His system, working remotely with shaky 4G Wi-Fi, churned slower than snails on an afternoon walk. He slammed his fist on the tablet as it stalled.

Frozen.

"Damn it!"

"Having some trouble?" a luxurious voice behind him called.

He raised his head only to catch Sage towering above him, her tall build looming like a skyscraper over a village. He'd barely noticed her ghost approach. She reached down her shirt and unhooked a small weapon from her blouse.

Jack shot to his feet.

He'd failed to realize how tall the arresting woman was. She arched back her hand, drawing on the thick band of a sophisticated slingshot whose accurate aim would only take a breadth of a second to sizzle through his forehead. She then reached her hand down her jumpsuit a second time and removed what looked like complicated ammunition–a steel arrow no longer than her hand.

She raised the lethal, steel dart, positioning it in the sling, then aimed steadily to fire.

A pulse beat and swelled at the base of his throat. Jack's hand slid down to the gun in his holster, his face beading with sweat under his headgear.

The dart sizzled from her aim.

Jack ducked, plunging to the concrete in a crouch.

She'd not missed. She was jesting with her prey. Sage drew back the elastic and discharged a second dart at Jack that landed in his good hand, bruising his bone. Violent discomfort stung through his arm.

A second dart fired at his tablet, wrenching it from his grip.

She wanted the tablet. Was his reversal working? Jack knew she was a mastermind behind Mason's hack - the whiz of the genetically enhanced trio, trained by GCHQ and ISTF specialists. Her brain could think like an NSA motherboard, her logarithms were impenetrable. Had she seen his hack?

The tablet had landed several inches from his boots.

He dove for it.

Sage chucked a steel rope she'd carried over her shoulders around his legs, tangling him in a firm knot. She progressed closer.

Jack dropped to the floor, the base of his head thumping the hard ground. He reached with his good hand and drew the gun from his holster and fired.

The bullet caught Sage in the shoulder, staggering her backward.

Jack heaved himself to a sitting position and uncoiled the steel from his ankles. Sage launched herself upward from where she'd fallen. Though the bullet had been accurate, it had landed in a platinum shoulder.

Her gaze squarely mocked his distress as she reached for her slingshot and aimed one last dart. Straight for his forehead.

CHAPTER 34

0719 hrs.

THE DART ZIPPED out of Sage's sling.

Jack closed his eyes.

It came from above. A thud, then a gloved hand stretched out an impenetrable steel plate in front of his face.

Nash!

Suited like the rest of the team, Nash drew into form. Sage lunged for him.

Nash stretched his left foot out in front of her. She tripped over his boot, slamming her jaw on the concrete, and landed with a thud.

Jack found his gun, and as she slung her metal whip at them, he fired in her arm.

She fell back.

Jack shot up and stood above her, he reached for the rope and together with Nash, they bound her in her own steel. Jack turned to his friend and set a hand on his shoulder. "Great timing, Nash."

He sneered. "She wasn't your type anyway."

A gunshot exploded in Mason's room.

"Calla's in there, with her parents," Jack said.

Nash narrowed his gaze at the door's lock and turned to the operatives who'd joined them. "Let's go!"

—

0721 hrs.

"What's it you want, Mason?" Stan said.

Mason pressed a button that opened a door in the far wall. Dena Laskfell, clearly unwell, lay like a vegetable on a medical bed. He tightened his squeeze on Nicole's neck. "Your wife here thought she could bolt her in her condition out of an institution in Texas, bring her here, so she can finish what she began years ago."

From the corner of her eye, Calla caught subtle movement as Nicole snapped the restraints around her hands. "To protect her from you."

"Liar!"

Nicole slammed the dart out of Mason's hand.

It trundled to the floor.

Anger welled in Mason's eyes as he reached for his pistol and discharged a high-speed bullet, zipping toward Calla.

Her eyes widened.

Time decelerated. Calla observed the propelling ammunition head toward her heart.

A breath of a second into her stare, they heard a second gunshot. The second bullet caught the first, and the two bullets collided, exploding in front of her.

She zipped her head behind her. Nash's arm remained stretched as his pistol's precision conquered Mason's bullet, having caught it midair in a fraction of a second. The shavings from the explosion hit her face, and she recoiled into Stan, closing her eyes. It was a feat few soldiers could master. Because Nash and Mason were close in height, their guns had been directed at similar levels and in the same line of action. The bullets had clashed at equal speeds.

Nash fired a second shot at Mason's gun and slammed it out of his hand. It landed meters from Dena Laskfell's bed. He then fired the restraints that confined Nicole to the bed, releasing her completely.

Nicole pulled up her arms, and Calla lurched forward to help her off the table. Mason retreated and found his machine gun from a nearby table. He flew toward the bed where Dena lay and ripped her limp body from the bed. Dena's body flopped over his shoulder as he darted through the back door.

Moments of pain and uncertainty transformed into a tear as Nicole stared at Calla.

She gawked back.

Nicole drew her into a hug. "Come with me, Calla. Let's stop what he started years ago."

Calla failed to form her words. Was the wait over? Was this the mother who'd left her? Should she feel anything for the woman who deserted them? Calla's lips trembled as she spoke. "Wh. .. where. .. have you been all these years? Why—"

"Did I leave you. .. and your father?" Nicole surrendered. "To protect you from that moron. Calla, the operatives, need a leader. That mantle always fell on the Cress family. Stan refused it, and that made you next in line. I didn't want that for you. And when Mason threatened to kill me when I was pregnant with you, I knew he would take your life the minute he found you. We made sure he didn't know you were ever born."

Nicole cupped Calla's face into her hands. "It was the hardest thing I ever had to do. And when the manuscript resurfaced, and Mason found out about you, I knew our one bargaining chip was getting to his mother."

Calla blinked at her uncomprehendingly, as if staring at an abstract painting. "What do we do now?"

"Get Dena Laskfell. It's our only ticket to Mason."

Stan stumbled toward Nicole's side bug-eyed as if he'd seen a howling phantom. A wife and partner he'd not seen in close to thirty years. Calla recoiled, watching as her parents reunited, a sting of emotion piercing at her eyes and threatening a choke.

Nash drew close and set a hand on her arm.

She turned to him and fell into his hold. "Thank you, Nash."

His eyes shimmered with conviction. "You're welcome."

With no time to explain, Nash laid a gentle hand on her cheek and turned to the group as more operatives filtered in. "Mason's getting away, we need to go. His mother is his hostage, and my guess is he knows we won't harm her. But I'm not so sure if he won't. We need them alive."

Nicole raised her eyes to him. "Nash, thanks for taking my call for help when I contacted you. Because of you, I identified her accurately among the many women in that prison, plus infiltrated her communication with Mason."

Nash stepped forward. "Mason's mother was kept in a Texas psychiatric prison since 1972. She'd been there for years for her crimes against humanity as she couldn't be confined in an ordinary prison. We don't know what drove her to the state she's in."

Nicole sucked air between her teeth. "That's why Mason wanted me. His mother and I had a fallout shortly before her arrest. Initially, we were on the same MI6 squad, both sent as moles to China. Then, she wanted the Hadrius Manuscript. I knew it was linked to you, so I refused. That's what started her madness. Calla, I couldn't let her misuse the manuscript for her own good. That would've seriously harmed you."

Stan rose and removed his headgear, rubbing absently at his arms as Nicole followed his movement. "I can't believe it's you."

"It is, Stan."

Stan's eyes revealed pain. "Why?"

"I'm so sorry, I should've never left you both," Nicole said, reaching for his arm. Can you forgive me? "

Stan stood stunned as if he'd been hit by a propelling projectile. "Nicole. .. I—"

Words failed him as he drew his wife into a long embrace before releasing her. "You're as determined and stunning as the day I last saw you."

"Then let's finish this together this time."

His eyes smiled at her. "Okay." He turned to the others. "Mason has watched what justice has done to his mother, and it's hit a raw nerve. He's mirrored his virus to the insanity she suffered. Let's go!"

Nicole sauntered to a far cabinet and pulled out some resources. She handed Calla a gun.

"I don't use these," Calla said, catching Nash's gaze.

Nicole nudged her. "Take it."

"No."

"I don't do guns. I never have."

Nash's look told Calla that he was wondering whether this was the best way to meet her mother. They heard the revving on a Jeep.

Stan shot to the door and turned to the operative team waiting at the entrance. "Let's move!"

CHAPTER 35

OUTSIDE THE BASE
0730 hrs.

MASON'S LUNGS STUNG with fire from heavy breathing. He wasn't as fit as he'd once been.

He had to get his mother from the lunatics. They were poison.

Delirious with medication, Dena's strides weakened, but she kept breathing steadily. Her body enfeebled from the jerks at her arms.

Mason shoved her into his Range Rover. For a second, he glanced at her ashen face and her sunken eyes. He could end if for her. Going back to prison would be death for her. If they were caught, authorities would haul them back to the dungeons of justice, and if he'd read the look in Shields face correctly, they'd ask for the worst kind of sanction.

He labored on with heavy legs and shuffled to the driver's seat. The triplets would have to fend for themselves. They knew the docking point at the harbor not far from Akrotiri.

Strained sunlight broke briefly through the clouds. Mason peered through the windshield and roared the engine into gear when he saw the operatives descend on them led by Cress and Shields. The car negotiated a tight bend and accelerated toward Akrotiri.

One glance in the mirror told him the operatives would not back down. His pursuers hunted him in a set of military Jeeps that saw them head South West on the sovereign, British overseas territory. He'd charted a yacht to take him to his next destination if only he could get to the harbor they used to use in the sixties. Was it still there? Would his captain find it?

He stepped on the gas and lost his pursuers near Kolossi. Soon the flat-paved surface of a rundown, isolated, military harbor drew in sight. He careered toward an old lighthouse, towering in the center of the blown-out building. That was the meeting point. The rustic location of *Mildred Mines,* the code agents had used decades ago to reach the numbers station.

He caught sight of his ride, four-hundred meters away in the Mediterranean Sea, where an electric boat with a catnapping ruffian waited for them. He drew his mother out of the car and dragged her toward the boat, waving at the dozing man, who'd tired of waiting.

He heard boots thudding behind him and zipped his head. He couldn't run the entire length to the boat without a fast shot from Shields, who stood with his firearm directed at his neck.

He reached over and grabbed Dena's neck. Just one wrench, then she'd be free.

"Stop!"

Nicole appeared from behind three operatives, her stance weak after enduring his brutality at the station. "Mason, we need to take her to the hospital. You've had her off her medication for more than thirty minutes. She won't survive."

Calla shot to her mother's side. "Let her go, Mason."

Nash's pistol remained level. "Mason, last warning."

"What? And rob the world of the justice it deserves? That's not your style, Shields." His hand tightened around his mother's neck. "Get back!"

Mason rotated his hand around the frail skin. "Sorry to disappoint you. But I have less sentiment for family."

He squeezed.

Nash fired, slamming Mason's hand from Dena's neck.

His hand oozed crimson, so red it stained her thin clothes. Mason dropped her to the concrete and drew a firearm from his combat pants. *Where are they?* From behind a lighthouse, a man's silhouette appeared, then two more with straight aim targeted at his tormentors, Ridge, Kane, and one more face.

Lascar.

Kane lunged for Calla and set a sharp *chikram* to her skin. She leaped with pain. It was charged with electricity as he'd engineered.

Mason signaled to Lascar and Ridge. "Get rid of them all!"

MILDRED MINES HARBOR, CYPRUS
0803 hrs.

Nash watched the fuming face draw into view. The daring operative who'd blown up his house, stolen Calla from him and impersonated her mother on his phone. Lascar had done enough, and frankly, Nash had taken ample harassment for a fortnight. His eyes widened with rage as Kane and Ridge tightened steel cords around Calla. They looped her hands through the rusty ladder that had probably been there since God knows when.

From her cries, he knew the cords burned her skin, yet not a single scratch or tear appeared.

What sort of cords were they?

Each step either he or Stan took toward helping her, the bionic twins stretched the cords tighter, and Kane's *chikram* sent sizzles of bolts through her. For the first time in his marine career, Nash was helpless.

The rain began a steady descent, and as it hit the cords around her, it sent high bolts of energy through her perspiring skin. Her breathing slowed rapidly. That's when he knew Mason would kill her without hesitation.

Nash's eyes caught hers. She tugged and writhed at the cords until her body fell limp over the charged rods. Beads of sweat formed on her brow, which each attempt at struggle. With the sting of anger burning his eyes, Nash's body broke into a cold sweat. He shot one glance at Stan and Nicole, who'd scurried to Dena's side where Mason had discarded as he fled to the boat waiting at the pier.

Dragging in a raged breath, Nash fisted his hands. He'd only lost focus for a second when a clenched fist landed in his stomach and pitched him to the wet concrete. His gun flew from his hand and catapulted several meters until it spattered in the sea.

His combat suit weighed down with the downpour, and as he glanced up, Lascar towered him with the sneer of egotism masking his face. Lascar gripped his hair and pulled him up. He slammed another blinding blow into Nash's jaw, and splitting pain smoldered through his head. Nash caved to the ground once more, his hand to his bleeding jaw. He shook his head for focus and watched Lascar come in for further assault.

Nash waited until he was about a meter away.

Lascar's lugged strides toward him were confident and arrogantly marked. Nash shot his full weight up and struck out with his closest weapon–a mud and oil mixture leaking from the old filling pipe, leading from the lighthouse to the sea. He cast it into his attacker's closest target–choleric eyes.

Lascar crumpled backward and moped the mud mixer from his vision. Kerosene stinging his opponent's eyes gave Nash enough time to rise, holding on to the piping around his feet for support. He brought another sharp blow at Lascar's neck nerve, causing temporary mental stunning and motor dysfunction in the operative for five seconds.

Lascar's muscles spasmed and set him off balance at the unexpected chop. He shot back with a violent boot to Nash's shin.

The pain agonized through Nash's whole limbs. He captured a breath and jumped swiftly to his feet. He gripped Lascar by the shoulder, and slugged pointed fingers to his neck, once more immobilizing the operative.

Lascar slithered to his knees, his back against Nash's chest. With acute agony searing through Lascar's limbs, and possible cramping of his right arm and hand, Nash knew he had debilitated him.

It was time for answers.

"You sent those messages, didn't you?" Nash said.

Seething through angered breaths, Lascar glared into him. "You don't deserve her."

"Bark up another tree, genetic boy."

Lascar blinked from mental stunning for about three seconds, before Kane tossed his *chikram*, slicing past Nash's leg. He shot a second missile that caught Nash's thigh.

The violent agony made him release his grip on Lascar.

Kane, followed by Ridge in full *shinobi* charge, pounced on Nash and heaved him on to a wet boat belt on the concrete. The slippery surface beneath, used to dispense boats into the sea, met Nash's pained back as he stared down at blood pouring from his wounds. The ninja set the gear of the rusted belt in motion and an old boat, with its nose toward Nash, geared into movement, clanking and grinding on the rusted iron as it slid along the rubber belt toward him. Ridge seized each of Nash's shoulders and pasted him to the ground as the decaying boat gravitated toward his head.

Nash's limbs were paralyzed with pain. From strained eyes, he watched Lascar tower above him with a victorious air, his hair dripping with grime and his chest heaving under his combat suit.

Mason shot into view behind the operative and handed a gun to Lascar. "Be done with him. The marine knows more about me than he should."

Nash's eyes narrowed into Lascar's eager face, then at the washed out stares of Stan and Nicole, who could not raise a hand to help without sending him and Calla to their deaths. He peered through the downpour at Calla. Nash was certain she'd fallen unconscious.

Mason took another pistol and directed his aim at Calla's failing body. "If you're not man enough to finish off a marine, Lascar, then she has ten seconds to live! One. .. two. .."

"The deal was not to harm her, Mason!" Lascar bellowed, his voice pleading in the rain.

"Three. .. four. .."

He stopped. "It's up to you. If you want her, then you don't need him."

Nash raised his chin, glaring through agonized eyes at Lascar. "You're an operative, not a murderer."

The engines of the churning boat continued their advance and progressed inches from Nash's head.

"Now!" belted Mason.

Lascar's body jumped slightly at Mason's command as Ridge pushed down harder at Nash's shoulders.

Nash could feel the air begin to leave his lungs. Either way, the boat or the bullet would get him.

Lascar's hand trembled as he aimed the firearm at Nash's neck.

Spit and blood choked in his throat as Nash took one last

pained glimpse at Calla. Lascar's knuckle whitened around the trigger, then he pulled.

A whiff of sulfur suffocated the air as the bullet sizzled out of Lascar's firearm. The boat steered the last centimeters toward Nash's bound body before Ridge and Kane leaped off the belt track as the rusty boat accelerated ahead toward the sea.

And then.

Silence.

CHAPTER 36

0804 hrs.

THE SOUND OF THE fired gun resonated in the trees as perched birds took flight at the sound of the shot. Lascar glanced down. The boat belt stood bare. Lascar's bullet had hit Ridge slicing his neck.

Mason's gun went off with sudden discharge and ripped into Kane's chest. The two assailants plunged to the wet ground, still gripping their weapons tightly as their lives expired with the two shots.

Lascar shot Mason a terrified look. He'd never missed a shot in his life at such close range. Both men turned their eyes to where Calla had been detained on the railroad crossing.

Not a sound.

Not a movement.

Empty.

The cords lay at the foot of the lighthouse.

Stan, Nicole, and Dena waited at one end of the empty harbor, their questioning glances bared. For several seconds, Lascar and Mason gawked at each other, their faces masked with bewilderment.

In one abrupt movement, they raised their guns at one another, terror streaking their eyes.

A slam from above caught Lascar in the neck, and he plunged to the ground.

Nash stood behind him.

Lascar swiveled and collapsed to the ground gripping his injured neck, his eyes questioning the last few seconds.

"Ever wonder what a blind spot is, Lascar?" Nash said, grunting as he spoke.

Lascar's eyes told Nash he had no words. Nash drew in a tight breath. "That's when a soldier takes his eye off the target."

Calla stepped forward. "That would be me, the target. You, scoundrels, paid too much attention to the previews, you missed the movie. It took me two seconds to break free from your pathetic restraints." She swiveled to face Mason. "Oh, and remember Spain? I now know why I could resist your pathetic attempt at hypnotism."

Mason observed Calla as she shot in front of him. He took a step back as she inched closer, a fighting confidence in her face.

He raised his hand to strike.

It stopped midair, as if an invisible force had restrained it.

He went in for another punch.

That, too, remained in the air.

Mason gravitated back, hands raised until he was up against the same ladder Calla had been strapped to.

With the charge of electricity revitalizing her operative genes, the energy gave her the confidence to face the truth she'd been trying to avoid. She was telepathic, exactly like her impaired opponent, only she could read his mind, before he could register his own thoughts. His weakness in processing human emotion was her strength at channeling human behavior.

She'd read his mind and broken his blows midair before he could advance. Mason had used the same methods in his cell with his victims. He'd been blinded by ambition and failed to draw and route strength from them.

Nash had been right. *Always use the attacker's strength against them, whatever that strength is.*

Only minutes earlier, she'd read Lascar's mind and willed him to fire his rage at their assailants–Ridge, then Mason's own fury had turned on Kane. She'd controlled the criminal's mind as easily as he'd manipulated those of his victims, with the same abilities they shared, genes fashioned for decades, possibly centuries from the same operative technology science.

Calla sidled her boots over the wet, uneven ground, her eyes fixed into Mason. The more he resisted, the stronger her telepathic ability.

No words were spoken, but Mason heard the words as clearly as if they'd been audible.

"Not as easy when you are on the other side. I'm just as telepathic as you, only mine surfaces in heightened danger situations. This one's for stealing my parents from me."

She swung her leg into a roundhouse thud that landed in his out-thrust chest.

"This one's for global technology systems, which from now on, will be protected by me."

A knee to the groin.

Mason shot up, coughing and gripping his agonized wounds.

"This one's for Veda."

A third strike hit Mason in the jaw.

"This one Mason is for wasting my time!"

Another strike to the groin.

"And lastly, Mason, the worst thing you could have ever done. .."

Her lips had not moved once, yet he could hear the words she related. *"This one is for going after the man I love."*

The last thud jolted Mason back like a bolt of current. He landed on the concrete and watched as she moved toward him. The pain from her vengeful strikes singed like fire. He couldn't see or think straight. His hands were on his temple. The agony made him surrender a pained yelp.

"Enough! Just finish me off." Mason felt round for his gun and handed it to her slowly. He couldn't will his brain to pull the trigger. Death would be easier than a maimed mind. The mind is where life begins. Without it, he would be nothing.

She eased the weapon from his hands and directed it at his chest.

Her other hand reached in her pocket, and she made a phone call. "Reiner, send the men through."

Mason barked out in pain. "Please, Cress!"

Was this the torture he'd put his victims through? The thudding of boots signaled the arrival of the ISTF tactics team and the operatives. Some stopped to attend to Stan, Nicole, and Dena, and one army paramedic advanced toward Nash's side. Three operatives restrained Lascar.

She turned her attention back to Mason. "Death is too easy for you. You need a real sting. Now that I have the coordinates from the caves of your mind to reverse the hack, I can proceed."

Calla called Jack on her SWAT radio. "Yes, Jack, here are the coordinates." She proceeded with the code as Jack crossed the tiny harbor, with his phone to his ear and his fingers flashing over his tablet. "Those will reverse the hack program, and by the way, he was hiding a lock in his brain, one that would make further attacks irreversible. Here are the coordinates for that."

Calla clipped off her phone, her gun still aimed at Mason's

brow. Reiner joined her as she hovered over her enemy, digging the gun into his skin. She suddenly withdrew and handed Reiner the pistol. "Here you go, Reiner. I don't do guns."

The rain stopped as the clouds cleared, and the sun peered through the glistening palm trees surrounding the harbor. Calla stepped away from Mason as he lay cowering on the ground. Reiner and several men bound him for transportation.

She hurried to Nash's side to check on his injuries. When she reached him, her eyes met his. She opened her lips to speak. Nash placed a gentle finger over her lips. "No words." He gently eased off his bulletproof vest as if it constricted his breathing.

Jack advanced toward them. "The systems are back. I was just on the phone with ISTF headquarters. We have to communicate with the affected parties."

"Thanks, Jack," Calla said.

"No, thanks to the team. We do what we do best—when we *stick* together." He winked and settled a kiss on her forehead before turning to his wounded friend.

Nash let out a weak smile as pain agonized his thigh. His eyes suddenly narrowed into alarm.

Calla followed his stare.

A weak Mason, barely responsive, freed his right hand, reached for the poison dart he'd held over Nicole only hours earlier, and drew it from his army vest. He raised the dart to his lips and prepared to send it sizzling toward Calla's chest.

Nash seized the gun from Jack's holster in one sudden movement, but before he could release a bullet, a shot fired from one of the ISTF tactic team members.

Mason plunged backward with the force of the charged bullet.

Then. .. stillness.

They watched him roll to his side. Then as silence seized the harbor, he breathed his last.

Calla marched toward the SWAT member. "I said we wanted him alive."

The agent dragged off her helmet and goggles. Hair flung out as the woman behind the headgear stared at the still body of Mason Laskfell.

Margot Arlington strode to the lifeless frame of the man she once loved. "This makes us even, Mason." Her voice trailed with a vengeance.

Margot suddenly turned her head toward Nash, leveled her aim once more, and fired a bullet to his front. She dropped the gun at her feet. "That, marine, is for disobeying orders."

LONDON, UNITED KINGDOM
72 HOURS LATER

He opened his eyes and studied the ceiling. It did not look familiar. Nash searched his surroundings. His eyes fell on her. Calla slept in a chair, with a wool blanket over her. He glanced out the window. Predawn light hit his face and from the view of the Shard skyscraper in the distance, the disproportionate rooftops of London greeted his groggy eyes. He was in a hospital room of some sort and from the pain in his neck and thigh, he must have sustained colossal injuries.

Nash had rarely been in hospitals as a patient, even when he'd been in the military. Then it came to memory. The way he'd fought Lascar, an operative with possibly twice his strength, and how Ridge and Kane had slammed him in the shoulder bone and rib cage.

And then the boat. Mason had been there and Arlington as well.

Nash raised a gauzed hand to his tender jaw and realized he wore a pair of his own pajamas–just the bottoms. A patch monitoring his vitals had been placed on his chest. He followed the length of the cords and caught sight of a screen indicating his critical health signs were sound.

How long had he been here?

Calla stirred, and her hair unfastened, covering half her exquisite face. She had two plasters on her wrists, and one just below her left eye. As if sensing his stare, her eyes opened and caught his. Relief struck her face, curling her lips into a welcoming smile. She sprang up and ambled to him, taking a seat in the chair next to his bed. "Nash, you're awake."

His throat was dry. It must've been the central heating that parched him. Or was it the medication? Instinctively, Calla reached for some water and raised the glass to his lips. He let the cool stream flow down his thirsting throat.

"Where am I?" Nash said.

"In a private military hospital near London Bridge. With ISTF Special Services on watch."

"Was that your doing?"

"Yes." She managed a tired smile. "How do you feel?"

He slowly sat up and watched her carefully. "I'll live."

She smiled and edged closer, her eyes deciphering volumes, yet the words wedged in her throat. *What's she trying to say?*

His hand ran down the side of the bed until it found hers. Hushed creaking at the door startled them. The door opened, and a cheerful nurse minced in with a tray of breakfast, smoked salmon, eggs Benedict, Muesli, fresh mango, kiwi slices, and low-fat yogurt. "Well. .. well, looks like you've resurfaced special agent. You took quite a hit and have been asleep for close to three days."

Nash shot her a glance. "Three days?"

"Yes, sir. But you've been in good hands. This young lady has been here every hour but one, when she went to your house to collect some personal items. She's been looking after you herself. Shaving you in the mornings, personally selecting your diet and food items, and administering the tube feeds herself when necessary. Making sure your room was secure. I wasn't allowed to feed you. She took care of you on her own. Your own personal nurse."

Calla ran a nervous hand through her hair as she watched the nurse set the breakfast tray down and check the machines.

"You seem fine and can perhaps have this tray yourself. I'd brought it in for your *nurse* here," the nurse said to Nash.

Nash glanced over at Calla, his drugged eyes softening. *No one's ever done that for me. Not even my own family.*

He let a pang of guilt shoot through him for a second, followed by admiration for Calla. The nurse left with a promise to bring in another tray. Calla took the tray and hoisted herself against the edge of the bed. In silence, she set a fork through the mango portion, slit it in half, and brought the fresh fruit to Nash's lips. He took a bite and chewed it down. She repeated the gesture in silence until half the tray was almost consumed. Nash's eyes never left her once. He reached for her feeding hand.

Calla set the tray on the bed rest as Nash pulled her close to him, and his hand caressed her flushed cheek, before brushing a gentle kiss across her forehead. Several seconds later, she pulled away. She paused, looking into his eyes. "Nash, I almost lost you in Cyprus."

"But, you didn't."

"I'm also so sorry about China and how we left things. You've always put me ahead of yourself and taught me some incredible lessons. I was selfish and unfair to you, unintentionally. I'm sorry." She raised her eyes to his. "Nash, I love you. You come first. .. above everything."

He stroked her hair. "I couldn't leave you in Gibraltar, even when it hurt the most. I had to find my way back to you."

"You saved my life, Nash, more than once and brought my family back together. I can't do life without you."

"Where's your family?"

"My mother is with my father in the Costwolds. After twenty-eight years, my mother is trying to make sense of her life. They need to work out so many things. They have to start over. .. getting to know each other again."

"It can take a lifetime."

"Nash, how do you feel? After you were shot three days ago, the paramedics gave up, almost pronouncing you gone by the time you arrived here."

"Nash rubbed a hand on his sore chest, recalling the shot from Arlington's pistol. "What happened to me?"

"When we got back to London, I gave Vortigern an ultimatum. I went to the London cove, one of the operatives' largest headquarters, and raided their medical research labs for anything to stop heart failure. Only God knows how you stayed alive. The bullet had been so close to your heart."

"It never stopped beating for you," he said. "You know that."

She smiled. "The operatives have medical and research procedures many years ahead of modern science. I told Vortigern to send me his best team of surgeons and supplies. At first, Vortigern resisted. I told him, he can have me lead the operatives with you in my life, or he'd never see a Cress again."

Nash raised an eyebrow. "What'd he say?"

"He had no choice. Without the Cress family, the operatives are vulnerable. It has always been Merovec's warning."

He squeezed her hand. "I've always wanted you to know your family."

"I want you to be part of it. More than you know."

She'd said more in those few seconds than all the years he'd known her. He nodded, and with a soft sigh, he planted taunting little kisses along her cheek before settling his lips on hers.

Nash pulled back slightly. "What happened to Arlington?"

"The US government is waiting for your recovery before they tackle her. They believe you are best qualified and should be involved in whatever next steps are determined."

"I see."

"By the way, I learned that from Masher. He came to see you himself when ISTF told him about Arlington."

So the old man is fine, after all.

Nash's exhausted eyes smiled at her. "Cal, there's still one more thing. What're you going to do about the operatives' mandate?"

"Can I decide that with you? Will you help me find Merovec?"

CHAPTER 37

BAIE ROUGE
FRENCH CARIBBEAN ISLAND OF ST. MARTIN
ONE MONTH LATER

NASH MOVED TO the edge of the cliff, a few paces from his new villa–a 7,500 square foot, roofed living space. Curved ceilings merged with a long terrace, surrounded by white columns and archways. Slightly raised, the villa commanded a stunning and pronounced view of Anguilla, and the narrow channel separating both Caribbean islands.

The warm sun beat on his face as he pondered. Being with Calla had its challenges, but not once did he anticipate that the people he was trying to protect, her people would be the ones to turn on him seven months ago. They'd begged her to leave him. *Begged? Commanded.*

Calla took a seat on the rock next to him and allowed the wind to rake through her hair. "Soldier, you're quiet."

She glared out to the sea as the sunset was about to set in. The auburn sun touched her soft face and turned her eyes amber green in the process. He drew her into a hug. "Sorry, we couldn't find Merovec after trying every possibility your mother could think of. He must have come to her and not the other way around."

She sighed deeply. "It only matters if we take on the mandate. Hey, let's just take in this place. Must be nice to have a new safe house."

He grinned. "You've no idea."

"Quite a change, isn't it? A bit opposite in climate?"

"Better. Besides, it brings out the olive color in your skin very nicely."

He drew in the gentle scent of unexpected combinations of grapefruit, gardenia, and vanilla in her hair. "Happy here, beautiful?"

Calla's eyebrows knit. "Never been better, Nash." She smiled. "Soldier, I'm keeping you."

"Even when the operatives told you to doubt me?" He saw the slight flicker of uncertainty for a moment behind her eyes, then it disappeared. "Your father guessed they would try to take you from me."

"I never believed them. I wanted to get away from all the operatives and what the mandate asked of me. Besides, look at what Lascar turned out to be, a traitor to his own mission. Vortigern hasn't been heard from since I saw him last. It must've been too embarrassing for his son to turn against the operatives." She took a deep breath. "For me, the choice between the mandate and you was always clear."

His eyes smiled at her. "That means giving up everything for me. I know what the mandate asks of you. I can't let you walk away from your destiny. It's really important."

Calla slid her head into his chest. "Nash, sometimes standing still and embracing your current destiny, is more important than chasing one. You might miss life." She paused. "You're important to me. And I never agreed with Vortigern and Allegra. I don't care that we're different.

Besides a few boosts in genes on my side and a little help from the galaxies, we're two beings with feelings, emotions, and passion."

He gently stroked her hair as it fell like a curtain on his shoulder. "What do we do now with the mandate? It sits on your head like a bad dream that won't go away. Are you sure you don't want it? "

"She does!"

The insistent voice cut harshly through the crashing of the waves beneath them. They zipped their heads around and caught eyes with a tall man. A noble and spirited face, with fair and faintly wavy hair, and black bending eyebrows. Intense, probing blue eyes accompanied by an expression of authority, stared at them. "I heard you were looking for me. I'm sure you know Taiven."

Taiven's frame drew into form behind the man.

Calla stood to his level. "You are him. .. ?"

Merovec glanced over at Nash, who rose slowly from the rock. "Nash Shields, this concerns you too."

Nash ambled to them.

"Now, Calla," Merovec began. "I admire the courage you have to stand up to me. A Cress determination that I saw from the first Cress who penned the Hadrius Manuscript. Now I'm here to let you know that you are free to do as you will and can walk away from the mandate. Alternatively, you can be part of history. The Cresses' mandate is to preserve history, look after the world's technology systems and scientific balance. You saw a fraction of what a global attack on technology systems can do. We're only at the beginning of a digital underground. Cybercriminals are on the loose crippling systems, creating data breaches, social networking threats, and the list goes on. It takes one new piece of software for ten security threats to surface on its log in password." He glanced at Nash. "You know that."

"What's your angle?" Nash asked, a protective streak ringing in his voice.

"This is the new attack on this world, not famine, not hunger and other disasters, but technology because the world depends on it more than anything else. Think about it. It even dictates the food brought to your table. Next time, look at your plate and decide how many items made it there without a megabyte. I need you to take that on with the operatives and offer you much influence and decades of research. If you refuse, well I guess I could try something else, but—

Nash interjected. "But she's one of the smartest and bravest operatives you've ever had, and you know it to the core–one that can stand up for both the average person and the operatives as a unit."

Merovec watched Nash, his eyes strangely impersonal. "I see why you chose him. I like him."

"Then why did you impose an alliance embargo between operatives and non-operatives," Nash asked.

Merovec tilted his head. "It's not my embargo, but nature's warning. I'm sure you met Laskfell's triplets."

Nash nodded.

Merovec rose. "They were the result of such an association. You'd think that the offspring of an operative and non-operatives would be a weaker breed of each. Not in this case. The possibilities with your offspring, as you saw with the triplets, are bewildering. Somehow, it reproduces a stronger version of the two–taking the best from both sides and creating an unstoppable being."

Calla glared him in the eyes. "Why's that such a bad thing?"

"A force that's not nurtured is a disaster waiting to happen. Now multiply that. I'll leave the results for you to ponder, but I must warn you that this is what you two are in danger of. I'll wait till next July for you to consider. Now, good day."

Merovec and Taiven began a descent toward the house.

"Wait!" Nash said.

They turned around. "Is Merovec *really* your name?"

Merovec grinned. "I go by many. Merovec is the one you need to know."

"Who are you, really?"

He drew in a deep breath and took a step toward Nash. "If you ever want to know who she is and where I come from, I can only leave you codes. H 13-2 and P 91-11. That should give you sufficient knowledge of me and why Calla is really here. You're a smart cryptanalyst, you can figure it out."

Merovec and Taiven headed away from the beach as Calla turned to Nash, looking for any reaction from his face. When she turned to follow his gaze after the two, their visitors had disappeared.

"You get your wish. You found him," Nash said.

She lifted her face. "Nash, Merovec himself said the only way this mandate can be released from me is to pass it on to another Cress." She suddenly went quiet, churning thoughts around her mind. "Eloping with you to Colorado was the best thing I ever did."

"You know we couldn't tell anyone about us getting married. It was too dangerous. We'd never have heard the end of it from the operatives. .. and possibly, my mother." He let out a little laugh. "Are you having second thoughts?"

"Not at all, Nash, remember when I said it would just be *us*. Nash, I couldn't do it. I couldn't go ahead with the operation. I knew it would break your heart and. .. mine."

Nash tossed her a smile. "Let's take our time."

"I don't think we can, Nash." She slowly took his hand and placed it on her abdomen. "This next Cress is going to need the protection and determination of a strong father."

EPILOGUE

NASH FOUND HIS tablet after Calla had retired for the night. He pulled out the microchip he'd rescued from Masher's office. He had not wanted to send this earlier, and now he knew he could not.

For days, he'd agonized over Merovec's numbers, their significance. Nothing made sense. At first, he'd thought they were coordinates, longitude, and latitude for Calla's ancestral origins, He'd even considered the numbers DNA or gene signatures. He also ran them through every decrypting system he knew, and at the NSA, there were many. Was Merovec referring to a year? An element in geology?

Damn it! What was it!

The fragments stared at him, blankly as he knotted his palms behind his head.

H 13-2
P 91-11

His eyes fell on a book he'd not seen or touched since he was a boy. It had been given to him by his maternal grandmother on his fifth birthday. Scratching his head, he drew it from the shelf and fingered through it. It was then that he understood. Merovec was referring to a code in this book. *Well, I'll be damned!*

The book was in two volumes. He flipped to volume two, then to the nineteenth book. Its title began with H and when he flipped to the thirteenth chapter and the eleventh section. It was clear to him. He read the words.

For some have entertained messengers unawares.

There the answers were in the most read book on the globe. He sat at his desk for three hours and began one of the strangest e-mails he'd ever written. Several hours later, he stared at what he'd written. The information it contained would be harmful to operatives. He reread the e-mail he had drafted several times but never sent to the head of HORIZON, the newly classified paranormal activity project launched at the NSA.

He called a number in the US.

"Shields?" the man said. "Judging from the fact that you've called me signifies that you could prove the theories that we investigated. What do you have for me?"

"Sir. It's been a false alarm. There's no paranormal or physic activity that would be of interest to the NSA."

"Then how do you explain the two NSA men who had superior minds, more telepathic than anything we have seen? They intercepted a signal we couldn't track. Not to mention the technology they used, though theirs was light-years ahead of the NSA's. We both know that NSA technology is at least forty-five years ahead of anyone's."

"I don't know what I can tell you, sir."

"All right. Can you at least send me your research? Your first analysis of the case? As you know, only four people know about HORIZON, you, I, the president and the British PM. It will stay in this circle."

"I need more time, sir."

"All right, Shields. Let me know if you come up with anything new."

"Good night, sir."

The fresh breeze blew through the open windows. Calla was asleep. He read the e-mail draft again.

CLASSIFIED

TO: Rodney Cook, Head of Psychic Spy Program,
National Security Agency
FROM: Nash Shields
SUBJECT: Investigation of Superior Intelligence Behavior on US Soil
STATUS: DRAFT
CC: White House, 10 Downing Street

Dear Sir,

On July 21, I was asked to investigate three of our own agents into what appeared to be superior behavior and extended capabilities when it came to weapon handling, military defense, and technology use.

As per your request to investigate two NSA officials connected to the two events on US soil, I can now confirm that what I'm about to reveal, should stay classified for the rest of history. Though there is much we can learn, I doubt our world is ready for the intelligence contained in this report, for you have to ask yourself what you really believe. Whereas I deal with facts, I will say that my beliefs have been challenged in the last several months. I'm now certain about the facts. Though vague, I have been a witness to activities deeply connected to our history and our future. I'm now at liberty to conduct my final review of the operatives.

My intelligence analysis took me to London, where I came in contact with people who, for the purposes of this report, I'll call 'operatives'. In fact, that's what they call themselves. Operatives are a strange breed of the natural, the unnatural, and science. I understand that HORIZON's key interest in the operatives stemmed from our government's interest to investigate claims of psychic phenomena with potential military and domestic purposes, particularly "remote viewing" where individuals claim the ability to psychically envision events, sites, or information from a great distance.

Operatives have the minds and capabilities of the supernatural, the anatomy and reasoning of everyday people, and the superior knowledge and capability to bridge the two. They are in every way humans who've tapped into a great source that's beyond mine and anyone's comprehension. As we stand, the operatives have acquired their original capabilities, and the question is, are they friend or foe?

We would be foolish to pick a battle with them, they watch over the world in many ways, and the ones I have had the privilege of working with are responsible for history, world technologies, and science, particularly ensuring they stay balanced and do not destroy humanity. These operatives could not only help the NSA as their technologies are far superior to anything we've seen at the NSA or ever will.
As you can see, we face a great dilemma. We can let them 'get on with it', or tickle their feathers and begin a battle we can never win. But with anything, there is vulnerability. A

weakness that can impair them. I think I've found it, but you'd probably have to kill me for it.

Sir, it's time to ask yourself what you believe, for, by my count, we're in the presence of strange messengers that were left to fend for themselves, and the only way they knew how was develop science and technology at a rate we never could.

Nash Shields
Senior Intelligence Analyst, NSA
Military & Security Adviser, ISTF (Gray Jaguar)

Nash's finger hovered over the delete button. His child would be better protected than Calla ever was. They would have a normal life. The more he read it, the more he was certain he couldn't share its contents with anyone.

And as much as it pained him, not even with Calla.

GET THE NEXT BOOK IN THE SERIES

The Decrypter: Digital Eyes Only
(A Calla Cress Technothriller)

The third book in the explosive bestselling technothriller series

"A female James Bond with a Matrix twist." Amazon Reviewer

Encrypted. Stolen, Ransom

A hi-tech encrypted device, with a list of codes detailing far-future technologies, goes missing from the NSA's vault of secrets.

When the British Prime Minister's private accounts are hacked, museum curator, turned cyber-defense agent Calla Cress is called on to decrypt a mysterious cipher left in the Prime Minister's home. Soon a series of encrypted ciphers surfaces on a darknet site, the Vault, whose inception is steeped in the mysterious history of the Maltese Knights. As Calla gets closer to not only unearthing the Vault's interlaced web of secrets but also discovering the identities of the darknet masters, she learns that technologies aren't the only thing the darknet intends to auction.

Calla has no idea how far the quest will plunge her and NSA agent, Nash Shields, into the past, and how much preventing a cyber war will hold the world ransom at a price much higher than she's willing to pay.

In a fast-paced, cyber-espionage, technothriller from the streets of London to the coves of Malta, from the glitzy allure of Monte Carlo to Spain's royal complex of the Alhambra fortress, Calla must end the sale of the NSA list, but with every attempt at annihilating the digital auctions, she risks exposing her dearest secret.

The Decrypter: Digital Eyes Only is Book 3 in the Calla Cress Technothriller Series but can be read as a stand-alone story.

JOIN THE ADVENTURE

SHORT REVIEW

Thank you for joining Calla, Nash, and Jack on this adventure!

As an author, I highly appreciate the feedback I get from my readers. It helps others to make an informed decision before buying.

It only takes a few minutes. If you enjoyed **The Decrypter and the Mind Hacker** please consider leaving a short review where you bought the book or by going here.

www.rosesandy.com

BE THE FIRST TO KNOW

Be the first to learn about new releases and other news from Rose Sandy, by joining **Real Time with Rose Sandy**, a podcast and fun e-update. See you there by going here: LINK -
>

https://rose-sandy.ck.page/afd6f12477

JOIN THE CONVERSATION

While you are at it, swing by the official Rose Sandy Facebook page (www.facebook.com/rosesandyauthor) to join a community of adventurers, history and technology enthusiasts.

Finally, if you enjoy pictures of travels, book inspirations, historical mysteries, science and technology thrills, check out my feed @rosesandyauthor on the Instagram app.

IN THE DECRYPTER SERIES

Book 1: The Decrypter: Secret of The Lost Manuscript
Book 2: The Decrypter and The Mind Hacker
Book 3: The Decrypter - Digital Eyes Only
Book 4: The Decrypter - The Storm's Eye

She's a museum curator, a doubter, and a skeptic. It all changed when the British government asked her to decrypt a code written in an unbreakable script on an ancient manuscript whose origin was as debatable as the origin of life. Then there was the issue of her long-lost parents.

Using her knack for history and technology, she bands with two faithful friends and is thrown into a dangerous journey of cyber espionage investigating the criminal, the unexplained, the scientific and the downright unthinkable.

More here: https://rosesandy.com/the-decrypter-series/

What Readers Are Saying About The Decrypter Series

"Takes you on a ride and refuses to let you off until you reach the very end."

"A brilliant read! I recommend this to anyone who enjoys mystery, suspense, thrillers, or action novels. The detail is astounding! The historic references, location descriptions, references to technology, cryptography…. this author really knows her stuff."

"An action-packed adventure, technothriller across several continents like a Jason Bourne or James Bond movie, but with an actual storyline!"

"Brilliantly written. I loved the very descriptive side, which was a good way of visualizing and getting to terms with each new place, as the action takes place in several different countries."

"The description is so rich, so immensely detailed that it just draws you in completely to its world."

"There is great tension and chemistry between the two main characters, Calla and Nash, that has you begging for more."

The historic references, location descriptions, references to technology, cryptography…. this author really knows her stuff."

"There is great tension and chemistry between the two main characters, Calla and Nash, that has you begging for more."

IN THE SHADOW FILES THRILLERS

A Crossfire Between Technology, Science, and International Espionage

Book 1 - The Code Beneath Her Skin
Book 2 - Blood Diamond in My Mother's House

A series about intelligent women caught in the crossfire between technology, science, politics, international espionage, and the men who drag them there.

Guaranteed action adventure in each book, you'll fill the need for thrills, savor satisfying cliffhangers as you follow a secret organization, **The Shadow Files,** and two of its former agents around the globe.

Sworn enemies, one is on a mission to safeguard the globe from economic corruption, and one swears he'll protect the victims.

Each book can be read as a stand-alone story. More here: https://rosesandy.com/the-shadow-files-series-2/

ABOUT THE AUTHOR

Rose Sandy never set out to be a writer. She set out to be a communicator with whatever landed in her hands. But soon the keyboard became her best friend. Rose writes suspense and intelligence thrillers where technology and espionage meet history in pulse-racing action adventure. She dips into the mysteries of our world, the fascination of technology breakthroughs, the secrets of history and global intelligence to deliver thrillers that weave suspense, conspiracy and a dash of romantic thrill.

A globe trotter, her thrillers span cities and continents. Rose's writing approach is to hit hard with a good dose of tension and humor. Her characters zip in and out of intelligence and government agencies, dodge enemies in world heritage sites, navigate technology markets and always land in deep trouble.

When not tapping away on a smartphone writing app, Rose is usually found in the British Library scrutinizing the Magna Carta, trolling Churchill's War Rooms or sampling a new gadget. Most times she's in deep conversations with ex-military and secret service intelligence officers, Foreign Service staff or engrossed in a TED talk with a box of popcorn. Hm... she might just learn something that'll be useful.

For more books and updates.

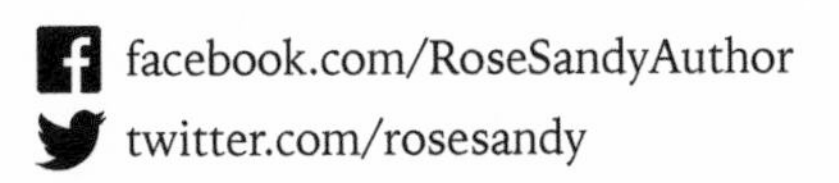

Ingram Content Group UK Ltd.
Milton Keynes UK
UKHW041422260523
422400UK00004B/266